ARKWRIGHT

ARKWRIGHT

ALLEN STEELE

TOR®

A TOM DOHERTY ASSOCIATES BOOK

NEW YORK

ARKWRIGHT

Copyright © 2016 by Allen Steele

Interior illustration © 2016 by Allen Steele and Rob Caswell

All rights reserved.

Parts of this novel were first published, in substantially shorter and different form, in *Asimov's Science Fiction* in 2014 through 2015.

A Tor Book
Published by Tom Doherty Associates, LLC
175 Fifth Avenue
New York, NY 10010

www.tor-forge.com

Tor® is a registered trademark of Tom Doherty Associates, LLC.

The Library of Congress Cataloging-in-Publication Data is available upon request.

ISBN 978-0-7653-8215-3 (hardcover)
ISBN 978-1-4668-8643-8 (e-book)

Our books may be purchased in bulk for promotional, educational, or business use. Please contact your local bookseller or the Macmillan Corporate and Premium Sales Department at 1-800-221-7945, extension 5442, or by e-mail at MacmillanSpecialMarkets@macmillan.com.

First Edition: March 2016

Printed in the United States of America

0 9 8 7 6 5 4 3 2 1

For Greg Benford and Jim Benford

CONTENTS

Prologue   11

Book One: The Legion of Tomorrow   15

Interlude: Affair with a Dreamer   108

Book Two: The Prodigal Son   127

Interlude: Ghost of a Writer   191

Book Three: The Long Wait   199

Interlude: Arrival   261

Book Four: The Children of Gal   267

Epilogue   330

Acknowledgments   333

Bibliography   335

ARKWRIGHT

PROLOGUE

He awoke and knew that he was dying.

He didn't know why he woke up at all. He should have passed away without ever regaining consciousness, effortlessly slipping from sleep into death. Yet something—perhaps the arrhythmic beating of his heart or the abrupt shortness of breath, or maybe just a realization from deep within his subconscious mind that his final hour had come—caused him to open his eyes for one last time.

He lay alone in his darkened bedroom with only the sullen red glow of a night-light near the door for company. No one else had shared his bed since his wife died more than thirty years earlier, but in this moment, he missed her more keenly than ever before. Judith would have held his hand just as he'd held hers, stroked his cold forehead, spoken quiet words of comfort . . . but she wasn't there, and never having been a religious man, he had no faith in the notion that he'd soon be reunited with her.

His chest was in agony. No surprise. His doctors had told him months earlier that cardiovascular disease brought on by a lifetime of cigarettes and infrequent exercise had deteriorated his heart to the point that he probably wouldn't make it to the end of the year, if a seizure didn't take him before then. Surgery wouldn't have solved anything; at best, it would have prolonged his life for only a little while. Judith had passed away in a hospital, and the memory of those awful last weeks had decided things for him. He'd go home and wait for the end there.

And now it had come.

A buzzer rested on the bed beside his right hand. Sterling, his live-in housekeeper, had insisted upon having it installed. One touch of its big red button, and Sterling would wake in his bedroom on the other side of the house. But his housekeeper would only dial 911, and even if an ambulance arrived in time, it would have just meant that he would die in a cold, sterile hospital room, with tubes in his nose and an EKG incessantly beeping above his head and fluorescent lights in his eyes, instead of here, in warm and silent darkness. A dignified death. He left the buzzer alone.

His breath was getting shorter, the pain greater. There was a clock on his bedside, but his vision was becoming blurred, and he couldn't clearly make out the digits. Was it 2:21 or 3:21? Didn't matter, really. His eyes turned toward the French windows beside his bed. Sterling had wanted to pull the drapes shut, but he'd stopped him. The sky was clear, and the autumn stars were out tonight, and lately he'd enjoyed gazing at them as he fell asleep. The stars had always fascinated him, and he took consolation with the knowledge that Perseus would be his companion in his time of dying.

Where was Hak Tallus? He wasn't real and never had been, but in this moment, it was easy to imagine him striding across the light-years, blaster at his side and the Galaxy Patrol at his back. Hak was out there, all right . . . and he felt tears gliding from the corners of his eyes. Tonight, his imagination wasn't enough. Now, as never before, he wanted to *be* Hak Tallus.

The pain was no longer as sharp as it had been, but the stars were beginning to dim, and each breath had become a mighty labor. The buzzer was a temptation that he wouldn't accept. He'd lived long enough. Time to let it go. Besides, he no longer had the strength to find the button and push it. So he gazed at Perseus and took comfort in the fact that, although Hak wasn't really out there, human-kind would nonetheless venture to the stars.

One day.

"Forward the Legion," he whispered, and then his eyes closed. Very soon after that, he felt nothing more.

No one was around to hear the last words of Nathan Arkwright. But his closest friends would have known what he meant.

BOOK ONE

The Legion of Tomorrow

1

When Kate Morressy's grandfather died on October 5, 2006, his passing made the front page of the next morning's *Boston Globe*. The headline—NATHAN ARKWRIGHT, SCIENCE FICTION PIONEER, DIES— appeared in the bottom-right corner below the fold, and it was the first thing Kate saw when she picked up the paper from the front stoop of her Cambridge apartment house.

Still wearing her robe, Kate stared at the newspaper in her hand for a long time before she carried it back into her apartment. Pausing to pour her first cup of coffee, she lay the paper down on the kitchen table and read the lead:

> *Nathan Arkwright, the science fiction author best known as creator of the Galaxy Patrol, died Thursday at his home in Lenox, Massachusetts.*
>
> *Arkwright, 85, is considered to be one of the "Big Four" sci-fi writers of the twentieth century, along with Robert A. Heinlein, Isaac Asimov, and Arthur C. Clarke. His 23 novels and five collections of short stories have been translated into dozens of languages and have sold millions of copies world-wide, and many readers credit him with sparking their interest in science.*
>
> *Arkwright's most famous creation was the Galaxy Patrol. Beginning in 1950 with the novel of the same title, it became*

a long-running series of space adventures that eventually consisted of 17 novels until its final installment, Through the Event Horizon, *appeared in 1988. The Galaxy Patrol was the basis for a radio drama, a CBS television series, three major motion pictures, and a daily comic strip. Many astronauts claim that they were inspired by the Galaxy Patrol, and a complete set of the novels is aboard the International Space Station.*

Born March 18, 1921, in Brooklyn, New York, Nathan Arkwright was . . .

Kate stopped reading. She ran a hand through her sleep-tangled red hair, slowly let out her breath, and then picked up the phone. Her mother lived in Milton, just south of Boston, and she was already up when Kate called.

"Grandpapa's dead," Kate said when her mother picked up the phone.

"Yes, he is." Very matter-of-fact, as if she'd just been given the weather forecast.

"I found out about it from the paper. Why didn't you call me?"

"I tried, but you were out of town."

"I was in Vermont." Kate glanced at the phone. Its message center displayed a zero, just as it had late last night when she'd returned home. "You didn't leave a message. You could have called my cell."

"How was Vermont? It's lovely this time of year, when the leaves are changing."

"Mom . . ." Kate shut her eyes and tried to count to ten but only made it to three. "Don't you think I would've cared that Grandpapa passed away?"

"Well, maybe you would, but . . ."

Sylvia Arkwright Morressy didn't finish the thought, and she didn't need to. She had stopped speaking to her father before Kate was born, for reasons that she'd never made clear. Indeed, Kate had met her grandfather only a few times in her life. The last occasion had been when she was a student at Dartmouth. Her boyfriend at the time, upon discovering that she was the granddaughter of Nathan Arkwright, had badgered her into driving down from New Hampshire so he could meet the famous author. They were met at the front door by the housekeeper, who allowed them to come in only so far as the front hall, where they waited until Grandpapa emerged from his study. He obligingly signed the boyfriend's wrinkled paperback copy of *The Galaxy Patrol* and then ushered the two college students who'd dropped in uninvited back out to the driveway, where Kate's secondhand Volvo was parked. Her mother had been outraged that Kate would do this, and Kate herself was embarrassed. That was eight years earlier . . . no, more like nine . . . and she'd stayed away from Grandpapa ever since.

"Are you going to the funeral?" Kate asked.

A pause. "No."

"Mom—"

"You can go if you'd like. Maybe there'll be someone you'll know."

Kate knew what her mother meant by this. Her grandmother had passed away before she was born; so as far as she knew, there were no other living members of his immediate family. "It would have been nice if you'd told me."

"I didn't find out until his agent called." Her tone hardened even further. "Her name's Margaret. Tell her I said hello."

Until she said that, Kate hadn't given much thought to attending her grandfather's funeral. Grandpapa was very nearly a stranger, a member of her family in name only. But her mother's indifference resolved the matter; she'd make the trip to Lenox because Nathan Arkwright's only child refused to do so.

"I will," she said.

"Very well, if you think must. Let me know if he left us anything. I kind of doubt it, but he might."

"I—" Kate bit off a response that wouldn't have done either of them any good. "Bye, Mom," she said instead, and she hung up.

2

Kate's trip to Vermont had been to do research for a magazine article she was writing about a nuclear power plant near Brattleboro that the local residents wanted to shut down. The only thing she had in common with her grandfather was that she, too, was a writer, although she'd chosen freelance science journalism instead of science fiction. She spent the rest of the day transcribing the interview tapes and incorporating them into her piece, but she took a break to make a call to *The Berkshire Eagle* and find out from the obits desk the place, date, and time the funeral service would be held. Kate's editor agreed to push back the deadline a few days to let her make the trip—indeed, he was impressed to learn that she was related to *the* Nathan Arkwright and even tried to talk Kate into writing a story about it. Kate told him she'd think about it, which was a polite way of saying no, and the next day she put on a black dress, got in her car, and drove west on the Massachusetts Turnpike into the Berkshires.

Although Nathan Arkwright had been an atheist, the funeral was held in a Congregational church. Kate would later learn that the pastor was big fan of Nathan's and had practically begged for the honor of hosting the memorial service. Thanks to GPS, Kate had little trouble locating the church; parking was another matter entirely. She wished that she'd left home earlier; both sides of the street were lined with cars for three blocks, with local police officers directing traffic.

The church was a big Gothic edifice built sometime in the 1800s, but by the time Kate got there, its oak pews were packed tightly, and people were standing against the walls. Nathan Arkwright may not have had much in the way of an immediate family, but he made up for it with fans, some of whom were apparently unaware of the proper way of dressing for a funeral; amid the dark suits and dresses, she spotted a few dress uniforms of the Galaxy Patrol, mainly worn by people who wouldn't have lasted a week in the Galactic Academy. Many had brought copies of the Patrol novels as if expecting the author to rise from his casket and give one last signing before he went off to the crematorium.

The casket itself rested in front of the nave, surrounded by so many wreaths and bouquets that every florist in town had probably been cleaned out. Its lid was closed, for which Kate was quietly grateful—she'd never been able to stand the sight of a dead body, even one tastefully arranged by a mortician—and instead a portrait photo of her grandfather was propped up on an easel. It was the same picture that had appeared on the dust jacket of every book Grandpapa published since 1972: Nathan Arkwright, a thick-set, red-haired man in his early fifties, smiling slightly as he regarded the prospective readers from behind wire-rimmed glasses with eyes both kindly and wise. Not the annoyed glare he'd given his granddaughter when she'd come to visit him.

The ushers were beginning to turn people away when Kate arrived, but when she quietly explained that she was a family member, she was escorted down the center aisle to the two front pews, which had been roped off with a red velvet cord. A few people were already seated in this section, older folks whom Kate recognized as distant cousins whom she barely knew; they nodded to her, not really recognizing her, either. She sat down by herself in the first pew and looked around. As she'd expected, Sylvia Morressy had made good her promise not to attend her father's funeral.

Once again, Kate wondered what her grandfather had done to

earn his daughter's hatred. She'd never said what it was that had caused her to avoid her father or to keep Kate away from him as much as possible. Even Kate's father didn't know why; Kate's mother filed for divorce before she ever gave him a satisfactory explanation.

The pastor had just emerged through a side door and was preparing to step up to the pulpit when four people approached the front pew. The youngest was a middle-aged man Kate recognized as Grandpapa's housekeeper; she remembered that his name was Mr. Sterling, and he looked very nearly the same as he had when she'd met him years earlier. The other three were two men and a woman, Grandpapa's age or thereabouts; one of the men sat in a wheelchair pushed by Mr. Sterling.

The usher who'd escorted Kate to her seat hurried up to meet them. As she watched, he quietly explained that the section was being reserved for family members. The woman—thin, petite, and silver haired but nonetheless bearing an inarguable presence—looked him straight in the eye and said something that Kate couldn't hear but which caused the younger man to hastily apologize. He pulled aside the cord and helped Mr. Sterling assist the woman and the taller of the two men into the pew; the man in the wheelchair remained seated in the aisle.

Kate didn't have the foggiest notion who they were, but it seemed as if the woman immediately recognized her; when she turned to glance at Kate, there was a look of surprise on an otherwise stoical face. The tall man—gaunt and gray, with jug ears and a nose like a beak—barely noticed her, but the man in the wheelchair, who'd lost most of his hair but still sported a trim white mustache, studied Kate as if trying to place her.

The woman stared at Kate so intently that it made her uncomfortable. Kate nervously looked away, but she could feel the old lady's eyes upon her. Kate was about to introduce herself when the pastor mounted the steps to the pulpit. An expectant hush fell upon the church, and Kate decided that any conversation would have to wait until later.

The opening prayer was ecumenical, and the hymnals remained untouched in their pew pockets, with the congregation instead invited to stand and sing the *Galaxy Patrol* theme song from the original TV series, the lyrics of which were conveniently printed in the program everyone had been handed upon walking in. Kate felt silly singing a song once popular on grade-school playgrounds, but apparently it was a bittersweet moment for many of the people seated behind her; she heard quiet sobs and choked voices when they reached the line "We boldly set forth for the stars," and she glanced back to see people dabbing tears from their eyes. *Whose idea was this?* Still, she had to admit, it was more suitable than "Amazing Grace" or "Shall We Gather at the River." Grandpapa was famously nonreligious.

The pastor's sermon was much like *The Boston Globe* obit, both respectful and impersonal. While it was clear that the pastor had met Nathan Arkwright and admired him, he didn't know him well enough to say anything reflecting anything more than a passing acquaintance. Instead, the pastor spoke of his novels and stories and how they'd entertained and inspired generations of readers. He said that Nathan had preferred solitude, particularly after his wife, Judith's, death, but he added that his correspondents had included scientists, authors, astronauts, and celebrities who'd been inspired by his books. He read bits from messages he'd received from famous people: a former NASA chief administrator, an *Apollo* moonwalker, the actor who'd portrayed Hak Tallus in the *Galaxy Patrol* movies. He ended the service by reading a passage from Grandpapa's last novel, *Through the Event Horizon*—a book that had made the *New York Times* Best Seller List and stayed there for nearly three months—which once again provoked sighs and tears from the congregation.

Before the service ended, the pastor announced that a private reception—"for family members and close friends only, please"—would be held at the deceased's residence. Only those who'd received invitations would be allowed to attend; another reception for members of the public would be held that afternoon at the local library.

Kate hadn't received an invitation, so it appeared that she'd be having fruit punch and cookies with Hak Tallus look-alikes if she decided not to drive home at once. The prospect wasn't particularly appealing. She'd just risen from her seat, though, when Mr. Sterling handed her an engraved invitation. Directions were printed on the back, just in case she'd forgotten how to get there.

Kate was still indecisive about going to the private reception; it was a three-hour drive from Lenox to Cambridge, probably longer now that it was leaf-peeping season and the Mass Pike was jammed with tour buses. But as she followed Mr. Sterling and the three old people up the aisle, the woman stopped and turned to her.

"You're Kate, yes?" She offered a hand. "I'm Margaret Krough, your grandfather's literary agent."

"Oh, yes." Kate recognized her name from the acknowledgments pages of Grandpapa's books. "Pleased to meet you, Ms. Krough."

"Maggie." A faint, almost enigmatic smile. "This is Harry"—she gestured to the man in the wheelchair—"and George." The tall man nodded, favoring her with an elfin grin. "Will you be at the reception?"

"Umm . . ."

"Please come. I'd like to have a little chat with you." Maggie turned back to Harry and George, who waited for her with the polite impatience of the elderly. "All right, gentlemen," she said, "let's be off."

Mr. Sterling continued pushing the wheelchair, but not before Harry raised a gnarled fist. "Forward the Legion!" he exclaimed.

The others laughed out loud. Kate had no idea what was so funny.

3

Nathan Arkwright's home was located just outside Lenox on a twenty-acre spread at the foot of the mountains. It was a sprawling, single-story manor built in a '70s-modernistic style that was sort of a cross between traditional New England saltbox and midwestern ranch house, with cedar siding and a steep, slate-shingle roof. Once past a front gate marked with a No Trespassing—Private Property sign, Kate followed the gravel driveway as it wound through maple-shaded meadows glowing with autumn wildflowers until she reached a circular turnaround surrounding an abstract iron sculpture.

Several cars were already parked off to the side of the driveway, and she'd barely pulled into the turnaround when a valet in a black windbreaker walked out to open the door for her and ask for the keys. She watched her eight-year-old Subaru with missing hubcaps go away to be parked next to a Lexus and a BMW and knew at once that she was the poor relation both literally and figuratively.

Mr. Sterling had already returned from the services. He met her in the front hall just as he had many years ago, yet this time he was friendlier, addressing her as Kate instead of Ms. Morressy as he hung up her overcoat in the foyer. He led her to the living room and had a tuxedoed caterer offer her a champagne flute and then excused himself.

The living room was large and broad, with a high ceiling and tall cathedral windows looking out upon the Berkshires. Modernist butcher-block furniture surrounded a circular central fireplace; upon oak-paneled walls were framed cover paintings from Grandpapa's books—the better ones by Emshwiller, Freas, and Whelan. The obligatory vanity bookcase contained multiple editions of his novels and collections in several languages, crowned by an acrylic cube: the Grand Master Nebula he'd received from the Science Fiction & Fantasy Writers of America a few years after he'd unofficially retired from the field.

The house looked like a million bucks. Kate had little doubt that it had probably cost that much too. The Galaxy Patrol had made its creator a wealthy man.

Drink in hand, Kate strolled through the room, surrounded by people and yet alone. Aside from the distant cousins she'd briefly met at the funeral, she knew no one. It was likely that many of those here were editors and publishing executives who'd come up from New York, while others might be fellow authors; she wasn't part of that world, though, so none of their faces were familiar. Kate was Nathan Arkwright's granddaughter, but the truth of the matter was that—aside from all his books and stories—she'd barely known him at all.

Drink your champagne and go home, she said to herself. *You've fulfilled your family obligation. No one will even notice that you've left.*

"Kate?"

Turning around, she found Margaret Krough standing beside her. The old lady had approached her so quietly that she hadn't seen her grandfather's agent until she spoke her name. "Ms. Krough."

"As I said, it's Maggie." Again, the same direct gaze, with emerald eyes unfaded by age. "So glad you made it. I've been expecting you."

"Yes, well . . ." Kate fiddled with the glass in her hand, her drink still untasted. "Just dropping by, really. I've got a long drive home and—"

"Oh no! Not yet. I'd really like to have a word with you, and so would George and Harry." Maggie took her by the hand. "Come this way, please . . . where we can talk in private."

For a woman in her eighties, Maggie was surprisingly spry. Walking quickly, she led Kate across the room, and as she did, Kate noticed how many eyes turned their way. Margaret Krough was plainly a figure of respect among this crowd. A small, birdlike man whose suit that probably cost more than Kate made in a month swooped in upon them, but Maggie frosted him with a tight, drop-dead-thank-you smile and moved on before he could do more than open his mouth.

"Who was that?" Kate murmured.

"One of Nat's publishers. Probably wants to renegotiate. I'll deal with him later." Maggie opened a door beside a baby grand piano and ushered Kate inside. "Come, dear."

Maggie closed the door behind them and turned the deadbolt lock. Kate hadn't been in this room since she was a little girl. It was her grandfather's office. Amid oak bookcases, a glass display shelf holding globes of Earth, the Moon, and Mars, and an antique brass telescope stood an L-shaped desk, the older-model IBM computer resting upon it surrounded by untidy stacks of paper. The windows faced the mountains, but the curtains were shut; the only light came from floor lamps beside the frayed leather armchairs and a couch that looked as if he'd regularly used it for naps. The magician's den.

George stood before the shelf, idly inspecting the Mars globe. Harry sat in his wheelchair, leafing through the papers on the desk. Kate had once been spanked for doing just that, during the only Christmas get-together she and her parents had ever attended, but Harry didn't seem the slightest bit embarrassed to be caught in the act.

"Looking for an idea to steal?" Maggie asked, her tone playfully scolding.

Harry made a rude sound with his lips. "You kidding? He stole his best ideas from me."

"So you've always said." George turned away from the globes and picked up the drink he'd left on an end table. "You're just jealous he . . . well, never mind. Hello, Ms. Morressy. So happy you've come. I'm just sorry we haven't met until now."

"No, we haven't. But I've never met any of Grandpapa's friends, so I guess that figures." The two men were strangers to her but obviously old acquaintances of her grandfather's. "Maggie told me your names, but I don't—"

"Harry Skinner," Harry said. "One of Nat's colleagues. We got started at the same time." A wry smile as he carefully returned some typewritten pages to their place on the desk. "I seldom wrote under my own name, though. Most readers know me as Matt Brown."

He gave her an expectant look, as if hoping that she'd recognize his byline. "I'm sorry, Mr. Skinner—"

"Harry."

"But I haven't read much science fiction except my grandfather's."

A sad smile, accompanied by an even sadder sigh. "Story of my life," Harry said quietly. "Thirty-nine books, and I'll probably be forgotten ten minutes after I'm dead."

"I always said you should have picked a better pseudonym." Maggie walked over to one of the armchairs and lowered herself into it. "Something more memorable than the shade of paint you put on your house."

"George Hallahan." George carried his drink to the couch. "Not a writer . . . or at least not science fiction."

Kate nodded, and then something tickled the back of her mind. She remembered a piece she'd written a couple of years earlier when she'd covered a conference at MIT regarding interstellar exploration; several speakers had made reference to the work of a former Manhattan Project scientist, a physicist from the Institute of Advanced Study by name of . . .

"Dr. George Hallahan." She stared at him. A legend in the theoretical physics community. "You knew Grandpapa."

"An old and dear friend. He'd call from time to time when he needed help with something." Seeing the astonished look on her face, George grinned. "No, you won't find my name in any of the acknowledgments. The security agreements I'd signed when I was doing

28

military research at General Atomics would have meant getting a visit from the FBI if they'd learned I was telling a science fiction writer how nuclear rocket engines worked. Besides, it didn't hurt Nat's reputation to let his readers believe that he dreamed up that techy stuff all by himself."

"Not to mention his plots," Harry muttered.

"Hush. Not true, and you know it." Maggie turned to Kate. "It doesn't sound like it, but Harry and Nat were best friends, practically brothers. What you're hearing is the sound of sibling rivalry."

Kate discreetly glanced at her watch. It was almost one o'clock. If she stayed much longer, she'd hit the weekend traffic on the pike going back to Boston. "Well, it's been a pleasure to meet all of you, but—"

Maggie held up a hand. "This is important, and I promise we won't take much more of your time. It concerns your grandfather's will."

"Oh?"

An apologetic smile. "I wish I could tell you otherwise, but it's not what you think, if you're thinking what I expect you'd be. Nat's lawyer let me take a look at it, so I'll spare you the anxiety of waiting to hear from him. Your grandfather left nothing to his family. Not you, not your mother, and not any of the relatives hanging around outside." A dry laugh. "Mr. Sterling found a case of *The Galaxy Patrol* in the basement. Signed Gnome Press first editions, just a little brown around the edges. Quite valuable. He'll be giving them to everyone here, just so no one goes home empty-handed."

"Bet half of them wind up on eBay," Harry said.

"Disappointed?" George seemed to be studying Kate's reaction.

She shrugged. "Not really. I barely knew Grandpapa, and he and Mom didn't get along at all. I really shouldn't expect that he'd leave us"—she waved a hand around the office—"all this."

"No." Maggie crossed her legs. "The house is being put on the market. The furniture will be auctioned. His books are being purchased by an antiquarian book dealer in New York, and we're negotiating with science fiction art collectors in Chicago and Alabama for his paintings. His savings will be liquidated, as well, once the estate's debts are settled. Fortunately, there are not many. Nat was nothing if not frugal." She smiled. "Even his papers are going somewhere else . . . the Eaton Collection at the University of California–Riverside. No cash for that, I'm afraid, but the estate will be getting a nice tax write-off."

"I see. And who's getting the money?"

"The Arkwright Foundation."

"The what?"

"Nat stated in his will that a nonprofit foundation is to be established in his name to underwrite various worthy projects. As executor of his literary estate, it will be my responsibility to make sure that all future income from his books—royalties, reprint sales, residuals from his media properties, and so forth—will be funneled directly into the foundation, where it will be invested into various enterprises that will increase the income over time."

"Uh-huh. I see." Kate set down the champagne and folded her arms together. "And what's to prevent the Arkwright Foundation from becoming your own money market account?"

Maggie's lips pursed, and her eyes became glacial. George cleared his throat. "You have a right to be suspicious," he said, quietly diplomatic, "but I assure you, on both my word of honor and the memory of our friend, that nothing of the sort will happen. In fact, that's the reason we've asked you here. We'd like to ask you to join us on the foundation's board of directors."

"Me? But I—"

"Barely knew him," Harry said, finishing her thought for her. "Yeah, we know. Believe me, Nat regretted this more than you'll ever know."

"I'm going to have to believe you, because he sure didn't let me know."

"Your mother stood in the way," George continued. "Their enmity is something we can't undo, but we can step around her by asking you to be the family's representative in the Arkwright Foundation."

"I see," Kate said, although she really didn't. To buy herself a moment, she picked up her drink. The champagne had lost its sparkle, but it wet a throat that had gone dry. "You still haven't told me what the foundation is all about. What's its purpose? Establish a wild bird sanctuary? Save whales? Provide free science fiction books to underprivileged kids?"

None of the three said anything for a few seconds. Harry and George looked at Maggie, silently deferring to her.

"We could tell you," Maggie said at last, "but it's a long story and one you might not believe if you heard it here and now. Perhaps it's better if you found out yourself."

Standing up from her chair, Maggie walked over to the desk. Opening a drawer, she pulled out a white cardboard box. "This is the last thing your grandfather wrote," she said, carrying it across the room. "An autobiography he'd been working on over the last several months or so. He didn't finish it . . . and frankly, I'm glad he didn't. I asked him not to write the damned thing, but he wouldn't listen."

Kate took the box from her and opened it. Inside lay a short sheaf of typewritten paper, probably no more than sixty or seventy pages in all. The cover sheet read *My Life in the Future,* with her grandfather's byline below it. "Why didn't you want him to write it?"

Maggie hesitated. "There are things about him that shouldn't be published."

"She's right," Harry said. "Your grandfather had secrets that shouldn't have been revealed while he was still alive . . . while a lot of people are still alive." George nodded in agreement.

"It's an incomplete manuscript, though, so no doubt you'll have questions." Maggie returned to her seat. Groaning softly, she bent down to pick up her handbag from where she'd left it on the side table. "You'll probably want to call us," she went on, opening it to fish out a silver card holder. "Here's my card. Harry and George will give you theirs too."

"I don't have one," Harry said, "but my number's in the Philly phone book." Catching a look from Maggie, he shrugged. "So I'm cheap. Sue me."

"I can be reached at the institute," George said. "I'll tell my secretary to put you through if you call."

Kate glanced at the card Maggie handed her: KROUGH LITERARY AGENCY, with a Park Avenue address in New York. "Why don't you just tell me?" she asked.

"Think of this as investigative journalism," Maggie replied. "Just don't publish the results."

"Okay, but how do I know you'll tell me the truth?"

"You can trust us," George said, a sly smile upon his face. "We're the Legion of Tomorrow."

4

My Life in the Future sat untouched on Kate's desk for the next couple of weeks while she worked on the nuclear power plant story. Autumn winds were pulling the leaves from the trees before she had a chance to pick it up again; by then, the conversation she'd had with her grandfather's friends had faded to the back of her mind, becoming little more than a curious incident.

Her mother didn't apologize for skipping the funeral, but she seemed a little more interested when Kate told her about having met Maggie, Harry, and George. She didn't know the two men but told Kate that she'd known Maggie over the years; apparently, she got along with Grandpapa's agent, because she asked how she was doing.

Yet she wasn't surprised that her father hadn't remembered either her or Kate in his will and was only mildly put out to discover that he'd left everything to the Arkwright Foundation.

"Figures he'd do that," she said, sitting across the breakfast nook from Kate when her daughter came to visit her. "Even in the end, he cared nothing for his family."

Hearing this, Kate remembered something Maggie had said: how her grandfather had actually cared for her but that her mother had stood in the way. "Mom, why didn't you and Grandpapa get along?" she asked. "What did he do that was so terrible?"

Her mother stared down at her coffee cup. "It's better that you don't know."

Kate hesitated. "Did he . . . umm . . . touch you, or . . . ?"

"No." Sylvia Arkwright shook her head. "Grandpapa may have been many things, but child molester wasn't one of them." She picked up her coffee, and Kate noticed that her hand trembled slightly. "But he was cold toward me most of my life, and I knew even as a young girl that he really didn't love me. It wasn't until she was dying that your grandmother told me why."

"And that is?"

Her mother said nothing for a few moments and instead gazed out the kitchen window. "She made me swear that I wouldn't tell you until Grandpapa was gone," she said at last. "I'm not sure I'm ready to break that promise yet. It's a little too painful, and I'm just not willing to share that with anyone. Even you."

It was this conversation that reignited Kate's interest in her grandfather's unfinished autobiography. Upon returning home, she picked it up from her desk and carried it into the den. There was a message on her phone from the guy she'd been dating for a while; he complained that he hadn't seen her in a couple of weeks and wanted to know if they could get together soon. Kate had never been good at maintaining relationships, but she realized that if she didn't let him know that she was still interested in him, he'd slip out of her life the way so many of her other former boyfriends had. All she needed to do was make a quick call and promise to get together with him for dinner and a show.

Of course she would. Then she turned to the first page of Grandpapa's autobiography, and that idea faded from her mind.

5

"My life changed," Nathan Arkwright would later write, "the day I picked up the June 1939 issue of *Astounding Science Fiction* and read in 'In Times to Come' that there would be a convention of science fiction fans in New York during the first week of July. Since it was intended to coincide with the New York World's Fair in Flushing Meadows, it was being called the World's Science Fiction Convention. Although I knew at once that I had to go, little did I realize that it would shape my destiny . . ."

Sunday morning church bells were still echoing through midtown Manhattan when Nat strolled down West Fifty-ninth Street. He didn't know exactly where Caravan Hall was, but that was where the piece in *Astounding* had said the convention was being held. As it turned out, it was a couple of blocks from the Hudson River waterfront, and he didn't have to look hard to find it. A handful of young men standing out front holding copies of the latest issues of *Amazing, Astounding,* and *Thrilling Wonder* told him that he'd come to the right place.

Oddly, two police officers stood beside the steps leading to the front door. They were eyeing everyone who walked in, and Nat couldn't help but notice that one of them was tapping his nightstick against his leg. This didn't look good. Nat decided that he'd better make sure he was in the right place, so he approached three guys standing across the street from the hall. One of them, a skinny fellow with a row of protuberant front teeth, gazed at Nat as he stepped up to them.

"Excuse me, but—" Nat began.

"You're looking for the World's Science Fiction Convention?"

Nat nodded.

"Upstairs. Second floor." He nodded toward the door. "Who are you?"

"Nat Arkwright, from Brooklyn."

"Fred Pohl, from Queens." He offered a handshake as he nodded to the others. "Don Wollheim and Cyril Kornbluth."

Nat shook hands with each of them, trying not to show his nervousness. He recognized Wollheim and Pohl as bylines from stories he'd read; they weren't major writers, to be sure, but he was envious to meet fellows not much older than himself who'd succeeded in selling stories to the pulps. But it wasn't just that. Nat had never before met anyone else who shared his passion for science fiction; no one else at Brooklyn High had the slightest bit of interest in this sort of thing, and he found himself anxious to fit in.

"How did you find out about this?" Cyril asked. He was a big, broad-shouldered fellow whose sharp eyes peered at Nat from behind horn-rimmed glasses.

"Saw a bit about it in that magazine." Nat pointed to the copy of *Astounding* tucked under Cyril's arm. It was the new issue, with a cover story, "Black Destroyer," by someone he'd never heard of, A. E. van Vogt. "Close enough to where I live, so I decided to drop in."

"Oh, so you're new to this," Don said. "Lucky for you. They're banning the Futurians."

Nat gave him a baffled look. "What's a Futurian?"

The other three were already chuckling over this. "Maybe it's better you don't know," Fred said. "But you may want to move on. If someone sees you with us, they might not let you in."

Putting two and two together, Nat determined that these three fellows were Futurians, whoever they might be. He looked across the street at the cops. "Is that why they're here?"

"Uh-huh." Cyril followed Nat's gaze; one of the cops stared back, and neither the cop nor Cyril dropped his eyes. "Sam . . . that's Sam Moskowitz, the convention chairman . . . saw us coming and wouldn't let us in. We tried to rush the door, and he called the cops—"

"*You* rushed the door," Fred said pointedly. "I was still at the dentist."

"Yeah, you got here late and missed everything." Don was grinning like the proverbial cat. "That, and Cyril punching Forry Ackerman in the stomach—"

"He had it coming." Cyril smiled at Nat and then suddenly balled a fist and feigned a lunge at him.

It wasn't the first time someone had tried to fake him out this way; Nat didn't flinch but simply glared at him instead. Disappointed, Cyril relaxed, and Nat turned to Fred again. "What does Sam have against you that makes him want to—"

"Never mind. Long story." Fred shook his head. "Go on up and have fun. Just don't let anyone know you've met us, if you know what's good for you."

Nat hesitated and then turned and walked across the street. The two cops watched him, and sure enough, before he set foot on the stairs, one of them moved to block his way. But then a kid about Nat's age who'd been standing behind tapped the policeman on the shoulder and whispered something in his ear. The cop nodded and without a word stepped away, swinging his nightstick to let Nat know that it was okay to proceed. Letting go of his breath, Nat walked upstairs and through the door.

Caravan Hall was a single large room with a bare wooden floor and walls painted in a pseudo-Egyptian art-deco style, the sort of second-floor loft usually rented out for lodge meetings and private dances. Although the balcony doors were open, the room was stuffy with the trapped heat of a summer day; the only concession was a water-cooler off to one side, with a coin dispenser that sold paper cups for a nickel. One look at it, and Nat decided that he'd rather go thirsty; the dollar he'd coughed up at the folding paper near the door represented half of what he'd earned last week in commissions from the part-time job he had at his family's shoe store, and he'd need the pocket change he had left for a meal and the subway ride back home.

The room was filled with young men—mainly in their teens and twenties, most of them wearing jackets and ties—but, so far as Nat could tell, only two or three girls. They chatted with one another, leafed through the hectographed fan publications set out on display tables, studied the garish cover paintings from pulp magazines that had been placed on easels. A projection screen had been set up at the far end of the room, and the program sheet he'd been handed told him that *Metropolis* would be shown that evening.

Nat had heard of the movie but had never seen it; he wondered if his father would mind too much if he stayed late to catch it. Probably. His father wasn't crazy about his son's fascination with trashy pulps, let alone his aspiration to write for them. This might be the only day he'd be able to spend at the convention, and only because the store was closed on Sunday. Nat wandered through the crowd, determined to make the best of it but still at a loss as to how.

He noticed a small group standing off toward one side of the room and walked over to see what was going on. He discovered that they were all looking at a tall guy with a goofy smile who had shown up wearing a fin-shouldered outfit that looked as if it had come straight out of a *Buck Rogers* strip; the crowd was both admiring and laughing at his costume, and the chap wearing it was basking in the attention. As he moved closer to get a better look, Nat bumped shoulders with a teenager just a year or two younger than himself.

"Sorry," Nat said, and the other youngster smiled forgivingly. "Will you get a load of that?" he added, trying to strike up a conversation.

"Yeah, it's something, isn't it?" The boy wore an open-collar shirt and no tie; his casual attire and midwestern accent told Nat that he wasn't a New Yorker. "Forry made it all by himself. He wanted to wear it on the bus, but I wouldn't let him."

Nat figured that this must the same Forry whom Cyril Kornbluth had punched earlier. He wondered if it was because of the costume or simply because Cyril liked punching people. Whatever the reason, he decided not to mention it. "Where did you come from?"

"Los Angeles."

"You took the bus all the way from California?" Nat was incredulous. The boy nodded happily. "How long did it take you to—?"

"Just who the hell do you think you are?" a voice demanded.

At first, Nat thought someone was addressing him. When he looked around, though, he saw that the voice belonged to someone standing directly behind him and the guy from California. Another teenager, he was directing his anger at a man in his late twenties.

"The convention chair, that's who," the older man replied, just as angry as the kid. "And if you're going to be passing out those things"—he pointed to a bunch of red pamphlets in the youngster's hand—"then I reserve the right to tell you to take a hike."

"Me? What are you coming at me for?" Stocky and a head shorter than the man who'd confronted him, with a peach-fuzz mustache grown in an obvious attempt to make himself look older, the kid had the pugnacious attitude of someone who'd grown up on the street; Nathan's ear picked up a Philly accent. "They're not mine, pal. I just found them stashed under the radiator and thought—"

"You'd be a good guy and hand 'em out?" The convention chairman—this must be the Sam Moskowitz, Nat figured, whom Cyril Kornbluth said had called the cops—reached to take them away. "Fat chance I'm letting you Futurians pass around your commie filth. Give 'em here!"

The kid backed away, and as he did, one of the pamphlets fell from his hands. Curious, Nat bent down to pick it up. He barely had a chance to read the headline—BEWARE THE DICTATORSHIP!—before Sam snatched it away from him.

"Hey!" Nat exclaimed. "I was looking at that!"

Sam ignored him. By then, several people who'd been admiring the man in the futuristic costume had turned their attention to the argument. From the corner of his eye, Nat noticed that one of them was a pretty girl about his own age, one of the few females in the room. Nat hoped that he wasn't embarrassing himself.

"Surely, just reading the material isn't grounds for expulsion." This from another bystander, a tall chap with a beak nose and ears like pitcher handles. He gestured to the pamphlet Sam had taken away from Nat. "If you don't want to be accused of being a dictator, perhaps you shouldn't behave like one."

The convention chairman cast him an angry glare, and in that moment of distraction, the girl moved in. "May I have one of those, please?" she asked the kid, politely holding out her hand. "I'd like to see what it says."

The kid grinned and started to give her a pamphlet, but Sam blocked him. "Oh no, you don't! Try that again, and I'm throwing you out with the rest of the Futurians!"

"Oh yeah? Then how come you let Asimov in?" He pointed to a fellow wearing a bow tie who stood nearby. "He's one of them too, y'know."

"Hey, leave me out of this," Asimov said.

"He agreed to behave himself and not bring politics into the convention."

"Politics, or just politics you don't like?" The kid gave him a look of contempt. "You're about as bad as Herr Schicklgruber, you know that?"

Sam's face went red, his lips pulling back from his teeth. Nat saw his hands start to curl into fists, and he knew that a punch was coming.

"Hey, now, wait a sec," he began, stepping forward to place himself between the two combatants.

But Sam was already in motion, and all Nat managed to do was get in the way. Caught off balance, he fell to the floor; a second later, he found himself at the young lady's feet. She had nice legs. He looked up to find her staring down at him, both aghast and amused, and he was trying to find something clever to say—how would Cary Grant handle this?—when another guy rushed forward to push the chairman and the kid away from each other.

"Okay, break it up!" he demanded. "No fighting in here!"

"Get 'em out of here, Willie!" Sam snapped, pointing to both the kid and Nat. "Throw 'em out, both of 'em!"

Nat stared at him. "Now just a minute! I didn't—"

"No, he did not." The girl stepped over Nat to confront Willie. "He was trying to stop a fight, that's all. Your friend—"

"Her too!" Sam snapped his fingers toward the door. "Out! Now!"

Willie started to reach for the girl, but she slapped the back of his wrist. "Mitts off, buster!" He winced and yanked his hand back, and she turned to Sam. "If this is the way you intend to run this convention, then I'll be happy to leave."

By then, Nat was beginning to sit up. "And even if you were giving me a choice in the matter, I'd join her, anyway."

She glanced down at him and gave him a lovely smile. Yeah, that was the right thing to say. Nat started to struggle up from the floor and found himself being helped to his feet by the kid. Now it was the three of them against the convention chairman and his friend. This wasn't the way Nat intended to make friends here, but there was no backing down now.

"I'm not a Futurian," Nat said to Sam, "but could you point them out to me so I can ask to join?" Not waiting for an answer, he patted the kid's shoulder. "C'mon, friend. Let me buy you a cup of coffee."

"I'll buy you both lunch," the girl said. "There's a place across the street. Let's go."

Nat and the kid shared a surprised glance. A free lunch from a swell-looking girl was an offer they couldn't refuse.

"After you, madam," the kid said, giving her a gallant bow.

"Thank you, kind sir." She fell in step with them as they walked away. Ignoring the stares and scattered applause of those who'd witnessed the altercation, they made their way through the crowded hall and down the steps, but it wasn't until they reached the sidewalk that they discovered a fourth person had joined them, the tall fellow who'd tried to defend them.

"What are you doing here?" Nat asked. "They didn't throw you out."

"No, they didn't." The tall man reached into his jacket pocket and pulled out a briar pipe. "But hanging around with the three of you looks like more fun."

The restaurant across the street from Caravan Hall was an Automat, appropriately futuristic for the World's Science Fiction Convention. Vending machines with little glass doors dispensed sandwiches and pie slices for a nickel apiece, leaving the waiter with only the job of coming around to pour coffee. For Sunday noon, the place was crowded; all the tables were taken.

The girl—whose name was Margaret Krough, although she insisted that they call her Maggie—made good her promise to buy lunch for Nat and the kid. His name was Harry Skinner, and it was clear that, although he seemed to be just as poor as Nat was, he was perfectly willing to take advantage of her generosity; he let Maggie plug nickels into the machines until he had a submarine sandwich, a Boston cream pie, and a carton of milk on his tray. Nat settled for a chicken salad sandwich and told Maggie that he'd repay her later. The tall chap, whose name was George Hallahan, bought his own lunch; Maggie's offer hadn't been extended to him, but he didn't seem to mind. A little older than the rest of them, he was also the most reserved, yet Nat detected a keen and swift intelligence behind his quiet, perpetual smile.

Once they'd collected their food, they waited a few minutes for a group to vacate a table so they could take their place. "I think half the convention has moved over here," Nat said, looking around as they settled into chrome-frame chairs. Everyone in the room appeared to be the same sort of young men whom they'd left behind.

"Not surprised," said Harry. "There's a feud going on among the fans who organized the convention. The Futurians are the guys who lost, so the other guys voted in an exclusion act to bar them from coming in." He motioned toward a large group who'd pulled together several tables; Nat recognized among them Fred, Cyril, and Don. "But they showed up, anyway, and that's got the people inside hot under the collar."

"So what is it about them that's upset the other guys?"

"The Futurians believe that science fiction can change the world," Harry said. "They think it should do more than just entertain people and instead present ways in which science and technology can solve social problems. The other guys—the so-called New Fandom, although most of them are just diehards from the old Science Fiction League—only want monsters and mad scientists and claim that the Futurians are nothing but a bunch of communists." A lopsided grin. "They're half-right, really. Some of the Futurians are reds . . . or at least they used to be."

Nat nodded. Although he wasn't interested in joining the Communist Party, he had to agree that science fiction needed to get past its adolescent tendencies. "And the leaflet you were handing out?"

"Dave Kyle wrote it. It's a statement of the Futurian position." Harry bit into his sandwich. "He must have tried to ditch 'em under the radiator," he added, speaking around a mouthful of food. "I found 'em and decided to hand 'em out, anyway." An unhappy shrug. "Fat lot of good that did me."

Nat frowned but said nothing. He was beginning to regret his decision to step up for Harry. Wasting a dollar was bad enough; it now appeared that he'd made enemies with the convention chairman, as well. He hoped that incident wouldn't hurt his goals of becoming a writer, but it appeared that he might have picked the wrong side.

"Sounds like you know a lot," Maggie said. From her accent, Nat pegged her as another New Yorker, but it wasn't hard to tell that her neighborhood wasn't in any of the boroughs. From the nice outfit she wore and the casual way she pulled lunch money from her purse, it wasn't hard to guess that she lived somewhere on the Upper East Side. "You know these people?"

"Some of 'em. I've been coming to meetings of the Philadelphia Science Fiction Society for about a year now; that's where this whole thing was hatched." Harry put aside the sandwich and reached for the carton of milk. "What about you? Why are you here?"

"I like science fiction, that's all." There was a hint of defensiveness in her tone.

Nat opened his sandwich, inspected the wilted lettuce leaf on top, and decided that it hadn't turned bad enough to make him sick. "I guess what he means is, y'know, I didn't see many girls in there. I didn't think any of them read this stuff until I met you."

Maggie gave him a sharp look but then cooled down a little when she saw the smile on his face. "I suppose not many do," she admitted. "But I'll read anything that looks interesting, and there are some good stories in those magazines, particularly *Astounding*, ever since it got a new editor."

"John Campbell." Nat nodded in agreement. "Yes, he's changed the magazine quite a bit since he's come aboard. I'd like to—"

He stopped himself before he could finish what he was about to say: *I'd like to send him one of my stories.* He was reluctant to identify himself as a would-be writer, particularly not with three people whom he'd just met.

But Maggie was eyeing him curiously, as if she'd caught what he'd almost let slip. Picking up her fork, she played with the garden salad she'd bought. "I think I wouldn't mind working for a magazine like that," she said. "Perhaps as an assistant editor."

"Is that what you do?" George was ignoring the sandwich he'd bought and instead had lit his pipe. He sat back in his chair, carefully blowing his smoke away from their faces.

"That's what I'd like to do one day," Maggie said. "I'm entering Columbia in the fall as an English major. I'm hoping it will lead to a job at one of the publishers here in the city."

"Really?" Nat said. "I'm starting school next semester too. Boston College, engineering." He didn't add that he was only able to attend because he'd managed to get a scholarship while in his senior year at Brooklyn High. Maggie's family obviously had enough money to send her to school; his didn't.

"That's interesting." George smiled around the stem of his pipe. "I'm in my third trimester at MIT as a physics major. That'll practically make us neighbors."

"Not going to college." Harry looked down at his tray as if he'd just admitted something embarrassing. Then he brightened and smiled at Maggie. "But hey, once you get a job at *Astounding*, maybe you'll buy a story I'll send you!"

Maggie looked interested. "You want to be a writer?"

"I already am a writer," Harry insisted. "I just haven't sold anything yet."

"I'm writing too," Nat blurted out before he could stop himself. Maggie raised an eyebrow, and Harry cast him an incredulous look as if to say, *Yeah, sure you are.* "No, really. I've been trying to get something in at *Amazing*, but haven't had any luck yet."

"Shouldn't be too hard," Harry said dryly. "Palmer will publish anything."

Nat felt his face burn. *Amazing* had been declining lately, its new editor evidently preferring cheap melodramatics to scientific accuracy. But he caught the wry grin on Harry's face and realized that the jab hadn't been intended to be mean. Harry might be a potential rival but might also be a friend.

"So I guess we're Futurians now," Maggie said. "Or at least fellow travelers, so far as the convention organizers are concerned." She looked dejected at the fact that they'd been thrown out of the hall.

"No, we're not." Harry shook his head. "Look, I know what I said back there about joining 'em, but they've got their own little group already, and they're not going to let us in just because I started handing out their pamphlets." He gave Nat and Maggie an apologetic look. "Didn't mean to get you guys tossed out. Thanks for sticking up for me."

"No sweat," Nat said. "I don't like bullies, that's all."

"Besides, we're not missing anything," Maggie said, and she smiled when the other three regarded her with disbelief. "I mean, we've met each other, haven't we? That's worth my dollar."

"Yeah, maybe you're right." Harry nodded in agreement. "Who needs the Futurians? Maybe we should start our own little club."

George closed his eyes, turned his face toward the ceiling. "The Legion of . . . Space."

"Naw." Harry shook his head. "Uh-uh. Jack Williamson wrote a story with that name some years ago."

"I know." George grinned. "I really liked it. And that's what I'm interested in—space."

"So am I." Nat smiled at him. "Y'know, this might sound crazy, but I really believe there's a chance someone might go to the Moon. Maybe even by the end of the century."

A nod and a knowing wink from George. "Sooner than that, I think."

"I like that name," Maggie said. "The Legion of Space, I mean."

"Okay, but Harry's right. It's got to be something else." Nat thought about it for a moment. "The Legion of Time."

"Jack Williamson again." Harry used a fork to spear an olive from

Maggie's salad and fling it across the table at Nat. "C'mon, there's got to be—"

"The Legion of Tomorrow," Maggie suggested as she moved her salad away from him.

No one said anything for a second. The four of them looked at one another, tasting the name on their tongues. "I like it," Nat said. "I like it a lot."

"All right, then . . . that's who we are." Maggie held out her hand, palm down. "The Legion of Tomorrow."

Nat didn't hesitate. He reached out his hand, placed it on top of Maggie's. George grinned and extended his own hand to rest it on top of Nat's. Harry gave the other three a look, bemused that anyone would take him seriously, but then he joined the circle with his own hand.

"Forward the Legion," he said. Then he leaned back in his chair and yelled to the group of Futurians sitting nearby. "Get that? The Legion of Tomorrow is coming for you!"

Don Wollheim stared at him. "Who?"

6

Later that day, Sam Moskowitz offered a compromise with the Futurians: he'd let them into the hall, provided that they promised to behave themselves and not cause any problems. All but five—Don Wollheim, Fred Pohl, Cyril Kornbluth, Bob Lowndes, and Jack Gillespie—accepted the olive branch and went in, but Sam's attempt to make peace didn't make much difference. The following day, the Futurians announced a counterconvention in Brooklyn for July 4, and that's where most of the writers went for the final day of the World's Science Fiction Convention.

I didn't know about this. Monday, July 3, was another day at the shoe store for me. So while my new friends Harry, George, and Maggie took advantage of Sam's amnesty pact to return to Caravan Hall for presentations about science and its role in the glorious future to come, I was measuring some restless tyke's feet for a new pair of Buster Browns. My father noticed that I was unhappy, so he made me a deal: if I'd stop sighing and gazing forlornly out the window, he'd close the shop for Independence Day and let me attend the rest of the convention.

The final day of what would later be called Nycon 1 wasn't at Caravan Hall, though, or even in Manhattan. Instead, the official event of the last day was a "Science Fiction Softball Game" at Flushing Meadows Park in Queens . . .

John W. Campbell, Jr. loosened his necktie, rolled up his sleeves, and spit in his palms. In no hurry at all, he bent down to pick up the baseball bat from where it had been dropped by the last player. He ambled to home plate, where he crouched low over the sandbag, hefted the bat high above his shoulder, and glared at the young man standing atop the pitcher's mound.

"Awright, kid," Campbell growled. "Show me your stuff."

The fierce look and icy voice with which he challenged the pitcher were the same he used on countless writers who'd cowered on the other side of his desk. But he wasn't in *Astounding*'s office in the Street & Smith Building, and the young fan from Philadelphia who stood on the mound had no desire to sell him a story. He sized up the burly older man pinch-hitting for the Queensboro team and then gazed past him at his catcher. The other Philly player lowered a hand between his knees and pointed a finger at the ground. The pitcher nodded slightly, understanding the catcher's signal. He juggled the softball in his mitt, making Campbell wait a second while he stole a sly glance over his shoulder to make sure that the last

Queens player at bat was still on second—there had been enough base stealing in the game already. Then he whipped back around and, with no warning at all, snapped the ball straight toward the catcher's glove.

It was an underhand pitch, but Babe Ruth couldn't have done better. Campbell was unprepared. He swung the bat wildly but didn't even come close. The bat hadn't completed its arc when there was the leathery smack of the ball slamming into the catcher's glove.

"Strike one!" the umpire yelled.

"Hell!" Campbell snarled.

Laughter from the bleachers, although the few writers who'd shown up for the game were wise enough to cover their mouths with their hands. Campbell was a big cheese in the pulp business, and no one wanted to risk getting on his bad side. The game had been listed in the convention program as being "Science Fiction Professionals vs. Science Fiction Fans," yet so few writers had actually shown up that the lineup had been changed at the last minute. Now it was between the Cometeers of the Queens Science Fiction League and the Panthers of the Philadelphia Science Fiction Society. Everyone was seated together in the wooden bleachers, players and spectators alike; indeed, the Panthers had to pull some of its players out of the stands when too few members of the Philadelphia club showed up for the game.

"You don't think he's going to strike out, do you?" Maggie asked.

Nat thought it over. Campbell was older than almost everyone else out on the field, but he had the physique of someone who'd spent too much time at a desk. Just before Sam Moskowitz had talked him into coming down from the bleachers to take a turn at bat for the home team, he'd been smoking a cigarette from a long ivory holder. Just the way he held the bat was proof that this was the first time he'd played ball in many years, perhaps even since grade school.

"Probably," he replied, keeping his voice low. Maggie quietly laughed, and Nat gave himself points for saying something funny.

He'd been disappointed to have taken the El all the way out to Queens just to find that most of the authors had gone to Brooklyn instead, but the fact that the Legion of Tomorrow had come out for the ball game made up for it.

Well, no . . . he had to admit, it wasn't just the Legion he was glad to see again but Maggie Krough in particular. She looked good this afternoon, in tan cotton slacks and a sleeveless light-blue shirt that showed off her figure. The way other fans kept glancing in their direction made him realize that he was fortunate to be sitting beside her, even if he did have share her with the two other guys.

"Strike two!"

Campbell didn't swear this time, but the expression on his face hinted his regret at letting himself get pulled into this.

"I think you may be right," Maggie said, and Nat was about to add something when she glanced past him. "Oh, thank you, George, that's very kind of you."

Nat looked around to see George Hallahan return from a nearby pushcart with a couple of ice-cream cones. "My pleasure," he said as he carefully handed the chocolate one to Maggie, keeping the vanilla for himself. "Sorry, Nat," he said as he sat down beside them. "Only have two hands."

"You mean you can't grow another one?" Nat asked.

"Not even at the science fiction softball game." George shifted his fedora to the back of his head as he licked the top of his cone. "Speaking of which, what have I missed?"

Nat hadn't been keeping track of the game. He gazed over at the scoreboard. It was being tended by the kid from California he'd met the other day—his name was Bradbury, he'd learned this morning, Ray Bradbury—and he'd looked like he was getting ready to change the number of Os in the Visitors box from two to three. "Queens is up seventeen to seven," he said, "but I don't think they helped themselves very much by pulling Campbell out of the bleachers to bat an inning."

"Well." George shrugged. "As I said, it's supposed to be a science fiction game."

Nat gazed at the convention members with whom he'd traveled to the Meadows. None of the writers he'd seen Sunday morning were here; besides Campbell, the only author he recognized was Ross Rocklynne, who apparently hadn't heard that most of his colleagues were in Brooklyn. He wondered why Campbell had bothered to show up. Good public relations with the fans, he supposed. After all, they were the ones who bought the magazine. All the same, he expected that Campbell would quietly excuse himself once he'd met his obligation as a celebrity player and head down to Brooklyn to meet with his authors.

Still, the setting was scientifictional enough. Out past right field, beyond the low fence that bordered the diamond, lay the World's Fair. The Perisphere and the Trylon towered above the pavilions, reflecting pools, and promenades of the fairgrounds, symbols of the fantastic world that awaited everyone if only they could pull themselves out of the Depression and, with any luck, avoid getting into another European war. When the game was over, everyone was supposed to go over there to have dinner and watch the Fourth of July fireworks, the last official activity of the World's Science Fiction Convention. Nat had already visited the fair, but he was looking forward to going again—this time, he hoped, with Maggie on his arm.

If she didn't find someone else instead.

The sudden crack of the bat brought his attention back to the field. Campbell had managed to hit the ball on his third try. It sailed up and over third base, describing a parabolic trajectory that carried it well into left field. Campbell had dropped the bat and was leisurely jogging toward first, confident that he'd just scored a home run; meanwhile, the Queens player who'd been on second was already sprinting for third, intent on rounding the bases and getting home.

Harry Skinner was playing left field for the Panthers, and until now it appeared that he wasn't going to do much out there except work on his tan. But Campbell's fly ball was a gift sent special delivery. Harry barely had to strain himself as he ran forward to catch it, and Campbell had just received the bad news from the first baseman when Harry hurled the ball to second, where his teammate got it in his glove just in time to tag the Cometeer trying to get back to where he'd started.

"Oh yeah!" Maggie nearly dropped her ice cream as she shot to her feet. "Go, Harry! Forward the Legion!"

Harry must have heard her above the uproar of disapproval from the Queens fans, who outnumbered the Philly contingent nearly two to one, because he grinned and waved to her. Nat tried not to be jealous, but he had to admit that, if Harry was his rival for Maggie's attention, he'd just scored a few points. And he looked good too, stripped down to his undershirt, his muscles shining with sweat. Nat had already figured that Harry was a working-class kid; his build was proof that he didn't spend his days in a shoe store.

The double play brought a sudden end to the fourth inning, and Harry sauntered in with the rest of his team. On the way, he walked past Sam. Nat saw him say something to the convention chairman, who this afternoon was doubling as captain of the Queens Cometeers; he couldn't make out the words, but Sam cast him an angry glare, which Harry took with a smug grin.

"What did you just say to him?" Nat asked when Harry joined them.

"I just asked if he'd found something to do with all those pamphlets." Harry was still smiling. "I don't think he can take a joke."

Nat and George shared an upraised eyebrow. It was bad enough that Sam had been forced to extend his amnesty to the teenager who'd openly challenged him in the convention hall just the other day. But Harry had also rubbed it in by volunteering to play for the

Panthers. So even though the Philly club was being trounced by the Queens team, Harry was finding a way to get revenge.

There was a lot of that sort of thing going on today. It wasn't hard to tell that there was a rivalry between the two fan clubs, and although they'd had dinner together last night at the Wyndham Restaurant—those who could afford the $1 banquet ticket, that is—the conflict between the Futurians and New Fandom was making itself felt on the ball field. In just the first few innings, players had traded sides, rules had been bent, and accusations of cheating had been made. Perhaps this was why most of the writers had fled to Brooklyn: the smart ones like Isaac Asimov wanted to keep above the fray, while the out-of-towners like Jack Williamson didn't want to get mixed up in what was essentially a turf battle among unruly East Coast teenagers.

"You're certainly tempting fate, aren't you?" Maggie asked, a wry smile on her face. She nodded toward John Campbell, who was wiping his face with a towel as he chatted with some fans. "I mean, he might remember who it was who stopped him from getting a homer."

Harry stopped grinning. He gave Campbell a worried look. "I dunno . . . you think I ought to go over and apologize?"

"If he rejects stories on the basis of who scores against him in a softball game," George said, "then he's a pretty poor editor. Besides, he'll probably have forgotten all about it by the time you send him another story." He shrugged. "Either way, I wouldn't talk to him, if I were you."

Sound advice, and yet Nat was tempted to walk over and introduce himself to Campbell. He wanted very badly to sell a story to *Astounding*. Perhaps if he approached its editor the right way . . .

"I think he's more interested in good stories than good sportsmanship," Maggie said, "if you know what I mean."

He didn't know how she'd guessed his intent, but the wink she gave him confirmed that she had. Nat stayed where he was. "Still, if I just knew what he was looking for . . ."

"What do you want to write?"

"Why, science fiction, of course."

"Yes, but what kind of science fiction?" Her expression became serious. "There are many different types, you know. Do you have something particular in mind?"

Nat gave Harry a wary glance. He liked Harry well enough, but he didn't know yet whether he trusted him not to steal an idea from him. But Harry had leaned away from them to tap another Philadelphia fan on the shoulder and beg a swig from the pint bottle of peach brandy he was carrying, so Nat answered her. "I've been kind of thinking about doing a space adventure story," he said, lowering his voice a little. "I got a title: *The Galaxy Patrol*. It's about—"

"Sounds like E. E. Smith. Or Ed Hamilton."

"Or Weinbaum or Leinster or Williamson," George added, leaning in to join the conversation.

"Well, yeah, sure. Those are my favorites, so—"

"What makes you think Campbell will want a story that's like what those other guys are already writing for him?" Maggie was unapologetic about interrupting him. Nat was learning that she was clearly a girl who wasn't afraid to speak her mind. "I mean, every time *Astounding* publishes another Lensman serial, their sales jump. Stanley Weinbaum is no longer around, but there are probably a half dozen writers trying to replace him. So what's so different about your story that Campbell isn't going to find it somewhere else?"

Nat opened his mouth and then closed it. Out in the field, the Cometeers first baseman had just tagged out the Panthers player who'd slugged a ground ball to the pitcher, but he barely paid attention. Maggie had a point. There was nothing in the story he planned to write that was much different from anything he'd read in *Astounding, Amazing, Startling,* or any of the other pulps.

"Let me ask you something." George slid a little closer to him. "The spaceships in your story . . . do they travel faster than the speed of light?"

"Umm . . . yeah, sure."

"Uh-huh." George nodded. "And what's the speed of light? I'll settle for an approximate figure."

"Uh—" Nat had to think about this for a moment. "It's about 186,000 miles per second, isn't it?"

"Close enough. However, Einstein clearly stated in his general theory of relativity that the speed of light is a maximum value, and nothing—*nothing*—may exceed it. Not even the spaceships in all those stories we read."

George pointed to the baseball diamond. "Let's say that this field is the solar system. Earth is home plate, and the Moon is the pitcher's mound. Okay?" Nat nodded, and George went on, "Well, on that scale, Mars is way out there past center field, the asteroid belt is the fence, and Jupiter is the Perisphere."

"It's not that far away!" Harry had tuned in on the conversation.

"Yes, it is, and Pluto is somewhere in the Bronx." George was still speaking to Nat. "So, with that scale in mind, where do you think the nearest star, Alpha Centauri, is located?"

Nat looked around, saw the distant Manhattan skyline to the west of the ball field. "The Empire State Building?"

"That's a pretty good guess. I would've said New Jersey, but we'll go with that. Now, providing that the speed of light is absolute and nothing can travel faster, no ship we'll ever build could reach the nearest star in less than four and half years. So you can pretty much forget Smith's or Hamilton's ships reaching the center of the galaxy in only a few days."

"Yeah, but so what?" Harry was determined to become part of the conversation. "It's just a science fiction story."

George sighed, shook his head. "Let me try it this way . . . when you go up to bat, you've got a good chance of hitting the ball over the pitcher's mound. You might even score a home run by knocking it all the way over the fence. But it's physically impossible for you to hit the Empire State Building. Not even Superman could do that."

"Superman could hit the Empire State Building," said a Queens fan sitting nearby.

"Shut up, Julius," Harry said, scowling at him.

"The point is, just about everyone who writes about space travel *gets it wrong*!" George intently stared at Nat over the top of his glasses. "You know, when I let one of the profs at MIT know that I read science fiction, he asked me why I was wasting my time with that trash . . . that's what he called it, not me. I asked him if he'd ever read any, and he told me that he had, but he's given up on it because, most of the time, the people who write it either pay no attention to science or simply get it wrong. He said, 'If those writers produced science fiction that got the science right and still told a great story, people might pay more attention to that stuff.'"

"So you're saying . . . ?"

"If you want to distinguish yourself from all the other fellows who are writing science fiction, do it better than they do. Get the science right." He pointed to the field. "Rockets are like softballs. You'll never going to get out of the ball park if you keep playing with those. If your Galaxy Patrol is going to other stars, they're going to need something on a whole different order of magnitude."

"Such as what?"

"Ever heard of Paul Dirac's theories about antimatter? Or the Einstein-Rosen Bridge?" Nat shook his head, and George smiled. "I'll tell you later. And remember, next semester, I'll be just across the Charles River from you."

"That's great!" Harry was grinning broadly. "Can I ask you for help too? I'm—"

"Skinner!" The fan who was managing the Philly team was yelling to him from the batter's box. "Your turn! Get down here!"

"Coming!" Harry stood up and started to climb down from the bleachers, and then he stopped and turned to Maggie. "Hey, sweetheart, if I can hit this ball all the way to Mars, can I take you to the fireworks tonight?"

Maggie laughed. "Sure! You're on! Knock it to Mars, and I'm your date."

"But you'll never break the speed of light," Nat said.

"I won't need to." Harry winked at Maggie. "If I score a run this inning, I'll be a bigger hero than Kimball Kinnison."

"He'll never do it," Nat said quietly as Harry walked away.

He was wrong. Harry's next ball went over the fence, and although the Cometeers beat the Panthers 23–11, Maggie went with him to the fair that evening.

But the conversation with George changed his life.

7

Maggie had warned Kate that her grandfather's memoirs were incomplete, but she didn't realize just how much was left untold until the narrative came to an abrupt halt shortly after the first World Science Fiction Convention. Nathan wrote about making his first sale to *Astounding* just a few months after he entered Boston College and how a subsequent series of short stories had helped pay his way through school and also made him one of the magazine's regular contributors during science fiction's Golden Age. But he'd just finished telling how a failed induction physical had kept him out of the wartime draft when the manuscript came to an abrupt end.

Perhaps her grandfather's failing health had stopped him, or maybe he'd heeded his agent's advice and decided not to write his life story. In any case, Kate came away from *My Life in the Future* only knowing how he'd met Maggie, Harry, and George and that they'd become this Legion of Tomorrow that they appeared to take so seriously even after sixty years. If she wanted to learn more, obviously she'd have to get it from them.

When she tried calling Margaret Krough, though, her assistant informed her that she was out of town; she'd flown to Germany earlier in the week for the annual Frankfurt Book Fair and would be there for a couple of more days. Kate was frustrated until she remembered that Harry had told her that he was available too. Directory information had his number in Philadelphia, and a phone call resulted in an invitation to visit him. A few days later she boarded the morning Amtrak train from Boston, and by midafternoon a taxi had dropped her off at the address he'd given her.

Harry Skinner lived in a large brick apartment building on Pine Street in the Washington Square neighborhood, a former row house that had been converted for use by senior citizens. A wheelchair ramp had been installed beside the steps leading to the front entrance, and a typewritten sheet of paper taped to a wall in the foyer gave the days and times when van service would be available to residents who wanted to go shopping. Kate pushed the button above Harry's mailbox; his voice came through the intercom a minute later and invited her to come up, advising her to take the elevator.

It wasn't Harry who answered the door, though, but a young man about Kate's age. One look at him and she had a clear impression of how Harry must have looked many years ago; the family resemblance was unmistakable, even though he'd substituted a goatee for a mustache. He welcomed her with a warm smile and a handshake and introduced himself as Jim Skinner, Harry's grandson.

Harry's apartment was small but not uncomfortable; the living room furniture was old yet well made, the rugs a little worn out, the bookcases as stuffed as one would expect of a lifelong reader. Like his late friend Nathan, Harry was evidently a widower. Kate noted several framed photos atop the fireplace mantel, pictures of Harry with a woman who could only have been his wife, the most recent of them only a few years old. It wasn't hard to guess that he'd moved here after she passed away.

"Gramps is in the bathroom," Jim said as he showed Kate in. "I just dropped in for a visit. I'll be off soon." A meaningful glance at an antique wall clock. "Almost time for me to go to work."

"This late in the day?"

"I'm an ER physician at Pennsylvania Hospital, just a few blocks away." A shrug and a grin. "Evening shift this week . . . lucky me."

She was about to reply when the bedroom door opened and Harry emerged. He wasn't in his wheelchair today but instead stood upright, leaning upon a wheeled stroller. "My grandson, the doctor," he said as he pushed the stroller into the living room. "When my ticker gives out and they rush me in, his nurse gets to be the one to say . . ."

"'It's dead, Jim.'" His grandson rolled his eyes at what was apparently an old joke. "Not for a while, Gramps."

"Yeah, but I hope I'm around to hear it. God, I love that line."

"Yeah, you should have written for *Star Trek*." Jim helped his grandfather to an armchair near the window and then picked up his overcoat from the nearby couch. "Can I get you anything before I leave, Miss . . . ?"

"Kate . . . just Kate. No, but thanks, anyway." She couldn't help but give him her best smile. "Very nice to meet you, Jim."

"Pleased to meet you too." He paused to bend over Harry and give him a quick kiss on the top of the head. "Tomorrow, same time?"

"Sure. Bring some women next time." Harry cast a mock-surprised look in Kate's direction. "Oh! Never mind—I've got one already!"

"Watch out for him," Jim said to Kate. "He's a dirty old man." Then he headed for the door. "Bye."

Harry waited until the door closed behind him before he turned to Kate. "I'll have you know that he's single, straight, and very much available."

Kate had already noticed the absence of a wedding ring. "I'll keep it in mind."

"Just saying." Harry pushed away his stroller, stretched out his legs. He wore a baggy cardigan and old jeans and looked a bit frailer than he had at the funeral. Kate wondered if it had been Jim's idea to move his grandfather into senior citizen housing near the hospital. "So . . . still persuing the life and times of Nathan Arkwright, are we?"

"I read his book—what there is of it, anyway. He didn't get very far, but he did talk about how he met . . . um, the Legion of Tomorrow."

Harry grinned. "Like the name? I know it's kinda childish, but that's what we've called ourselves ever since."

"I'm a little surprised, I guess, that you've continued to get along after all these years. I can understand why you and Grandpapa still know Maggie—she became your agent, after all—but he makes it sound like you and he were rivals from the start."

"Well, yeah, we were, sort of. I made my first sale to *Startling Stories* just a few months before he broke into *Astounding*, so we came in at the same time. But Nat was never drafted, so he was able to keep writing while most of us—Bob Heinlein, Ted Sturgeon, Isaac Asimov, Sprague de Camp—either got shipped off or were otherwise involved in the war effort. Your grandfather did his bit by working as an engineer at the navy shipyard here in town—he and Bob shared an office, in fact—but otherwise, he remained a civilian."

"So he came to Philly?"

Harry nodded. "After he got his degree, he moved here for a while. That was when—"

He suddenly stopped. Looking out the window, he was quiet for a few moments. "Damn," he said quietly. "You'd have to bring that up, wouldn't you?"

"I'm sorry, but I don't—"

"Did he mention that Maggie and I were an item for a little while?" Kate shook her head, and Harry shrugged. "Guess that's something he didn't feel was worth mentioning. Or maybe it was a little too close to something he didn't like to talk about." He sighed and went on. "Yeah, anyway, Mags and I started seeing each other just before the war. Nat was in Boston by then, but a degree from Central High was the furthest my formal education went. My folks couldn't afford to send me to college, so I went to work in my dad's machine shop instead. But every now and then, I'd take the train to New York on the weekends to see Maggie, and it wasn't long before we became pretty serious about each other. But then Pearl Harbor happened, and since my family's always had some navy blood, I didn't wait for Uncle Sam to draw my number. I kissed my best girl good-bye, went to the nearest recruitment office, and got in the fight."

He gestured toward the shelf where Kate had noticed pictures of him and his wife. "See that one on the end?" he asked, pointing to a small black-and-white snapshot of a group of bare-chested young men standing beneath the wing of a B-29 Superfortress. "That's my Seabee group in the South Pacific. I spent the summer of '45 on a small island in the Marianas." He paused meaningfully. "Does the name Tinian ring any bells for you?"

"No, it—" Then she remembered history, and her eyes widened. "Oh, my God. You mean you were there for . . . ?"

"Yes, I was. And so was George."

8

The Army Transport Command C-53s from Albuquerque began arriving in late afternoon. One at a time, only a couple of minutes apart from each other, the Dakotas touched down on the broad, two-mile-long landing strip navy construction crews had spent the last few months bulldozing and paving down the length of the small island. The transports followed three B-29s that had flown in earlier that day from Kirtland Air Force Base in Texas; just offshore, the USS *Indianapolis* lay at anchor, having arrived from San Francisco shortly after dawn.

It was July 26, 1945, and Harry Skinner had a gut feeling that something big was about to happen.

PO First Class Skinner leaned against a jeep, idly smoking a Lucky as he watched the most recent plane taxi toward a nearby row of hangars. The largest hangar was specially air-conditioned, and although no one except flight crews and aircraft engineers were now being allowed in there, everyone knew what they were doing. A B-29 from the 509th Composite Group, *Enola Gay*, was parked inside, and it was rumored that its bomb bay had been specially converted to carry a larger-than-usual payload.

Harry had an idea what it was, but he carefully kept his mouth shut. It wasn't just the fact that he didn't want to draw the ire of navy intelligence officers. Over the past few years, he'd discovered that it wasn't wise to show how smart he was. Most of the guys he worked with were much like himself, working-class kids from the East Coast; they were often poorly educated, and some of them had just enough brains to operate a bulldozer or a crane. Harry didn't want to have to try explaining his suspicions to them; they probably wouldn't have understood or believed him, anyway.

The last C-53 came to a halt in front of *Enola Gay*'s hangar, its twin props winding down. Unlike the others, this one apparently carried passengers; Harry could see them through the side windows. He watched as a ground crewmen pushed a ladder to its hatch, and he immediately stood up and buttoned his shirt when he recognized the first passenger to emerge from the plane. General Curtis Le-May had visited Tinian many times over the past several months and was notorious for chewing out enlisted men for sloppy appearance even though they were working in the island's broiling heat. Harry dropped his cigarette and was about to make himself look busy when he caught sight of one of the men who followed LeMay down the ladder.

"Oh, man," he muttered. "That can't be."

Yes, it was. George Hallahan.

George wasn't in uniform but instead wore civilian clothes, a fedora pulled low over his head. He was standing beside the plane, waiting for the rest of the passengers to disembark, when Harry walked across the field toward him. George turned around just as Harry was about to tap him on the shoulder, and at first it seemed as if he didn't recognize him. Then his mouth fell open, and a smile stretched across his face.

"Harry Skinner . . . well, I'll be damned."

"George, you old . . ." Harry was about to grab his friend in a bear hug, but then he caught a sidelong glance from General LeMay and stopped himself. "What are you doing here?"

The smile faded slightly; too late, Harry realized that he'd said the wrong thing. "Can't really talk about it," George murmured as he offered a handshake. "I'm . . . well, a consultant. Call it an inspection."

Harry nodded. That was probably as accurate a description as George could give without revealing too much. "It's been ages," he said as they shook hands. "Last time I heard from you, you were still at MIT."

"Yes, well . . ." The smile returned, albeit a bit more tentatively. "I received my doctorate just in time to be recruited for an advanced research program."

"Uh-huh. I see." Harry looked past him. LeMay was no longer paying attention to them. "The same sort of operation I've been working on here, I take it."

George didn't reply at once but instead glanced over his shoulder at the other passengers coming off the plane. For the moment, no one was looking their way. "Let's take a little walk," he said quietly. "You can show me the field."

They strolled away from the C-53, heads lowered as if they were examining the runway apron. Nearby was a long, shallow pit that the Seabees had excavated in the concrete hardstand; its purpose was to allow a ground crew to load an unusually large payload into a B-29's underbelly. Harry guided George toward it.

"No one's come right out and told us what's going on," Harry said, keeping his voice low as he pointed out the pit, "but I think I know."

George hesitated. "I'm under security restrictions not to discuss what we're doing," he said at last, "so I can't say anything, but—" He stopped to think about it a little. "Let me ask you something. Have you been keeping up with *Astounding* lately?"

The question, seemingly off topic, caught Harry by surprise. "Uh . . . yeah, sort of. My dad sends it to me. Mail always takes a while to get here, so I'm a few issues behind, but—"

"Did you read a story called *Deadline*? It was by Cleve Cartmill, and it was in the March issue last year."

Harry had to think back a bit. "Isn't that the one about the two alien races who are fighting a war, and one of them devises an atomic—"

"That's the one." George cut him off before Harry could say something he shouldn't. "Reread it if you get a chance, and keep in mind that it caused enough concern among some of my colleagues that army intelligence officers paid John Campbell a little visit to ask how Cartmill might have gotten his information."

Reading the story again was out of the question. Magazines sent from home tended to get passed around the barracks before ending up as toilet paper; Harry seldom kept the issues of *Astounding* and *Amazing* his father put in the mail. Nonetheless, he whistled under his breath. "No kidding?"

"No kidding . . . and that's about as much as I can tell you."

Someone yelled George's name, and they looked back toward the hangar. The rest of General LeMay's group were starting to go inside; an MP was walking toward him and Harry. "Better head over there," Harry said. "I'll walk with you."

"All right." George nodded as they turned away from the loading pit. "Let's keep what we were talking about to ourselves, okay?" Harry nodded, and George changed the subject. "I'm sorry to hear about you and Maggie. That's a real shame."

Harry gave him a sharp look. "Come again?"

"I heard that you broke up. Nat told me in a letter that he and Maggie were . . ."

Harry felt his heart suddenly go cold. He stopped walking. "What about Nat and Maggie? I haven't heard anything from her in weeks, and Nat hasn't written me in almost a year."

Harry had seen Nathan Arkwright's stories in *Astounding*. The Galaxy Patrol series in particular had become popular among readers, and he'd figured that Nat was too busy writing for Campbell to send a letter to a buddy in the service. But when he saw the surprised and . . . God help him, *pitying* . . . look on George's face, he realized this assumption was in error.

"Oh no." George's face became pale, his eyes wide. "Oh, God . . . Harry, I didn't know. She told me she'd written you a letter, and I thought . . . I assumed . . . you'd received it already."

"The mail is slow getting here. I told you, it sometimes takes . . ." Harry swallowed something hard that had formed in his throat.

"Are you telling me that Maggie has started . . . you mean, she and Nat are . . . ?"

George looked down at the ground, slowly nodded. "I'm so sorry. I thought you already knew."

"I . . . I . . . Maggie's going out with . . . ?"

"Dr. Hallahan?" By then, the MP had caught up with them. "General LeMay wants you to come along." He gave Harry a hard look, silently admonishing the lowly petty officer for distracting a civilian scientist from an important task.

George nodded and then turned to Harry again. "Look, I have to go. Maybe we can get together again, okay?"

"Yeah, sure," Harry murmured. "Go."

George gave his arm a brief squeeze that was meant to be commiserative, and then he fell in beside the MP as they returned to the hangar where *Enola Gay* was being kept. Harry watched them walk away. All at once, the sun was no longer hot, he could barely feel the ground beneath his feet, and New York was on the far side of the Moon.

9

"I got Maggie's letter the day after the bomb dropped on Hiroshima." Harry continued to stare out the window; his gaze hadn't left the street since he'd begun to tell Kate the story of what happened on Tinian sixty years earlier. "It was addressed to me and not someone named John, but it was pretty much the same."

Kate slowly nodded. Even after all these years, it was clear that Harry still recalled the pain he'd felt that day. "I guess you never forgave my grandfather for that, did you?"

"No, I eventually did." Harry finally looked at her again. "By the time I got out of the service and returned to the States, Maggie and Nat had already broken up. It was kind of a foolish fling for her, really. She was lonely, I'd been gone for four years, and since Nat was there . . ." Another shrug. "I couldn't blame her. Hell, I couldn't even blame Nat all that much. It just . . . well, happened, that's all."

"My mother told me that my grandparents met during the war."

"That's true. Nat did meet Judith around that time . . . but it wasn't until after he and Maggie broke up. Maggie and I never got back together again, although she eventually became my literary agent." Then he grinned. "Her first client was Nat, and her second one was me. I guess she had a thing for taking on old boyfriends."

"That was kind of her."

"Kindness didn't have anything to do with it. Maggie's an agent. Her bread and butter come from being a go-between for authors and their publishers. Nat was her most successful client, sure, but she couldn't have made a living from his work alone, so she also had to represent lesser lights like me." Kate started to object, but he held up a hand. "No, it's true. In the Legion, all the luck rolled downhill and landed in Nat's lap." His gaze wandered over to the bookcase packed with paperbacks and book-club hardcovers bearing Matt Brown's name. "I just consider myself fortunate enough to have been able to make a living at this for as long as I did. Better than factory work, and it took me to some interesting places."

From the street below, she could hear the sound of traffic picking up. The urban evening rush hour was beginning; she'd have to start thinking soon about getting a cab to the train station. "I'm sure you have, but—"

"Let me tell you about one of them." Harry sat back in his chair, crossing his ankles together as his gaze returned to the window. "Back in '72, a science writer by the name of Richard Hoagland— you've probably heard of him, he later made a big deal about the whole 'Face on Mars' thing—had a brainstorm: charter a cruise ship to anchor off Cape Canaveral and then get a bunch of scientists and science fiction writers to play host for the *Apollo 17* launch. He got all the big names, and a few guys like me, as well."

His tone became reflective. "It was an eventful evening, in more ways than one."

At the midnight hour, the moonless night was clear and filled with stars and unexpectedly cool for the Florida coast even at that time of the year. A little while earlier, a couple of stewards had moved through the crowd gathered on the aft pool deck of the SS *Statendam*, passing out wool lap blankets to anyone who wanted them. Harry had almost taken a pass, but the December chill won out over pride. Sitting in a lounge chair on the starboard side, he draped the blanket over his legs and then buttoned up his sport coat and tucked his hands into his pockets.

"If they delay this thing any longer," he muttered, "I'm going to ask for my money back."

Leaning against the rail, Nat looked at him in surprise. "I thought you got a free ticket."

"I did. I'm talking about NASA." Harry turned to George. "Can't you guys get anything right?"

"Don't blame me. I'm not working there anymore." George was also huddled into his coat; he clasped a steaming cup of hot chocolate between his gloved hands. Harry kicked himself for forgetting that George's job at the Marshall Space Flight Center had ended the day *Apollo 17* was rolled out from the Vehicle Assembly Building. "Be patient. These things don't get off as efficiently as they do in your stories."

Harry grunted and said nothing. Instead, he gazed across the dark ocean at the distant lights of Cape Kennedy. Seven miles away, both illuminated and miniaturized by the crisscrossed beams of searchlights that lanced high into the heavens, the Saturn V was a tiny white *i* rising from the seaside mound of Pad 39-A. *Apollo 17* was supposed to have lifted off at 9:38 P.M., but the countdown had been halted at T-minus thirty seconds. According to Walter Cronkite, who was narrating the launch on the TV in the ship's bar, there had been some sort of onboard computer glitch. That was over two and a half hour hours ago. It was now twenty after twelve, and Harry was beginning to wonder if Becky had the right idea by going to bed early.

What a foolish thought. Harry gazed down the length of the cruise ship's aft deck. Gathered around the swimming pool, which deckhands had covered with a canvas tarp once it became obvious that the night was going to be too cold for anyone to take a dip, was science fiction's old guard, the writers who'd imagined space travel long before it became a reality, socializing with the best and brightest of American intelligentsia. Near the stern, Fred and Carol Pohl chatted with Isaac Asimov and his new wife, Janet. Seated at a table beside the pool was an unholy quorum of Art Clarke, Marvin Minsky, and Carl Sagan. Ted Sturgeon was huddled with *Analog*'s new editor, Ben Bova—Ben had been running the magazine formerly called *Astounding* for nearly a year now, but Harry was still getting used to the fact that John Campbell was gone—while former astronaut Ed Mitchell and NBC anchorman Hugh Downs were having a drink and a laugh with Bob and Ginny Heinlein.

The only person who was out of place was Katherine Anne Porter. *Playboy* had commissioned a piece from her about the launch, and it had become clear that she disdained the science fiction writers with whom she'd been forced to share a sea cruise. She remained aloof to everyone, deigning to speak only to Norman Mailer, the one other mainstream author aboard. Mailer was here because he'd written *Of a Fire on the Moon*, but Porter had no interest in space; apparently, someone at *Playboy* thought it would be cute to send the author of *Ship of Fools* on this particular assignment. Harry had already decided to skip the article when it came out.

Apparently, Nat alone, hardy New Englander that he was, had the foresight to bring a heavy sweater and a scarf to Florida; everyone else was trying to keep warm by drinking coffee or bourbon. The only person unfazed by the cold was Robert Heinlein, who wore a dinner jacket and tie as if this were nothing more than a balmy evening in Colorado Springs. Aside from a handful of wives and children who'd given up and gone to bed, though, no one was letting the late hour cause them to miss the launch. They didn't even want to go into the pool bar where it was warm, as some had done, lest they risk giving up their places on the deck.

An elite lineup of writers, scientists, and intellectuals . . . and a disaster. The *Statendam* had accommodations for six hundred and fifty, but only about a hundred or so had paid to get on the ship. Heinlein and Asimov had both swallowed Dick Hoagland's line and had invested in the cruise; Nat might have, too, if Maggie hadn't talked him out of it. As capital ventures went, this one was a bust.

But, Harry had to admit, it was fun. He'd moseyed through the crowd a few minutes earlier, wandering in and out of conversations. Some of it was shop talk—Ben was trying to persuade Ted to send a story to *Analog*—and some of it was mildly scandalous—Isaac and Fred had been speculating about the intentions of the young lady in the bikini who'd been flirting with all the writers earlier in the day—and a little bit had been truly head spinning, like the conversation between Clarke, Minsky, and Sagan about the possibility of machine intelligence in the universe. But in the end, he'd found his way back to Nat and George . . . his closest friends, the Legion of Tomorrow, as they still privately referred to themselves even after all these years.

"You're unusually quiet," George said.

"What do you mean 'unusually'?" Harry gave his old friend a mock-serious glare and then raised a hand to his mouth to pat back a yawn. "You trying to make something of it?"

"Not at all." George sipped his hot chocolate. "It's just that, by this time, you and Nat are usually going at it like a couple of wet cats."

"Just wish this thing would get a move on. It's past my bedtime." Even as he spoke, Harry hated how he sounded, like a cranky, middle-aged man.

"I wouldn't be in such a hurry if I were you," Nat said quietly. "This may be the last time we'll see anyone go to the Moon for quite some time to come."

He was still standing at the railing, but now his back was to the Cape, and he'd lifted his eyes to gaze up at the sky. There was a pensive expression on his face, and deck lamps seemed to illuminate a bitterness that had emerged from a person who, Harry had lately realized, had developed a tendency to keep his true feelings buried deep inside.

"Nixon cut NASA's funding for the last two missions," Nat went on, still staring up into space. "*Apollo 18* and *19* aren't going to the pad. Isn't that right, George?"

"I'm afraid so." George nodded. "The president claims he's concerned about the federal budget, but the hardware's already been built, and the infrastructure is almost a decade old. The money the government is saving by scrapping those last two missions is negligible in the grand scheme of things." He shrugged. "I suspect he's trying to get back at Kennedy after all these years. Apollo was JFK's signature program, and Nixon still hasn't forgiven him for the '60 election."

"Whatever the reason, this is the final Apollo mission." Nat lowered his head, rubbed the back of his neck. "Maybe we'll get the new space shuttle. Maybe a space station too. But I wouldn't count on anything more than that."

"But there's Mars," Harry began.

"No. Not anymore." George shook his head. "Before I resigned, everyone at Marshall got the word from Washington HQ—Mars is off the table until further notice. We've still got the two *Viking* missions in a few years, but no one there is to even talk about manned missions."

"I still think you had your best shot back in the '50s with Freeman Dyson's Orion proposal at General Atomics." Nathan blew into his cupped hands and stuck them in his jacket pockets. "You're right; without support for NASA, no one's going to Mars. I kind of wonder if we ever will."

Harry was having a hard time believing what he was hearing. Like everyone on the boat, Nathan Arkwright had always been a tireless promoter of space exploration. The Galaxy Patrol books and TV show were often cited as being a major influence on America's interest in space; together with Heinlein's juveniles, Nat had introduced an entire generation to the grand adventure that lay ahead. Until *Star Trek* or *2001: A Space Odyssey*—Harry had seen Art's movie a half dozen times already—nothing had whetted public enthusiasm for space as much as Nat's books.

Harry briefly wondered if Judith had something to do with this. Nat's wife had stayed in Massachusetts, with Nat covering for her by claiming that she was prone to seasickness, but it was becoming apparent that Judith was ill and Nat didn't want to talk about it, not even with his closest friends. But no, this newfound skepticism was coming from somewhere else.

"If I didn't know you better," Harry said softly, "I say this was heresy."

"Not heresy—just cold, hard reality." As if he'd known what Harry was thinking, Nat cocked his head toward Heinlein. "Bob's been pushing space longer and harder than any of us, but even he's seen the writing on the wall. Of course, he blames the Democrats for the budget axe—Proxmire in particular—but like George says, it's really a bipartisan effort. And let's face it . . . the public's just not all that interested anymore."

"I'll say." Harry glanced at the window of the nearby bar. Through the curtains, he could see a handful of passengers who'd retreated from the cold to watch the launch coverage on TV. "What do you want to bet they got a lot of angry calls when they preempted *Medical Center*?"

"So what do you do about it?" George asked. "I mean, isn't that your job, getting people excited about space?"

"My job is selling books to—"

On the other side of the bar window, the people watching TV suddenly broke into applause and excited shouts. Someone put down their drink and ran to the door. "They're coming off the hold!" he shouted to the people on deck. "They're picking up the count where they left off . . . T-minus thirty seconds and counting!"

More shouts and applause from the pool deck as everyone dropped what they were doing and crowded toward the portside railing. Harry briefly thought about running upstairs to wake up Becky, but *Statendam*'s captain solved the problem by blowing a long, loud blast from the liner's single funnel. No one could possibly sleep through that.

"Guess they must have fixed the computers." Harry stood up from his chair, stretched, and walked over to the railing. It seemed as if the salt breeze was waking him up, but he knew better; it was the anticipation of what he was about to see. Looking down the railing, he saw the same on everyone's faces. Isaac, Fred, Bob, Ted, Ben, even Mailer and Porter . . . they were like children who'd been sitting up late on Christmas Eve, waiting to see if Santa would come down the chimney.

George was right. This was his true purpose in life—not to sell paperbacks, for he could have written mystery or western novels and accomplished the same thing, but to sell the future. That was how he'd come to be there, standing on the deck of a cruise ship with a privileged view of history. But when he looked over at Nat, there was a dark scowl upon his best friend's face that he'd seldom seen before, as if . . .

Light blazed across the western horizon, a false dawn coming from the wrong direction. In hues of bright orange and fiery crimson, it illuminated the vast plumes of smoke rising from either side of the distant rocket. At first, there was no sound; the ship lay at anchor seven miles from the launchpad, Harry reminded himself, so the primary ignition of the five first-stage engines wouldn't reach them for another sixteen seconds. But as the Saturn V cleared its skyscraper-size launch tower and rose upon a white-hot lance, a thunderclap rolled across the ocean, so loud that he had to clap his hands over his ears even as he felt the deck tremble beneath his feet.

All around him, his friends and colleagues were staring in rapt fascination as *Apollo 17* roared into the midnight sky. It seemed to pass directly overhead as it arched out over the Atlantic, the rocket itself an invisible mass at the head of a man-made comet. The noise gradually diminished, yet it left behind a tinny ringing in Harry's ears. As if his hearing wasn't beginning to go bad, anyway.

He watched as the fireball sailed out over the ocean, growing smaller with each passing second. A brief flare as it jettisoned the first stage, and then the second stage ignited, and the rocket became a bright star that finally moved out of sight. By then, the applause and excited yells that had accompanied the liftoff had subsided. Everyone lowered their eyes from the heavens to grin at one another; Santa had come down the chimney, after all.

"To the bar!" Bob shouted. "First round's on me!"

Laughter greeted this announcement, but when Harry and George started to step away from the railing, Nat stayed behind. He continued to watch the place where the Saturn V had vanished, as if he could actually see *Apollo 17* discarding its second stage and going into parking orbit around Earth.

"Nat?" he asked. "What?"

"We can't let this die." Nat's voice was low, choked with emotion. Harry couldn't tell for certain, but it seemed as if there were tears on his face. "Whatever we do, we can't let this be the end."

"That's always been a special memory for me," Harry finished. "Not just the launch, but also because . . . well, it was one of those few times, once we got older, that your grandfather let us see his real self."

Kate looked at her watch. If she were going to catch the late-evening train back to Boston, she'd have to hurry. "Look, I don't mean to be obtuse, but why are you telling me this? What's that got to do with the Arkwright Foundation?"

"Nothing. Everything." Harry was quiet for a moment. "You're going to have to get the rest from Maggie and George. I could tell you, but I think it's better that you speak with them. Particularly Maggie."

Kate was a little irritated. She'd come a long way just to hear an old man tell stories. It was clear that Harry was done, though, and she had a train to catch. "Well, I appreciate it," she said, standing up. "Is there anything I can do for you before I go?"

"Nothing at all, thanks." Harry pulled over his stroller and used it to balance himself as he rose from his chair. "Give Margaret my best when you see her."

He escorted her to the door, slowly pushing himself along. As she opened the door, he said one more thing. "Y'know, it just occurred to me . . . you've got Nat's red hair."

"Uh-huh." Kate stopped to look back at him. "There's not a lot of family resemblance, but at least there's that."

"But Sylvia doesn't have red hair."

"No. Mom was a brunette before her color changed."

Harry nodded. "Must have jumped a generation. Genes are funny that way, aren't they?" He turned away. "Anyway, have a good trip home."

10

It didn't seem like she was getting anywhere with her investigation, so Kate put it aside to begin her next assignment, an article about the effects of deep-ocean dumping. She'd just begun making her way through a stack of reports from Woods Hole when the phone rang. It was Maggie.

"I hear you've been down to Philly to see Harry. Did you have a good chat?"

"If you know that, then you must know what he told me." Kate leaned back in her office chair. "I guess I'm a bit shocked to know that you and Grandpapa once had an affair."

"It didn't last long. Just a few months. Then he met Judith and, well, that was that." A pause. "I knew Harry would tell you. He got over it a long time ago, but it's still something he remembers."

"I bet." Kate paused, trying to find the right way of saying what she meant to say without being offensive. "Look, Ms. Krough . . . Maggie . . . this is all very interesting, but I've got a lot going on just now. I have another story deadline in front of me, and I can't spend more time hearing about my grandfather's personal life. If you've got something to tell me—"

"I do, and I promise that I won't take up much more of your time. But it's something I can't tell you over the phone. Can we get together for lunch?"

Kate shut her eyes. Why did everyone think that freelance writers were never busy? "I can't come down to New York just now. I—"

"I mean in Boston. I have business up there next week, and I'm thinking we could get together at the Four Seasons. My treat."

It was an offer she couldn't refuse. She could afford to take a couple of hours away from the desk, and lunch at one of the best restaurants in town was not something to lightly pass up. So a few days later, she found herself sitting across from Maggie in the restaurant of the Four Seasons hotel, waiting for the lobster salads they'd each ordered. Outside the window beside their table, people walked along Boylston, coat collars turned against an unseasonably chill wind that whipped through the Commons across the street.

"So what is it that you wanted to tell me?" Kate pulled the straw from her glass of iced tea. The niceties had been dispensed with, the small talk about the weather said and done.

Maggie didn't respond at once. She gazed out the window, hands clasped together in the lap of her tweed business suit. Kate reflected that, even in her eighties, Margaret Krough was still a very attractive woman. Sixty years ago, she must have been stunning; no wonder both Harry and her grandfather fallen in love with her, if only for a short time.

"As I recall, Judith passed away just a few months before you were born," Maggie said at last. "That would be sometime in"—she closed her eyes for a moment—"1977, yes?"

Kate blinked. That wasn't something she was expecting. "Yeah, 1977. I was born on November 10. Grandma was already gone by then."

"I remember it well." Maggie slowly nodded. "I was with her and your grandfather the night she died. So was your mother." She shook her head and sighed. "It was a very bad night for all of us."

11

There was a small lounge just down the hall from the room where Judith Arkwright lay dying, and this was where Maggie led Nathan once his wife had fallen asleep again. The doctors at Bay State had warned them that the drugs would do this; she would fade in and out of consciousness during her final hours, but in the end, leukemia would claim her life, and there was nothing anyone could do but wait for the inevitable.

Sylvia was on her way to Springfield, but she was probably being held up by midsummer traffic on the pike, so Maggie decided to take Nat to the lounge until she showed up. When Judie's illness had reached the terminal stage, he'd brought her in from Lenox and since then had been at her side almost constantly. Maggie arrived from New York to find him unshaven and haggard, sitting beside his wife's bed with her hand clutched in his. He hadn't eaten or slept in a couple of days and wouldn't even step into the bathroom to put a razor to his face, but at least he'd listen to his agent and lifelong friend. So when Maggie told him to get up and come with her to the lounge for a little while, Nat obeyed as she'd known he would.

As it turned out, the lounge had a TV, and when they came in, it was showing a late-night news story about the *Star Wars* craze sweeping the country. The movie had been out for over six weeks, but the lines at the theaters weren't getting any shorter. Maggie was about to turn it off, but then she noticed that Nat was paying attention and left the TV on. He sat down and stared in fascination at the brief clips from the movie—Imperial fighters attacking the *Millennium Falcon*, Luke Skywalker handling his father's light saber, Darth Vader stalking through the Death Star—and Maggie knew that, at least for a moment, he'd been transported away from the tragedy of this long, dark night.

"Have you seen it yet?" she asked.

"Twice. Great movie . . . even if they stole some stuff from me." He pointed to a shot of X-wing fighters in combat. "I've got ships just like those in the Patrol books, y'know."

"Yeah, I noticed the same thing. And Han Solo is quite a bit like Hak Tallus, isn't he?"

"I should sue." He glanced at her. "Do you think we should sue?"

"You wouldn't get anywhere. The studio would just sic their lawyers on you, and even if you won in court, you'd spend more money on the case than you'd get from the settlement." Maggie forced a smile. "Besides, this could be good for you. Science fiction is hot right now, and you practically invented this sort of thing."

"Ed Hamilton and Doc Smith invented it. I just improved it." He was quiet a moment. "You think you might be able to swing a movie deal?"

"I don't see why not. The books have never been out of print, and everyone remembers the old TV show. Let me get in touch with my contacts in Hollywood and see if I can work out an option for—"

There was a knock at the door, and they'd just looked around when it swung open and Sylvia marched in, all but pushing aside the nurse who'd led her there. Sylvia stared at her father in open-mouthed disbelief.

"I love it. Mama's dying, and you're in here talking business with your agent." She gazed up at the ceiling and shook her head. "Incredible. You're just incredible."

Had she overheard the conversation, or did she simply make an assumption? Either way, it was hard to deny what they'd been doing.

"Sylvia," Maggie began, "it's not what you think. We were just talking—"

"Butt out, Margaret," Sylvia snapped. "This is between Papa and me." The nurse left, frowning but saying nothing as she quietly shut the door behind her. Sylvia fastened her glare on Nat. "Why aren't you in there with her? Don't you care that she's—"

"Sylvia, calm down." Nat spoke to her with the resigned patience of a father who'd fought with his daughter so many times that it was hard to remember when they didn't quarrel. "I've been with her ever since she was brought in. She's sleeping right now, and I needed to take a break."

Sylvia opened her mouth, but Maggie interrupted her. "It's true.

Your father has been at her side the entire time. If you want to blame anyone, blame me. I suggested that he come in here for a few minutes."

Sylvia didn't say anything for a moment, giving Nat a chance to rise from his chair. "I'm so glad you came," he said as he took a step forward, raising his arms as if to embrace her in an awkward hug. Sylvia visibly recoiled, and he stopped himself. "Did you drive yourself, or did Hank?"

"Hank's downstairs in the florist shop. He'll be up in a few minutes." A smile twitched at the corner of her lips. "No, he wouldn't let me drive. The baby's fine, thanks for asking."

Her hand ran down the small, round bulge pressing against the front of her dress. Maggie couldn't help but stare at it. Sylvia was six months pregnant with the child she was having with Hank Morressy, the Boston architect she'd married a couple of years earlier. Nat was looking forward to having a grandchild, but Maggie wondered if he'd ever get to know her. He and Sylvia had never been very close, but Judith had always managed to bridge their mutual animosity. Now that she was going away . . .

Not for the first time, Maggie regretted the fact that Sylvia didn't know the truth. She was an adult now, but she still needed a mother, just as the baby would need a grandmother. If only Nat had told his daughter . . .

"Sit down, please." Nat offered the chair he'd just vacated. "You shouldn't be exerting yourself. Can I get you some water?"

"No. I want to see her." Sylvia turned and left the room before her father could stop her; as the door swung shut, Maggie heard her out in the hall, calling for a nurse.

Nat stared at the door. He suddenly looked older, pitiful, no longer a successful, middle-aged writer but a man who'd spent too much time at the typewriter and suddenly emerged from the imaginary world he'd spent decades building to find his wife dying and his daughter resentful of years of neglect.

"This isn't the way I wanted it to be," he said softly. "I never thought she—"

His voice broke. His head went down, and his shoulders began to shake. Maggie stood up and, at a loss for what else to do, took him in her arms. It was the first time in many years they'd embraced, but this time it was as old friends, not lovers. She held him and waited until the tears passed, and then she found a handkerchief and let him dry his face.

"All right," she said once he was calm again. "I'm here for you. Now let's go see Judie."

When they returned to the hospital room, they discovered the door was shut and Sylvia nowhere in sight. Hank stood outside, bouquet in hand. He and Nat gave each other a polite nod; they'd never become more than acquaintances, and Sylvia had probably told him nothing but the worst about his father-in-law. Maggie liked Hank; he was courtly, reserved, and completely the opposite of his wife. She suspected that the marriage wouldn't last.

Maggie went to the door, but before she could open it, Hank stepped in front of her. "She's awake," he said to her and Nat, "and Sylvia's in there with her, but"—he hesitated—"the nurse came out and said that her mother wanted to speak to her in private and asked us to wait out here."

Maggie stared at the door and then turned her gaze toward Nat. The color had left his face. His mouth was open, but nothing was coming out. Nat looked back at her; no words were necessary, for in that instant, they both knew what Judith was telling Sylvia.

Maggie felt her legs become weak. She instinctively grabbed Nat's elbow for support. All of a sudden, this was the last place in the world she wanted to be.

The only thing they could do was wait.

The three of them stood together in the hallway, ignoring the hospital staff walking around them, the occasional cryptic announcement coming over the PA system, for what was probably only a few minutes but seemed much longer. Then the door opened, and Sylvia came out.

She stood for a moment in the doorway, her face just as pale as her father's. No one spoke for several seconds, and then Nat stepped forward.

"Sylvia, I . . . I'm so sorry, I—"

Her hand shot up. She slapped him across the face. "That's for never telling me," she said, her voice an angry croak, and then she turned to Maggie.

Maggie braced herself, but while Sylvia's hand trembled, it remained at her side. Instead, she looked at Maggie, her mouth opening, closing, and then opening again. Maggie waited for her to speak, and at last the words came.

"That woman in there is my mother," Sylvia said. "It'll never be you."

12

Kate stared at the woman seated across the table. "That can't be true."

"It's true." Maggie's expression couldn't have been more serious. "I can show you the birth certificate. I'll even consent to a DNA test, if you insist." She paused. "Or you can call your mother. Sylvia will confirm everything I've told you now that she knows that you know."

Kate looked down at the table. Sometime in the last few minutes, the waiter had delivered their food. The lobster salad was utterly revolting. The room felt too warm, and the other restaurant guests sounded as if they were shouting at one another. Bile, acidic and bitter, rose from her stomach into her throat; realizing that she was about to be sick, she shoved back her chair, stumbled to her feet, and hurried out of the restaurant.

As luck would have it, the ladies' room was vacant. Kate slammed open the door of the nearest stall and, bracing her hands against the wall, leaned over the commode and opened her mouth. But nothing came out. She gasped for air and willed herself to throw up, but either there was nothing in her stomach or the panic attack was beginning to subside.

After a couple of minutes, her breathing returned to normal, and her heart no longer pounded. Kate went to the sink, where she rinsed her face and tried to comb her hair as best as she could with her fingers. Then she straightened her blouse and skirt, took a deep breath, and went back to the restaurant.

Margaret Krough was still seated at their table. "Are you okay?" she asked when Kate returned. There was a look of concern on her face that could only be described as grandmotherly. "I thought about coming to see if you were all right, but, well, I figured you might want to be alone."

Kate nodded as she sat down. The lobster salad was still there, but she'd lost her appetite; she covered the plate with her napkin. "I'm sorry. I didn't mean to—"

"No." Maggie shook her head. "I should be the one to apologize. I hit you hard with something you weren't expecting. There was no other way to tell you, but I can't blame you for being upset."

Kate gazed at her, trying to see her in a different way yet having trouble doing so. She'd never known her grandmother—or rather the woman she'd grown up believing to be her grandmother—but nonetheless, it was difficult to accept the new truth with which she'd been confronted: her grandmother was alive, and sitting across the table from her.

"So what am I supposed to call you?" she asked. "Grandma?"

"If you'd like, but I think we're past that now. Maggie is fine." A sad smile. "To tell the truth, though, there were times when I wished you knew me and could call me that name. But that's the choice I made, and I had to live with it."

"Why did you do it?"

Maggie let out her breath as a quiet sigh. "Please understand, when I discovered that I was pregnant from my affair with Nathan, I was in my early twenties and working as an assistant editor at Street & Smith. I had my eye on a publishing career, perhaps even starting my own literary agency. Even while I was having a relationship with your grandfather, I was coming to realize that getting married and having a child was the last thing I wanted to do, and in fact, I never did. But having an abortion was . . ." She closed her eyes and shuddered. "Well, it wasn't a pleasant prospect. They were far more dangerous back then than they are today. So I was between a rock and a hard place."

She absently ran a fingertip around the rim of her water glass. "Fortunately, Nat took responsibility for what had happened. We'd just broken up when the doctor told me the news. It really was just a fling, although for a little while, I'd thought it was serious enough that I made the mistake of writing a letter to Harry, but Nat accepted the fact that the child was his, and it was up to him to do something about it. He and Judith had met by then, and their relationship was serious enough that engagement was inevitable, but she'd already accepted me as an old girlfriend who was still one of her beau's best friends."

"That was rather forgiving of her," Kate said.

"Judie was a saint. I was at the party where she and Nat met, and . . . look, it's a long story, but what it boils down to is that I was trying to figure out how to break up with him without hurting him too badly when they met. Nat liked me well enough, but with her, it was love at first sight. All I had to do was step aside and let nature take its course."

"So the three of you stayed friends."

"That's right. And that made it easy for the three of us to sit down and work things out."

"So my grandparents—Grandpapa and Judith, I mean—"

Maggie smiled. "If you still want to call Judie your grandmother, you can. I understand."

"So they decided to adopt my mother once she was born."

"That's correct." Resting her elbows on the table, Maggie clasped her hands together. "I took a leave of absence from Street & Smith—I hadn't yet begun to show, so they accepted my story that I was having a 'case of nerves' and needed a sabbatical—and moved up to New Hampshire, where my family had a summer cottage on Lake Winnipesaukee. My parents were sympathetic to my situation, and my mother came up to take care of me. In the meantime, Nat and Judie tied the knot and then moved up to Boston where Nat had a teaching position waiting for him at Boston College. Judie bought some maternity clothes and started wearing pillows beneath them, and because she wouldn't let anyone touch her belly and stayed home as often as she could, everyone accepted their story that she was pregnant. When the time came, they took a weekend trip up to New Hampshire, where she allegedly gave birth to her child."

"In a vacation cabin on the lake, with a country midwife who happened to live nearby doing the delivery." Kate slowly nodded. "That's what I was told, growing up. And it was all a lie."

Maggie shrugged. "I prefer to think of it as a plausible fabrication."

"And no one else knew?"

"The only two other people who knew were Harry and George, and they promised to keep it to themselves." She raised a hand before Kate could ask the obvious question. "Because they belong to the Legion of Tomorrow, and we've never kept secrets from each other . . . well, almost never."

"So Grandpapa adopted Mama, and Grandma raised her as her own child. And you—"

"Maintained a discreet distance." Maggie gazed out the window. "It was actually a fairly pleasant arrangement. Once I became an agent and took on Nat as my first client, I was able to watch Sylvia grow up. She always thought of me as the lady who took care of her father's business, and I was even her babysitter a couple of times." Her face darkened. "But Nat never really warmed to her. Because of the circumstances in which she was born, I think he had trouble accepting her as his legitimate child, and after he quit teaching to become a full-time writer, he paid more attention to his work than he did to her. That hurt their relationship even more. And when Judie told her the truth just before she passed away—"

"I think I understand everything now."

"No, you don't." Maggie shook her head. "Only part of it, the part where you know why Nat, Harry, and I share a bond that goes back many years and how the Legion of Tomorrow has become the basis for the Arkwright Foundation."

"*How*, sure, but not why." Despite everything Maggie had just told her, Kate found herself thinking like a reporter again. Of the "five Ws" that had been drilled into her back in journalism school— *who, what, when, where,* and *why*—she'd learned the first four; the all-important fifth one was still missing.

"You're right. You should know this too." The waiter came by, and Maggie motioned for him to take away the plates. "I guess it really started just a few blocks up the street, during the 1989 World Science Fiction Convention." She paused, and a bleak smile crossed her face. "Come to think of it, that was almost exactly fifty years after Nat, Harry, George, and I first met."

13

It should have been a good weekend for Nat. In the end, though, Maggie realized that bringing him there had been a mistake.

The line for his autograph session began forming an hour before he actually showed up. By the time Maggie escorted him up the escalator to the promenade of the Hynes Convention Center where author signings were taking place, nearly four hundred people were waiting for him. Nathan Arkwright stared at the line snaking down the broad upstairs mezzanine, and for a moment, Maggie thought he was going to turn and beat a hasty retreat to the curb where his housekeeper, Mr. Sterling, had dropped them off just a few moments earlier.

"My god, Maggie," he muttered. "Who are all these people here for?"

"You, my love," she whispered, and then she took him by the arm and led him to the table.

This was the first science fiction convention Nathan had attended in years. Indeed, if it hadn't been in his own state, he probably wouldn't have shown up at all. But the mass-market paperback of *Through the Event Horizon* had just come out, and since the book was a *New York Times* hardcover bestseller last year, his publisher was putting a major push behind it, and they wanted Nat to make at least a couple of public appearances to promote the book. Showing up for one day of this year's Worldcon shouldn't have been much of a burden, but even so, Maggie had had to practically drag Nat out of his house. He'd become a recluse since Judith's death, and invitations to attend SF conventions had been routinely ignored.

Once Nat sat down at the table—by himself, thankfully, with no authors he didn't know sitting beside him—things got better. One by one, fans stepped before him, each bearing copies of his books to be signed, mainly *Beyond the Event Horizon*, but some also brought old and valuable editions of his earlier books, including one collector with a mint-condition copy of the May 1940 issue of *Startling* where he'd made his debut. Nat was standoffish at first, saying little if anything to the people who approached him, but he gradually warmed up to the task. He began talking to the fans, chatting with them as he signed his name with the onyx Montblanc fountain pen that Maggie had given him when he'd signed his first million-dollar contract, even talking a little bit about the Galaxy Patrol books although this was a subject he was usually reluctant to discuss with anyone who wasn't professionally involved with their production.

As she quietly sat beside him, Maggie saw a glimmer of the Nat she used to know. Deep down inside the lonely old man still mourning the death of his wife was the young writer she'd met at the first Worldcon a half century earlier. It was a pleasure to see him return, if only for a few minutes.

The signing went well, and when it was done, she escorted him up another level to the greenroom so he could get out of the public eye for a little while before his next program event. But even there he was the center of attention. Once they heard that he was in the building, longtime friends who hadn't seen him in many years— Hal Clement, Robert Silverberg, Kelly Freas—made a point of coming by, while younger writers for whom he was only a legend either shyly came up to shake his hand or stood off to the side, pretending to play it cool but actually delighted to be in the company of one of the Big Four. Nat sat on a couch, sipping a Diet Coke as writers, artists, and editors gathered around him, and for a little while, it seemed to Maggie that the Nat she knew and loved was coming back.

It didn't last. A couple of hours later, Nat made the second of three appearances the convention had scheduled for him that day, a panel discussion with the vague title "The Future of the Future." Again, Nat was among friends: Bob Silverberg and Fred Pohl, along with the moderator, Stanley Schmidt, the *Analog* editor for whom Nat had written a rare Galaxy Patrol short story a couple of years earlier. The panel was held in the main ballroom, and it was filled to capacity; every seat was taken, and fans stood along the walls and sat in the aisle. So things should have gone well.

Yet they didn't. Once again, Nat was the center of attention, but what had been a novelty earlier in the day was now an unwanted task. From the first row, Maggie watched as Nat seemed to fade before her very eyes. As the hour went by, he slumped lower and lower in his chair, and he seemed incapable of engaging the other panelists in conversation but instead spoke past them, veering off topic to talk about things that had little to do with the subject at hand. When Fred spoke about emerging awareness of an electronic dominion called cyberspace, for instance, Nat responded with a rambling complaint about how hard it was to find someone in the Berkshires to repair his daisy wheel printer when it broke down. But it wasn't until the hour was nearly over that matters went from bad to worse.

A bearded fan with Brillo Pad hair and wearing a black T-shirt and baggy jeans—seeing him, Maggie mourned the bygone era when no self-respecting young man would go out in public without a haircut and a tie—had stood up to ask why anyone even bothered to write about space anymore. "It's all about computers, y'know," he said. "The *Challenger* disaster just shows how dangerous space is. Can't we do the same thing with robots and not make astronauts risk their lives going up there?" A shrug and a know-it-all smile. "Space travel . . . y'know, that might have been great for the '40s or '50s, but now it's the '90s, and it's a whole new world."

Bob Silverberg leaned forward to speak, but Nat cut him off before he could utter a word. "That is probably the stupidest thing I've ever heard," he said with a slow, disgusted sigh.

A collective gasp went up from the audience. A few scattered laughs, a boo from way in the back, but mainly a shocked, shared *ohhh*. Fred's eyebrows raised, and Bob gave him a sharp look. Stan was stunned, as well, but before he could gain control of the mike, Nat hunched forward to stare the astonished youngster straight in the eye.

"No, really," he went on, "that's amazingly imbecilic. I have a computer too, but do I really think that it could anything I can do? Hell, no. It can't even make coffee. So this idea that computers are going to be the end-all and be-all of everything is just moronic." He shook his head.

"Nat," Bob began.

"No, let me finish." Nat turned his back to him and Fred. "As for the rest, do you seriously believe the astronauts are marched out to the launchpad at gunpoint?" He made a pistol out of his fingers and jabbed it at the audience. "G'wan . . . get in that shuttle, or I'll kill you!" A few people chuckled, and Nat went on, "It is an incredibly brave thing that they do and couldn't possibly be replicated by any computer or robot, no matter how sophisticated they may be. And even if people could be left on the ground, why would we want them to be? The future is a frontier that's not going to be explored by sitting in front of a computer screen, eating potato chips. It's *life*, and life requires an effort. The astronauts know this, and that's why they're willing to accept the danger. And maybe if you got off your butt, you'd understand these things!"

By then, the ballroom had gone quiet. The laughter had stopped, and everyone was staring at Nathan as if he was a beloved grandfather who'd suddenly scolded his family for no apparent reason. The fan who'd asked the question was pale; not knowing whether to sit down or remain standing, he nervously shifted back and forth on his feet.

"You want to see the future?" Nathan demanded, still glaring at him. "You want to know what things are going to be like in the next century? Then turn off your TV, put down your computer games, drop the Star Trek book you're reading, and go out there and *create it yourself!* Science fiction is just that—it's *fiction!* Made-up stories! You've got to . . . got to . . ."

Nathan blinked and stammered as if he'd suddenly lost his train of thought. As abruptly as it had begun, the storm passed. Stanley Schmidt took over the mike and tactfully changed the subject, and Nat said nothing more for the rest of the hour. When the panel was over, Maggie hurried to the stage. She took Nat by the arm and ushered him out a side door before anyone could corner him. Mr. Sterling had been given the afternoon off and wasn't supposed to pick them until that evening, so she flagged down a cab on Boylston Street and pushed Nathan into the back of it.

Maggie asked the driver to take them to a small neighborhood bar she knew about in the Back Bay area, one where they were un-likely to encounter any fans or other writers. Once they were settled into a booth, she pulled out her portable phone—an expensive toy that she'd fortunately thought to put in her shoulder bag before com-ing up to Boston, just in case a client or an editor needed to reach her—and used it to call the convention's guest liaison. The young lady with whom Maggie spoke was sympathetic when she was told that Nathan Arkwright was canceling his reading later that afternoon; apparently, she'd already learned about Nat's panel blowup. Maggie simply told her that Nat wasn't feeling well; she apologized for the inconvenience and then disconnected and hailed a waiter.

Through all of it, Nat was silent. Stunned by his own behavior, he'd allowed Maggie to spirit him out of the convention and into the dark anonymity of the bar, where he could become just another old guy having a drink. There was a ball game on TV, but the Red Sox weren't playing, so the few other people in the place weren't paying much attention. Maggie waited until their drinks came, and then she reached across the table to take Nathan's hand.

"Okay, you," she said. "What happened back there?"

"I don't know." Nat picked up his whiskey and soda, took a sip, and put it down again. "I was doing okay, I think . . . well, maybe I wasn't . . . but then that brat starts in with . . . I don't remember, but it was something stupid, and it just set me off." A wry grin. "Scared the hell out of him, didn't I?"

"You scared the hell out of *me*."

Nat started to laugh, but then he saw the expression on her face, and the grin disappeared. "Sorry. Didn't mean to do that to you." He looked down at his drink and shook his head. "No, I don't know what got into me. Maybe I'm just frustrated about a lot of things, and I took it out on the first guy who rubbed me wrong. Coming here might not have been such a good idea, after all."

"Yes, well, I think that goes without saying." Then she shook her head. "No, no, that's not true. You were doing fine during the signing and had a great time in the greenroom. In fact, it's the happiest I've seen you in years. But then you got up in front of all those people and . . . oh, for god's sake, Nat! What were you thinking?"

Nat looked away. His gaze turned toward the TV, and for a minute or so, he watched the baseball game with detached curiosity, perhaps not really seeing it at all.

"This isn't my scene anymore, Maggie," he said at last. "Science fiction, I mean. I come to this convention, and it's filled with strangers. Sure, I still know a few people, but the rest . . . they're just children, kids who aren't interested anymore in anything I've got to say."

"That's not true. Your books sell better than they ever have. You have the fans to owe for that."

He gave her a sidelong look. "C'mon, you know better. Fans aren't most of my readers. They're not even the core. They're a subset, a little circle off to the side of a big Venn diagram. So maybe I ought not care what they think, but . . ." Again, he shook his head. "I do because, in a way, the kid may be right."

"How's that?"

"No one cares about space anymore. The fans are now into . . . what did Fred call it, cyberspace? . . . and if it isn't that, then it's dragons and elves. If the Galaxy Patrol stories are still selling well, it's because I've been writing them for almost fifty years and have the TV show and the movies too. But I'm bored with them. I really am." He paused to pick up his glass. "This book is the last one, Maggie. I'm done with the series."

"Don't say that."

"Sorry, old girl, but you'll have to find a new meal ticket. I'm done with the Patrol books. Sharecrop 'em if you want—I'm sure you'd have no trouble finding writers who'd beg to do them—but I'm sick of the whole thing." He took a drink, hissed between his teeth. "In fact, I'm sick of writing, period. Half of a century is long enough."

Maggie wished Harry or George were there. She could have used help from the rest of the Legion just then. But Harry was ailing, and George was busy at the Institute for Advanced Study, so she had to handle Nat by herself. "So what are you going to do? Sit around the house and do nothing all day?"

"No, not at all. I want to continue pursuing my interests, just in a different way, that's all." Nathan put down the empty glass, pushed it away. "I'm thinking about putting all that money I've made to good use and underwrite the things I believe in. Projects that will get people into space—private companies, university research, stuff like that."

"You'll have a lot of people knocking at your door."

"Not if I do so anonymously. I might even set up a nonprofit foundation and fund it with profits from investments in space business." He shrugged. "I'm still working it out in my mind. But the point is, I've finished writing. I'm retiring."

"Writers don't retire, Nat. They just quit for a while." Maggie picked up her drink. "You'll be working on another book before long."

"Only if it's my memoirs, sweetheart." He cocked an eyebrow.

"Come to think of it, that's not a bad idea. Fred and Isaac have written their autobiographies. Why can't I?"

She'd just taken a sip of her vodka and tonic when he said this; it took a lot to keep from sputtering. "Please don't," she said, wiping her mouth with a napkin from the table. "If you tell the truth, no one will ever forgive you."

"The truth? About what?" And then he caught the look in her eye and understood. "Oh, yeah, that. Well, one day, she'll be old enough to understand."

"So if Grandpapa had finished his memoirs . . ." Kate began.

"You would have learned the truth about your mother and me," Maggie finished. "And so would have the rest of the world. Fortunately, he never did, and he never will."

"Okay, I understand. But everything else you just told me?"

"Will make sense if you'll be patient just a little while longer." Maggie raised a hand, signaling the waiter to bring the check. "I told you that I'm here on business, and that's the truth, but the business is you. I want to take you someplace."

"Where?"

"Why, to see George, of course, so he can tell you the rest of the story."

14

Maggie had hired a town car to bring her up from New York. It was parked at the curb outside the Four Seasons, a black Audi sedan in which the driver sat reading a paperback. He got out to hold the back doors open for Maggie and Kate and then slid behind the wheel again. Apparently, Maggie had already told him where to go, because he didn't ask for directions as he weaved his way through the midday traffic.

Kate was surprised when they got on the expressway and even more surprised when they followed it out of the city. They picked up the Mass Pike and left Boston behind; Maggie refused to answer her questions but instead sat primly in her seat, hands folded in her lap as she gazed straight ahead. There was a sly smile on her face, but she said little.

They got off the pike at the Framingham exit and were soon driving through leafy Boston suburbs, passing industrial parks belonging to high-tech companies: software designers, medical equipment manufacturers, biotech research firms. They entered the driveway of one such park and approached its first building, an anonymous two-story glass wall with a FOR LEASE sign posted on the front lawn.

"They should have taken that down," Maggie said disapprovingly when she noticed the sign. "We've rented the entire second floor."

"The foundation?" Kate asked, and Maggie nodded. "Why do you need this much space?"

The car came to a stop in front of the building, and the driver climbed out to open the doors for them. "Come in and see," Maggie said as he helped her out of the backseat.

A couple of service vehicles and a delivery van were parked beside the building; in the ground-floor hallway, Maggie and Kate had to move aside to make room for a workman pushing a hand truck out of the elevator.

"I must apologize for the mess," Maggie said as they rode upward. The car's walls and floor were covered with brown wrapping paper to prevent them from being scratched. "We're still moving in, as you can see."

The entrance was a plate-glass door upon which a hand-lettered sign, *Arkwright F.*, had been taped. A reception desk had been installed in the front foyer; the carpet was covered with canvas tarps, and the walls were being repainted, but a young black woman sat at the desk, working at a Mac that looked like it was fresh out of the box.

"Ms. Krough! Good to see you again!" She stood up as they walked in. "Dr. Hallahan is waiting for you in the boardroom. Can I bring you coffee?"

"Thank you, Barbara. Tea would be nice. Kate?"

Kate shook her head. From hallways leading in opposite directions away from the reception area, she heard hammers, drills, and the muffled voices of workmen. Sawdust was in the air. She figured that the foundation had been there only a couple of weeks. They had probably moved in right after the first check from her grandfather's estate cleared the bank.

Barbara escorted them to a room halfway down the hallway to the left of the reception area. The boardroom appeared to be finished, at least; the walls had a fresh coat of eggshell-white paint, with a forty-two-inch plasma TV on one of them. The oval conference table was covered with papers and file folders, though, attesting to the fact that the room was being used as a temporary office, and seated behind an Apple laptop was George Hallahan.

"There you are. I was wondering when you'd show up." George wore a bow tie today, making him even more professorial than before. He stood up and walked around the table, pausing to give Maggie a quick buss before shaking hands with Kate. "I hope you had a good lunch with Margaret. She didn't bore you too much, did she?"

Kate couldn't tell whether he was joking or not. "It was . . . quite interesting," she managed to say.

A grin and a devilish wink. "I imagine it was, indeed." He quietly regarded her for a second, as if divining her thoughts from the expression on her face, and then stepped back. "Well, if you'll take seats, please, I shall begin."

Kate and Maggie settled into brand-new office chairs across from where George had been sitting. Barbara returned with a tea mug for

Maggie and then left, shutting the door on her way out. George remained standing, hands clasped behind his back.

"Well, now," he began. "I think it's safe to assume that Maggie has filled you in about . . . um, parts of your family history of which you were formerly unaware, yes?"

"She did." From the corner of her eye, Kate could see Maggie watching her. "I'm still trying to absorb this, but yes, I know."

"Good." He paused. "I'm sorry we made you find out in this manner, by having you read Nat's biography and then speak to Harry and Maggie in turn. Had we told you everything after your grandfather's funeral, though, there's a chance you wouldn't have believed us."

"Three crazy old people," Maggie said. "That's probably what you would have thought of us."

Kate started to object and then realized that she was probably right. If a woman she'd only just met had told her that she was really her grandmother, she would have chalked it up as senile dementia. Harry's tales of what happened on Tinian and the *Apollo 17* launch would have been no more than an old man's recollections, and her grandfather's memoirs . . . interesting, but inconsequential. "I understand," she said.

"Good, very good. Now let me tell you about the last time I saw Nat, when I visited him earlier this year."

15

Summer had come late to the Berkshires, but it had come, anyway. From the sundeck of Nathan's house, George watched an eagle as it rode the thermals above the nearby mountainside, searching the forests below for prey. There were new leaves on the trees and dragonflies in the air, and the meadows were green again.

A lovely day. Despite the warmth of the afternoon, though, Mr. Sterling had wrapped a light shawl around Nathan's thin shoulders before leaving them on the deck to talk. Nat sat huddled in his rocking chair, his shoulders bowed slightly forward, and George reflected that his friend had become disturbingly frail since the last time he'd seen him. That had been quite a few years ago, but even so, there wasn't any way to get around it. Nat Arkwright wasn't much longer for this world.

"Have you read about that asteroid?" Nat asked. "The one that was in the papers lately?"

The abrupt change of topic caught George off guard. Only a moment earlier, they'd been chatting about the kinds of raptors that nested in the Berkshires; Nathan couldn't quite make out the eagle, but George could, and that was what prompted the conversation. Now, all of a sudden, Nat wanted to talk about something else. He'd always had a tendency to do that, though, and George was one of the few people who could keep up with him.

"Which asteroid?" he asked.

"The one that may hit Earth in about twenty-five years."

George liked to think of his mind as a mental card file; he quickly flipped through it until he located the correct card. "Ah. That would be 99942 Apophis, a near-Earth asteroid that was discovered, um, fairly recently." At the last second, he decided not to inform Nat that Apophis had actually been discovered nearly eighteen months earlier, with the newspapers reporting its possible trajectory about six months later. No point in reminding his old friend that his memory was giving out along with the rest of his body. "I wouldn't worry about it too much."

Nat peered at him. "Why not? For God's sake, you know what something like that could do if it hit us."

"*If* it hit us. As I recall, it's been calculated that Apophis will probably miss Earth when it swings back by in 2029." He smiled. "In any case, I shouldn't worry about it too much. I doubt either of us will be around by then."

In the old days, Nat would have appreciated the macabre humor of what he'd just said. He might have even laughed. Now he simply cast George a sullen glare. "I'm concerned with human history after I'm gone, you know. I don't believe the universe will cease to exist the moment I die."

"Of course it won't." George shifted uncomfortably in his chair. This conversation was taking a more serious tone than he expected or liked. "But there's not much you can do about that, is there?"

"There isn't? Or perhaps there is."

For the first time since George had arrived at Nathan's house this morning, after his assistant had driven him up from Princeton, a smile appeared on Nat's pale and lined face. A few weeks earlier, George had received an unexpected phone call from him, an invitation to spend a couple of days at his place in western Massachusetts. George hadn't seen Nat in a long time, and a little weekend getaway to the Berkshires sounded like fun.

Nat had been moody the moment George showed up, though, and it wasn't until this moment that he showed any sign of his old self. There was a familiar twinkle in Nat's eye, a certain slyness that meant he'd been playing with an intriguing idea that had come to him lately, some notion that he wanted to bounce off "the Legion's genius-in-residence" (as he liked to call George). In the past, this sort of thing usually occurred when Nat had a brainstorm for a new Galaxy Patrol novel. Yet it had been nearly twenty years since Nathan Arkwright had published his last novel, and George doubted that he was about to produce a new one, even as the final act of a life that was coming to a close.

"What's on your mind, Nat?" George sat back in his chair and cupped his hands together. "Why did you ask me to come here?"

Nat was quiet a moment. Gazing up, he appeared to finally notice the eagle roaming the sky above his home. "Have you read Martin Rees's *Our Final Hour*?" he said at last.

"Yes. Fascinating book."

"What do you think of his prognosis? That the human race has only a 50 percent chance of surviving the twenty-first century and that if we don't or can't change our ways, we're doomed to extinction by our own hand?"

George pursed his lips. "I think Sir Martin's being a tad pessimistic in his odds, but—" He paused, weighing his words. "I'm afraid he may be right. Even if an asteroid doesn't clobber us, global climate change could very well do us in. Or nuclear war. Or a plague we ourselves created and transmitted. Any of a number of different things."

"And does this bother you?"

"Of course it does." A wry smile. "That's one of the reasons why I've continued my line of research all these years. We can't afford to have all our eggs stuck in one basket, can we?"

"No, we can't." Nat slowly nodded. "All of us have been working toward the same objective all along, haven't we? The Legion, I mean. Harry and I wrote stories about the human race leaving Earth and going out into space, Maggie made sure that they got published, and you've been trying to accomplish the same thing in real life."

"We've come a long way since Caravan Hall, but don't give me too much credit. I haven't been all that successful." George looked away toward the nearby mountains. "I thought we had a good idea with Project Orion when I worked on it at General Atomics, but we lost the funding for that. Same thing happened in the '70s when I was involved with developing the NERVA engine at NASA. We could have been on Mars by 1990 if we'd built nuclear rockets. Each time we came close, though, either Congress or the White House would pull the plug for one reason or another."

"That's my understanding of it, yes." A breeze drifted across the meadows. Nathan pulled his shawl a little closer, as if feeling a chill. "The problem isn't technological or even willingness; it's always money."

"That's right. We know what it takes to go into space. We know what it takes to colonize another planet. We could even start building starships within this century, if we put our minds to it."

"Starships?" Nat raised an eyebrow. "Really?"

"Sure. The British Interplanetary Society came up with its Daedalus design as far back as the '70s. Lately, other people have revisited their work and come up with a second-generation design called Icarus. But it doesn't need to be nuclear fusion. There's also been quite a bit of work done on beam propulsion, either laser or microwave. It would be very big and very expensive, but so far, there's been no showstoppers . . . well, almost none."

"What's the problem?"

"People." George stretched out his legs. "We don't know how to keep people alive in space for the length of time it would take a vessel to travel to another star system. Even if we could accelerate a ship to half light speed, which is remotely feasible with a beamed-power system, it would take the ship almost five years just to reach Alpha Centauri. Anything farther away than that could take decades, even centuries."

"Generation ships."

"Great idea for science fiction stories, but it falls apart when we try to figure out how to make it work in real life. The biggest hurdle is building a reliable, foolproof, closed-loop environmental system that can sustain itself almost indefinitely. Look what happened to Biosphere II. It had its own greenhouse effect within months, and they finally had to pull the residents out of there. You might be able to make something like that work on the Moon or Mars, because you can fix the problems with assistance from Earth, but once a ship leaves the solar system, it's on its own." George shrugged. "Besides, when you think about it, even in science fiction, most generation ships end in disaster, don't they?"

"Then hibernation—"

"A bit more feasible, but you're still talking about keeping people alive for long periods of time, even if they're in an artificially induced coma. Low-temperature freezing can damage brain tissue, and warm-sleep methods are conjectural at best." George shook his head. "Space is a very dangerous environment, completely unforgiving. I love reading science fiction and always have, but guys like you and Harry often underestimate how hard is to live out there."

Nathan was quiet for a few moments. "Do you think interstellar travel is impossible?" he asked at last. "Tell the truth."

"No, just very, very difficult. It may be something that living beings will never be able to do. Unmanned probes, yes, but nothing with a crew aboard." He thought about it for a moment and then added, "Of course, there is an alternative."

"An alternative? Do you think it would work?"

"Yes, it might. It involves—"

Nathan lifted a hand that had become gaunt and spotted. "Explain it to me in a moment. Let me tell you why I've asked you here."

George was curious about that very thing. It had been quite a while since Nat had invited him or anyone else from the Legion for a weekend stay. Even Maggie did most of her business with him by phone or email. And although George still liked to attend science fiction conventions on occasion—quietly, as a fan who was seldom recognized—it had been many years since the last time Nathan Arkwright had made a public appearance. Something had gone out of him when Judith died; he'd continued writing for another ten years and then gave it up and contented himself with living off the royalties and residuals being generated by the Galaxy Patrol franchise.

Nat let his hand fall to the armrest of his chair. "Here's an inescapable fact of my own," he said quietly. "I'm dying."

George wasn't surprised. His eyes hadn't missed anything over the past few hours he spent with his old friend, and he was too good a scientist not to accept the evidence of his observations. Yet when he started to ask the obvious question, Nat shook his head. "Don't ask me about the details," he said, his voice taking on a phlegmy rasp.

"That's the only part of it that depresses me. The rest I can take, but—"

"I understand. How much longer do you think you've got?"

"A few months. The doctors don't think I'll make it to the end of the year. 'Til then, I'm going to just get weaker and weaker." A strained smile. "I guess that pretty much kills the book I was writing. Not that anyone would want to read my autobiography, anyway."

George let out his breath. "I'm sorry, Nat. I . . . I really don't know what to say." He'd never been able to handle death well, and Nathan was one of his oldest friends. "If there's anything I can do—"

"Yes, yes, in fact, there is." Nathan looked straight at him. "I'm like you. I want the human race to go to the stars. I think I've worked out a way how. That's going to be my legacy, and you and Maggie and Harry can help me."

George stared at him. "How?"

"First things first." Another smile, a little stronger now. "I've just had my lawyer revise my will. Here's what I'm doing . . ."

16

George was interrupted by a polite knock at the door. Barbara came in, and first Kate thought she'd come to offer coffee again. Instead, she stepped aside to let two people into the room: Harry Skinner and his grandson Jim.

Kate was apparently the only person in the room surprised to see them. Maggie merely smiled, and George glanced at his watch. "Very good. Right on time, and the timing's perfect. I was just about to tell Kate about Nat's final bequest." He turned to her again. "Your grandfather—"

"Wait a minute." She looked at Harry and Jim. "I saw you just a few days ago. Did you know you were going to be here?"

Harry was riding a three-wheel scooter today. He leaned forward in the saddle seat to lay his arms across the handlebars. "'Fraid so. We didn't know exactly when Maggie was going to bring you here, so we had to play that part by ear." He cocked a thumb at Jim. "I'm lucky that he was able to take a day off and borrow a van from the hospital. Otherwise, I would've had to take the train up, and it's getting hard for me to travel."

"Okay, I get that, but why?"

George cleared his throat. "If you'll let me continue . . ." Kate nodded and he went on, "Your grandfather decided to amend his will to establish the Arkwright Foundation. Until then, he was going to leave his estate mainly to charity, with a token amount going to you and your mother. But in his last few months, he came up with a different idea—using his fortune to underwrite that which had fascinated him his entire life."

"Space travel," Kate said.

"No, not just space travel—space *colonization*. And not just in the local neighborhood, either. He was far more ambitious than simply putting people on the Moon again or sending them to Mars. He wanted to provide seed money for a serious effort at interstellar exploration."

"It's actually a continuation of something he's been doing for quite some time," Maggie said. "When he retired from writing, he turned to quietly tracking and observing space development on several different fronts, in particular small start-up companies and private research groups. When he saw someone doing something that was particularly promising, he'd send them a check with the stipulation that the donation was to be kept anonymous, with no one knowing except the company president or research team leader."

"Only Maggie knew about this," George added. "Nat didn't let either Harry or me know. But over the last twenty years or so, he's been quietly underwriting a lot of nongovernmental space efforts, particularly those concerned with interstellar exploration."

Kate stared at him, not quite believing what she'd just heard. "Interstellar . . . you mean, as in building starships?"

"Yes, exactly." George was utterly calm, as if it were the most logical thing in the world. "You're a science writer, so I'm sure you're aware of the recent discoveries of extrasolar planets. So far, what's been found are largely hot jupes, superjovians, or smaller planets that aren't in habitable zones, but everyone working in this area believes it's only a matter of time before we find Earth-mass planets whose orbits are just the right distance from their primaries and that those stars will be close enough to Earth to make traveling to them a possibility."

"That's what the Arkwright Foundation is all about." Maggie picked up the thread of the conversation. "Its purpose is to underwrite and support an ongoing program of research and development aimed at building the first starship within the next one hundred years, if not sooner. This office is just the first step. Once we're settled in, we're going to start making contact with individuals, private companies, and organizations that share our same goals and enlist their help, with everything being coordinated from here."

"We'll be doing this quietly," Harry added. "It won't be made public, and there won't be government involvement, either. We don't want this to become another NASA project that gets scuttled because Congress can't get off its dead ass and give it decent funding. So we're going at it alone."

"Well, good luck with that." Kate didn't mean to come across as skeptical, but she couldn't help it. "Look, Grandpapa was rich, but I doubt you'll get very far depending on his royalties."

"We know that," Maggie said. "That's why I've been working on a long-range program that will funnel the assets and future earnings of Nat's estate into various investments, including some of the technologies we'll need to draw upon. We figure that, with careful management, we'll be able to provide the foundation with a permanent financial base that will grow with time, from millions to billions, if we play it right."

"And how long do you think it'll take? To build a starship, I mean."

"Oh, decades, at least," Harry said. "Even generations." He gestured to Maggie and George. "We'll be long gone by then, of course, which is why we'll be leaving the foundation to you and Jim once we're not in the picture anymore."

Kate looked at Jim Skinner, who'd taken a seat at the other end of the table. He smiled and nodded; apparently, he'd already agreed to work with the foundation. No wonder Harry was so keen on having her meet him; their brief encounter in Philadelphia hadn't been an accident.

Despite her misgivings, Kate found herself becoming less skeptical. It sounded goofy at first, but the more she thought about it, the more this plan made sense. Everything Maggie, George, and Harry told her made sense.

No. Not everything. "I still don't get it," she said. "I mean, why come to me? I hardly knew my grandfather, and I'm not all that interested in interstellar travel. You could easily find someone else to sit on the board of directors. I don't have anything to contribute."

"Actually, you do," George said. "In fact, other than your mother, you have something quite unique, something we'd like to have very much. Your—"

He abruptly stopped, his face turning red as if he'd been about to say something embarrassing. Harry laughed out loud. "Oh, c'mon. I can't believe you're such a prude!"

"We'd like to have your eggs," Maggie said. "Just as we'd like to have Jim donate some of his sperm."

"*What?*"

"We're working from an assumption that the ship we build won't have a living crew." George was obviously more comfortable discussing engineering than human reproduction. "As I told Nat, that's been the sticking point of every proposal for interstellar travel—keeping the crew alive and sane for the long time it'll take a ship to reach its destination. So we're asking a different question entirely . . . why send people at all?"

He reached forward to tap a command into his laptop's keyboard. The plasma-screen TV on the wall behind him lit, showing a diagram of a female oocyte being fertilized by a male sperm and gradually developing through the zygote and blastocyst phases into an embryo. "We believe we can develop the means by which this process could take place in an artificial uterus," he continued, "one that would be aboard the starship and regulated by the onboard AI. Of course, there would be more than just one. The ship would carry enough egg and sperm specimens, each from an individual donor, to establish a colony at its destination."

"But who would raise the children once they're born? You can't seriously intend to send a bunch of infants down to an uninhabited planet, can you?"

"Of course not. That's one more thing that needs to be worked out." George shook his head. "I'm not going to pretend to have all the answers. But that's the purpose of the foundation—to take the long view and make our plans over the course of years. No crash program like Apollo, but instead a gradual research-and-development effort with a long-term objective."

"All right, I understand. But you still haven't explained why you want Jim and me to be donors."

"Isn't it obvious?" Maggie nodded toward Harry and George. "We'd be donors ourselves were it not for the fact that we're long past reproductive age. But Jim carries Harry's genes, while you—"

"Carry both yours and my grandfather's."

"Exactly," George said. "I never married or had children, but many years ago, I donated a sperm specimen for a research project involving cryonic preservation of genetic material. I checked on its status and found that it still exists and can be made available to me."

"So the Legion of Tomorrow will make the trip, if only indirectly." Harry grinned. "Just as well. I've never been crazy about long-distance travel."

Maggie steepled her fingers together. "If it makes any difference, I'm thinking that we might be able to offer you a permanent position here. The foundation will need an executive director once it's up and running, someone who can shepherd things along. It'll be a full-time job, of course, unless you're too busy scratching out a living as a freelance writer."

"It's a tempting offer," Kate said.

"How 'bout it, kiddo?" Harry asked. "Ready to sign up with the Legion of Tomorrow?"

Kate didn't reply at once. Instead, she gazed around the table, looking at Maggie, Harry, and George. Four friends had grown old together yet continued to share the idea that the future could be made better by feats of the imagination. It was a notion born in a less cynical time, and perhaps it was a little wide eyed and maybe even naïve, but nonetheless they continued to believe in it.

One of their number was now gone, but in his memory, the others had dedicated themselves to fostering the legacy he'd left behind. The ideals they'd believed in all these years would survive, carried into the future by their grandchildren, and their children after that, and so on through generations to come.

She'd been invited to join them, to dedicate her life to its cause. Kate knew that she couldn't refuse. She finally understood what their slogan meant.

"Forward the Legion," she said.

INTERLUDE

Affair with a Dreamer

"I believe it should be the goal of the United States to build and launch the first starship and to do so within this century."

Senator Clark Wessen stood at a speaker's podium, his hands folded together on its glass surface as he addressed the debate moderator and, behind her, the audience of the University of New Hampshire campus auditorium. On either side of him, the five other candidates from his party who desired to be the next president of the United States watched in stoical silence as their rival from Indiana continued to speak.

"A project of this magnitude would take decades, and yes, it would cost a considerable amount of money. However, it would pay itself back with the development of new technologies in several different areas while providing long-term goals . . . um, an objective . . . for many major . . . um, industries . . . companies, that is." The senator stumbled over his own words; speaking without a prompter was obviously something to which he wasn't accustomed. *"And in the end, it will—"*

"Five seconds, Senator," the moderator said.

"—provide not just our country but the human race as a whole with a new frontier, a new world it can—"

"Time's up, Senator."

"—explore and colonize in years to come. Thank you."

A smattering of applause from the audience, like dismal raindrops falling on a barn roof. Wessen offered a quick, nervous smile in return. The other candidates were careful to keep their expressions neutral. All except Robert Jacques Bolivar. The Georgia governor had a gleam in his eye as he turned to regard the older man standing beside him.

"Pause," Marty said.

The 3-D image on the holoscreen froze on the two-shot image of Wessen and Bolivar; they looked like a pair of dolls on display in a recessed shelf on Marty's office wall. Alphonse Martino, whom everyone at *The Dirty Truth* called Marty, leaned back in his chair and looked over at the young staff writer sitting on the other side of his desk.

"You caught that part, didn't you?" he asked.

"Nope. Didn't watch the debate." Jill Muller sipped the latte she'd brought in with her; it was lukewarm already, and she didn't want to have to go back down to the lobby to buy another. She caught the annoyed expression on Marty's face and shrugged. "Politics isn't my beat, you know that. And how many debates do they have during primary season, anyway?"

"Too many," Marty admitted. "They're like kindergarten beauty pageants, although not nearly as mature." He pointed to the holo. "But I thought this would've caught your attention—what he said, I mean, about wanting to build a starship."

"Sure. I read our site, y'know." Jill took another sip, reluctantly decided that she was just going to have to let her coffee go cold, and placed it on the corner of the managing editor's desk. "Bolivar pounced all over it, and so did . . . um, what's his name, the bald guy, the Hawaii congressman?"

"Gosling."

"Yeah, Gosling. But Bolivar got him worse. Chided him for wanting to spend money on building a starship when the National Coastal Barrier Initiative is over budget and behind schedule, made him sound like a complete airhead." Jill grinned. "What did *The Daily News* call him? Senator Stardust?"

"Senator Stardust, yes. And I just got this from the op-ed desk." He picked up a slate, ran his finger down its screen, and then turned it around and held it up for Jill to see. Displayed was a cartoon by one of the *Truth*'s staff cartoonists: a caricature of Senator Wessen, bent intently over the handlebars of the tricycle he was riding, 1940s-style space helmet on his head and toy ray gun held aloft. In the foreground, a happy-looking man wearing a WESSEN IN '36 button proclaimed, *"And here he comes, folks . . . the next president of the United States!"*

"Cute." Jill couldn't help but smile, though. "I imagine his campaign is going to be just thrilled to see that."

"They're going to see worse." Marty put the slate down. "Wessen's little remark was one of the high points of last night's debate, and if he isn't in enough trouble after a fourth-place showing in Iowa, this is going to hurt his chances of landing anywhere near the top three in New Hampshire. And forget about taking it away from Bolivar. The primary's in two weeks, and the latest straw poll puts the governor ahead of Gosling by five percentage points and Wessen by eight."

"Okay, Wessen said something stupid last night. Why ask me about it?" Jill absently flipped her long blond hair back over her shoulders. "I'm on science desk. You got six people covering the campaign already who know more about this stuff than I do."

"Yes, I do, and one of them turned up something I'd like to have you check out." Marty leaned forward, clasping his hands together atop his desk. "Would you like to know why Clark Wessen would say something like that during a presidential campaign?"

"He's trying to sound like President Kennedy?"

"You know your history. I like that." A smirk. "Nice to see you're interested in something else up there other than nerd stuff."

Jill tried not to bristle. She'd come to realize that, for Marty, "nerd stuff" was any subject where he wasn't likely to find a scandal of one form or another, which was the only thing he was interested in reporting, really. But she said nothing as he shook his head. "We thought that too. However, the guys covering the Wessen campaign have been doing a little digging and just last week discovered a couple of things that weren't very interesting until last night."

Marty held up a finger. "One . . . about three weeks ago, Wessen introduced a bill on the Senate floor, a routine measure requesting an exemption from a bill Congress passed a couple of sessions ago—namely, he put forth an amendment to the Domestic Space Access Act, requesting an exemption on behalf of something called the Arkwright Foundation."

"What's—"

"Two." Marty held up another finger. "When our people checked Wessen's public statement of campaign contributions, they discovered that, in the five months since he officially declared his candidacy, he's received nearly $400,000 from . . . want to guess where?"

"The Arkwright Foundation?"

"Bull's-eye. Give the lady a prize." His fingers became a pistol that he aimed and fired at her—a pet expression and gesture that he used just often enough to be obnoxious. "So our people wanted to know the same thing you do—what is the Arkwright Foundation? They did a little checking and found out that it's a nonprofit organization based in the Boston area that—and I quote—'advocates the research and development of near-term interstellar travel.'"

"Sounds like they want to build a starship."

"Uh-huh and that's just about all anyone knows about them. So far as we can tell, they don't do much public outreach. No membership drives, no magazines or newsletters, a website that tells as little as they can get away with." Marty picked up a rubber band, began playing with it. "For an advocacy group, they're awfully quiet. And for a nonprofit, they must have a lot of money to throw around if they're able to give that much to the campaign of a candidate no one seriously believes has much chance of winning the nomination."

"Yeah, it's a mystery." She frowned. "Let me guess—you want me to check them out, right?"

"Uh-huh. Fly up there and see what you can find out about them. Who are they? Why are they bankrolling Wessen? Why did he introduce a bill on their behalf?"

"All right, but"—Jill hesitated—"why me? This is a political story, Marty. I'm a science writer. Why don't you want one of your political reporters to handle this instead?"

"Because every one of them is working double time covering the New Hampshire primary, and this has enough of a science angle to it that you should be able to tackle it." A condescending smile. "Besides, it's not like you've got a lot to do around here, is it?"

"Since you mention it—"

"Whatever else you've got on your plate, you can add this to it." His smile vanished. "If you can't handle two stories at once, I'm sure there are a lot of unemployed writers who can."

Jill didn't answer that. Much like the pistol gesture, this was something that Marty said often enough that she no longer found it threatening. Since she'd been working at the *Truth*, seldom had a week gone by that he didn't make the pretense of being about to fire her. If he'd sexually harassed her, it wouldn't have been as annoying as having him wave the job termination stick every time they had a disagreement.

On the other hand, they both knew that the science beat at *The Dirty Truth* was something of a fifth wheel. She'd come here straight out of journalism school at the University of Missouri, and in the last year or so, stress and overwork had been the least of her concerns. Privately, she'd lately begun to wonder if she should begin looking for another job. Unfortunately, she knew that there were few to be found. She'd been keeping up with her classmates, and more than half of them had failed to find work in the journalism field. Like it or not, she had been very lucky to land a position at a Washington-based investigative news site . . . even if it meant working for a toad like Alphonse Martino.

"Since you put it so nicely . . ." Jill pushed back her chair to stand up. "How much do you want, and when do you want it?"

"Six thousand words yesterday, but I'll settle for the same this time next week." Marty turned toward his desk comp. "Go see Angie about a train ticket."

South Station in Boston was a mess. Construction work on the terminal from the new transcontinental maglev had resulted in a chaos of sawhorses, plastic sheets, jackhammers, and concrete dust, and getting from the Amtrak platform to the sidewalk was like running a gauntlet. And it didn't get any better once she reached the cab stand. It had been just three weeks since the temporary seawall outside Boston Harbor had burst, and the city was still cleaning up from the flood. The downtown streets smelled of seaweed and dead fish, and Jill had step over a gutter filled with standing water to reach the cab at the front of the line.

So Framingham was something of a relief. Her appointment turned out to be on the second floor of a wooded, ivy-grown industrial park that looked like it had been there for decades; she spotted the names of a couple of well-established high-tech firms on the sign out front. Inside was a reception area that could have belonged to a venerable old charity: wood-panel walls, an impressive painted mural of the Milky Way, faux-leather furniture that looked comfortable enough to sleep on.

Which she nearly did. The receptionist, an older lady named Barbara, took her name, tapped her ear jack and repeated it to someone at the other end, and then asked her to take a seat and offered a cup of coffee. Believing that the person she was supposed to see would soon come out to meet her, Jill politely declined the coffee and sat down on the couch. Barbara smiled and turned to her desk screen. After a few minutes, Jill pulled out her slate and checked her questions. A few minutes after that, she turned to her notes. Once that was done, she decided that it couldn't hurt to look at her email. It was late afternoon and her train trip from Washington had been long, and before she knew it, her eyelids were beginning to feel heavy and her neck boneless and weak, and her head lolled forward and . . .

"Hello? Am I disturbing you?"

The light pressure of a hand on her knee and a quiet voice snapped her back to awareness. Startled, Jill sat up at once. "Oh, my god! I'm so sorry, I—"

The rest caught in her throat. Standing before her, bent over to shake her awake, was a young man about her own age, fair skinned with rust-colored hair and a closely trimmed beard, and lively blue eyes that played mischievously behind a pair of rimless glasses. There was an amused but not unkind smile as he studied her.

"Not at all," he said, and his smile became apologetic as his hand fell from her leg. "I'm the one who should be sorry. I was on a conference call that took longer than I'd thought, and, well, at least you found a comfortable place to wait."

Jill's face burned. Dozing off just before an interview is not good form. At least there was no one else in the room to witness her embarrassment except Barbara, who'd diplomatically turned away. At a loss for what else to do, she stood up and stuck out her hand. "Well, then, hello," she said. "I'm Jill Muller, staff writer for *The Dirty Truth.*"

"Benjamin Skinner, media representative for the Arkwright Foundation." Rising from his crouch, Skinner took her hand. He was tall and well dressed, and Jill decided that he was just about the most attractive male she'd met in quite a while.

"Pleased to meet you," Jill said, "but . . ." She hesitated. "I'm sorry, but I thought my interview was going to be with someone else named Skinner—Kate Skinner, the foundation president."

"My mother, yes." He nodded. "She extends her apologies for not being here herself. Something came up at the last minute that required her attention."

Ordinarily, Jill might have been irritated to find herself being brushed off by the person she was scheduled to interview, but if it gave her a chance to spend a little time with this handsome specimen . . .

Knock it off. You're here on business. "That's quite all right, Mr. Skinner. Thanks for taking the time to see me."

"Not at all. My pleasure." He extended a hand toward the hallway leading to the back. "If you'll follow me." He started to turn away, and then he stopped to turn and add, "Oh, and by the way, it's Dr. Skinner, but I'd be happy if you'd call me Ben."

"Okay, Ben," she said, "and you can call me Jill."

Ben led her to a small, windowless office down the hall that didn't look like it was used all that often. She suspected that it didn't actually belong to him or anyone else but mainly functioned as a place for meetings such as this. He closed the door behind her and then sat down behind an immaculately clean desk, stretched out his legs and folded his hands together, and calmly let the interview begin.

Most of the answers he gave were just as routine as the questions themselves but nonetheless interesting. The Arkwright Foundation, he explained, was a private, nonprofit organization devoted to the research and development of the first interstellar vessel. It had been founded thirty years earlier by Ben's great-grandfather, the science fiction author Nathan Arkwright—Jill wasn't familiar with his name until Ben mentioned that he was the creator of the Galaxy Patrol—who'd left his literary estate as a bequest to provide seed money for the foundation. Since then, the Arkwright Foundation had grown exponentially, using that money to provide capital investments for companies perfecting the enabling technology needed for interstellar exploration and then using the profits from those investments for the foundation's primary goals.

"To build a starship?" Jill asked, and Ben nodded. "In the near future . . . say, this century?" He nodded again. "Are you serious about this?"

"Oh, yes," he replied, not at all insulted. "We're quite serious. In fact, we already have a design in mind for such a vessel, an unmanned ship called *Galactique*."

Ben slid a hand across his desktop and tapped its inlaid keypad. The wall behind him dissolved into a starscape panorama. On display was, at first glance, what appeared to be an open, horizontal parachute; whiskery cables towed a tiny cylindrical object behind it. Ben tapped the keypad again, and the image became animated. The parachute began to slowly move forward, and as it did, the background stars faded to a light shade of blue and stretched out into long, thin rays.

"It's going to be a beamship," Ben said, turning in his chair to point to the image behind him. "That is, a spacecraft that doesn't carry its own engines but instead is propelled by—"

"Lasers."

He gave her a surprised look. "Microwaves, actually. A phased-array satellite positioned at Lagrange Point Four will transmit a 120 terawatt beam—"

"That powerful? Really?" Jill raised an eyebrow. "And where are you going to get that much power?"

"Solar powersat in the same Lagrange-point orbit. It'll beam electrical energy to the beamer, which in turn will convert it to a steady-state microwave beam." She started to ask the obvious next question, but he beat her to it. "When the powersat comes into eclipse, storage batteries aboard the beamer will continue supplying power. The beam will continue uninterrupted throughout the ship's boost phase, however long that will be."

"Okay." Jill paused to write a few notes in her slate. Ben politely waited until she was ready; she could feel his eyes on her, but oddly enough it didn't bother her as it might have if it had been anyone else. "So, um . . ."

"Yes?" Not impatiently, but in expectation, as a good listener would be.

She briefly considered continuing in a technical vein—she'd love to know why they were opting for an unmanned craft instead of one with a crew—but decided to close in on the real point of the interview. "This is going to cost a lot, isn't it?" she asked, and he nodded. "Where does the foundation think it's going to get the money for all this?"

"As I said, it'll be from investments in the technology developed by the companies who'll be doing the work for us. Powersats, of course, we already have, although we believe the market could stand an improved design. But the big one will be the beamer. Once it's sent *Galactique* on its way—we're still in the process of selecting a destination from a list of candidate stars—it can then be utilized for interplanetary missions within our own solar system. With something like this, we'll be able to send spacecraft to the outer system— for instance, the asteroid belt or the Jovian moons, where the best commercial opportunity lies—in just weeks or even days. So the economic payback will be sufficient to maintain the foundation's operations for decades to come."

"But in the meantime, you still need to raise money, yes?"

Ben crossed his arms. "We're doing well," he replied.

Was it her imagination, or had he just become a little more guarded? She looked down and pretended to look at her notes, but she really wanted to make him sweat just a little. "So what's your connection with Clark Wessen?"

He shifted a little in his seat. "How do you mean?"

"Well, a few nights ago during a debate in New Hampshire, the senator came out in support of a project very much like what you're suggesting. As it turns out, the Arkwright Foundation has made considerable cash contributions to his campaign—"

"It wasn't cash."

"Excuse me?"

"It wasn't a cash contribution. It was a check." He grinned like a kid. "I watched my mother fill it out myself. Four hundred thousand dollars."

"That's a rather large amount, don't you think?"

A casual shrug. "Not as much as others make."

"Why did she—the foundation, I mean—make it?"

"We approve of the senator's stance on various issues, and we think he'd make a great president."

"Uh-huh. And the fact that he's asked for an exemption to the Domestic Space Access Act on behalf of the Arkwright Foundation . . . ?"

"What a remarkable coincidence. All the more reason for us to support his campaign."

The smile was still there. She might have been annoyed if he wasn't so charming. "So why would the foundation want an exemption? Why would you ask the senator to—"

"May I ask a question? A personal one?"

"Well, yes, I suppose. What do you—"

"What are you doing for dinner tonight?"

Jill was so startled the stylus fell from his fingers.

"Oh, I'm sorry," Ben said, instantly apologetic. "I didn't mean to . . . I mean, I didn't—"

"No, no, that's quite all right." She nervously scooped up the pen and was glad that the movement let the hair fall down around her face to obscure the blush she felt coming on. "I just . . . I didn't—"

"That was a bad question. Sorry. I shouldn't have asked that." He let out his breath, looked away.

Jill studied him. Without a doubt, there was something about Ben Skinner she found irresistible, a strange collision between intelligence and innocence. Had his mother anticipated a hard line of questioning from a *Dirty Truth* reporter and sent her attractive, awkward son to deflect her? No, no one was that clever. He was what he was, and that was more intriguing—and to be honest, sexier—than just about any other man she knew.

What the hell. Go for it, kid.

"I haven't made any plans," she replied. "Why? Do you have something in mind?"

They went out to dinner together. Later that evening, she accepted his request to come home with him. That wasn't surprising, really; by the time dessert arrived, Jill Muller had decided that Benjamin Skinner was someone with whom she could easily become infatuated, and apparently the feeling was mutual. So of course she took him up on his proposition.

It was the second proposition he made later that surprised her.

Jill had expected the dinner conversation to be a continuation of the interview, but they spoke very little about the foundation or its goals. Instead, by candlelight in the Revolution-era tavern in Sturbridge where he'd taken her, they talked about themselves. She learned that Ben's work at the Arkwright Foundation was only part-time and that he was actually a systems engineer at NASA. He didn't expect to be there very much longer, though, seeing how the space agency was being downsized into nonexistence, an unexpected consequence of the Domestic Space Access Act. Once the Galactique Project was under way, he planned to tender his resignation and work for the foundation full-time. And no, he wasn't married and didn't even have a girlfriend, although he was hoping that might change any day now.

For her part, Jill told him about her frustrations at being a science writer at a muckraking news site that had little interest in science; she'd been hired only because the publisher thought they needed a science desk, but most of the time, all she did was cover press conferences. She admitted, perhaps a bit rashly, that she'd been put on this story because of its political angle, not because the *Truth* had any real interest in space exploration. Perhaps her candor had come from the nice bottle of merlot Ben ordered, but probably not. She liked him a lot and didn't want to deceive him by pretending any longer that this story was about anything else than what it was. In any case, she was so busy wondering if he'd ask her to come home with him that she let slip the fact that she'd gladly find another job if only one was available.

However, she didn't entirely forget why she'd come to Boston in the first place. And so, quite some time later, when both of them were naked and sweaty but not exhausted enough to fall asleep, Jill rolled over on his living room rug, pulled up the sheet he'd thrown over them, and propped her chin upon his chest.

"So let me ask you one thing," she said.

"Yes, of course I can," Ben said as he slid his hand across her buttocks.

She snickered. "Right answer, but the wrong question."

"Ohhh, I'm so sorry to hear that."

"No, really"—she hesitated—"why did the Arkwright Foundation give all that money to Senator Wessen?"

Ben didn't reply at once. Instead, he rolled over on his side and gazed past her at the warm embers of the fake fire not really burning in the hearth a few feet away. "Let me ask you something first," he asked after a moment. "If I tell you, am I going to read it on your site?"

That *was* a good question. "Maybe . . . oh, god, I don't know." Jill sighed, let her head fall to the floor. "This isn't ethically proper, is it? Sleep with a guy and then try to get him to say something that could get him in trouble?"

"I don't know. Was that your intention?"

"No!" She quickly sat up, looked him straight in the eye. "That's never what I wanted to do! But if I don't come back with something—"

"Okay, sure. I understand." Ben rolled over on his back. "How about this? I'll tell you what you want to know on the condition that, when I'm done, you'll let *me* ask *you* a question. After that, you can decide how you want to handle what I've told you. Okay?"

Jill gazed down at him. "You'd trust me that much?"

"Uh-huh." He gently stroked her thigh. "I think you'll do the right thing."

"All right. Sure."

Ben sat up, pulling his end of the sheet across his lap. "Yes, the four hundred Gs the foundation contributed to Wessen's campaign was a payoff," he said as he reached for the bottle of wine he'd taken from the kitchen. "It's pretty obvious that we wanted him to submit a bill exempting the foundation from the law requiring all American-based space companies, including nonprofits like the Arkwright Foundation, to launch their spacecraft from U.S. launch sites. And you can probably figure out the reason we'd want that."

"Uh-huh." Jill watched as he poured dark-red petit noir into their glasses. "The Domestic Space Access Act had the best intentions, but it backfired. The coastal launch sites in Florida, Texas, and Maryland are going underwater, and that's caused the commercial sites in New Mexico and California to become overbooked."

"And that means they can charge as much as they want for their services." Ben passed a glass to her. "It's going to take at least four launches for the foundation to get all the starship's components into orbit—that's not counting the powersat we'll have to build at L-4—and we won't have money to spare on rate hikes and surcharges. But we've already got a nice site picked out in the Caribbean, so if we can get the exemption—"

"Then you can launch from down there." Jill placed the glass on the floor beside her without tasting it. "And that took bribing a senator, of course."

"It's not a bribe. Not technically, anyway." Ben sipped his wine. "We're just fortunate to find a presidential candidate who also happens to be a ranking member of the Senate science committee. He's got sufficient clout to move the bill out of committee and to the Senate floor, and once it's there, I have little doubt that it'll move to the House. It's a routine measure, really—unless, of course, the *Truth* calls attention to it."

"Uh-huh." Jill watched the holographic flames for a moment, thinking over what he'd just said. "Okay, I can see why you'd pick Wessen. A contribution to his presidential campaign wouldn't look like an obvious bribe. But he called attention to it himself when he made that comment during the debate. If he hadn't, no one would've known what you guys were doing. So was he just being dumb or—?"

"No." Ben put down his glass and then arched his back to stretch. "He wasn't being dumb. In fact, I'd say he was downright clever."

"Really?" Jill squinted at him. "From what I've heard, he just about killed his chances of winning New Hampshire with that comment."

"And if he does badly enough in New Hampshire, he'll probably have to get out of the race." Ben smiled. "Tell me something . . . do you think every politician who runs for president actually intends to win the election? Or even get nominated?"

"Sure, of course," she replied, and then she frowned when he shook his head. "I don't follow. Why wouldn't they?"

"Look, there are six guys from Wessen's party in the primary, plus four from the other side and two independents. That's twelve candidates altogether. Only one of them is going to the White House in November—maybe two, if another of them gets picked as the running mate for the winning ticket. That means ten or eleven will have raised a lot of money, only to drop out between now and the conventions. So ask yourself—what happens to the unspent campaign funds once a candidate drops out of the race?"

"It goes to pay off their bills?"

"Yes, but what if a candidate has kept his expenses low and then drops out early in the race? Say, after a dismal showing in the New

Hampshire primary after saying something ridiculous during a debate?"

Jill stared at him. "Are you joking?" He didn't reply, only smiled back at her. "But wouldn't he have to repay his major donors if he drops out?"

"Nope. They knew they were taking a risk when they put money in his war chest. Sure, I imagine some of them are wondering if they bet on the wrong horse, but there's nothing they can do about it now. And Wessen is no fool. He knows he doesn't have a snowball's chance of winning the nomination. So if keeps his expenses low, which he is, and leaves after a bad showing in New Hampshire, he might walk away with . . . oh, I dunno. A few hundred thousand dollars, maybe even a million. Tax-free."

"Did you know he was going to—"

"No, not at all. We were just looking for a senator who'd do what we wanted. Wessen saw an opportunity and went with it." Ben lay back down on the rug and folded his hands behind his head. "He gets what he wants, and we get what we want. Works out pretty well, don't you think?"

Jill slowly nodded. "Yes, it does. So what makes you think I'm not going to write about this?"

"Well, for one thing, judging from what you've told me about *The Dirty Truth*, it won't be your story for very much longer. If you take it back to Washington, your editor—Marty, is it?—will probably just take it away from you and reassign it to his political team. You won't even get a byline out of it."

Jill picked up her glass and, gazing into the fire, took a long sip of wine. Like it or not, Ben was right. At best, she'd get a brief acknowledgment at the end of another writer's article, a little feather in her cap that no one would remember a month from now. It was a bitter—and yes, a dirty—truth that she'd have to accept.

"Hell," she murmured.

"Sorry. But let me offer you a proposition."

"I think you have already." She smiled despite herself. "Glad I accepted. At least something nice will come out of this."

"Good. I'm happy you feel that way. Maybe you'll like this one too. Come work for us."

Jill was about to take another sip when Ben said this. She nearly dropped the glass. "What did you say?"

"You heard me. Come work for the Arkwright Foundation." He reached forward with his left hand to stroke her leg. "I'm doing this job only because we don't have anyone else just now, and to tell the truth, I'm not very good at it. We need someone to handle media relations."

"You'd take me?"

"Why not? You obviously know what you're doing. If I put in a good word for you, I'm sure my mother would hire you in flash." He grinned. "She'd probably like you. She used to be a science writer herself, way back when."

Jill gazed back at him, still not quite believing what she was hearing. "You're serious?" she asked, taking his hand in hers. "You'd hire someone you just slept with because—"

"I want to hire someone to represent the foundation who doesn't think that building a starship is impossible. Call this a job interview if you like."

"I *don't* like!" She half-playfully slapped his chest. "I don't want to get this job just because . . ."

"Ow! Okay! Cut it out!" He caught her wrist before she hit him again. "No, of course not. But I . . ." He hesitated. "I just don't want this to be a one-night stand. This way, well . . ."

"You'd see me a little more often, is that it?" Jill let him pull her a little closer.

"Why? Is that a problem?"

"No." She crawled forward to swing her left leg over him, straddling his body between her thighs. "No, I don't find that objectionable at all."

His hands rose to her hips. "Then you'll think about it?"

"Uh-huh," she whispered as she let the sheet fall away. "I'll give you an answer in the morning."

She already knew what it would be.

BOOK TWO

The Prodigal Son

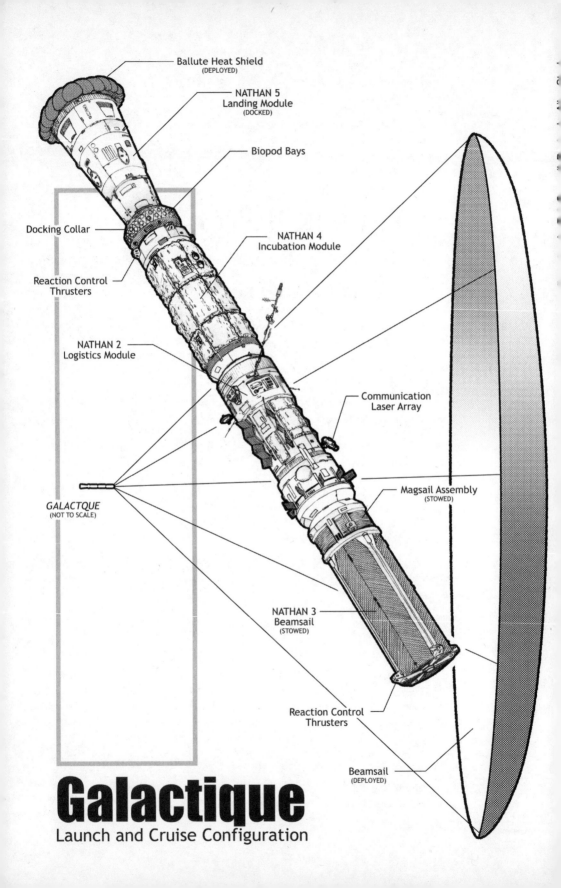

Ballute Heat Shield
(DEPLOYED)

NATHAN 5
Landing Module
(DOCKED)

Biopod Bays

Docking Collar

NATHAN 4
Incubation Module

Reaction Control
Thrusters

NATHAN 2
Logistics Module

Communication
Laser Array

GALACTQUE
(NOT TO SCALE)

Magsail Assembly
(STOWED)

NATHAN 3
Beamsail
(STOWED)

Reaction Control
Thrusters

Beamsail
(DEPLOYED)

Galactique
Launch and Cruise Configuration

1

The Gulfstream G8 was an old aircraft on the verge of retirement. Its fuselage creaked whenever it hit an air pocket, and the tiltjets had made a rattling sound when it took off from San Juan. At least the Caribbean looked warm. Matt figured that, if something went wrong and the plane had to ditch, he and the other passengers wouldn't freeze to death in the sun-dappled water that lay below. Provided that they survived the crash, of course.

Matt looked away from the window to steal another glance at the young woman sitting across the aisle. She'd said nothing to him over the past couple of hours, and he couldn't decide whether whatever she was studying on her slate was really that fascinating or if she was merely being standoffish. The aircraft jounced again, causing her to briefly raise her eyes from the screen. She caught Matt looking at her, favored him with a polite smile, and then returned her attention to the slate.

She was beautiful. Dark-brown skin and fathomless black eyes hinted at an Indian heritage. Her build was athletically slender, her face solemn, yet her mouth touched with subtle laugh lines. And there were no rings on her fingers.

"Rough flight," he said.

She looked up again. "Excuse me?"

"Rough flight, I said." Searching for something to add, Matt settled on the obvious. "You'd think the foundation could afford a better plane. This one looks like it came from the junkyard." He picked at the frayed upholstery of his left armrest.

"They're trying to save money. This is probably the cheapest charter they could find."

Her gaze went back to her slate, her right hand pushing away a lock of mahogany hair that had fallen across her face. She was plainly uninterested in making conversation with a fellow passenger—or at least the young guy about her own age seated beside her. But Matt had learned how to be persistent when pursuing attractive women. Sometimes, the direct approach was the best.

He stuck out his hand. "Matt Skinner."

She eyed his hand for a second before deciding to take it. "Chandraleska Sanyal."

"Chandalre . . ." He fumbled over the syllables.

"I'll settle for Chandi."

"Okay. So what are you doing with the . . . y'know? The project."

"Payload specialist, *Nathan 4*. I'm with the checkout team." She nodded toward the handful of other men and women sitting around them. Most were in their late twenties or early thirties, although two or three were middle-aged or older. "Same as everyone else— except you, I suppose."

"Oh yeah . . . checkout team." Matt had no idea what she meant by that other than it had something to do with the rocket carrying *Galactique*'s components into orbit. Leaning across the armrest, he peered at her slate. Vertical columns of numbers, a bar graph with multicolored lines rising from left to right, a pop-up menu bar. They could just as well have been Egyptian hieroglyphics. "Fascinating."

Chandi wasn't fooled for a second. "I didn't know tourists still visit Ile Sombre. Or are you the new kitchen help?"

It was an insult, of course, but at least she was talking to him. "Oh, no," he said. "I'm coming down to visit my parents. They work on the project. Ben and Jill Skinner . . . maybe you know them?"

Matt had the satisfaction of watching Chandi's eyes widen in surprise. "Dr. Skinner's your father?" she asked, and he nodded. "That means you're with the Arkwright family."

"Why, yes. That's my middle name—Matthew Arkwright Skinner." He said this with deliberate casualness, as if it was the most unremarkable thing he could have mentioned. "Nathan Arkwright was my great-great-grandfather. He started the Arkwright Foundation about seventy years ago, when—"

"I know the foundation's history. I've even read a few of his novels." Chandi nodded toward the other passengers. "It's a good bet everyone has. Which book was your favorite?"

The soft chime of a bell saved Matt from having to admit that he'd never read any of Nathan Arkwright's science fiction novels. The seat belt lights flashed on, and the pilot's voice came through the speakers. "We'll be coming in for landing, folks, so if you'll return to your seats and stow your belongings, we'll have you on the ground in just a few minutes."

The other passengers began collapsing their slates. Matt felt his ears pop. Chandi saved her work and slipped her slate into her travel bag. "If you look out the window, you might see the launch site."

Matt turned to look. For a moment, he saw nothing, and then the plane banked to the right, and Ile Sombre came into view. He caught a glimpse of a *ciudad flotante*, one of the floating towns common in the coastal regions of the Southern Hemisphere; this one was Ste. Genevieve, a collection of prefabs, huts, and shacks built atop pontoon barges above the flooded remains of the island's former capitol. Then the aircraft moved away from the coast, and he saw, rising from the inland rainforest, something that looked like a giant yellow crayon nestled within a gantry tower: a cargo rocket perched atop its mobile launch platform.

"*Nathan 2.*" Chandi leaned across the aisle to gaze over his shoulder. "Scheduled for liftoff the day after tomorrow—if all goes well, that is."

Glancing back at her, Matt couldn't help but see down the front of her blouse. It was a pleasant sight. "That's . . . um, the microwave beam thing, isn't it?"

Chandi noticed the direction he was looking and quickly sat up straight again. "No. The beamer went up six weeks ago on *Nathan 1*. It's being assembled in Lagrange orbit and should be ready for operation in about four months. *Nathan 2* is carrying the service module."

"Oh, okay. Right."

A bump beneath their feet as the landing gear came down, followed a few seconds later by the trembling shudder of the engine nacelles swiveling upward to descent position. About a thousand feet below, a paved airstrip came into view. Chandi gave her seat belt a perfunctory hitch to make sure it was tight. "Mind if I ask a personal question?"

Matt smiled. "I can give you the answer. Yes, I'd love to have dinner with you tonight."

She didn't return the smile. "What I was going to ask was, why are you here?"

"Come again?"

"I mean, it's pretty obvious that you don't know anything about *Galactique*. This is no vacation spot. The island lost its beaches years ago, and there's no one at the hotel except the launch team. So trying to use your family name to pick up girls isn't going to get you anywhere."

Matt's face became warm. "I didn't . . . I wasn't—"

"Sure you weren't." Chandi's expression was knowing. "So what brings you here?"

He suddenly found himself wishing the plane would crash, if only because death might save him the embarrassment of this moment. Chandi was watching him, though, waiting for an answer, so he gave her the only one he had that was honest.

"My grandmother thought it was a good idea," he said.

2

Matt's grandmother was Kate Morressy Skinner, the Arkwright Foundation's executive director, and as Matt stood in the customs line of what was laughably called the Ile Sombre International Airport, he once again reflected that it had been a mistake to call her asking for money.

He'd always gotten along well with Grandma, but he should have known that her wealth was an illusion. The foundation had been established by a bestowment left by her grandfather; it was worth billions of dollars, but all of it was tied up in investment capital associated to its principal goal: building and launching the first starship from Earth. Grandma had been made its director when she was about Matt's age, and although she received a generous salary, she was hardly rich. So she shouldn't have been expected to give her grandson a "loan" they both knew would probably never be repaid.

Matt watched the customs inspector open the backpack he'd brought with him from the States and begin to carefully sort through his belongings. The airport terminal was a large single room in a cinder block building; customs was a row of folding tables behind which the inspectors stood. The place was humid, with the ceiling fans doing nothing but blowing hot air around. It was springtime in this part of the world, but it felt like midsummer anywhere else. Through the open door leading to the airstrip came the roar of another battered Air Carib jet taking off. Except for the passengers who'd disembarked from Matt's flight, everyone in the building was black; he'd later learn that the native inhabitants were descended from African slaves who'd escaped from French and Spanish plantations elsewhere in the Caribbean and made their way to this remote island just south of Dominica, which the Europeans avoided because it had once been a pirate stronghold.

Grandma had done enough for him already by lining up his most recent job as an orderly at the Philadelphia hospital where Grandpa had worked as a doctor before he passed away. But that job lasted only about as long as all the others before it: part-time actor, recording studio publicist, store clerk, a couple of positions as assistant associate whatever. He'd keep them until he got bored and his boss noticed his lack of commitment, and then the inevitable chain of events would follow. The carpet. The warning. The second warning. The final warning. The unapologetic apology, the dismissal form, the severance check. And then the move to another city, another apartment, and another job found on another employment website.

When the hospital fired him, Matt called his grandmother in Boston and asked if she could front him a few hundred bucks. Just so he could make ends meet until he found work again. She'd sent him a plane ticket to Ile Sombre instead, telling him that his parents had a job for him down there. Which was why a customs inspector was now asking him to empty his pockets.

Matt pulled everything from his jeans and denim jacket and put it on the table. Cell, wallet, key ring holding keys that no longer belonged to anything he could unlock except a storage locker in Philadelphia, a lighter, and a pack of Denver Highs. The inspector, a tall black man with a purple-dyed 'fro, picked up the smokes and glared at him.

"This is not allowed, sir," he said, his deep voice inflected with a Caribbean accent.

"I thought marijuana was legal here. It is where I come from."

"You're not in America. Do you have any more, sir?"

"No. That's my only pack."

The inspector turned to another uniformed man standing behind the table and said something in French Creole. The other islander gazed at the pack and shook his head. "We will let you go, sir," the inspector said to Matt as he dropped the pack in a nearby waste can, "but you'll have to pay a fine. One hundred dollars, American."

"I only have sixty."

"That will do."

Matt removed the last money he had in the world from his wallet and gave it to the inspector, who carefully counted the bills before tucking them in his shirt pocket. "Thank you, sir." He handed Matt's passport back to him. "You may go now. Have a pleasant visit."

Third-world graft. The inspector probably would have shaken him down for something else if he hadn't found the smokes. Matt zipped up his pack, slung it across his shoulder, and headed for the exit door. At least he wouldn't spend his first night on Ile Sombre in jail.

Chandraleska Sanyal had already gone through customs. She was standing outside with the other new arrivals, waiting to board a dilapidated solar van parked at the curb. Matt caught her eye, and she gave him a brief smile. Apparently, he hadn't turned her off entirely. He was about to go over and make an excuse to spend more time with her by seeing if he could hitch a ride on the bus when a woman's voice called his name.

He looked around, and there was his mother walking toward him. "Hello, sweetheart," she said as she wrapped her arms around him. "Have a good flight?"

Jill Skinner was in her early fifties, but the gene therapy she and her husband had undergone a few years ago had erased at least a decade from her apparent age. She now looked more like she could have been Matt's older sister rather than his mother. "Okay, I guess," he said, returning the hug. He decided not to tell her about the customs hassle. "Where's Dad? He's not coming?"

"He's busy at the space center. *Nathan 2* goes up in a couple of days, or haven't you heard?" She glanced at his pack. "Is that all you brought with you?"

"Didn't think I'd need anything else." No sense in letting her know that it contained nearly everything he had left. The stuff in the storage locker would probably be auctioned once he failed to pay the rent. "Where are you parked?"

"This way." She turned to lead him across the airport's pitted car park. "I'm afraid I'll have to drop you off at the hotel. I'm needed at work too, although I'm hoping I can get you to start helping me after *Nathan 2* gets off."

Matt's mother was the Arkwright Foundation's press liaison at the Ile Sombre launch site; his father was mission director. Matt had grown up with the foundation, but he'd never shared his parents' commitment to it. This was the first time in many years Mom had even intimated that she'd like to have him join her and Dad.

"Yeah, well, I was sort of thinking I'd just like to take it easy for a while." He didn't look at her as they crossed the car park. "Kinda catch my breath, decide what my life's goals should be."

His mother didn't answer that, or at least not at once. Instead, she pulled a key remote from her shorts pocket and thumbed it. A short distance away, a Volksun beeped to remind her where she'd parked it; its engine was already humming by the time she opened its hatchback and let her son throw his pack in.

"Twenty-eight is a little late to be making up your mind what you want to do, isn't it?" she said as she got in behind the wheel. "First there was journalism school—"

"That was your idea, not mine."

"Then there was acting, then the music business, then the idea of working in a hospital while going to med school—"

"A lot of guys I know take a while to settle into something." Through the side window, Matt spotted the van in which Chandi was riding; it was pulling away from the terminal, heading for parts unknown.

"A lot of guys you know probably aren't flat broke." His mother didn't look at him as she backed out the parking space. "Oh, yes, I know . . . Grandma told me you'd tried to hit her up for money."

"It was just a loan."

"Maybe, but I promise you, you're not going to get a dime from her, or your father and me, either, unless you work for it. So don't count on getting a tan while you're here." She left the car on manual control and started driving toward the airport gate. "You've been a grasshopper for much too long. Time for you to become a busy little ant, just like the rest of us."

Jill Skinner had always been fond of *Aesop's Fables*; she'd been referring to the tales for as long as he could remember. Nothing ever changed. Matt slumped in his seat and regretted letting the customs inspector take away the only thing that might have made this trip bearable.

3

The Hotel Au Soleil was a former resort dating back to the last century, when tourists still came to Ile Sombre for winter getaways. That era had come to end just as it had for much of the Caribbean; rising sea levels and catastrophic hurricanes had wiped out scenic beaches and pleasant seaside villages, and the subsequent collapse of the cruise ship industry had been the final blow. Fortunately, the Au Soleil was far enough away from the water that it hadn't shared the same fate as Ste. Genevieve. The port town lay submerged beneath the *flotante* anchored above its ruined buildings and streets, but the hotel had survived. Run down and in crying need of a fresh coat of paint, it now functioned as living quarters for the space center that, along with coffee and citrus, had become one of Ile Sombre's principal industries.

The hotel was modeled in the plantation style and sprawled across ten acres abutting the island's undeveloped rain forest. Shaped like an H, its two-story wings surrounded gardens, tennis courts, and a swimming pool. Matt was pleased that he'd been given a poolside cabana room until he discovered that it wasn't quite as luxurious as it sounded. The room was small, its bed not much more than a cot, and the pool itself had long since been drained and covered by a canvas tarp. His parents, on the other hand, had taken residence in one of the cottages that had once been reserved for the wealthiest guests and were now occupied by senior staff.

"That's where we're staying," Jill said, pointing out the cottage to him as she led him down the outside stairs to the cabanas. "Sorry we can't give you one of the spare bedrooms, but your father and I are sharing one as an office, and the other one is used by Grandma when she visits."

Matt watched as she ran a pass card across the door scanner. "Is she here often?"

"Not really. She doesn't like to travel very much these days." His mother stepped aside to let him press his thumb against the lock plate; the door beeped twice as it registered him as the room's rightful occupant. "But she's planning to come down soon. Probably when we launch *Nathan 5*. She wants to be here when we send *Galactique* on its way."

Matt thought that his mother was going to leave him alone to unpack and maybe catch a nap, but she had other plans. He had just enough time to cast off his unneeded jacket, drop his pack, and give his quarters a quick look-see before she hustled him out the door and back to the car. By then, it was almost dusk. He hadn't eaten since he'd changed planes in Puerto Rico, and he asked if they'd be getting dinner anytime soon.

"We'll be coming back here to eat," she said as they drove away from the hotel. "Everyone has their meals together in the dining room—buffet-style, but it's still pretty good. Right now, I'm taking you to Operations and Management. Your father would like to see you."

The Ile Sombre Space Launch Center was located on a high plateau about five miles from the hotel, not far from the island's eastern coast. Matt's mother passed the time by telling him about the place. It had been established earlier in the century by PanAmSpace, the consortium of South American countries that provided launch services for private space companies in the Western Hemisphere. For several decades, it sent communications, weather, and solar-power satellites into Earth orbit, but then Washington moved to protect the American space industry by passing the Domestic Space Access Act. When the DSAA came down, Ile Sombre lost most of its business. The launch center fell into disuse and might have been abandoned altogether had it not been for the Arkwright Foundation and the Galactique Project. It had taken some shrewd political manipulation by the foundation to gain an exemption from the DSAA, but in the end, they'd won. Ile Sombre was now *Galactique*'s principal launch site; it was from there that the starship's microwave propulsion system had been sent into space, soon to be followed by its four-module hull.

A chain-link fence surrounded the space center, its entrance gate guarded by islanders in private-security uniforms. As Jill slowed down for the checkpoint, Matt noticed a handful of people squatting beside a couple of weather-beaten tents erected just outside the fence. Hand-lettered plywood signs that looked as if they'd been through several tropical showers leaned haphazardly on posts stuck in the ground: *Stop Galactick!!* and *God Will Never Foregive You* and *Earth Is You're Only Home*. The protesters were all middle-aged white people; they glared at the Volksun as Matt's mother flashed her ID badge and the guards waved her and Matt through.

"Who are they?" he asked.

"Morons." She said this as if it explained everything, and then she caught his questioning look. "They're from the New American Congregation, a fundamentalist megachurch in North Carolina. They've been opposed to the project from the beginning. Shortly after we began launch operations, they sent down some so-called missionaries to give us a hard time." She shrugged. "They're harmless, really. Just don't talk to them if you happen to run into them."

She drove to Operations and Management, a flat-roofed building not far from the hemispherical Mission Control dome and, a short distance away, the enormous white cube that was the Vehicle Assembly Building. Work had ended for the day, and men and women were streaming through the front doors, each of them wearing badge lanyards over linen shirts and spaghetti-strap dresses. Jill stopped at the security desk to get a visitor's badge for Matt—"We'll get you a staff badge tomorrow"—and then they went upstairs and down a hall to a door marked *Mission Director*. She didn't bother to knock but went straight in, and there was Matt's father.

Like many sons, Matt had often wondered if he'd resemble his father when he got older. Now he was sure of it. Dr. Benjamin Skinner had taken retrotherapy as well and so didn't look his age, and the cargo shorts and short-sleeve polo shirt he wore were more suitable for a younger man. Only a few strands of gray in his mustache attested to his true years. His office, though, was the sort of cluttered mess only a senior project engineer would have, its shelves choked with books, the desk buried beneath reports and spreadsheets; his father still preferred to read paper. Through the corner windows could be seen the distant launchpad. The sun was going down, and floodlights at the base of the pad were coming on to bathe *Nathan 2* in a luminescent halo.

"There you are." Ben stood up and walked around the desk, carefully avoiding a stack of binders on the floor. "Good trip down?"

"It was all right." Matt shook hands with him. "You need to get a better plane, though. I thought it was going to fall apart."

"Yeah, isn't it a heap? But we made a good deal with Air Carib, and every penny we save goes to what counts." He cocked his head toward *Nathan 2*.

"Maybe you should write a press release about that, Mattie." Jill picked up a pile of books from an armchair and sat down. "It could be the first job you do for me."

Matt didn't know which he liked less, the prospect of becoming a media flack or being called by his childhood name. "I don't know if I'm going to be here that long."

"Did Grandma send you a round-trip ticket?" Ben asked, and he smiled when Matt shook his head. "Well, there you have it. You can't go home until you can buy a ticket, and you can't buy a ticket unless you work for us." A shrug. "I don't know what's so bad about that. There are dozens of people who'd love to be working here . . . even writing press releases."

"I gave up that stuff when I quit the music business."

"Got fired, you mean." His mother wasn't letting him get away with anything. As usual.

"It's a job, son, and I bet you'll come to like it if you'll give it a chance." Ben crossed his arms and leaned against his desk. "We're making history here. Launching the human race's first true starship, sending our species to a new world twenty-two light-years away . . . I don't know how anyone can't be excited about a chance to participate in this."

Even after all these years, his father still didn't get it. His dream—his lifelong obsession, really—wasn't shared by his son and never had been. Matt had grown up in a family that had devoted itself to a goal that his great-great-grandfather set out for them, but he'd never understood why. They could have lived a life of ease with the money the Arkwright Foundation had earned over the years from its investments in the launch industry, asteroid mining, and powersats. Instead, he'd watched his father, mother, and grandmother throw it all away on—again, he glanced out the window at the distant rocket—*that*.

"Yeah, well . . ." He looked down at the floor. "So long as I'm here, I guess I'll try to get *excited* about it." He knew what they were thinking. He'd been through this countless times already, even before he'd left home to find his own way in the world.

"The prodigal son returns," his mother said dryly.

"What?"

"Never mind." She pushed herself out of the chair. "I'm sure you're hungry, and it's almost dinnertime." Jill looked at her husband. "Honey, c'mon—time to go home and eat. Sorry, but I'm not letting you get dinner out of the vending machines again."

"Guess you're right." Ben looked at the papers on his desk, obviously reluctant to leave his job even for a little while. "I can always come back later, I suppose." Standing up, he took his son by the arm. "The food at the hotel is actually pretty good. We cheaped out with the airplane but spared no expense with the people we hired to cook for us."

Matt remembered the remark Chandi had made when she'd suggested that he might be someone who was coming down to take a job in the kitchen. "So I've heard."

4

"T-minus ninety seconds. The launch director has given permission to end the hold and resume countdown."

The voice from the ceiling speakers was accentless, almost robotic; Matt wondered if it was computer generated. Although he was seated on the other side of a soundproof window separating the visitors' gallery from the launch control center, he could see his father. Benjamin Skinner stood behind his console in Mission Control, his gaze fixed upon the row of giant LCD screens arranged in a shallow arc across the far wall of the windowless room. In keeping with a tradition established by mission directors of the NASA era, he wore an old-fashioned necktie from a collection of atrocious ties.

Matt had seen this particular tie earlier that morning at breakfast: a topless Polynesian girl in a hula skirt, dancing beneath a palm tree. He thought it was amazingly stupid, but apparently, his father believed that it would bring them good luck.

All the other controllers were decked out in dark-blue polo shirts with the Galactique Project logo embroidered on the breast pockets. Their attention was focused entirely on the data stream coming from *Nathan 2*. In the center wall screen, the cargo rocket stood upon the launchpad, wreathed in hydrogen fumes seeping from ports along its canary-colored hull. Above the screen, a chronometer had come alive again: -00:01:29, the figure getting smaller with each passing second.

"Why did they stop the countdown?" Matt asked.

"They always go into hold at the ninety-second mark." Chandi cupped a hand against her mouth even though no one in the firing room could possibly hear them. "Gives the controllers a chance to catch up with their checklists, make sure they haven't missed anything."

"I thought computers controlled everything."

"At this point, they pretty much do." She smiled. "But only a fool would completely trust a computer when it comes to something like this."

Matt glanced at his slate. It displayed the *Nathan 2* fact sheet his mother had sent him a little while earlier. *Galactique*'s service module—the 110-foot segment containing the ship's guidance and control computers, fission reactor, maneuvering thrusters, laser telemetry, and sail control systems—was being transported to geosynchronous orbit 22,300 miles above Earth by an unmanned Kubera heavy-lift booster manufactured in India by Lokapala Cosmos, the kind used to launch solar-power satellites.

The rest was data: reusable single-stage-to-orbit, 233 feet in height, gross liftoff weight 4,750 tons, powered by eight oxygen-hydrogen aerospike engines. All four of *Galactique*'s modules were designed to fit snugly within its 115-by-45-foot cargo bay, which had a 400,000-pound payload capacity. Kuberas were reliable workhorses, built to be launched again and again with a minimum of ground-time turnaround.

That was how it looked like to an engineer, though. To Matt, the rocket resembled nothing more or less than an enormous penis. The Giant Space Wiener, worshipped by a roomful of people with a Freudian phallic fixation.

"Why is it yellow?" It was the only thing he could say that wouldn't have offended the young woman sitting beside him.

The people seated around them cast him patronizing looks, as if he were a child who'd asked an obvious question. "So they can find it easily when it splashes down after reentry," Chandi said, visibly annoyed. "Didn't your mother teach you anything?"

Matt almost laughed out loud. It wouldn't do, though, to explain what he thought was so funny. "That's something Mom and Dad are interested in," he said, keeping the joke to himself.

"T-minus sixty seconds and counting."

Chandi raised an eyebrow, and Matt distracted himself by glancing over his shoulder. His mother sat a couple of rows behind him, surrounded by the handful of reporters who'd flown down to Ile Sombre for the launch. She caught Matt looking at him and gave him a brief nod and then cupped an ear to the journalist who'd just asked her a question.

Matt knew that he should be sitting with his mother, learning the job he'd soon be taking. But he'd spent all yesterday with her doing what little he could to help the press office get ready for the launch, and he'd become tired of being attached to her elbow. So when he'd seen Chandi enter the gallery along with the other specialists who'd been on the plane, he contrived a reason to take the seat beside her: he'd told her that he wanted to watch the launch with someone who'd explain things to him.

Chandi didn't seem to mind, although he caught hostile looks from a couple of other guys who'd aspired to be her companion. Matt told himself that he didn't really have a crush on her. He might have even believed it, if he'd repeated it to himself long enough.

"*T-minus thirty seconds and counting.*"

"They're retracting the gantry arms," Chandi said quietly, bending her head slightly toward him as she pointed to the center wall screen. "The rocket's now on internal power."

"That means it's pulling juice from only itself?" Matt asked and she nodded. "Okay . . . um, so what happens if something goes wrong?"

"Shut up," growled an older man sitting behind them.

"Hey," Matt said, glancing back at him. "I'm just asking."

"Don't." Chandi scowled in disapproval. "It's bad luck." She paused and then went on, "They can abort the launch right up to the last two seconds, but that's only if the computers pick up a mission-critical malfunction. After main-engine start, we're pretty much committed to—"

"*T-minus twenty seconds.*"

She abruptly stopped herself, and Matt was startled to feel her nervously grab the back of his hand. She'd apparently meant to grasp the armrest only to find it already occupied, because she immediately jerked her hand away.

"It's okay," he murmured. "You can, if you want."

Chandi gazed at him, her dark eyes embarrassed. She returned her hand to the armrest without shaking him off.

"Thanks," she whispered.

"*T-minus fifteen seconds.*"

All of a sudden, she rose from her seat. "Follow me," she said, still clutching his hand.

"What are you—"

"Hurry!" She pulled him to his feet and then turned to push her way past the other people seated in their row. "Excuse me, excuse me . . ."

Matt dropped his slate, but Chandi didn't give him a chance to pick it up. He caught a glimpse of his mother's face; she stared at him in bafflement as Chandi tugged him toward the gallery's side entrance. Chandi let go of his hand to shove open the door; Matt followed her as she raced down the stairs leading to the control center's rear door. In seconds, they were outside the dome and running around the side of the building.

Although he was a newcomer, Matt was aware of the safety rules that mandated everyone witnessing a liftoff had to do so from inside Mission Control. The pad was less than three miles away; if the Kubera blew up, the dome would protect them from the blast. He knew he was going to catch hell for this from his mother, but Chandi hadn't given him any choice.

"*T-minus ten seconds.*" The voice came from loudspeakers outside the dome. "*Nine . . . eight . . . seven . . .*"

"Stop." Chandi grabbed him by the shoulders, halting him in midstep. "Watch."

"*Six . . . five . . . four . . .*"

They had a clear view of the launchpad. From the distance, the rocket was almost toylike, dwarfed by its gantry and the four lightning-deflection masts surrounding the pad. Matt had just enough time to regret no longer having the close-up view afforded by the control room screens when a flare silently erupted at the bottom of the rocket, sending black smoke rolling forth from the blast trench beneath the platform.

"*Three . . . main engine ignition . . . two . . . one . . . liftoff!*"

The Kubera rose from its pad atop a torch so bright that it caused him to squint. The eerie quiet that accompanied the ignition sequence lasted only until the rocket cleared the tower. The silence ended when the sound waves finally crossed the miles separating him from the rocket, and then it was as if he were being run over by an invisible truck: a crackling roar that grew louder, louder, louder as the rocket ascended into the blue Caribbean sky. Seagulls and egrets and parrots took wing from all the palmettos and coconut trees around them as *Nathan 2* became a fiery spear lancing up into the heavens. It was no longer the Giant Space Wiener but something terrifying and awesome that seemed to take possession of the sky itself.

Breathless, unable to speak, Matt watched as the rocket rose up and away, becoming a tiny spark at the tip of a black, hornlike trail forming an arc high above the ocean. The sudden, distant bang of the sonic boom startled him. He wasn't aware that Chandi was quietly observing him, savoring his fascination. It wasn't until the spark winked out and the loudspeaker announced main-engine cutoff and that *Nathan 2* had successfully reached low orbit that he remembered she was standing beside him. His ears were ringing when he looked at her again.

"That was . . . incredible," he said.

"Yes, it was." Chandi nodded knowingly. "Now you see why we're here?"

5

The launch team celebrated with a party that night at the hotel. Instead of the customary buffet in the former restaurant, a cookout was held by the swimming pool. A propane grill was brought out of storage, tiki lamps were lit, and a couple of hundred pounds of Argentine beef, purchased by the foundation and stashed away for special occasions, emerged from the kitchen's walk-in freezer. Hamburgers and steak fries and coconut ice cream and an ice-filled barrel of Red Stripe beer: *Nathan 2*'s foster parents were in the mood to party. Their child had finally left home.

Matt went to the party expecting to hook up with Chandi, only to find that she was less interested in him that evening than she'd been that morning. She smiled when he approached her and didn't object when he brought her a beer and asked if she'd join him for dinner, but no sooner had they sat down at one of the patio tables when a half dozen other scientists and engineers carried their paper plates over to their table. They sat down without asking if they were interrupting anything, and the conversation immediately shifted to technical matters: integration of *Galactique*'s sail within *Nathan 3*'s faring, the timeline for recovery and turnaround of the Kubera booster once it returned to Earth, the problems anticipated with meeting the schedule for final testing and checkout of the *Nathan 4* module.

Matt tried to keep up as best as he could, but it was all above his head. Within minutes, he was lost, and no one at the table was willing to stop and provide explanations. Chandi made a polite effort to include him in the conversation, yet it was as if he were a dull schoolboy who'd been mistakenly invited to eat at the teachers' table. No, worse than that: everyone at the table was his age, more or less, but some of them were probably earning their doctorates about the same time he was working in a convenience store.

After Matt asked Chandi if she'd like another beer—she impatiently shook her head and returned to the discussion of maintaining *Galactique*'s extrauterine fetal incubation system during the mission's cruise phase—he quietly picked up his plate and left. He tossed the plate in the recycling can, fished a couple of Red Stripes from the beer barrel, and found another place to sit, a neglected chaise longue on the other side of the pool. And there he proceeded to drink, listen to the reggae music being piped over the loudspeaker system, and wonder again what he was doing there.

He was on his second beer when his father came over to join him. Ben Skinner ambled around the end of the covered swimming pool and into the place where his son had chosen to hide. By then, he'd removed his dress shirt and absurd tie and replaced them with an equally ugly Hawaiian shirt, and he stopped at the foot of Matt's lounger to gaze down at him.

"Care for some company?"

"Sure." Matt regarded him with eyes that were becoming beer fogged. "Have a seat."

"Don't mind if I do." Ben eased himself into the chair beside him. "Saw you earlier. Thought you were making friends. Now—"

"Now I'm here," Matt said, finishing his thought for him. "They're nice enough, but . . ." He shrugged. "Y'know, you've heard one conversation about the quantum intergalactic microwave whoopee, you've pretty much heard 'em all."

"Oh, yeah, that. I think I read a paper about it in *BIS Journal* just the other day." A grin appeared and quickly faded when he saw that Matt wasn't appreciating the joke. "Can't blame you. If you're not on their wavelength, it's going to be pretty hard to understand what they're talking about. Here, let me see if I can cheer you up."

He reached into his breast pocket, and Matt was astounded to see him pull out a joint. "Dad? Since when did you—"

"Before you were born." His father smiled as he juggled the hand-rolled spliff between his fingers. "I don't indulge all that often, but I picked it up again when we came down here. I don't mind if anyone here smokes, so long as it's after hours and they don't do it at the space center. Got a light?"

"I thought marijuana was illegal here." Matt dug into his shorts pocket, searching for the lighter he habitually carried. "That's what the customs guys told me when they took away my smokes."

"Old island law from the smuggling days that's still on the books. Only time the cops enforce it is when they get it in mind to shake down a gringo. Otherwise, no one cares." Nonetheless, he gazed at the crowd on the other side of the pool, wary of anyone spotting him smoking pot with his son. "I don't do this very often, really. Just on special occasions. Then I go down to Ste. Genevieve and buy some of the local stuff."

Matt handed his lighter to his father. "I'll keep that in mind."

"Just be careful to take someone with you if you go. Someone who doesn't look like a white guy from the States." Ben flicked the lighter, stuck one end of the joint in his mouth. "Maybe the young lady you were with tonight."

"Chandi."

"Umm-hmm." The joint flamed as his father touched it with fire. It burned unevenly as he took a long drag from it. "Dr. Chandraleska Sanyal," he went on, slowly exhaling. "I recruited her myself, from Andru & Reynolds Biosystems. Very smart woman."

"Out of my league, you mean."

"No, that's not what I mean." Ben leaned over to pass the joint to him. "Sure, you'll have to run a little harder to catch up with her, but . . . well, she must see something in you if she'd taken the trouble of dragging you out of the dome during the launch."

"You know about that? Your back was turned to . . . oh. Mom must have told you."

"Yes, she did." His father frowned. "That's against safety regs, by the way. Don't let me catch you doing it again."

Matt drew smoke into his lungs. It was unexpectedly strong; not harsh at all, but still more robust than the processed and preserved commercial stuff to which he was more accustomed. He felt the buzz as soon as he let it out. *Nice.* "It was her idea."

"I'm not going to bust your balls over it. So how did you like it? The launch, I mean."

"It was . . ." Matt struggled for the right words. "Awesome. Just . . . I dunno. I've never seen anything like it."

His father smiled. "Yeah. I've seen a lot of rockets go up, but I've never gotten used to it." He paused. "Y'know, back when you were a kid and I was still working for NASA, you could have asked me anytime to take you to one of these things. I could have arranged for you to get a visitor's pass for a launch before they went bust."

It was an old story, Matt's lack of enthusiasm for that which his parents had devoted their lives. There was a brief period, when he was a child, when he had been fascinated by space. He'd even wanted to be an astronaut. But he'd left that behind along with his toy spaceships and astronomy coloring books. Now he was back where he'd started, and the last thing he wanted was to have his father pushing at him again.

"Guess I wasn't interested," he said.

"Hmm . . . no, I suppose you weren't." Ben took another hit from the joint and was quiet for a moment, as if contemplating the years gone by. "Maybe I made a mistake trying to get you involved with all this too soon. I've lately thought that . . . well, if you hadn't grown up with me and your mother constantly discussing this stuff over the dinner table, it might not have killed your interest. That and your grandmother—"

"I'm not blaming her for anything." The joint was half-finished, and he was enjoying the high he already had; he shook his head when his father tried to pass it to him again and reached for his beer instead. "Grandma's . . . y'know, Grandma. The foundation is her life. But you and Mom . . . I mean, with you two, this whole thing is like some kind of religion. The Church of *Galactique*. Praise the holy starship, hallelujah."

His father scowled at him. "Oh, c'mon, it's not that bad."

"Yes, it is," Matt insisted, "and you've had it for as long as I can remember. That's why I went away. I had to find something else to do with my life than follow this obsession of yours."

Despite himself, he found that he was getting angry. Maybe it was just a headful of marijuana and beer, but it seemed as if a lot of pent-up frustration was boiling out of him whether he liked it or not. On impulse, he pushed himself off the lounger, nearly losing his balance as he stood up again on legs that suddenly felt numb. "Maybe I'd better take a walk," he mumbled. "Get some fresh air or something."

"Sure. Okay." His father was hurt by the abrupt rejection, but he didn't try to stop him. "Whatever you want. But, Mattie?"

"Don't call me that. I'm not a kid anymore."

"I know . . . sorry." Ben shook his head. "Look, just a little advice, all right? You can knock this so-called obsession of mine all you want, but—" He lowered his voice as he cast a meaningful look across the pool to where Chandi and her friends were still seated. "If you want to get anywhere with her, you're going to have to learn to appreciate the things she's interested in. And she joined our religion a long time ago."

6

Even if he didn't care to follow his father's advice, Matt had no choice in the matter. His mother found him in the dining room the following morning, nursing a hangover with black coffee and an unappealing plate of scrambled eggs. The party was over, and so was any hope he might have still had of making this trip into a tropical vacation. It was time for him to go to work as her new assistant.

Before he'd left college to pursue a half-baked fantasy of becoming a movie actor, Matt had been a journalism major. That hadn't worked out, either, but he'd learned enough to know a little about what it took to work in a media relations department. This was Jill Skinner's job at the Arkwright Foundation, and even before Matt had decided to come down to Ile Sombre, she'd been complaining about being shorthanded. So his arrival had been fortunate—for her, at least. She now had someone to do scut work for her, giving her a chance to take care of more important tasks.

Over the course of the next several days, Matt tagged along with his mother as she went from place to place in the Ile Sombre Space Launch Center. A large part of her job involved keeping up with daily events and writing press releases about them for the news media; since she wanted him to start doing some of this for her, it was important that he learn the Galactique Project from top to bottom, beginning with the preparations leading up to launch of *Nathan 3*, scheduled for six weeks from then.

It was more interesting than he'd thought it would be. *Nathan 3* was being checked out in a dust-free, temperature-controlled clean room in the Payload Integration Building next to the VAB. The clean room was the size of a basketball court, and everything in there was spotless and white, down to the one-piece isolation garments that made everyone wearing them look like surgeons. Matt couldn't go in there, but his mother showed him where to stand quietly in the observation gallery overlooking the floor.

From there, he could see *Nathan 3*. Resting within an elevated cradle, it was an enormous, tightly wrapped cylinder made of tissue-thin carbon-mesh graphite, dark gray with the thin silver stripes of its lateral struts running along its sides, resembling a giant furled umbrella. *Galactique*'s microwave sail had been built and tested in the same Southern California facility that manufactured powersats, but it served a completely different purpose. Once *Galactique* was completed in orbit and ready to launch, the sail would gradually unfold to its operational diameter of a little more than sixty-two miles. It seemed unbelievable that something so big could be reduced to fit inside the Kubera's cargo bay, but it had a material density of only the tiniest fraction of an inch, and the sail itself had been designed on origami-like principles so that it would unfurl in concentric layers upon deployment. Still, it would take all the Kubera's thrust to successfully get it off the ground.

Three days after it carried *Nathan 2* into space, the cargo rocket returned to Earth. On Jill's insistence, Matt accompanied the recovery team when they set forth on an old freighter to the spot where the rocket splashed down in the Caribbean about a hundred miles east of Ile Sombre. There they found the Kubera floating upright on its inflated landing bags, looking very much like a giant fishing bob. He watched as divers in wet suits swam out to drag tow cables to the booster; once that was done, the ship slowly hauled the Kubera back to the island, where the freighter docked at Ste. Genevieve's commercial port. Over the next several days, the rocket would be lifted out of the water by derrick cranes, loaded onto a tandem tractor-trailer, and driven back to the space center, where it would be refitted for the *Nathan 3* mission.

Meanwhile, preparations for *Nathan 4* were under way. In another white room, *Galactique*'s incubation module was being checked out for its primary purpose, carrying cryogenically preserved sperm and egg specimens from two hundred human donors to the ship's ultimate destination, the distant planet still officially known only as Gliese 667C-e.

When Matt's parents had explained the foundation's plan many years earlier, he'd had a hard time understanding it. Why send sperm and eggs when, with a bigger ship, you could send living people instead? But he was thinking in terms of the science fiction movies he'd seen as a kid, where huge starships carrying thousands of passengers easily leaped between the stars with the help of miraculous faster-than-light drives. Reality was another matter entirely. FTL drives didn't exist, and they never would. Furthermore, the larger the ship was, the more energy would be required for it to achieve even a fraction of light speed. If its passengers were to remain alive and conscious during the entire flight, such a vessel would have to be several miles long, a generation ship capable of sustaining these passengers and their descendents for a century or more. So even if a ship that large were built—such as from a hollowed-out asteroid, one early proposal—the amount of fuel it would have to carry would comprise at least half of its mass. It would be like trying to move a mountain by providing it with another mountain of fuel.

Making the issue even more complicated was the fact that no one knew how to build a closed-loop life support system that could keep people alive for such long periods of time. The sheer amount of consumables they'd need—air, water, and food—was daunting and could not be produced or recycled, without fail, for decades or even centuries on end. No one had successfully come up with a means of putting people into hibernation and reviving them again many years later, either. Perhaps one day, but now . . . ?

The solution to all this was obvious: remove people from the ship entirely and instead build a smaller, lighter vessel that could carry human reproductive material to the new world, where it would be gestated and brought to term within the extrauterine fetal incubators. This process was better understood and more feasible and therefore made it more likely that a starship could be built if it didn't have to devote so much of its mass to keeping its passengers alive. And since *Galactique* wouldn't have its own engines but instead rely on the microwave beamer in Lagrange orbit to boost the ship to .5c cruise velocity, it would be able to make the voyage to Gliese 667C-e in a little less than half a century.

Even so, there was nothing simple about *Galactique*'s EFI module. Just as large as *Nathan 2* and *3*, the cylinder was an AI-controlled, robotically serviced laboratory. From the observation gallery, Matt watched as clean-suited technicians worked on the module from the outside. This was the most heavily shielded part of the starship and the most complex; through the open inspection ports, Matt could see the tubes in which the fetuses would be gestated to infancy before being loaded aboard the lander. There was only a small crawl-space running down its central core, and that had been provided more for the spidery robots that would maintain the ship than for the humans who'd built it.

Galactique's final module, *Nathan 5*, was still being assembled in Northern California. It contained two major segments: the ninety-foot landing craft that would transport the newborn infants to the planet surface, where they would be raised by what were affectionately being called "nannybots" until they were old enough to fend for themselves, and the biopods that would precede them, aeroshells containing first the bioengineered "genesis plants" capable of transforming Gliese 667C-e into a human-habitable planet and then later the fledgling flora and fauna that would populate the new world.

Next to the vessel itself, this was probably the most challenging aspect of the project, one that was pushing human technology to its furthest limits. It was hoped, though, that the Galactique Project would bootstrap a new era of space exploration. Aside from brief missions to Mars and the Moon and small-scale efforts to mine near-Earth asteroids, humankind was still largely confined to its native planet. The foundation believed that *Galactique* would demonstrate the viability of beamships and thus prompt private industry to use the project's beamer to send manned missions to the outer planets.

In any case, Matt liked visiting this place and often stole time from writing press releases or making travel arrangements for visiting journalists to view *Nathan 3* being prepared for its journey. But it wasn't just his growing interest in *Galactique* that brought him to the gallery. It was also being able to watch Chandi at work. Her outfit should have made her indistinguishable from the rest of her group, but nonetheless, he could always tell who she was; she seemed to move just a little differently from her colleagues. And although she acknowledged his presence with only a brief wave, that small gesture was enough.

They'd see each other in the evenings after dinner when the launch team would get together on the patio for drinks and perhaps a joint or two. By then, Matt had become better acquainted with some of the other people working on the project. They'd come to accept him as a nonscientist who had his own role to play, and he made an effort to keep his skepticism to himself in order to assure their friendship.

Yet one evening, something slipped out of his mouth that he hadn't meant to say. And that got him in trouble with Chandi.

Matt was sitting at a poolside table with her and a couple of other team members: Graham Royce and his husband, Rich Collins, both of them British space engineers who specialized in beam propulsion systems. The three men were sharing an after-dinner joint—Chandi didn't smoke but politely tolerated those who did—and watching the crescent moon come up over the palms. By then, *Nathan 3* was on the launchpad, with countdown scheduled to commence in just four days. The Brits were relaxed, knowing that their job was done for a little while; they wouldn't have to go back to work again until *Nathan 3* was docked with *Nathan 2* and the orbital assembly would attach the sail's rigging to the service module.

"You're hoping on a lot, aren't you?" Matt asked, passing the joint to Rich. "I mean, the way I understand it, the beamer has to fire constantly for . . . what is it, two and a half years?"

"Pretty much, yes," Rich said.

"Nine hundred and twenty days." Graham was the older of the two—although with retrotherapy, it was hard to guess his true age—and had a tendency to be annoyingly precise.

"Whatever. So for two and half years, the sail has to catch a microwave sent from Earth even as it's moving farther and farther away. Meanwhile, the ship's moving faster and faster—"

"Acceleration rate is 1.9 meters per second, squared."

"—until the ship is about half a light-year from Earth." Graham took a brief drag from the joint and gave it to his mate. "By then, it'll be well out of the solar system and traveling half the speed of light, so we can turn off the beamer and let the ship coast on its own. Any course adjustments will be accomplished by the onboard AI using maneuvering thrusters. When it reaches Gliese 667C-e—"

"Eos." Chandi smiled. "I think everyone's pretty much settled on that name."

"Until the International Astronomical Union approves," Graham said, "it's officially Gliese 667C-e."

Rich coughed out the hit he'd just taken. "You're such a prick, you know that?" Graham smirked, and Rich went on, "So what's your question—or did I miss something?" His eyes narrowed in stoned confusion.

"Well," Matt said, "it's just that it seems like you're counting on everything going exactly the way you've planned. The beam not getting interrupted or missing the sail entirely—"

"That's why the sail is so bloody big," Rich replied. "The beam spreads as it travels outward, so the sail has to be large enough to receive it."

"But if something punches through it, like a meteorite or—"

"Meteoroid," Graham said. "It's not a meteorite until it passes through Earth's atmosphere. The sail is large enough it can take a few punch-throughs without losing efficiency."

"The reason the beamer is being located in L-4 orbit is to minimize the number of occasions the beam will be interrupted by Earth's sidereal orbit around the sun." Rich handed the joint back to Matt. "Everything is being automatically controlled by synchronized computers aboard both the beamer and *Galactique*, so there's little chance of the beam getting lost."

"But you're still putting everything on faith." The joint was little larger than a thumbnail by then, and Matt had to gently pluck it from Rich's fingers. "I mean, it's almost like religion for you guys."

No one said anything. Although it was a warm evening, it seemed as if the temperature had suddenly dropped a few degrees.

"Is that what this seems like to you?" Chandi asked after a moment. "Religion?"

"Sometimes, yeah." Matt carefully put the joint to his lips, inhaled what was left of it. "I used to call it the Church of *Galactique* when my mom and dad were talking about it."

"Oh, bollocks." Graham shook his head in disgust. "No wonder they tossed you out of the house."

Matt glared at him. "I left on my own. They didn't—"

"There's a difference between religion and faith," Chandi said. "Religion means you've accepted a set of beliefs even if those beliefs would appear to be irrational to anyone who doesn't buy into them. Faith means you've chosen to accept something that you've given yourself the chance to question. It might still be something greater than you, or even God if you decide to go that way, but it's not irrational. So, yes, we're operating on faith, but it's faith in something we've done ourselves, not divine providence."

Matt was already regretting what he'd said. Especially since he'd spoken while under the influence of Ile Sombre marijuana. "But at some point, it's still something that's no longer under your control. Once *Galactique* gets away from here, by the time you hear about anything going wrong, there won't be much you can do about it." He grinned. "Doesn't make much difference if it's not God. You're still praying to a machine, right?"

"Oh, Holy *Galactique*, please render thy blessings—" Rich began, and then he shut up when he caught Chandi scowling at him. "Sorry."

"That's why we're working so hard to make sure everything aboard checks out while we've got a chance to lay our hands on it." Chandi was no longer looking at Rich; her dark eyes were angry as they fastened on Matt. "And that's not just a machine I'm working on. It's a vessel carrying what will one day be a human colony—my descendents included."

"Yours?"

"Yes. Mine." Chandi continued to stare at him. "I've donated my eggs too. So far as I'm concerned, I'm sending my children to Eos. So I'm doing everything I can to make sure they arrive safely, and I'm placing faith in my efforts and everyone else's that they will. So, no, this isn't religion to me, and I'll thank you to keep your bullshit analysis to yourself."

An uncomfortable silence. Rich broke it by clearing his throat again. "I could use some ice cream. Anyone care to—"

"Love to." Chandi stood up from her chair, crooked her elbow so that he could take it. "Lead the way."

Matt watched as Rich gallantly escorted her across the patio, heading for the dining room where desserts were customarily laid out at the end of the meal. He might have been jealous if he didn't know Rich was gay, but nonetheless, he disliked seeing her being taken away by another man.

"You rather stepped in it there, didn't you?" Graham idly folded his hands behind his head and leaned back in his chair. "Word to the wise, lad—never accuse a scientist of practicing religion with his or her work."

"I'll make it up to her."

"Sure you will. May I suggest how?"

"I'll apologize. Maybe some roses too."

"Apologies would be proper, yes, although I doubt you'll find a florist in Ste. Genevieve. Besides, I was thinking of something a bit more . . . um, symbolic, shall we say?"

"Such as?"

Graham smiled. "Donate a sperm sample."

Matt stared at him. "You gotta be kidding. Do you know what that sounds like?"

"I know what it would sound like if it was anyone else but her. In Chandi's case, though, it would mean that you're willing to believe in the same things she does . . . that you'll take the same leap of faith she has."

"That's too weird for—"

"Just an idea." Graham shrugged. "Think it over."

7

Graham's suggestion was strange, and Matt might have disregarded it as the sort of thing someone might have said while buzzed. Yet he remembered it the next morning, and the more he thought about it, the more sense it made. There was a poetic sort of appeal to the idea of donating sperm to the mission; as Graham said, it would mean that Matt had come around to Chandi's way of thinking to the point that he was willing to send his genetic material on the same journey. Together with an apology, it might go far to heal the wound he'd made.

Yet when he went to his father and told him what he wanted to do, Ben turned him down. "Sorry, son," he said, "but your seat's already taken by your grandparents."

"What?"

Ben Skinner stood up from his desk and walked over to the coffeemaker. "Grandpa and Grandma were two of the very first people to donate sperm and egg specimens to the mission, way back when the Arkwright Foundation was getting started. In fact, I think they did it right after they got engaged. You know the story about the Legion of Tomorrow, don't you?"

"That's the club my great-great-grandfather belonged to, isn't it? The one with all the science fiction writers?"

"Umm . . . sort of." His father poured another cup of coffee for himself and then held up the carafe and raised an eyebrow, silently asking Matt if he'd like coffee too. Matt shook his head, and Ben went on, "There were only four people in the Legion, and just two of them were writers, both of them your great-great-grandfathers. We named you after Grandpa Harry's pseudonym, in fact."

"I know, but what does this have to do with—"

"Because your grandfather and your grandmother both made donations, their genomes are already represented in *Galactique*'s gene pool. They're carrying the seed, so to speak, for three members of the Legion—Nathan Arkwright, Margaret Krough, and Harry Skinner. If any of their descendents were to also donate egg or sperm specimens, this would introduce an element of uncertainty to the colony. What if your descendents met and fell in love with your grandmother's descendents, and they decided to have kids?"

"I don't see how that would . . . oh. You're talking about inbreeding."

"Right. They wouldn't even know it, but they'd be effectively marrying within the family, and that would cause all sorts of problems in a small founding population." His father walked over to a bookcase, pulled out a thick binder, and held it up. "This is our record of everyone who has made donations. We've spent many, many hours making sure no one who did is directly related to anyone else. Your mother was allowed to make a donation because she doesn't belong to our bloodline, but I wasn't, as much as I'd love to. So I'm afraid you're out of luck."

"Oh, well; it was just a thought." Matt tried to hide his disappointment with a shrug.

"Nice to see that you've taken an interest in this, though." Ben returned the notebook to the bookcase. "May I ask why?"

Matt was reluctant to explain his reasons. He was afraid his father would have found them childish. "Never mind. Just something I thought I'd like to do."

"Yes, well . . ." His father sighed as he went back to his desk. "Believe me, I wish I could help you, but the EFI system is going to be dicey enough as it is. I'm a little afraid of how things are going to work out once *Galactique* reaches Eos and it gets a closer look at the lay of the land. The genetic alterations that may have to be made . . ."

His voice trailed off, but not before Matt's curiosity was raised. "What sort of alterations?"

Ben said nothing for a moment. Standing behind his desk, he turned to gaze at the launchpad. "It's not something we're really talking about in public—we've had enough trouble with the fundamentalists already—but it's possible that the specimens may have to be genetically altered in the preembryonic stage to suit the planetary environment. Gliese 667C is an M-class red dwarf, smaller and cooler than our sun, while Eos itself is about one-third larger than Earth, with an estimated surface gravity about half again higher. We know that it probably has a carbon dioxide atmosphere with traces of water vapor, but even after *Galactique* drops the biopods and the place becomes habitable, in all likelihood, any humans we put there will have to be changed in some very basic ways in order to survive."

"What sort of ways?"

"The AI will make that determination once it surveys the planet. We've supplied it with the necessary parameters and given it some options we believe are suitable, but—" His father paused. "Well, what comes out of the EFI cells will be probably different from what most people normally think of as human beings."

Matt felt a chill. He tried to imagine the sort of people his father described but could only come up with a race of deformed children, shambling and monstrous. "I can't believe you're doing this. Remaking humans, I mean."

"Really?" His father turned to give him an inquisitive look. "What do you think you'd see if you went back in time—say, four million years—and met your earliest ancestors, the australopithecines who were living in northern Africa? They didn't look very much like us, either. And they'd probably be shocked by us too. But evolution changed them. They adapted to their environment. That's much what we'd be doing here . . . just a lot faster, that's all."

Matt didn't know what to say to this. He was still searching for a reply when his father sat down again. "I'm sorry, but I've got a lot of work ahead of me. Like I said, thanks for the offer, but—"

"Sure, okay. No problem." Suddenly, Matt wondered if it had been such a great idea, after all.

8

As it turned out, his notion didn't make much difference, anyway. The next time Matt saw her, Chandi had apparently forgotten all about their quarrel—either that or she'd simply decided to put it behind her. In any case, she was friendly toward him again as if nothing had ever happened. He decided that it wasn't worth mentioning to her that he'd tried to donate sperm to the mission, and so nothing was ever said again about the disagreement they'd had.

Nathan 3 lifted off on schedule, a flawless launch that carried the Kubera and its payload away from Ile Sombre and into the black and airless ocean that *Galactique* would soon sail. This time, Matt watched the liftoff from inside the dome; he sat with his mother and the journalists they were hosting, but when the rocket cleared the tower and rose into the deep blue sky, he looked over to where Chandi was seated. Their eyes met, and she smiled as if she, too, were remembering the previous launch and the moment they'd shared. He realized then how much he missed sitting with her.

He saw her again at the postlaunch party that night, and this time he was able to keep up with the poolside conversation among the launch team members. Matt decided not smoke pot at the party—after all, it was marijuana that had caused so much trouble last time—and he nursed the one beer he had, and she seemed to appreciate that because she remained at his side most of the evening. In the warmth of a moonlit tropical night, she couldn't have looked lovelier. Matt was sorely tempted to whisper in her ear and ask if she'd like to come back to his room with him, but he held back. He didn't want to risk offending her again . . . and deep inside, he'd come to realize that he wanted more from her than just a one-night stand.

More journalists had traveled to Ile Sombre for the *Nathan 3* launch. Now that *Galactique* wasn't just a single module in geosynchronous orbit, the press was paying more attention to the project. The half-finished vessel was large enough to become a naked-eye object in the night sky, and Jill asked Matt to send a press release to the news media, telling them how to inform the public where and how to look for it. Before long, even those who'd paid little attention to the project became aware that a starship was being built above Earth, and suddenly *Galactique* became an object of interest to even those who didn't care much about space.

Not all the attention was welcome. Until then, the protesters from the New American Congregation who'd camped outside the Ile Sombre Space Launch Center had numbered no more than a half dozen or so, but when he came to work in the morning, Matt began noticing more tents, more signs, more people. He didn't know if they all belonged to the church or if some were opposed to the project for other reasons, yet technicians flying in from the States reported meeting protesters at the airport, and the ongoing demonstration outside the space center became increasingly aggressive, with angry shouts greeting launch team members as they approached the front gate. The foundation hired more security guards, but when some of the protesters began showing up at the Hotel Au Soleil to harass team members when they came home from work, private cops had to be posted there, as well.

And that wasn't all.

The day *Nathan 4* was finally transferred from the clean room to the VAB to be loaded aboard the Kubera, its checkout team decided to throw a little celebration of their own. It was noticed that they didn't enough marijuana for a proper party, though, so someone would have to go into Ste. Genevieve to acquire some local herb. Matt was tapped for the job, and he didn't mind; it wouldn't be the first time he'd bought weed, and he'd been told the name of an islander who regularly sold cannabis to project members and where he could be found. He borrowed his mother's Volksun and drove into town, but before he left, he asked Chandi if she'd like to come along.

His father had once suggested that he bring her because she wasn't a white male American and therefore might be able to get a better deal from the locals, but that wasn't the reason. He wanted to do something with her that would take them away from the project and its people, if only for a little while. It wasn't exactly a date, but at least it was better than sitting around the pool again. To his surprise, Chandi agreed. She was tired of seeing little else but the clean room and the hotel, and like Matt, she'd never been to Ste. Genevieve. So they left just after dinner, and as the sun was going down, they parked the Volksun at the municipal wharf and walked onto the floating pier leading to the *flotante*.

The inhabitants of Ste. Genevieve had saved their homes from destruction by rebuilding them atop a collection of rafts, barges, and pontoon boats anchored above the flooded remains of the original town. Narrow boardwalks kept afloat by barrels connected shanties and shacks, which in turn were tied together by submerged cables. In some instances, the upper floors of preexistent brick buildings were still being used, their rooftops supporting a forest of solar collectors, satellite dishes, and freshwater tanks that collected rain and distilled it. The walkways were illuminated by strings of fiber-optic Christmas lights strung across tar-painted poles, and rowboats, canoes, and kayaks were tied up in slips between buildings. Smoke rose from tin ducts that served as chimneys; the salt air held the mixed aromas of burning driftwood and fried fish.

Matt and Chandi made their way through the *flotante*, trying to locate the bar where the weed dealer was said to hang out. Hand-painted signs nailed to shanty walls showed them where Ste. Genevieve's original streets had once been located; Matt had been told to look for a place called Sharky's, located on what was still called Rue Majeur. Islanders sitting in old lawn chairs silently watched them; their expressions hinted at amusement, suspicion, or curiosity, but no one said anything. Foreigners from the space center didn't come to town very often, and while the locals didn't have anything against them, they didn't necessarily have anything *for* them, either.

Sharky's turned out to be the rusted shell of a double-wide trailer that had been relocated to a barge, with a wraparound porch outside and a screen door leading inside. A few island men were seated on the porch; they quietly observed the Americans as they stepped onto the barge, and it was clear that they appreciated seeing Chandi. She did her best to ignore their stares, but Matt wasn't surprised when she took his hand.

The barroom was small and dimly lit with shaded fluorescent bulbs and cheap beer signs. Incredibly, there was a state-of-the-art holoscreen on the wall; it was showing a soccer match, the volume turned down low. Everything else was run down, with the same particle-board tables and plastic chairs as the outside deck. The bar was little more than wood planks laid across a couple of oil barrels; the bartender impassively watched the visitors as they approached the bar, saying nothing as he continued to wipe clean a chipped beer mug.

"Hi. I'm looking for someone named Parker. Is he here?"

"Lots of folks named Parker." The bartender wasn't giving him anything. "You have a first name?"

"James Parker."

An indifferent shrug. "I know someone named James Parker. What do you want with him?"

"We understand he sells something we'd like to have."

The bartender finished cleaning the mug and then put it down and fished another one from the tub beneath the bar. "He'll be here soon. Have a seat, mon. Would you like a beer?"

"Yes, thanks. Red Stripe."

The bartender turned to a cooler and pulled out two bottles of beer. There were no stools, and Matt was beginning to look around for a place for him and Chandi to sit when a voice behind them asked, "Care to join me?"

Another man was in the bar, sitting at a table in the corner near the door. Surprisingly, he was the first white person they'd seen since entering Ste. Genevieve. Middle aged and thick set, with iron-gray hair and handlebar mustache, he had on the kind of outfit only a tourist would wear: khaki hiking shorts, a photographer's vest over a long-sleeve safari shirt, a bush hat, and waterproof boots. Like he was expecting to spend time in the jungle, hacking his way through the rain forest with a machete.

There was something about him that Matt immediately distrusted. He didn't know why, except perhaps that this character was even more out of place than he and Chandi. There was no polite way to refuse, though, so he led Chandi over to the table.

As they sat down, Matt noted a couple of empty Dos Equis bottles on the table, along with the one the stranger was currently drinking. Obviously, he'd been there for a while.

"Frank Barton," the stranger said as they sat down. "And you are . . . ?"

"I'm Matt; she's Chandi." Matt shook hands with him. "Down for some sightseeing?"

"Something like that." Barton picked up his beer. "I've come to see where all the action is. You folks work at the space center?"

"We're with the project, yes," Chandi said.

"I see." Barton took a long slug from his beer, wiped his mustache with a finger as he put it down again. "So what is it you two do there?"

"I'm an engineer. He's a consultant." Apparently, Chandi was suspicious, as well. Glancing at her, Matt saw the wary expression on her face.

"I see, I see." Barton slowly nodded. "I've heard you people sometimes come into town. I sorta figured if I sat here long enough, I'd eventually meet one of you." He smiled. "Guess I'm lucky . . . here's two."

Matt didn't like the way he said this. Now he noticed something else; half hidden within the open collar of his shirt was a silver chain holding a gold crucifix. It might mean nothing—he knew plenty of people who had crosses just like it—but it might also portend trouble.

"Why is that lucky?" he asked. "You want to know something about the project?"

"I already know all there is." Barton leaned back in his chair. "You, on the other hand, are in need of enlightenment, for the sake of your souls."

That settled it. Frank Barton belonged to the New American Congregation, and he'd staked out Sharky's in hopes of cornering someone from the project. Matt's father had warned him against engaging the church's "missionaries," and now he knew why.

Matt started to push back his chair. "Well, it's been nice to meet you, but—"

"What does my soul have to do with this?" Chandi made no move to get up. She leaned closer, resting her elbows on the table and propping her chin on clasped hands. "Please, *enlighten* me."

"Isn't it obvious?" Barton fixed her with an unblinking stare. "What you're doing is blasphemous. Sending forth the human seed into God's creation, there to foist our sins upon other worlds. We were never meant to—"

"Really? Where in the Bible does it say that?" She smiled. "I've been to church too, and I don't remember ever hearing space exploration was inherently sinful."

Barton's eyes narrowed. "God clearly intended Man to live on

Earth and Earth alone. He created this world for his chosen, and the other worlds were to be left alone."

"Again, where does it say that?" She looked over at Matt. "I must have missed something in Sunday school, because that's an interpretation I've never—"

"There are many interpretations of the Gospel." Barton clearly didn't enjoy being challenged. "For you to rip children from their mother's wombs and put them aboard rockets—"

"Oh, c'mon, do you *really* think that's what we're doing?" Chandi was grinning by then; she was toying with him and relishing every second. "Hate to say it, but you're the one who needs enlightenment. You've got everything wrong and don't even know it."

"So you're aware of the word of God, and still you commit a mortal sin!" Even in the bad light of the bar, Matt could see that Barton's face was becoming red. His anger was growing in proportion with Chandi's amusement. "I thought I could save you, but I see now that you're beyond redemption."

Matt closed his eyes. Barton was a familiar type: more than just a zealot, he was a cranky, middle-aged man who'd long since decided that he was right about all things and couldn't tolerate any difference of opinion. There was no point in arguing with someone like this, but Chandi wasn't giving up. She was enjoying herself too much.

"Yup. Sinner and proud of it." Chandi picked up her beer. "Better that than an old fart who thinks he speaks for God." She started to take a sip. "Jesus would've laughed his ass off if he'd ever met you—"

"How dare you take his name in vain?" Barton leaped up from his chair. Before Matt could stop him, he reached across the table to slap the bottle from Chandi's hand. "Miserable whore, you have no right to—"

It had been many years since the last time Matt punched someone, and the last time he'd been in a bar fight, he'd been ashamed of himself later for doing so. But not this time. There was something very satisfying about slamming his fist into Barton's hillbilly mustache, and it was even more gratifying when Barton fell back over his chair, hit the wall behind him, and sagged to the floor.

Chandi was still regarding Matt with wide-eyed shock when the bartender came out from behind the bar. "Out!" he yelled, half raising the cricket bat that had materialized from somewhere. "No fights in my place! Leave before I call the police!"

"Hey, look, he—"

"Let's go." Chandi took Matt's arm, pulled him away from the table. "You've done enough."

Matt looked down at Barton. He was still conscious but stunned enough that he wasn't going to get up for another minute or so. When he did, though, things would probably get worse than they already were, and Matt didn't want to have to deal with the island police as well as an angry bartender. It wouldn't be easy explaining why two Americans from the space center were in a dive like Sharky's.

He pulled a couple of dollars from his pocket and dropped them on the table by way of apology and then let Chandi lead him from the bar. The islanders sitting out on the deck must have heard the fight, for they were standing just outside the door, silently watching him and Chandi as they came out. Among them was a tall, skinny fellow with dreadlocks, who appeared as if he'd been just about to come in; Matt wondered if this was James Parker but decided not to stop and ask. There wasn't going to be a chance to buy weed tonight, that was for sure.

Neither he nor Chandi said anything to each other as they walked back through Ste. Genevieve. Matt's hand had begun to throb, and when he flexed his fingers, he discovered that he'd jammed his middle knuckle. He still had to drive, though, because the Volksun was key-printed to his touch. He'd also need to find some aspirin and maybe a bandage once they returned to the hotel.

The ride back was largely in silence. Matt tried to make a couple of jokes about what had happened, but they fell flat. From the corner of his eye, he could see Chandi quietly studying him; she said little, but her gaze never left his face. In the pale light from the dashboard, though, it was hard to tell her expression.

He parked near his parents' cottage. When he and Chandi climbed out, they could hear party sounds coming from the pool, just out of sight from behind the trees.

"They're not going to like it when I tell 'em I didn't get any weed," Matt murmured as he started to head for the flagstone path leading to the patio.

Chandi laid a hand upon his arm, stopping him. "We're not going to the party," she said quietly.

"We're not?"

"No. We're going to my room."

And then she pulled him close for a long, lingering kiss.

9

It didn't go unnoticed that Matt and Chandi failed to show up at the party. Every eye turned in their direction when they came down for breakfast together the following morning, and quite a few knowing smiles were cast in their direction. Although Graham gave him a salacious wink, no one said anything; it was if everyone had been quietly waiting for the two of them to pair up, with the only surprise being that it hadn't happened earlier.

It was not the one-nighter Matt had feared it might be. Chandi slept with him again the next night, this time in his room. She had a queen-size bed, though, and the cabanas were visible from the patio, so after that, they agreed her place was more comfortable and offered a little more privacy. He returned to his room each morning to shower, change clothes, and brush his teeth, but after a while, they decided that he might just as well move in with her, and that was fine with him; he never liked the cabana, anyway.

Their relationship was gloriously erotic, but it wasn't just the fun they had in bed that kept them together. It had been many years since the last time either of them had been in love. Like Matt, Chandi had had her share of failed relationships; she told him that she'd once been engaged but had broken up with her fiancé when she'd discovered that he was secretly having an affair with another woman. And until she'd met Matt, she'd never had anyone willing to stand up for her. Matt was relieved; his last girlfriend would have been disgusted if she'd seen him get in a bar fight, even if it had been to defend her.

They were ready for each other. Their meeting on the flight to Ile Sombre may have been a happy accident, but Matt's parents seemed to believe that Chandi was just the sort of person their son needed to have in his life. Matt was nervous when he reluctantly accepted their invitation to bring Chandi over for dinner—to be sure, they hadn't liked his previous girlfriends—yet it turned out for the better. His mother enjoyed meeting her, and while his father already had respect for her intelligence, he was apparently surprised to find that she was charming, as well. Matt hadn't been necessarily seeking their approval, but nonetheless, he came away from the dinner pleased that they thought well of her.

As it turned out, it was fortunate that he and Chandi hadn't waited any longer to begin a romance. *Nathan 4* went up a couple of weeks later, a perfect liftoff followed by a problem-free rendezvous and docking with *Galactique*. When this occurred, Chandi's role in the project came to an official end. There was no practical reason for her to remain on Ile Sombre; her contract with the Arkwright Foundation was fulfilled, and she was free to go. Yet she wanted to stay on the island until *Galactique* was completed and launched, and now that she and Matt were living together, his room could be taken over by one of the *Nathan 5* technicians scheduled to arrive soon. So Ben Skinner found enough money in the budget to allow her to stay on the payroll as a part-time consultant, and that problem was fixed.

It wasn't until then that Matt realized that he, too, could leave anytime he wanted. He'd saved up enough money not only to buy a plane ticket back to the States but also to pay the rent while he searched for a new job. But he no longer wished to leave, and when he thought about it, he came to the conclusion that it wasn't simply because of Chandi. Over the past months, he'd developed an interest in *Galactique* and the Arkwright Foundation that hadn't been there before. Although he was still skeptical about the mission's chances for success, his cynicism had disappeared; Chandi's enthusiasm had rubbed off on him. He found that he also wished to remain on Ile Sombre to witness the beginning of *Galactique*'s long voyage to Gliese 667C-e.

But after that? He and Chandi still had to figure out if and how they'd have a future together. This worried him, but it was far from the largest concern anyone had.

Until then, the schedule had proceeded smoothly. Each of *Galactique*'s modules had been launched and docked without any major problems, but their luck couldn't last. When the time came for *Nathan 5* to be launched, the project's good fortune ran out.

Construction work on *Nathan 5* had already run behind schedule. Ground tests of the landing craft's main engine had revealed flaws serious enough for subcontractors in California to dismantle the engine and replace several critical components, which in turn necessitated another series of tests before they were satisfied that the craft was flightworthy. Because of this, loading of *Nathan 5* aboard the freighter that would carry it down the Pacific coast to the Panama Canal and through the Gulf of Mexico was pushed back by more than a month, and this delay caused concerns of its own.

Galactique's launch schedule had been carefully timed to occur before the beginning of the Caribbean's annual hurricane season.

The drawback of using the Ile Sombre Space Launch Center was the fact that it lay within a tropical zone prone to major storms. Indeed, quite a few PanAmSpace launches had been postponed because of hurricanes that suddenly developed in the South Atlantic. The mission planners were aware this when they'd devised the launch schedule; they'd hoped that, if all went well, the last module would be sent into orbit before the weather interfered.

Now that the final launch was being postponed to late summer, though, there was an increasing risk of it being disrupted by a hurricane. Meteorologists had already noticed indications that just such an event may occur; the waters of the South Atlantic were warmer than usual, and several large tropical storms had already blown through the Lesser Antilles. The Kubera could be kept within the Vehicle Assembly Building until the weather was calm enough for a launch; what everyone dreaded was *Nathan 5* being at sea when the freighter carrying it was caught by a hurricane. The loss of the module carrying the biopods and landing craft would be a major setback; it would take years for replacements to be built, during which time *Galactique* would have to be mothballed in orbit, both of which would be very expensive.

Ben Skinner met with the other mission planners, and over the course of a six-hour boardroom session, they came up with a solution. Instead of putting *Nathan 5* aboard an ocean vessel, the foundation would rent a cargo jet to fly it down to Ile Sombre. There was just such an aircraft suitable for this purpose: the C-110 Goliath, built by Boeing as a heavy-lift military transport. Its cargo bay was 130 feet by 45 feet, more than big enough for the module, and as it turned out, Boeing maintained two Goliaths in Seattle for private lease.

There was only one problem with this. Until then, the previous modules had been brought to Ile Sombre aboard ships, where they could offload at the same port where the Kubera was retrieved. The port was protected by chain-link fences and armed guards and lay close enough to the space center that security had never been an issue. But if *Nathan 5* were flown in, the plane would have to land at the island airport, where the module would be offloaded onto the tractor-trailer rig used for transporting the Kubera and be driven across Ile Sombre all on public roads, where it could be easily blocked by the protesters who were steadily gaining numbers outside the space center.

"And to make matters worse, the rig's going have to go slow," Ben said, sitting at the end of the table where he'd just had dinner with his family. "You know the roads around here . . . they haven't been resurfaced in years. They're like washboards. So the driver will have to take it easy to keep *Nat* from being damaged en route from the airport, and if the protesters know it's coming—"

"They will. It's already in the news that we're doing this." Jill didn't pause in clearing away the dinner plates. "But I don't think they're going to give us much trouble. They'll probably just stand on the side of the road and wave those idiot signs of theirs. They've never been violent before."

Hearing this, Matt looked across the table at Chandi. They'd started coming over for dinner once a week, but he still hadn't told them about what happened that night in Ste. Genevieve. They weren't aware that at least one member of the New American Congregation was capable of violence.

Chandi didn't say anything, but she shook her head ever so slightly when their eyes met. "It might be smart to take precautions, anyway," Matt said. "Maybe get some of our people to walk alongside the truck to keep them away."

"Yeah, that could work." Ben slowly nodded. "Nice idea. I'll talk it over with the planning team." He picked up the bottle of merlot on the table and poured another drink. "Maybe your grandmother will have some other suggestions once she gets here."

"Grandma's coming down?"

"The week after next," Jill said. "I thought I told you." She smiled as she returned to the table. "In fact, I'm sure I did."

"Yeah. I just forgot." Matt shrugged. "I've been kinda busy."

"Yes, you have." Ben's gaze shifted from him to Chandi, and Matt could have killed him for the sly grin on his face. "In fact, I think she wants to have a talk with you about what you're going to do once we close down operations here. Have you given any thought to that?"

Again, Matt traded a look with Chandi. This had been something they'd discussed more than once lately, usually as late-night pillow talk. "A little."

"Yes, well, talk to Grandma when she gets here." Again, a coy smile. "I think she has a something in mind."

10

Grandma Kate had aged well for a woman in her eighties who'd never taken retrotherapy. Although she'd undergone the usual geriatric treatments available to the elderly, including cardiovascular nanosurgery and organ-clone transplants, genetic revitalization had come along too late for it to be effective for a woman of her years. So unlike her children, Kate Skinner looked her age, but nonetheless, she managed to get around, albeit slowly and carefully.

Matt and his mother met Grandma when she arrived at the airport. She was the last person to come off the plane, and once she endured the indignity of being helped down the stairs by a flight attendant, she gratefully took a seat in the two-wheel mobil that had been carried in the G8's belly compartment. Once in the chair, though, she returned to her old self. The customs official who'd given Matt a hassle a few months earlier quailed before the old woman who wasn't about to let him waste her time by opening each of her suitcases, and even her daughter-in-law knew better than to keep her waiting long at the curb for the van she'd borrowed from the space center to take her to the hotel. Kate didn't suffer fools gladly.

To Matt's surprise, though, Grandma treated him with a little more tenderness. She insisted that he ride with her in the back of the van, and once she'd dispensed with the small talk, she turned her attention to her grandson.

"So you took a job here, after all." Not a question; a statement of fact.

"I didn't have much choice, Grandma. The plane ticket was one way."

"I know. I bought it, didn't I?" A tight-lipped smile. "You didn't need a handout from me, kiddo. You needed a chance at a fresh start. Ben tells me you've done pretty well with it too."

"He has, Kate." Jill turned her head slightly without taking her gaze from the road. "I couldn't have done without Matt. He's done everything from writing news releases to managing press conferences to booking flights for reporters. Everything you'd want from a good right-hand man."

Matt said nothing. His mother was exaggerating; his first few weeks in the media relations department had been a train wreck, and even now he was still committing the occasional gaffe. Yet if she wanted to give Grandma a good report, he wasn't about to argue.

"Are you enjoying the work?" Grandma asked.

"Yes, I am." About this, he didn't have to lie. "I've learned a lot, and I think I've got a better appreciation of what the project is all about."

"Do you really?" She seemed to study him. "You're not just saying that, are you?"

He decided not to reveal his lingering doubts about the feasibility of terraforming a planet and populating it with children raised by robots. "I think *Galactique* will get there," he replied, and he hoped she'd be satisfied to let it go at that.

Apparently, she was, because she only nodded and shifted her gaze to the rain forest they were driving through. Yet the conversation wasn't finished. She picked it up again once they'd arrived at the Hotel Au Soleil and she was taken to the cottage she'd be sharing with her children. Believing that he was no longer needed, Matt was about to leave, but then she raised a hand.

"Stick around a minute. I want to talk to you a little more." She looked at Jill. "You can go now. He'll catch up with you later."

His mother was a little surprised by this, but she didn't object. She left the cottage, closing the front door behind her. Grandma waited until she was gone, and then she turned to Matt again. "So . . . thought about what you're going to do once we close up shop here?"

Matt remembered his father raising the same question over dinner a couple of weeks earlier. "I dunno. Do what everyone else is doing, I guess—go home and get another job. I might stay in media relations, turn that into a career."

"Yeah, you could do that. Your job here will be a short item on your résumé, but I'm sure it'll help you land a position somewhere. Maybe you'll even keep it for a while, if you don't get bored and quit. That's always been a problem for you, hasn't it?"

"Sort of."

"Sort of." She repeated what he'd said flatly as if she had little doubt that he would. "Well, if you want to go back to drifting, that's your right. I won't stop you. But I can offer you something better."

She paused, waiting for him to say something. When he didn't, she went on, "Even after *Galactique* is on its way, the foundation's work won't be done. It's going to take almost fifty years for the ship to reach Eos, but it's not like we're just sticking a note in a bottle and tossing it into the sea. It'll regularly report back to us, telling us what's going on, and even though those reports will get further and

further apart, we'll still have to listen for them just in case something happens that we should know about."

"You want me to do that?"

"I'd like for you to join the tracking team, yes. The foundation
is taking over an old university observatory in Massachusetts, out in
the Berkshires not far from where your great-great-grandfather used
to live. This is where the laser telemetry received by the lunar tracking station will be relayed. It's rather isolated, but we'll be keeping a
small staff there, paying them from foundation funds to maintain
contact with *Galactique.*"

"I don't know anything about—"

"You can learn. Ben can teach you. In fact, he's probably going to
be running the operation; didn't he tell you this already?" Matt
shook his head, and his grandmother sighed. "Oh, well, I guess he
was expecting me to tell you about it. Anyway, he'll be in charge, but
he's not going to be around forever. Sooner or later, someone will
have to take over for him."

Grandma gave him a meaningful look. Matt said nothing, for he
didn't know what to say. He'd been half expecting her to offer him
a job with the Arkwright Foundation, but a lifetime commitment
was something else entirely. He didn't know if he was ready to spend
years on a mountain out in the middle of nowhere, listening for signals transmitted from a spacecraft receding farther and farther into
the interstellar distance.

"I don't know," he began.

"You don't have to say yes or no right away." Grandma shook her
head. "Just think about it awhile, all right? The job's there if you
want it. We won't have any trouble finding someone else if you decide to give it a pass, but . . ." She smiled. "I'd like to keep it in the
family, if you know what I mean."

He did. But he was unsure whether he wanted to become part of
that legacy.

11

Nathan 5 arrived the following week, flown in aboard a Boeing C-110 so large that an Air Carib G8 could have fit within its bulbous cargo hold. The enormous tiltjet, resembling a cucumber that had sprouted wings, touched down at Ile Sombre International with a roar that rivaled a Kubera launch. A large crowd of islanders had gathered at the airport to witness the landing of an aircraft that they'd probably never see in these parts again; they watched from the edge of the runway as the Goliath made its slow vertical descent alongside the space center staffers who'd volunteered to shepherd its payload across the island.

Matt and Chandi were among them, as was Matt's father. The planning team had decided to take up Matt's suggestion and recruited members of the launch team to walk alongside the truck that would carry the module from the airport to the space center. At first, many people thought it was an unnecessary precaution, but those who still believed that only had to look over their shoulders, where a mob of protesters from the New American Congregation and their supporters waited on the other side of sawhorses erected and patrolled by island police. As Matt's mother had predicted, the protesters had known all along that *Galactique*'s landing module would be arriving by air instead of by sea, and they were taking advantage of this change of plan.

"Think we'll have any trouble from them?" Chandi eyed the protesters nervously.

"No doubt we will," Ben Skinner said quietly. "The question is, how much? If all they do is hold up their signs and yell, everything will be okay. But if they go further than that . . ." He nodded toward the private security force waiting nearby. Some carried sonics as well as the usual batons and stun guns. "They'll break it up if things get bad. I'm not going to worry too much."

Matt watched as the Goliath's bow section, three stories tall, opened and swiveled upward beneath the cockpit, revealing the cargo bay. The module lay on a wheeled pallet, sealed within an airtight plastic shroud. The tractor-trailer rig was already backing up to the plane, waved into position by the runway crew. The flatbeds had been jacked up to same height as the cargo deck; once the tandem trailers were in place, the pallet could be rolled straight onto the truck from the plane. Once it was tied down and covered with tarps, the module would be ready to leave the airport.

That was the easy part. At a walking pace, it would take a little more than an hour for the truck to make the trip to the space center. If only the roads were better, but that couldn't be helped. Like most Caribbean islands, Ile Sombre's public roads weren't maintained very well; the truck had to move slowly, or else the module might rock about and be damaged. To make matters worse, the road between the airport and the space center narrowed until it barely qualified as a two-lane thoroughfare; islanders were known to reach through open driver-side windows and briefly shake hands with friends whom they passed.

The island police were closing the road to local traffic, but nonetheless, it would be during this part of the passage that the truck and its precious cargo would be particularly vulnerable.

Matt hoped his father was right.

It was almost an hour before the truck was ready to depart from the airport. As the massive flatbeds slowly moved away from the plane, a pair of SUVs belonging to the island police took up position in front and behind the truck. They stopped and waited for the walking escorts to take their own positions on either side of the truck. Matt and Chandi found themselves near the front; he watched as his father climbed into the cab to watch the driver and make sure that he didn't go too fast. Private security guards were scattered among the walkers, carrying their sonics at hip level where they'd be visible but not necessarily threatening. There was another long pause while everyone got ready, and then there was a long blast from the truck's air horn, and the convoy began to creep forward.

The protesters were ready too. They'd remained behind the sawhorses the entire time, more or less quiet while the module was being offloaded from the Goliath, but when the truck slowly rolled through the airport's freight entrance, they rushed to the roadside, placards above their heads, voices raised in fiery denunciation. Police and security guards did their best to hold them back, but the protesters were only a few yards from either side of the truck, and it was impossible for Matt to ignore either their shouts or their slogans.

"You'll burn in hell for this!"

NO SIN FOR THE STARS!

"Repent! Destroy that thing!"

DON'T SEND BABYS TO SPACE

"Blasphemy! You're committing blasphemy!"

JESUS HATES SCIANCE!

"Repent!"

Furious eyes. Shaking fists. Someone threw a rock. It missed the canvas-shrouded module and bounced off the side of the truck instead, but immediately a security guard raised his sonic and aimed it in the direction from which the rock had come. He didn't fire—the guards had been ordered not to do so unless absolutely necessary—but the protesters in that part of the crowd quickly backed away. No more rocks were thrown . . . yet.

Chandi was walking in front of Matt, and although her back was to him, he could see her face whenever she turned her eyes toward the crowd. She was doing her best to remain calm, but he could tell how angry she was. The walking escort had been told not to engage the protesters, but he could tell that her patience was being sorely tempted. Chandi had little tolerance for the willfully stupid, and there, just a few feet away, were the very kind of people she detested the most.

He trotted forward to walk beside her. "Having fun yet?" he said, raising his voice to be heard.

Chandi's mouth ticked upward in a terse smile. "Loads. Hey, how come you can't take me on a normal date just once?"

"Do you like to dance?" he asked, and she nodded. "Okay, when we get back to the States, I'll take you to a place I know in Philly. You'll love it. Candlelight dinner, ballroom orchestra, just like—"

The truck horn blared, a prolonged *honnnk! honnnnnk!* that sounded like the driver pulling the cord as hard as he could. At first, Matt thought he was trying to get the protesters out of the way. Then a guard ran past them, and when Matt looked ahead, he saw what was happening.

A rust-dappled pickup truck, the kind used on the nearby banana plantations, had pulled out from a side road about fifty yards ahead of the convoy. As Matt watched, it turned to face the approaching tractor-trailer. It idled there for a few moments, gray smoke coming from a muffler that needed replacing—Ile Sombre was one of the last places in the Western Hemisphere where gasoline engines were still being used—while police and security guards strode toward it, shouting and waving their arms as they tried to get the driver to move his heap.

"The hell?" Matt said as the tractor-trailer's air brakes squealed as it came to a halt. Everyone stopped marching; even the protesters were confused. "Didn't this guy hear that the road's closed?"

Chandi said nothing but instead walked to the front bumper of the halted truck, shielding her eyes to peer at the pickup. "I don't like it," she said as Matt jogged up beside her. "Looks like there's something in the back . . . see that?"

Matt raised his hand against the midday sun. Behind the raised wooden planks of the truck bed was something that didn't look like a load of bananas. Large, rounded . . . were those fuel drums? "I don't know, but it looks like . . ."

All at once, the pickup truck lurched forward, its engine roaring as it charged straight down the road. The police SUV was between it and the tractor-trailer, but the driver was already swerving to his left to avoid it. Protesters screamed as they threw themselves out of the way; the police and security guards, caught by surprise, were slow to raise their weapons.

"Go!" Matt grabbed Chandi by the shoulders to yank her away from the tractor-trailer. The other escorts were scattering, as well, but the two of them were right in the path of the pickup truck, which nearly ran over a couple of protesters as it careened toward the flatbed. *"Run!"*

Yet Chandi seemed frozen. She was staring at the truck even as it raced toward them, her mouth open in shock. Matt followed her gaze and caught a glimpse of what startled her—the face of the driver behind the windshield: Frank Barton.

"Go, mon! *Get out of here!*" A security guard suddenly materialized behind them; he shoved Matt out of the way and then planted himself beside the tractor's bumper and raised the sonic in his hands. Other hollow booms accompanied his shots, but this was a time when old-style bullets would have been more effective; the truck's windshield fractured into snowflake patterns from the focused airbursts, but it still protected Barton.

"Chandi!" Matt had fallen to the unpaved roadside and lost his grasp on her. He fought to get back on his feet but was knocked down again by a fleeing protester. "Chandi, get—"

Then a well-aimed shot managed to shatter the windshield and cause Barton to lose control of the wheel. The truck veered to the right, sideswiped the SUV, tipped over on its side . . .

That was the last thing Matt remembered. The explosion took the rest.

12

Matt later came to realize that he owed his life to the guard who'd pushed him out of the way. That alone kept him from being killed when the gasoline bomb in the back of the stolen farm truck exploded. Matt escaped the blast with little more than a concussion and a scalp laceration from a piece of flying debris, but the guard had lost his life, while Chandi . . .

In the days that followed, as Matt sat by her bedside in the Ile Sombre hospital where the blast survivors were taken, his mind replayed the awful moments after he'd regained consciousness. One of the first things he'd seen were two paramedics carrying away the stretcher upon which Chandi lay. His father had been kneeling beside him, holding a gauze bandage against his son's head until doctors could get around to tending to the less critically injured. He'd had to hold Matt down when he spotted Chandi, unconscious, face streaked with blood, hastily being loaded into an ambulance parked alongside the tractor-trailer.

Everyone said that she was lucky. Five people died that day: the security guard, three protesters, and Frank Barton himself. There were numerous injuries, though, and hers were among the worst. The force of blast had thrown her against the tractor's right-front bumper, breaking the clavicle in her left shoulder and the humerus of her left arm and also fracturing the back of her skull. She might have died were it not for the fact that there happened to be a doctor on the scene who was able to stabilize her until the ambulances arrived. It was no small irony that the doctor also happened to be one of the protesters, and he'd put aside his opposition to the project in order to care for the wounded.

The Ile Sombre hospital outside Ste. Genevieve was remarkably well equipped, staffed by American-trained doctors. Chandi underwent four hours of surgery, during which the doctors managed to relieve the pressure in her skull before it caused brain damage and repair the fracture with bone grafts. Yet she remained unconscious, locked in a coma that no one was certain would end.

Matt stayed with her. He left the hospital only once to return to the hotel and change clothes before coming straight back. He sat in a chair he'd pulled up beside her bed in the ICU, where he could hold her hand while nurses changed her dressings or checked on the feeding tube they'd put down her throat. Sometimes he'd sleep, and every once in a while he'd go to the commissary and make himself eat something, but the next five days were a long, endless vigil in which he watched for the first indication that Chandraleska Sanyal was coming back to him.

So he was only vaguely aware that the landing module had been unscratched by the explosion or that once it arrived at the space center, clean-room technicians had worked day and night to make sure it was ready to be sent to the VAB and loaded aboard the waiting Kubera. Although the New American Congregation had formally condemned the attack, no one at the project was willing to bet that there wasn't another fanatic willing to try again. Matt's father and grandmother determined that the safest place for *Nathan 5* was in space; the sooner it got there, the better. The launch date was moved up by a week, and everyone at the space center did their best to meet the new deadline.

The day *Nathan 5* was rolled out to the pad, Chandi finally woke up. The first thing she saw when she opened her eyes was Matt's face. She couldn't speak because of the plastic tube in her throat, but in the brief time before she fell asleep again, she acknowledged his presence by squeezing his hand. Then the doctor who'd responded to his call bell asked him to leave, and he went to a nearby waiting room, fell into a chair, and caught the first decent sleep he'd had in almost a week.

Nathan 5 lifted off three days later. They watched the launch together on the TV in the recovery room where Chandi had been taken. It was still hard for her to talk, and the doctors had told him that it would take time for her to make a full recovery; Matt had to listen closely when she spoke. Nonetheless, when the Kubera cleared the tower and roared up into the cloudless blue sky, she whispered something that he had no trouble understanding.

"Knew it . . . it would go up," she murmured.

Matt nodded. He knew what he should say. He was just having trouble saying it.

13

A week later, *Galactique* left Earth orbit.

By then, *Nathan 5* was attached to the rest of the ship, and *Galactique* had become a cylinder 440 feet long, its silver hull reflecting the sunlight as it coasted in high orbit above the world. Its image was caught by cameras aboard the nearby construction station and relayed to Mission Control, where everyone involved with the project had gathered for their final glimpse of the vessel they'd worked so long to create.

Although the gallery was packed, with all seats taken and people standing against the walls, this wasn't where Matt and Chandi were. At Ben's insistence, Matt had pushed Chandi's wheelchair to the control room itself, where he parked it behind his father's station. His mother was there, and Grandma, as well. Seated in her mobil, Kate Morressy Skinner regarded the young woman whose shaved head was still swaddled in bandages with a certain reverence Matt had never seen before. At one point, she took Chandi's hands in her own and whispered something that Matt couldn't hear but which brought a shaky smile to Chandi's face.

The final countdown was subdued, almost anticlimactic. Although the mission controllers were at their stations, most of them had their hands in their laps. *Galactique*'s AI system was in complete autonomous control of the ship; the ground team was there only to watch and be ready to step in if something happened to go wrong.

At the count of zero, tiny sparks flared from the nozzles of the maneuvering thrusters along the service module. Slowly, the ship began to turn on its axis, rotating like a spindle. Then, all of a sudden, long, narrow panels along *Nathan 3* at the ship's bow were jettisoned, and cheers and applause erupted from the men and women in the control room and gallery as the first gray-black panels of the microwave sail began to emerge.

It took hours for the sail to unfold, one segment at a time, upon the filament-fine carbon nanotubes that served as its spars. As it did, the ship moved out of geosynchronous orbit, heading away from Earth and closer to the beamer. No one left the dome, though, and the control team watched breathlessly as the sail grew in size, praying that the spars wouldn't get jammed or that the rigging wouldn't tangle, which would mean that the assembly team would have to be called in. But that didn't happen. Layer after layer, the sail unfurled, becoming a huge, concave disk even as the ship receded from the camera.

Finally, the last segment was in place. The thrusters fired again, this time to move *Galactique* into cruise configuration behind the sail until it resembled a pencil that had popped a parachute. Once more, the thrusters fired, this time to gently orient the ship in the proper direction for launch. On the control room's right-hand screen, a plotting image depicted the respective positions of *Galactique* and the beamer.

A dotted line suddenly appeared, connecting the starship and the machine that would send it on its way. The microwave beam was invisible, of course, so only control room instruments indicated that it had been fired.

A few moments later, *Galactique* began to move, slowly at first, and then faster, until it left the screen entirely.

By then, everyone in the dome was shouting, screaming, hugging each other. Fists were pumped in the air, and Matt smelled marijuana as someone broke a major rule by lighting a joint. His grandmother was on her feet, pushing herself up from her mobil to totter forward and wrap her arms around her son and daughter-in-law.

Matt stood beside Chandi, his hand on her shoulder. They said nothing as they watched the departure-angle view from one of *Galactique*'s onboard cameras, the image of Earth slowly falling away. Then Chandi took his hand and pulled him closer.

"Still think . . . it won't get there?" she asked, so quietly that he almost couldn't hear her.

"No. It'll get there." He bent to give her a kiss. "I have faith."

INTERLUDE

Ghost of a Writer

The ballroom of the Hotel Au Soleil was filled nearly to capacity when Ben Skinner walked in with his mother, wife, and son. This particular part of the hotel was seldom used anymore, but in the past, it had been the setting for the dinner parties and receptions of Ile Sombre's wealthy seasonal visitors. Today, it was the location of another sort of event: *Galactique*'s postlaunch press conference.

Looking across the rows of reporters seated behind a small forest of tripod-mounted cameras—the ceiling wasn't quite high enough for minidrones, so Jill had requested that they not be used; flying cameras would simply get in the way—Ben was glad that his wife had decided to move the media briefing from the space center. There had been few enough reporters at the earlier launches for everyone to squeeze into a conference room, but when the foundation started getting flooded with requests for press credentials, it became apparent that *Nathan 5*'s liftoff and the subsequent orbital launch of the completed starship would be witnessed by a larger number of journalists.

And this was even before the violent events of a couple of weeks earlier. The truck bomb had done more than take the lives of five people and nearly kill Matt's girlfriend; it had also focused public attention on a story to which, up until now, relatively few people had been paying attention. Many of the journalists who'd flown to Ile Sombre for the launch had to camp out in the parking lot; only a lucky few had gotten rooms at the hotel, while others had been forced to scrounge for overnight accommodations at homes in Ste. Genevieve and the outlying villages, where the locals had made them pay even higher rates than the hotel.

So the ballroom was to be the scene of the latest—but not the last!—act of a play that was taking generations to perform. Ben smiled to himself as he watched Matt help Kate out of her mobil and up the steps of the temporary stage erected at the front of the room. Perhaps it was just as well. Glancing over to the left side of the stage, he confirmed that the diodes of the holoprojector set up over there were lit. For this final press conference at Ile Sombre, they had a little surprise, and it would work better in a larger room.

There were three mikes on the table, one for each person sitting there. Matt made sure that the mikes were active and there was a glass of water at each seat, and then he hopped off the stage and went over to the side of the room to stand near the door. The Arkwright Foundation logo was on the projection screen behind the stage; Jill stepped to the podium in front of it, and the murmur of voices gradually subsided.

"Good afternoon, and welcome to the last official press briefing for the launch of *Galactique*." As she spoke, Jill's gaze moved restlessly across the room. "As before, any remarks made from this stage will be on the record. The exception will be responses made to individual questions from the press that are to be answered in private, and those will be handled on a case-by-case basis. When we get to the question period, please identity yourself and your affiliation, even if I call you by name."

Nods from a few people, but most gave her blank stares. The vast majority of reporters here were pros familiar with the protocols. "For those who don't know me already," she continued, "I'm Jill Skinner, senior media liaison for the Arkwright Foundation. With me are my husband, Mission Director Dr. Benjamin Skinner, whom you've probably already met"—Ben smiled and gave a quick wave—

"and his mother, Kate Morressy, executive director of the Arkwright Foundation."

"Not to mention our son, Matthew Skinner, who's been working with his mother at the press office." Ben pointed over to Matt, who forced a smile but said nothing. The young man was embarrassed, but Ben couldn't help himself. Matt had come a long way in the past few months on Ile Sombre, and Ben was particularly impressed by the way he'd stuck by Chandi when she was in the hospital. If your dad couldn't brag about you just a little, then who could?

"Um, yes," Jill said, flustered that she'd been thrown off script but recovering quickly. "We've been having something of a family reunion. Glad you all could come."

Some appreciative chuckles, and Ben noticed several reporters jotting notes on their slates. He suddenly realized that this particular aspect of the launch would be a likely human-interest angle for the stories many of them would write.

Jill returned to the business at hand. For the next several minutes, she delivered a rundown of the major events of the liftoff and launch, beginning with *Nathan 5* clearing the tower and ending with *Galactique* deploying its sail, catching the initial microwave burst from the beamer, and leaving Earth orbit. Everyone who'd been in the launch control center had witnessed all this, of course; she was simply recapping them, supplying such details as exact times and technical names. She used the podium interface to throw flight data on the screen behind her and let the reporters download copies for themselves.

"I'll now take questions," she finished. "Anything I can't answer myself, I refer to Ben or Kate." A half dozen hands were already in the air. Jill pointed to a middle-aged black man seated in the first row. "George?"

"George Claxton, Reuters." The reporter stood up as he spoke. "As I understand, *Galactique*'s mission control operations will soon be shifted to another location now that it's been successfully launched. Could you tell us a little more about that, please?"

"Perhaps my husband can answer that. Ben?"

"Certainly." Ben hunched closer to his mike. "Once we close down our operations here, command and control of the spacecraft will be taken over by the foundation's tracking facility in New England. This is the former Juniper Ridge Observatory in Crofton, Massachusetts, which used to be owned by the University of Massachusetts until we took over the site and refurbished it. Juniper Ridge will receive telemetry relayed to it from the laser rectenna on the lunar far side, and our staff will continue to observe and communicate with *Galactique* while it's en route to Gliese 667C."

Claxton grinned. "You're going to be waiting quite a while." This brought a few chuckles.

"No doubt." Ben smiled in return. "But Jill and I are already planning to move out there, and we believe that we'll soon be joined by other members of our family."

As he said this, he couldn't help but glance in Matt's direction. His son didn't say anything but gave his father the slightest of nods. Ben had told Matt that he was welcome to join him and his mother on Juniper Ridge and that if he cared to make his relationship with Chandi permanent, she would be welcome as well. Matt hadn't yet given him an answer, but Ben had little doubt that it would be positive. It appeared that the boy was done with his wandering days and was ready to settle down, get married, and start a family. And the observatory, while somewhat remote, was the perfect place to do this.

Jill pointed to another raised hand. A young Asian woman in the back stood up. "Liu Hsing, China News Service. Now that the foundation has successfully developed a microwave propulsion system for long-range spacecraft, does it have any plans to use this system for other purposes?"

Again, Jill deferred to Ben. "Once *Galactique* ends its acceleration phase 920 days from now," he said, "we'll be temporarily shutting down the beamer. However, we won't be permanently taking it out of service, but instead will offer it for lease to commercial space companies interested in sending spacecraft to Mars and beyond. In this way, the foundation hopes not only to fund its operations at Juniper Ridge but also promote future deep-space initiatives."

Even as he spoke, Ben found himself saying as little as he could while still answering the question. There was already commercial interest in interplanetary beamships, yes, but also rumors that a few companies, including at least one in Hong Kong, were already planning to build their own beamers instead of leasing time on the foundation satellite. The Arkwright Foundation had done its best to protect its proprietary rights, but there was nothing to prevent competitors from building their own laser or microwave beamers from scratch or placing them in orbits closer than Lagrange points. So the less said, the better.

"Jason Floyd, Associated Press. Are there any plans to press charges against the New American Congregation for their role in the attack on your vehicle?"

Ben cupped his hands in front of his face to hide his expression. Every day since the attack, there had been questions from the press about that. It wasn't hard to see that many of the reporters in the room wouldn't have been there if Frank Barton hadn't tried to ram *Nathan 5* with a bomb-laden truck. From the corner of his eye, he saw Matt look down at the floor, and he was glad that Jill was here to handle that question. The tragedy was still fresh in everyone's mind, but especially his.

"Yes, the Arkwright Foundation will be pressing charges against the church," Jill said. "We believe that they're responsible for inciting one of their members to make the attack. However, on the advice of our legal counsel, this is all I can say at the moment." She looked around the room. "Next?"

The questions continued for another hour or so. Some were incisive, a few were highly technical, and one or two downright obtuse

("Is there any danger of *Galactique* colliding with an asteroid?"). Ben and Jill took turns answering them; his mother remained quiet, waiting her turn to speak when her turn came at the end of the session. At last, the questions began to wind down, and when it reached the place where no hands were being raised, Jill spoke again.

"We're almost done here, I think. If there are further questions, now or anytime in future, you have the foundation's contact information in the briefing material you were given when you arrived. But before we leave, we have one last little surprise for you. For that, I'll turn the floor over to my mother-in-law, Kate Morressy Skinner. Kate?"

Scattered applause as Jill stepped away from the podium. Ben stood up, and together, they walked off stage, leaving Kate alone at the mike. She didn't stand, though, but remained seated where she was. Once they'd joined Matt at the side of the room, Kate spoke for the first time since the press conference had begun.

"First, I'd like to thank all of you for making the long trip to Ile Sombre for the launch," she said. "For most of the foundation's history, we've worked quietly, shunning public attention as much as possible. We've done this to avoid the political interference that has hampered previous long-term space efforts, but we'd also hoped that, in the end, the world would pay attention to what we've achieved. Through you, that's become possible, and for that, you have our appreciation."

"While it lasts," Jill softly added, and Ben nodded. He knew what she meant. *Galactique* would probably remain front-page news for a few more days, and then something would come along to take its place. The news cycle would inevitably change, and the launch of humankind's first starship would slip from the top of the public agenda. It wouldn't be completely forgotten, but a year from now, most people would have to struggle to recall the details of a story that had held their attention twelve months earlier.

"The Arkwright Foundation was the legacy of my grandfather, Nathan Arkwright," Kate continued. "Nat was a visionary, a writer who used science fiction as an imaginary means of exploring space.

Many were written before the first rocket even left Earth's atmosphere. His Galaxy Patrol novels and the media franchise based on them made him rich, but he had little use for money, and so at the end of his life, he turned his wealth to a higher purpose—establishing a foundation that would further the goals in which he believed."

Ben looked at Matt and quietly nodded. His son reached into his shirt pocket and pulled out a remote. He held it ready at his side and waited for his grandmother to finish.

"Before he passed away," Kate went on, "my grandfather left a message. He had no idea when it would be heard, but it's directed to those who are here today." She paused. "Gentlemen, ladies . . . Nathan Arkwright."

Ben turned to the lighting control panel on the wall behind him and used the dimmer switch to tone down the ceiling panels. When the room was dark enough, Ben touched a stud on the remote. The two of them had rehearsed this just a little while before the press conference, and it worked beautifully. The room had just begun to dim when a shaft of light appeared on the stage to the left of the table, and within it was the seated figure of an elderly man, frail and ill looking, his hands folded together in his lap.

"*Hello,*" he said, his voice coming from speakers hidden beneath the stage. "*I'm Nathan Arkwright . . .*"

The image wasn't perfect. Life-size holographic technology wasn't widely available when Nathan had his friend George Hallahan make a digital recording of him just a few weeks before his death. The foundation had taken the recording to a Hollywood postproduction facility, where they'd transferred Nathan's features to a hologram of an actor dressed and seated just the way Nathan had been. In this way, they were able to make a reasonable facsimile of Nathan speaking to an audience in some future time he'd never live to see.

"*If you're seeing this,*" Nathan said, looking directly at the camera, "*then it means that, on this day, the Arkwright Foundation has achieved its primary goal—the launch of the first starship from Earth. Aboard is the genetic material of dozens of volunteers that, in time, will become the inhabitants of some distant world far from Earth. They will be the citizens of the galaxy . . . "*

Ben smiled. Every time he heard that line, he got a kick out of it. He wondered how many people in the room would catch the reference to Nat's favorite Heinlein novel. Probably about as many as those who'd realize that he'd lifted this entire scenario from a scene in Asimov's *Foundation*. No one appreciated the classics anymore.

"We can only imagine what worlds they'll discover out among the stars. In time, though, our descendants will meet them in the places where they've made a home for themselves. Because this is only the first step. This is the beginning of just one journey. Before us is an infinite and endless voyage . . . "

Ben always thought that part sounded just a bit hokey. When he'd suggested editing it out, though, his mother had just about ripped his head off. Great-Grandpa's last message would remain untouched, even if the old man had a taste for overstatement. Jill took Ben's hand, and when he looked at her, he caught the amused look in her eye. She felt the same way, but this was Kate's show.

"So today, we dedicate ourselves to the task of following them into the future. The foundation's work is far from finished. In fact, it has only begun . . . "

A smile crept across his aged face as he raised a hand. *"Thank you,"* Nathan said, *"and farewell."*

Matt stopped the projection, and Ben raised the lights again. Applause swept through the room, and a few reporters were sufficiently moved to rise to their feet. They'd all get a copy of the recording later, and Ben had little doubt that, by the end of the day, Nathan Arkwright's final public message would be heard around the world.

Ben glanced at his son, and Matt looked over at his mother. For a few moments, none of them said anything. Instead, they shared a quiet smile. Ol' Nat was right about one thing. The hard part was done, but their work wasn't over yet.

"Okay, then," Ben said quietly. "Let's pack up and head for the mountains."

BOOK THREE

The Long Wait

1

My name is Dhanishta Arkwright Skinner, and this is the story of my life. But to tell it correctly, I must begin not in the place where I was born but a long way from there.

On the day of my birth—February 7, 2070—humankind's first starship, the *Galactique*, was beyond the farthest reaches of the solar system, riding a microwave beam projected from a satellite in L-4 orbit approximately 238,000 miles from Earth. From the perspective of an outside observer—that far from Earth, there were none—the starship would have appeared to be an enormous disk, sixty-two miles in diameter but only a few fractions of an inch thick, parabolic in form and vaguely resembling a parachute. The carbon-mesh beamsail slowly spun clockwise on its axis, and dragged along behind it by threadlike nanotube cables was the vessel itself, a cylindrical collection of modules 330 feet long, with various antennae, including a small pair of barrel-shaped laser transmitters, protruding from its hull and the bell-shaped fuselage of a landing craft flaring at its stern.

This hypothetical observer would have caught only the briefest glimpse of *Galactique* as it flashed by. Although the ship began its journey at the stately rate of 1.9 meters per second, over the course of weeks and months, it had gradually gained velocity while Earth shrank to a tiny blue star and even Jupiter and Saturn became little more than small bright orbs. By the time *Galactique* passed through the orbit of Neptune and entered the Kuiper Belt, it was traveling at nearly a quarter of the speed of light and still accelerating.

Within the ship, all was dark, cold, and quiet. I wasn't aboard. In fact, *Galactique* carried no living crew. Its passengers—some of whom were destined to become my descendants—were sperm and egg specimens sealed within a cryogenic crèche, circular rows of stainless-steel tubes that looked like silver pens covered with a thin skein of frost. The only open space was a central passageway running down the length of the vessel, but even if I had been there, the shaft would have been barely large enough for me; it was there solely to provide access for the spiderlike robots that occasionally emerged from their cubicles to perform the routine inspection and maintenance tasks delegated by *Galactique*'s quantum-computer artificial intelligence.

The AI was a purely logical machine-mind. It possessed no soul and dreamed no dreams, its thoughts—if they could be called that—little more than digital processes of an unliving thing. It had great patience, though, because it was programmed to regard time itself as nothing but an abstraction, and it understood the language of its creators only when their words were translated to its own coded input. It maintained a log of its journey that was periodically pulsed to a receiving station on the far side of the Moon, but it wrote no poems, sang no sea chanteys. Although I often fantasized what it might be like to be a passenger, I'm glad I wasn't; *Galactique*'s guiding mind would have been lousy company.

So there was no one aboard *Galactique* who would have appreciated the fact that, on the very same day it achieved the cruise speed of half the speed of light, 0.6 light-years and 920 days from Earth, I was born.

2

Let me tell you about my home.

The Juniper Ridge Observatory rests atop a mountain in the Berkshires, just outside the small town of Crofton, Massachusetts. Built in 1926, it was a relic of astronomy's golden age, when the planets and stars were studied through optical telescopes in remote locations. Juniper Ridge was a planetary observatory established by Massachusetts State College—later the University of Massachusetts—and for nearly a century, students had traveled to it from the Amherst campus, where they assisted professional astronomers in such tasks as confirming Clyde Tombaugh's discovery of Pluto and continuing Percival Lowell's observations of Mars.

By the end of the century, though, Pluto had been reclassified as a Kuiper Belt object, American and Russian probes had discovered Mars to be nothing like Lowell imagined, and large instruments like Juniper Ridge's thirty-inch Cassegrain reflector had been made largely obsolete, first by radio astronomy and later by orbital telescopes. When UMass and four other western Massachusetts schools built the Five College Radio Astronomy Observatory near the Quabbin Reservoir, Juniper Ridge's usefulness for scientific research came to an end. The observatory remained open for a few more years as a place to teach undergraduate physics students and a location for star parties, but in 2012, the university closed Juniper Ridge for good. The telescope was dismantled and sold to the Museum of Science, Boston, and the aperture of its concrete dome was sealed.

The observatory and its adjacent buildings went up for sale and might have been eventually sold to a real estate developer and torn down to make room for a resort had it not been for the Arkwright Foundation. The Galactique Project was in its early planning stages by then, and the foundation knew that it would need a permanent location for their operations after *Galactique*'s components were launched on the Caribbean island of Ile Sombre and assembled in Earth orbit. A closed-down observatory would be an ideal site, and the fact that Juniper Ridge wasn't far from the former home of the foundation's benefactor and namesake appealed to the board of directors. So the foundation purchased the property and renovated it as the new Mission Control Center, and in August 2067, the Galactique Project moved in.

I came into the world on the very same day *Galactique* achieved its cruise speed of .5c, so my birth was overshadowed by the activity in Mission Control, located on the ground floor of the former observatory dome. At that point, it would be nearly seven months before the lunar tracking station received the laser telemetry from the distant starship and relayed it to Juniper Ridge, so the control team had to go by faith and previous reports that the ship was still on course. Nonetheless, they cheered when the mission director—my grandfather, Benjamin Skinner—issued the order for the beamer to be shut down. *Galactique*'s two-and-a-half-year boost phase was over; the vessel was now on its own.

While this was going on, a young midwife who lived in Crofton was handing a newborn infant (me) to the woman lying in an upstairs bedroom of the adjacent house (my mother). Despite my father's reservations, Chandraleska Sanyal Skinner had insisted upon giving birth at home and not in a hospital. She'd spent too much time in Bay State in recent years, undergoing long-term therapy for the head injury she'd sustained on Ile Sombre in the weeks just prior to *Galactique*'s launch—a truck bomb had gone off near the launch site, a story that I won't repeat here—and the less she saw of the place, the better. My father—Matthew Arkwright Skinner, another member of the control team—had gone along with my mother's wishes only reluctantly, and not until after my grandmother found a local midwife. Dad had become accustomed to Mom's mood swings; if it was less stressful for her to have the child in the house they shared with his parents, it would be better for everyone.

My father took a few minutes to cradle me in his arms and agree with my mother that my name would be Dhanishta—eventually shortened to Dhani, just as Mom abbreviated hers to Chandi—and that, like him, my middle name would be in honor of my great-great-great-grandfather, the author Nathan Arkwright. Then he surrendered me to Mom and went back to the observatory to tell my grandparents the other great news of the day.

And then he got in his car, drove down the mountain into town, walked into Crofton's one and only bar—a country roadhouse called the Kick Inn, which I'd grow up hoping would burn to the ground—and celebrated this momentous day by getting plowed. My family didn't see him again until late that evening, when his car brought him home after someone deposited him in it and set the autoreturn.

Sadly, this was something I'd come to expect from my dad.

By the time I was old enough to realize that he had a drinking problem, I'd become Juniper Ridge's child-in-residence. Seven people lived there: my parents, Matt and Chandi, and grandparents, Ben and Jill, who shared the two-story New England saltbox that had once housed the staff astronomers and visiting scholars, and Winston and Martha Crosby, a young couple who occupied a smaller cottage that once belonged to the observatory's maintenance staff. The Crosbys were childless, making me the only kid among a half dozen grown-ups. So while I had no siblings or immediate playmates, I didn't lack for adult supervision . . . which was fortunate, because my parents, while loving, had troubles of their own.

I once had a great-grandmother, as well, but I have no memory of her. Kate Morressy Skinner, the family matriarch, lived long enough to make one last trip from Boston to Crofton so she could hold her newborn great-granddaughter in her arms, and then she went home and, a couple of months later, quietly passed away in her sleep. When I got older, I learned that Grandma Kate was the person responsible for her family coming to live on Juniper Ridge. As the last surviving member of the Arkwright Foundation's original board of directors, she'd approved the purchase of the observatory and then delegated the task of monitoring *Galactique*'s voyage to my parents and grandparents.

From the start, I was a lonesome child. My mother, whose behavior was already erratic when she and Dad got married and moved to the observatory, became even more reclusive after I was born. The truck bomb had been set off by a member of something called the New American Congregation, and although they were no more—the Arkwright Foundation had sued them into bankruptcy—she continued to believe that another one of them would try to find us and finish the job. Paranoia was a legacy of her head trauma. The nearest public school was in another town twelve miles away, meaning that she'd have to travel there by car or bus every day, a commute that would take her from the familiar safety of the mountaintop retreat and into a world of strangers whom she increasingly distrusted. Once I finished preschool, she decided to homeschool me herself. Although Grandpa and Grandma argued against this, Dad didn't mind; he'd disliked making the twenty-four-mile round trip to my kindergarten five days a week and figured that Mom's new role as their child's teacher might help stabilize her precarious mental state. And since Uncle Win and Aunt Martha were willing to pitch in, Mom wouldn't have to do it herself, which was also just as well, because Dad was often too hungover to keep up his end of the bargain.

So after age six, I saw children my own age only occasionally. There were twin girls who lived on a horse farm three miles down the road from the observatory and a boy who lived with his father in a trailer a mile farther on, but the sisters were a little younger and the boy a couple of years older, and at that time of life, even a year in age difference can seem like an impassable gulf.

And it wasn't just that. In the constant company of six intelligent and highly educated adults, three of whom took turns every day as my teachers, I grew up in an intellectual environment. I was reading at middle-school level before I was nine and by the time I was in my teens, I was fluent in French, Spanish, and Indian, adept in higher forms of algebra and physics, knowledgeable of American and world history, and had read the most of the classics of Shakespeare, Poe, Hemingway, Marquez, Clarke, Swanwick, and Le Guin. I was a brainy little girl, but precocious children often don't have a lot in common with kids their own age, and that made me even more lonesome.

I also knew something most kids didn't know: the details of humankind's first starship, now bound for Eos—or, if you want to get technical, Gliese 667C-e, a terrestrial planet in close orbit around an M-class red dwarf twenty-two light-years from Earth. Every day, my family and the Crosbys took turns standing watch in the observatory, which we called the MC. Inside the dome, a ring-shaped array of computers, control consoles, and holoscreens had been installed on the ground floor, while on the newly installed second floor, a twenty-foot radio dish antenna had taken the place of the old telescope. Once the dome's aperture slot was open, the dish was able to slowly rotate on its pedestal, tracking a network of communications satellites across the sky. The comsats relayed information sent to them from another pair of satellites in orbit above the Moon, which in turn transmitted data gathered by the laser receiving station on the lunar far side.

This data was the voice of *Galactique*. The ship was already three and a half light-years from Earth the day my father took me in his lap and, in a moment of sobriety that was becoming increasingly scarce, patiently explained what he and Mom and Grandpa and Grandma and Uncle Win and Aunt Martha did for a living: they were listening for reports sent from a vessel on a long, long journey to a distant star, waiting for the day many years in the future— sometime in July 2135, in fact—when we would finally learn that it had safely arrived.

"See, everything the ship tells us about what it's doing comes to us here." Dad shifted me from one knee to another as he pointed to the holoscreen floating before us. "All those numbers are codes, and the codes let us know that the ship is doing just fine."

"Uh-huh." I gnawed the knuckle of my left thumb as I gazed at the glowing columns of letters and digits. "I don't know what they mean." I was pretty smart for a seven-year-old, but not *that* smart.

"Don't do that." Dad gently pried my thumb from my mouth. "It'll make your teeth crooked. Sure, you don't know what they mean, because they're in code—short for what the ship wants to tell us. But since *we* know what the codes stand for, we can figure it all out, and if they tell us something's going wrong, we can tell the ship how to correct itself and make things right."

"Although it takes a while," Grandpa added. My grandfather was seated in a chair on the other side of the ring, studying another display as he listened to us. "We can't tell at once what *Galactique* is telling us because it's so far away, and *Galactique* won't know what we're telling it for the same reason."

"I don't understand." I fidgeted in my father's lap, but nonetheless, I was fascinated. I tended to chew my thumb when I was trying to figure something out. "Why does it take so long?"

"How fast does light travel? Do you remember?"

"Umm"—I sought to remember what Uncle Win had taught me just last week—"186,000 miles per second."

"That's right! Good girl! And that's also how far the laser beam carrying data from *Galactique* travels in one second. It can't travel any faster because a laser is just a concentrated form of light, and . . . ?" He waited for an answer.

"Nothing moves faster than light!" I was proud of myself for knowing what Dad meant. "Nothing! Nothing at all!"

"Okay, so let's figure it out. How many seconds are in a year?"

"Ummmm . . ." I started to raise my knuckle to my mouth, and he pulled it away again. "A lot?"

"That's as good an answer as any. A lot. And if you multiply all those seconds by 186,000, and then take that number and multiply it by"—Dad paused to run his forefinger down the display, pulling up the figure for *Galactique*'s current distance from Earth—"3.523 lights, or light-years, that's how far away the ship is from us. Which means that it now takes three and a half years for us to hear anything *Galactique* has to say to us and another three and a half years for it to hear anything we'd have to say to it today."

I stared at the holo. "Three and half *years*?"

"Uh-huh. And getting longer all the time."

I remember that day well, for in that instant, I had an epiphany seldom experienced by little girls and sometimes never fully realized by quite a few adults: a sense of the vastness of space and time, the sheer enormity of the cosmos. Not only was the distance between the stars greater than I'd thought it was, but the implication that the universe itself was unimaginably huge was a revelation both awesome and frightening.

Suddenly, I'd become a tiny and inconsequential little thing. The bottom had dropped out from under me, and I was an insignificant particle of a far greater whole.

I shivered. The hollow concrete eggshell of the MC had become a cold and forbidding place. I had an urge to scramble out of my father's lap and run from the building, never to return again. But Dad put his arms around me and pulled me closer, and then he whispered something in my ear that I'd never forget.

"Do you want to know a secret?"

I looked at him. "What?"

Dad glanced over his shoulder to make sure that Grandpa wasn't listening in. Satisfied that he wasn't, he went on. "There's a little boy aboard *Galactique*."

"*Really?*" I was astonished.

"Shh!" Dad raised a finger to his lips. "Yes, there is. He's asleep just now and won't wake up until *Galactique* reaches Eos, but yes, he's there. And it's our job to make sure he gets safely to the place where he's going. Understand?"

"Uh-huh." I thought about this a moment. "Dad, what's his name?"

My father hesitated, and then he gave me an answer. "Sanjay."

3

Later in life, I'd often wonder why my father told me that this imaginary child was a boy and why he'd picked the name Sanjay. Perhaps it was only a spur-of-the-moment decision, the sort of embellishment a father would add to a fairy tale. Yet it's also possible that he might have been revealing a subconscious regret. Maybe he'd wanted a boy instead of a girl, and he would have named this boy Sanjay if things had been different.

Yet this didn't occur to me at the time. The revelation that there was a little boy asleep on *Galactique* provoked a different kind of wonder. As I lay in bed that night, the lights turned off and the blankets pulled up against the winter cold, I didn't sleep but instead gazed up at the ceiling, thinking about Sanjay. Dad told me very little about him, but it didn't matter; my imagination supplied the details, and before long, he became as real to me as any living person.

Sanjay was my age, naturally, and like me, he also had the dark skin and straight black hair of someone with an Indian-American heritage. He slept in what my father called "suspended animation" because that was the only way he'd be able to survive the half-century-long voyage to Eos, but I figured that, every now and then, he'd wake up, knuckle the crust from his eyes, and then rise from his little bed and wander through the ship just to see what was going on. In my mind's eye, *Galactique* was very different from what it actually was;

it was the kind of spaceship I was familiar with from the old science fiction movies I sometimes watched with Uncle Win, who had a fondness for such things. Sanjay would gaze through portholes at the passing stars, have a cup of hot chocolate and a cookie, check the instruments to make sure the ship was still on course, and then get sleepy and return to bed again.

No one knew about Sanjay except my father. The little boy was a shared secret that we tacitly agreed to keep from my mother, grandparents, and the Crosbys. And since I'd found that there was little I could talk about with the few other children I knew—the two girls, Joni and Sara Ogilvy, were only interested in their dolls and the pony they wouldn't let me ride, and I tried to avoid seeing the boy, Teddy Romero, who was scary and a little mean—I didn't reveal his existence to them. Which was just as well. Sanjay was just as lonely as I was, which made me feel a certain kinship toward him. He was the little brother I didn't have, the playmate I'd been denied. He became a friend I'd never actually met yet with whom I carried on many conversations, always when I was certain no one else was around.

As imaginary friends go, Sanjay was wonderful. Nonetheless, I was aware of the fact that my little chats were rather one-sided and that he wasn't really talking to me. I also knew that, even if he did occasionally wake from his long slumber, anything that he might actually want to say to me wouldn't be heard for years. Still, I wanted very much to speak to him. I considered the problem for quite a while, and then one day, I approached my father with my solution.

"I want to send a message to Sanjay," I said.

It was an afternoon in late spring. The winter snows had melted, and there were new leaves on the trees. My father was behind the observatory, standing on a stepladder to clean the solar panels that, along with a small wind turbine on a nearby hilltop, supplied Juniper Ridge with its electricity. His eyes were puffy—he'd slept on the living room couch again, having come home from the Kick Inn late the night before—but he managed a smile as he climbed down the ladder to patiently listen while I explained what I wanted.

"You know it'll take a long time for it to get there," he said when I was done.

"Yeah, I know. But he can hear it when he—" I stopped myself. Dad didn't know that Sanjay wasn't always asleep. "Whenever he wakes up," I finished.

My father nodded but didn't say anything as he wiped his hands on the cloth he'd been using to clear the spring pollen from the photovoltaic cells. "It's very expensive to send a signal to *Galactique*," he said at last. "If I let you do this, it can only be one time. And you'll have to make it very short—no more than a minute. Understand?"

A minute seemed much too short for everything I wanted to say to my friend. "All right. Just a minute. Please, Dad."

"Okay, then. We have to send some course data next Wednesday, anyway. Write down what you want to say and show it to me first, and if I think it's short enough, I'll let you record it, and we'll attach it to the next pulse." He paused. "But don't let anyone else know you're doing this, okay? Sanjay is still our little secret."

I grinned and happily nodded, and over the next week, I wrote a short script for what I wanted to say. Knowing that I had only sixty seconds, I rewrote it again and again, pruning unnecessary words and revising my thoughts, and then I carefully rehearsed it while keeping an eye on the clock to make sure that I didn't exceed the time limit. The following Tuesday, I showed the handwritten script to my father while he was standing watch in the MC. He liked what I had to say but made me read it aloud while he timed me. Satisfied, he told me to come back the next night, which was when he was scheduled to send the transmission.

The scheme almost fell through at the last minute. After dinner, I walked over to the dome at the appointed hour only to discover that Dad and I weren't alone. Uncle Win was there too, and while he and I got along just fine, when it came to *Galactique*, he tended to be rather humorless, often saying that keeping track of the ship was "a sacred trust." He wouldn't understand the notion of sending a nonessential video to the ship.

Dad caught my eye when I came in, and he silently placed a finger to his lips. I kept the message in my pocket and remained quiet while he and Uncle Win checked and rechecked the coded material they were preparing to transmit. Then Dad drained the last of the coffee in his mug, idly wished aloud that he had more, and asked Winston if he'd mind going back to the house and brewing another pot. Uncle Win was a coffee bug, and everyone was in favor of doing whatever it took to keep Dad away from the Kick Inn, so he was only too happy to comply.

As soon as he was gone, my father hustled me to a chair in front of the console where the videocam was located. He fitted me with a headset and did a brief mike check and then stepped out of range of the lens. "We're all set," he said, pointing to the keyboard. "Whenever you're ready, just push the Enter key and start talking."

"Okay." I spread the wrinkled notebook pages out on the console.

"You've only got one shot at this. Make it count."

"Okay. I will." I took a deep breath, nervously fussed with my appearance. I was wearing my nicest blouse and skirt and had even put a little yellow silk flower in my hair. Then I touched the key and looked straight at the lens.

"Hello, Sanjay," I began. "My name is Dhanishta Arkwright Skinner, and I'm calling you from Earth . . ."

4

Sanjay wasn't real, but thinking about him so much accustomed me to imagining *Galactique* in vivid terms, so it was easy for me to visualize what was happening there.

A little more than three and a half years later, my message was received by the ship, along with a related set of instructions my father hadn't told me about. Since they were prefixed as a nonessential communiqué not to be opened until after the ship reached Gliese 667C-e, the AI stored them in memory and then proceeded to the more important material.

Galactique's course was taking it in the general direction of the galactic center, just below the plane of ecliptic. By then, the ship's point of origin was no longer visible; Earth's sun, along with its family of planets and neighboring stars, had vanished into a conical zone of darkness that had appeared behind the ship. The same Doppler effect caused by the ship's relativistic velocity—a little more than 93,000 miles per second—caused the stars around and in front of *Galactique* to redshift, changing hues slightly as they seemingly migrated in the direction of travel, while at the same time causing infrared and ultraviolet sources to enter the visible spectrum as seemingly new stars.

If there had been any living passengers aboard, they would have been confused by the display. *Galactique*'s AI, along with the array of lesser computers it managed, was prepared for these phenomena. The navigation subroutines ignored the visual distortions and instead took their bearings from galactic coordinates, taking into account the parallax motions of the nearby stars. There was little chance that the ship would get lost on its way to Eos, but just to make sure, Juniper Ridge periodically transmitted navigational updates.

In turn, *Galactique* responded by confirming its status, using the twin high-powered lasers that had been elevated from its service module shortly after launch. The beamsail itself, no longer serving as the propulsion system, now performed a second role as the ship's receiving antenna, using sensors threaded through its carbon-mesh surface.

On the whole, though, the ship's navigation system was mainly autonomous. It had to be. Although the time dilation effect of .5c caused the hours to pass more slowly aboard *Galactique* than they did on Earth, many years went by between the moment the ship sent back its confirmation signal and the moment it was received on Juniper Ridge.

I was fifteen years old when I learned that the message I'd sent Sanjay had been heard.

5

This was one of the few good things that happened to me in that year of my life. When my grandfather, who'd read the message the night before during his watch in the MC, told me about it the following morning over breakfast, it came as a poignant reminder of one of the last fond memories I had of my father, who was no longer living on Juniper Ridge.

Dad had become tired of the observatory's isolation. As the years went by, he gradually came to regret leaving behind the freewheeling life he'd led before rejoining his family and sharing their commitment to the Galactique Project. He'd been a drifter before then, and as he approached his forties, he began to miss his old ways. My father still loved me, but relations with my mother had become strained. They still slept in the same bed, but days would go by when they wouldn't even look at one another, let alone share a kiss. The

Kick Inn had become the center of his social life, and there were nights when he didn't even bother to come home but instead crashed on the couch of one of his drinking buddies.

We didn't know it, but he'd also met a local woman, a lady named Sally Metcalfe, who liked single-malt whiskey as much as he did. Their friendship didn't become a full-blown affair for quite a while, but it wasn't lost on Mom that her husband's eye had begun to wander. She never fully recovered from the head injury she'd sustained years earlier, and her distrust of outsiders soon extended to Dad as well. I often heard my parents arguing from the other side of the wall that separated my bedroom from theirs, and although my grandparents tried to bring peace to the family, it was becoming increasingly obvious that, little by little, Dad was withdrawing from us.

One Saturday afternoon shortly after my fifteenth birthday, I went with Grandpa and Grandma on a shopping trip to Pittsfield, the nearest large town. Uncle Win and Aunt Martha were in California for an astrophysics conference at UC–Davis, and Dad claimed to not be feeling well, so we left Mom in the MC while we went to buy new clothes for me.

Pittsfield shopping trips were always special, and I didn't get new clothes as often as I would have liked. It was a happy day for me until we returned. The first thing we noticed when we pulled up in front of the house was that Dad's car was missing.

Mom was still in the observatory, analyzing the latest data received from *Galactique*, so she was completely unaware that, sometime in the last several hours, he had thrown his clothes into a couple of suitcases, left a brief, impersonal note on the kitchen table—*Going away for a while. Don't call me . . . I'll come back when I'm ready!*—and taken off.

Grandpa tried calling him anyway, but he never received an answer. Although my father's car was found in the parking lot of the Boston transtube station, his phone's GPS locator remained active for a few days, so Grandpa was able to track Dad's westward route on the tube through New York, Pennsylvania, and Ohio, until the signal vanished in Indiana. Apparently, Dad remembered that he could be traced that way and ditched the phone while changing trains at the Indianapolis station. Grandma went into Crofton and visited the Kick Inn, and from its denizens, she confirmed what Mom had suspected: Dad had been seeing another woman, and apparently she'd persuaded him to run away with her. Where they were headed, though, was anyone's guess. The drunks only knew that Sally used to live "somewhere out west" and that she'd often talked about going back.

I spent the next couple of days in my room, lying in bed with the blankets pulled up over my head, refusing to talk to anyone. Through the wall, I often heard Mom crying. Sometimes we both wept at the same time, but never together. Truth is, I had never been as close to my mother as I'd been to my father. Mom had always been a little aloof, preferring the role of tutor and disciplinarian, while Dad had been the one who gave me piggyback rides when I was little, took me hiking and swimming in the summer and snowshoeing in the winter (when he wasn't drinking, that is), and told me about Sanjay.

Although I'd long since learned the truth—there wasn't a little boy aboard *Galactique*; it was just a story my father had made up—deep in my heart, I always believed that Sanjay was real, if only in a metaphorical sense. But when my father broke my heart, he also broke what little faith I still had in that childhood fantasy.

My family was shattered by the loss, but we did our best to pick up the pieces. Yet things only got worse. Six weeks later, Uncle Win and Aunt Martha came to Grandpa and Grandma with news of their own. While they were at the conference, Uncle Win had learned about a teaching position that was opening up in UC–Davis's physics department. The job was tenure track, with a salary considerably higher than what he was earning from the Arkwright Foundation; without telling anyone except his wife, Winston had quietly submitted his résumé. Now the position was being offered to him, and the Crosbys had come to the conclusion that this was an opportunity too good to pass up.

I could be cynical and say that Winston Crosby's idea of the Galactique Project being a sacred trust apparently had an expiration date, but in hindsight, I can't blame him or Martha. Their titles as my aunt and uncle were honorary, after all, and although we'd always thought of them as family, they'd been on Juniper Ridge for almost eighteen years. Like Dad, they were pushing forty. My mother and grandparents didn't want to see them go, but they reluctantly agreed that the time had come for them to move on. Their car was the next to leave Juniper Ridge, never to be seen again.

Since the observatory was now staffed by my family alone, Grandpa and Grandma decided that I needed to take on some of the work in the MC. Perhaps it was just as well. Mom had become even more reclusive, if that was possible. A borderline agoraphobic by then, she seldom left the house anymore, and when she did, it was only to putter around the greenhouse that was attached to the main house, a silent communion with the cucumbers, radishes, and tomatoes she planted after Dad went away. In many ways, she was an invalid, but it was even worse than that; heartbreak had made her a ghostly presence, a specter of the woman she'd once been.

I was old enough to look after myself, though, and since there wasn't much else to do besides watch my mother silently suffer, I gratefully let my grandparents teach me what I needed to know: how to monitor the communications equipment, how to rotate the radio dish so that it could properly receive signals from the lunar tracking station, how to interpret the coded messages that periodically appeared on the screens. Grandpa still reserved for himself the crucial task of calculating the astrometric updates that occasionally needed to be transmitted to *Galactique*, but we both knew that responsibility would eventually become mine, as well. Despite the retrotherapy he and Grandma had undergone when they were younger, it was clear that the years were finally catching up with them. Their hair was graying, their postures were becoming stooped, and there were times when their short-term memories for little things weren't as sharp as they used to be. Perhaps they'd never leave Juniper Ridge, but they wouldn't outlive *Galactique,* either.

But I was getting older too, and I was no longer sure I wanted the role that was being put upon me.

6

My teens were not an extension of the idyll in which I'd spent my childhood (and it really was a happy time, all things considered). Although I was smarter than most kids my age, Mom had done me no favors by keeping me out of school. By the time I was sixteen, I'd become painfully aware that I was not only mostly friendless but also rather naïve.

I wasn't entirely lonely. I'd established my own online social network, and although I'd never met any of the other kids with whom I communicated, I knew who they were and what they were up to. They often hid behind avatars and screen names, but I realized that their daily lives were much different from mine. I knew nothing of what it was like to be in homeroom with a cute boy whom they really liked, and when sex came up, I had to pretend to be just as wise about it as they seemed to be (they probably weren't, but I didn't know that). They bought their clothes in malls; I went shopping maybe two or three times a year, and a big day for me was when I'd get a new winter parka. They dropped casual references to sock bands of which I was only dimly aware, let alone seen. Yes, I could explain the Drake equation or the Doppler effect, but how many teenagers want to hear about that? Next to them, I was either a country bumpkin in bib overalls or a virgin princess locked in a castle tower, depending on the way I felt that particular day.

Naturally, I began to rebel.

I lost the argument with my mother about going to school, but she couldn't stop me from using my feet. In the afternoons, I started walking down the road to Joni and Sara's house, where I made a deliberate effort to cultivate their friendship. The twins were both fourteen by then, but in some ways, the three of us were the same age; I'd learned to dumb down a little bit when talking to them, and in return for helping them with their homework, they introduced me to music and movies and girl stuff that I wouldn't have been exposed to otherwise. Sara continued to be a bit snooty—the Ogilvys had money, as she seldom missed an opportunity to remind me—but Joni and I became close friends. In years to come, that friendship would become valuable.

And I introduced myself to sex. Let's be honest about this: I had no interest in being a thirty-year-old virgin. I wanted to get laid and wasn't very particular about how I'd go about it. Which was just as well, because the only likely prospect was Teddy Romero. His father was another regular habitué of the Kick Inn, and Ted himself was just a few years away from elbowing up to the bar alongside his old man. He had the necessary equipment, though, and that's all that really mattered. He was a bit surprised when I started coming down the road to the double-wide where he and his father lived and practically threw myself at him, but he obligingly took me out on a couple of dates and didn't mind too much that I wouldn't drink with him (liquor was something I'd shun my whole life, for obvious reasons). Two or three nights like that, and I finally got what I wanted from him; he drove me out to an abandoned granite quarry on the outskirts of Crofton and did the deed.

Losing my virginity wasn't the rapturous experience I'd been led to believe it would be. Ted fumbled with my bra until I helped him open it, and he ruined my nicest pair of panties; he had beer on his breath, and he handled my breasts like they were wads of dough. I was glad I'd insisted that he wear a condom. Altogether, it was messy and rather degrading, but at least my curiosity was satisfied. Yet I had to brush my teeth twice to get the taste of his mouth out of my mouth, and I came away from the experience wondering why everyone made such a big deal about sex.

That was it for Ted. My mother was locked in her own little world, so she was unaware of my brief affair, and my grandparents obligingly looked the other way. I think they knew what I was doing and why, though, because when Ted showed up at the observatory a couple of nights later, Grandpa chased him away and told him not to come back again. I saw Teddy a few times after that, and he'd favor me with a leer and a wink, but after a while he lost interest in me, and in years to come, I'd occasionally spot him while I was in town, usually when he was lurching in or out of the Kick Inn.

By then, I had other things to worry about.

7

When I was eighteen, two things happened: I left home, and the Arkwright Foundation got in trouble.

College was both inevitable and welcome. I'd earned a GED after passing the state exams with such high scores that the local board of education made me take the tests again, this time under close supervision, just to make sure that I wasn't cheating. They had a hard time believing that a girl who'd been homeschooled since age six could still manage to land in the top 1 percent of all students in a state known for the quality of its public education. Not only did I ace the GED exams but also the SATs, and those scores got me into UMass.

I would have liked to have gone to school a bit farther away than Amherst, but my mother wasn't willing to loosen the leash quite that much. So I compromised with her; I'd spend two years at UMass, and if my grades held up and I still wanted to move on, she'd let me transfer to an out-of-state college if I could get into one. Which was fine with me. I intended to major in physics, and I had my eyes set on UC–Davis. Although the Crosbys had long since left Juniper Ridge, my family had kept in touch with them, and Uncle Win promised me that he'd put in a good word for me with the admissions office.

Try to understand: I'd lost interest in *Galactique*. I'd grown up hearing about the ship, but it had been years since I'd believed in the little boy I'd once thought was aboard. For me, the Arkwright Foundation was something that was started by my great-great-great-grandfather and now belonged to Mom and my grandparents. I'd be an old lady by the time *Galactique* reached Gliese 667C-e; the last thing I wanted was to find myself still sitting around the observatory, waiting for a weak signal from a distant star. My father was gone, the Crosbys had moved away, and now it was my turn to do the same.

So I packed my bags and kissed Mom and Grandma good-bye, and then Grandpa drove me down from the mountains. Compared to where I'd come from, the UMass campus was like a major city, and the dorm I moved into was more alien than the starship now a little more than nine light-years from Earth, but within a few weeks, I'd almost entirely forgotten about *Galactique*.

Unfortunately, the rest of the world didn't do the same.

I'd settled into undergraduate life and was making friends with my fellow students—I was shy at first but soon discovered that I wasn't that much weirder than anyone else there—when the Arkwright Foundation found itself receiving unwanted attention. A couple of years earlier, Grandpa had come to the realization that the foundation was beginning to run low on funds. From the beginning, it had depended on investments made into various private enterprises, mainly the space companies that had developed the technologies upon which the Galactique Project depended. The seed money for those initial investments had come from the royalties and licensing rights of Nathan Arkwright's work; the foundation derived its start-up income from the Galaxy Patrol books and movies, and for a long time, the cash flow had been sufficient for the foundation to pursue its objectives.

But *Galactique*'s enormous development, construction, and launch costs had drained the funds. Since then, the investments that once provided a stable source of income had dried up when the supporting companies either folded or were bought out. The plan to lease the foundation's beamer to private industry fizzled when several companies in the United States and China formed a consortium, SolEx, to build its own beamer in geosynchronous orbit. Although not as powerful as the foundation's, the SolEx beamer was closer and easier to service than the old one at L-4. The Arkwright Foundation had hoped that the Galactique Project would spur the development of the solar system, but it was only partly successful. SolEx used its new beamer to venture out into space, but it went no farther than Mars, with commercial asteroid mining operations remaining close to Earth.

To add insult to injury, even the Galaxy Patrol franchise had sputtered into oblivion. No one but old people remembered Hak Tallus anymore. Nathan Arkwright became a writer many people had heard of but few actually read.

For a short while, there had been talk of building *Galactique II*, but the money simply wasn't there. And although the foundation no longer had to pay for anything except Juniper Ridge, even those costs had become burdensome.

So Grandpa, who'd become the foundation's president and chief financial officer as well as *Galactique*'s mission director, decided to take the unprecedented step of approaching the federal government for financial assistance. He'd made a request to the National Science Foundation for an annual grant of $500,000 on the grounds that *Galactique* was an interstellar probe launched for the benefit of all humanity and that the world would benefit from whatever knowledge we eventually learned. *Galactique* was well known to everyone, of course—the book Grandma had written about the project had been a bestseller—so the NSF had no trouble agreeing to Benjamin Arkwright's request, and soon Juniper Ridge had a new source of funds to support itself.

Then some tightwad junior congressman from a red-dust state caught wind of this particular line item in the federal budget, and although $500,000 was barely worth a mention in the grand scheme of things, he decided that it was worth investigating. He claimed that the money would be better spent on drought relief in his district, but I suspected that he was looking for a way to bolster his own political career. In any case, he sicced his staff on the foundation, and they dug deep into its history, and within the dim shadows of the past, they discovered a dirty little secret: it seemed that the Arkwright Foundation had once bought a senator.

My grandparents didn't tell me about the subpoena they'd received. They were worried that it might distract me from my studies, and besides, they didn't take it very seriously. And my mother, of course, was mostly oblivious to the whole thing. So I was unaware of what was going on until my advisor happened to read about it in the news, and when he told me about it, I immediately called Grandma.

"What the hell is going on?" I demanded.

"Oh, it's nothing to worry about," she said as breezily as if we were talking about the unseasonal nor'easter that had just dumped six inches of snow on our part of the state. "Some fool in Washington sticking his nose where it doesn't belong, that's all. You shouldn't be concerned about it."

"It's a subpoena, Grandma! It means you and Grandpa are going to have to testify before Congress!"

"Just a subcommittee hearing, dear. Grandpa's doing the talking, and he's getting a lawyer to help him with the testimony—"

"A lawyer!" The only time my family had ever hired a lawyer was when a contractor had done a lousy job installing a new septic tank for the house. We'd smelled trouble then, and I was getting the same kind of stench again.

"Just to give advice. Honestly, Dhani, it's—"

"And what's this about the foundation paying off a congressman to get an exemption from"—I stopped to glance at the news article I'd pulled up on my slate—"the Domestic Space Access Act? No one ever told me about that."

A pause. "That was a long time ago, and it's not what it sounds like. The press have got it all wrong, and so does the subcommittee." Another pause. "Honey, I really can't talk about it. Besides, you know how bad the phones are out here."

The phones at Juniper Ridge had always worked fine. Grandma was giving me a hint that she suspected they might be tapped. Something cold slithered down my back. "Do you want me to come home?" I asked. "I can get out of classes and take the bus back if you—"

"Oh, I don't think that's necessary." Another pause; this time, I heard Grandpa say something in the background. "Well, it would help if you could come back for a few days and keep your mother company when we're in Washington. Do you think you could do that?"

"Sure. Of course." After Dad went away, we'd been careful never to leave Mom alone for very long. My mother's mental state was too fragile for us to expect her to take care of herself. "When do you want me to come home?"

"Two weeks from tomorrow." Grandma's voice brightened again. "Really, Dhani, it's nothing to worry about. We've got the situation well in hand."

A couple of weeks later, I took a few days off from school and returned home, catching an omnibus from Amherst and getting off in Crofton, then hiking the rest of the way to the observatory. My grandparents had left for D.C. only a few hours earlier, and Mom was already beside herself; it took an hour or so just to calm her down and convince her that she hadn't been abandoned. Besides gardening, the one thing she was still capable of doing on her own was standing watch in the MC, but I checked anyway to see if there were any new messages. The last was a routine status report transmitted nearly twenty years earlier and received just the previous week. All was well. I went back to the house and made dinner for Mom and me.

Next morning, we sat together in the living room and watched the subcommittee hearings. They were being carried live on one of the Fedcom sites; I put it up on the holo, and it was almost as if we were in seated in the hearing room. As Grandma told me, Grandpa was the one doing the talking; a young woman not much older than I was seated at the witness table beside him, and while only a handful of people were visible in the background, I spotted Grandma directly behind Grandpa and his attorney.

They were outnumbered by the members of the House Ways and Means oversight subcommittee. The chairman wasn't the same congressman who'd made the accusations against the foundation; that was Representative Joseph Dulle (pronounced "doo-lay," unlikely as that was), a moon-faced guy with a flattop haircut who looked like he'd probably spent his adolescence yanking up the underwear of smaller kids.

The chair yielded the floor to Representative Dulle, and he opened with a broadside attack. After it had come to his attention that the Arkwright Foundation had been the recipient of over $1 million in federal outlays—"for a project of dubious value even in terms of scientific research"—his staff had investigated the matter and discovered that, even though the foundation was claiming to be a nonprofit organization, it had derived most of its income from investments in some highly profitable enterprises, "making its nonprofit status suspicious at the very least." To make matters worse, his staff discovered that, during the 2036 presidential election, the foundation had contributed $400,000 to the presidential campaign of late Senator

Clark Wessen when he'd unsuccessfully sought his party's nomination. Wessen, in turn, had not only publicly come out in support of the Galactique Project—"an unusual thing for a presidential candidate to be addressing when there were far more important matters on the agenda"—but also introduced and pushed through a Senate bill granting the foundation an exemption to the Domestic Space Access Act, thereby allowing it to use the Ile Sombre Space Launch Center instead of U.S. launch sites "as another means of avoiding having to pay federal taxes and user fees."

"Now the Arkwright Foundation has found another means of fleecing the American taxpayer," Dulle continued. *"Get it to pay millions of dollars to support a space probe that was launched over twenty years ago. In essence, we're being asked to spend money on an abandoned observatory occupied by the surviving members of the family who started the foundation in the first place, who use technical jargon and high-minded promises as a way of misappropriating taxpayer funds for their own use."*

Dulle was staring straight at my grandfather when he said this, as if expecting his angry gaze to cause Grandpa to hide under the table. If so, he must have been disappointed. My grandfather listened with an amused smile and patiently waited until the congressman was done. Then the chair gave the floor to him, and Grandpa switched on his table mike and began his defense.

Grandpa held his ground well. While maintaining a respectful tone, he managed to be just patronizing enough to sound like a respected scientist lecturing a political hack on the nuances of public policy. He pointed out that, while he appreciated the subcommittee's interest in these matters, the fact remained that the principal figures in this investigation were long gone; Senator Wessen's presidential campaign was a footnote in the history books, my great-grandmother Kate Morressy Skinner had passed away nearly twenty years ago, and they were not still around to defend themselves. He then went on to say that, under the federal laws of the time, nothing either of them had done was illegal. The Arkwright Foundation's contributions to

Senator Wessen's PAC had been in the interest of a public servant whose social agenda the foundation agreed with; likewise, there had been no pressure on the senator to support the Galactique Project or introduce legislation that would make its launch operations more viable from Ile Sombre than if they had been conducted at similar facilities on American soil. The foundation's investments had been completely legit, with the profits being wholly devoted to research and development of *Galactique,* and since most of those companies were no longer supporting the project's operations in western Massachusetts, the foundation had been forced to request modest funding from the federal government.

"This isn't a free ride for us, Mr. Dulle," Grandpa said. *"This isn't an attempt to fleece anyone. Galactique is an ongoing effort to expand the human presence into the cosmos, to establish a new home for our race. Until recently, the Arkwright Foundation has succeeded in doing this with the barest support from the American government. The money we've received from the National Science Foundation keeps the lights on in our Mission Control center and allows the three people who monitor the spacecraft to live there full-time. You're welcome to visit us at any time, and you'll see that we're hardly in the lap of luxury."*

It was a good defense. I thought Grandpa's testimony was a superb takedown. But as he finished, my mother spoke up for the first time.

"He's right, you know," she said quietly.

"Of course he's right." I was grinning. "Grandpa kicked his—"

"No, I mean *he's* right." She pointed to Dulle, who was taking a moment to study his notes. "He knows the truth. Ben's just covering up."

I stopped grinning. "You're saying the project's just a scam? Mom, you know better than that."

She glared at me. "Of course it's not a scam. I built *Galactique* with my bare hands, didn't I?" She often said that, even though it technically wasn't true. "But your great-grandmother told me the whole story after I married your"—she stopped herself before she could mention Dad, which she no longer did—"after I got married. Yes, the foundation bought off Wessen. The money was funneled through his PAC, but I bet he didn't spend a dime of it on his campaign. Everyone knew he didn't have a chance, anyway. He got knocked out of the race in the New Hampshire primary."

This was the first time in ages my mother had spoken much about anything except radishes and tomatoes, but I hardly noticed. "So you're saying there really was a payoff?"

"Senator Wessen was the best politician money could buy, and we had him in our pocket." Then she smiled at me. "I think I'd like some tea, dear. Would you make some?"

I didn't know what else to say or do, so I got up from the couch, went into the kitchen, and put the teapot on the stove. I stood there for a long time, watching the steam slowly rise from the spout as I played with the teabag between my fingers. No one had ever told me any of this. Until a couple of weeks earlier, I'd never even heard of Senator Wessen. And while I could hardly blame my great-grandmother for doing what needed to be done in order to get *Galactique* off the ground, it was still disturbing to learn that the Arkwright Foundation had indulged in some rather sleazy tactics to achieve its goals.

The subcommittee had begun to question Grandpa when I returned to the living room. Representative Dulle had distributed copies of Senator Wessen's campaign records to the other members, and they were coming at my grandfather from all sides. Suddenly, Grandpa didn't look so certain of himself. Behind him, Grandma sat stiffly in her chair. Although her face showed no expression, I could tell that she was nervous.

"Better hope those guys don't have the goods on us," Mom said as I handed the tea mug to her, "or we're screwed."

But they did. And we were.

8

The congressional investigation was the beginning of the end of federal funding for the Arkwright Foundation. Despite Grandpa's best efforts, Dulle got his way. He had allies on both sides of the hill, and under pressure from the House and Senate, the National Science Foundation cut its appropriation, as meager as it really was. Once again, Juniper Ridge was on its own, but even as my grandparents scrambled to find a way to make up for the loss, worse things were happening far, far away.

About the same time this was going on, *Galactique* was approaching a star system about midway to Eos: Gliese 832, an M-class red dwarf 10.5 light-years from Earth. This nameless little star didn't have much going for it: a couple of gas giants, but no Earth-mass planets within its habitable zone. The ship would pass through the outermost reaches of the system, though, so the mission planners had decided to have the ship conduct a brief survey as it swept by, just in case there was anything there worth noting. Besides, it would give them a chance to calibrate the ship's sensors and make sure they were functioning the way they were supposed to once *Galactique* reached Gliese 667C, even though it would take more than a decade for the results to reach Juniper Ridge.

Galactique's beamsail had long since ceased its primary function, but since then, it had become useful for something else—a shield against the interstellar dust that would have chewed the ship apart if the sail hadn't been there. The sail was probably riddled with pinholes by the time *Galactique* made its flyby of Gliese 832, but it should have deflected anything that might have damaged the ship.

It didn't.

We'll never know exactly what happened, because the AI didn't report a specific cause, so we can only guess. The most likely scenario is some bit of transient debris in the outer system—a tiny piece of a long-dead comet, a miniscule fragment of a stray object—came in an oblique angle that caused it to miss the sail entirely and, in a one-in-a-billion chance collision, hit the ship. It couldn't have been very big, or else it would have destroyed *Galactique*; in fact, it may have been not much larger than a piece of gravel.

Size doesn't matter when it comes to something like this, though, because the effect was catastrophic. It knocked out communications with Earth.

Galactique carried two 1,250-watt lasers, powered by the ship's nuclear reactor and mounted side by side outside the service module. The reason for this redundancy was that, even if one laser went dead, the other would continue to function. Yet it wasn't the lasers themselves that were hit but something else: the electrical bus that supplied juice to the array. That was in an exposed part of the service module outside the hull plates protecting the ship's interior components. Perhaps the lasers should have been independently mounted, each with its own bus, but no one can predict every possible contingency; we can't blame the engineers too much for failure of foresight.

In any case, our hypothetical little rock clipped the line. In that instant, *Galactique* went dark.

The AI would have detected the problem immediately, if not the precise cause, and acted upon it. The array was withdrawn into the service module, where the spider-bots went to work on it. By the ship's internal chronometer, the repair job probably took only a few days, but time dilation made it seem much longer to observers back on Earth. We didn't even know about the accident for more than ten years.

By then, a lot had changed back home.

9

I met Robert in the second semester of my sophomore year, which I'd originally intended to be my last hurrah at UMass. If it hadn't been for him, I might have gone ahead with my original plan to transfer to UC–Davis and move out west.

By then, I felt comfortable enough about matters at home to think about leaving Massachusetts and setting out on my own. Although the Galactique Project was no longer receiving federal funds, Grandma came up with the idea of turning the Arkwright Foundation into a publicly supported nonprofit, thus allowing them to sell memberships, conduct fund-raising drives, and otherwise do whatever it took to keep the MC open and maintain the communications lifeline with the ship (it would still be many years before we learned about the accident). My mother found a new pastime in running the foundation website, and Grandma took to writing a monthly newsletter that told the foundation's supporting members what was happening on Juniper Ridge.

Representative Dulle continued to harass us—not satisfied with depriving the Arkwright Foundation of NSF funding, he was also determined to have the Justice Department open its own civil investigation—but we were assured by the foundation's attorney and our own congressman that he wouldn't get far. With Senator Wessen's buy-off decades in the past and the principal figures involved with the scandal long since deceased, no one was taking Dulle very seriously. The bastard got his pound of flesh, and he'd just have to be happy with it.

The foundation was just scraping by, but Grandpa was confident it would survive. I came home for the summer and helped around the place, but already I was itching to leave. During my freshman year, I'd taken weekend trips with my friends to Boston and New York, where I'd gone on gondola rides through flooded downtown streets and caught plays at rooftop theaters. I'd seen a side of life far different from tiny little Crofton, and I wanted more of it. And although Mom still wanted me to stay close enough for her to feel as if I was safe from the sinister forces she persisted in believing were ready to pounce—Dulle had replaced the New American Congregation as her nemesis—Grandma assured me that she was getting along well enough that I didn't need to be concerned about her. If I still wanted to go to California, no one would stand in my way.

Then I met Robert.

As these things sometimes happen, it was entirely accidental. Some oaf brushed up against me as I was leaving the serving line in the student union cafeteria and caused me to drop my tray. The carton of milk on it fell upon the shoes of the student behind me, and as I stammered my apologies, he stooped down to help me clean up the mess. I looked up and found a pair of quiet gray eyes regarding me with amusement and just a bit of interest. He put aside his own tray, asked me to wait a minute, and then went back into the line and replaced everything I'd lost, running his thumb across the scanner to pay for them. And then he asked if I'd join him for lunch.

That was Robert Ignatz. Not Rob or Bob, and never Bobby—Robert. He was tall and kind of skinny, with a thatch of dark-brown hair that was comb resistant and a shyness that was almost as deep as my own. He was an art student studying holosculpture with a minor in industrial design, which is why we'd never shared a class. Indeed, if it hadn't been for the cafeteria accident, we probably would have never met. Speaking to girls had always been a problem for him, so he took the fact that I'd soaked his shoes with milk as a heaven-sent opportunity to meet one.

Hell if it didn't work. Robert and I had lunch together, and when it was over, I gave him my number and let him know that I wasn't doing anything special that weekend, and that was how things got started. I'd met a few guys during the last couple of years at UMass, but none were especially attractive. Indeed, most reminded me of Teddy Romero; ten minutes with them, and it was obvious what their intentions were. I'd begun to wonder whether I was a lesbian or destined to become a nun when I met Robert, who didn't even try to take my hand until I took his first and nearly fainted when I stopped him on the sidewalk outside the theater where we went for our third date and told that I wouldn't mind a kiss.

Besides social awkwardness, Robert and I had a couple of other things in common. The first was little previous sexual experience. When we finally mustered the courage to go to bed together—I kicked my roommate out for the night; she didn't argue, just went down the hall to shack up with her own boyfriend—I discovered that it didn't matter very much that I'd only once before been with a guy, because that was one time more than my dear sweet Robert had been with a girl. But he was as tender as Teddy had been callous and also delightfully indefatigable. We didn't sleep much that night.

The second was that he'd also come from a broken family. His mother had left when he was young, and his father never seemed to care very much for him. Although they lived in Connecticut, he went back as little as he could; his dad considered the presence of a grown-up son to be an impediment to his new life as a roaming stud. So Robert had made the UMass campus his home, and he'd already decided that he'd remain in Amherst after graduation; he liked it there, and he already had a line on getting a job at an industrial design studio in Springfield, where he worked part-time as an intern.

When he told me this, I knew that I was going to give up California. If the choice was between transferring to UC–Davis and or staying at UMass with Robert, then it was obvious which way I'd go. No regrets. By the second semester of our junior year, we'd left the dorms and found an off-campus apartment, and when we graduated a year and a half later, I walked away with a diploma under one arm and the other around my best friend, lover, and chosen companion for life.

So I didn't move out west but instead remained in New England. That's another reason I was lucky to have met Robert. The decision to stay close to home changed my life when Na came.

10

Everyone who was alive at the time remembers where they were and what they were doing when the world learned of the existence of 2099 NA-2.

I was twenty-nine years old, a science teacher at Amherst High, and living with Robert in a two-century-old farmhouse in the nearby town of Leverett. We'd never married and saw no real reason to do so; our relationship was solid, and since we both had parents whose marriages had ended badly, we didn't want jinx things by repeating their mistake. Robert worked out of the house; his rising reputation as a holosculptor had enabled him to leave his job at the design firm a couple of years earlier to set up his own studio, where he earned a little extra money teaching students the fine art of painting with light. We had no children, but that was something we were considering; in the meantime, we were happy contributing to the education of other people's kids.

So I was in the faculty room between classes, having coffee and glancing over the homework my students had just sent me, when another teacher said, "Oh, my god, *no!*" I looked up. The wall screen was logged on to a newsnet, and the first thing I saw was something that looked like a fuzzy little white blob against a black background.

From my childhood on Juniper Ridge, I'd learned to recognize a space telescope image when I saw it. My first thought was that it was a star or perhaps a newly discovered exoplanet somewhere many light-years from Earth. But it wasn't either, and it was much closer than that. It was the monster we'd all come to know as Na.

When it was first discovered four months earlier by Spaceguard's orbital telescope, 2099 NA-2 appeared to be just another near-Earth object whose elliptical orbit would carry it past to our world. There are nearly countless NEOs like it, but the vast majority of them come no closer than the Moon. This particular asteroid was a little more than half of an astronomical unit from Earth when it was first spotted, and it was first believed that it would come no closer than the Moon; as a matter of routine, it was classified as a potentially hazardous object, worth watching but probably no more hazardous than any of the many PHOs discovered every year. Shortly after this particular asteroid crossed Mars orbit, though, planetary astronomers reexamined the data and came to the realization that it was much more dangerous than that. A Spaceguard alert team at the Lowell Observatory in Arizona was assigned to study 2099 NA-2, and what they found caused them to immediately contact their counterparts in Hawaii and ask them to confirm their findings. A few days later, the Maui observatory delivered its verdict, and it was grim indeed.

First, 2099 NA-2 was on collision course with Earth. Traveling at 27,000 MPH, in two and a half months, it would sail straight into our planet.

Second, and worse, this was a *big* asteroid. A class-C carbonaceous-chondrite rock shaped like a potato, it was about half a mile wide and a little more than a mile long—as newscasters would become fond of calling it, "a flying mountain" (the name *Na* came a little later; the phonetic pronunciation as "nah" was irresistible). It wasn't going to be another dinosaur killer like the one that turned *Tyrannosaurus rex* into an interesting fossil, but nonetheless, June 17, 2099, was going to be a very bad day for every living creature on Earth.

Typically, the public was the last to know. The highest echelons of the world's governments were the first to receive the information, and as conference room lights burned late in capitols from Washington, D.C. to Beijing, it was secretly agreed that the news would be withheld until the various defense and science ministries got their acts together and all the options were studied. By then, it had been determined that Na would likely come down somewhere in the Pacific, which was both good news and bad—good because it would miss any major land masses, bad because of the potential long-term effect on the global climate, not to mention the immediate consequences for the coastal areas and islands in the region.

There was one mitigating factor: Na was still far enough away that something could be done about it. Obviously, the coastal population centers and island chains of the Pacific would have to be evacuated in advance of the inevitable tsunamis. Yet there was also the possibility, however slim, that Na might be diverted. In fact, when the first news conference was held, it was announced that the *Comstock*, an asteroid-mining spacecraft belonging to Translunar Resources that was currently operating just beyond the Moon, was already on its way to deep-space rendezvous with Na. Once it arrived, *Comstock*'s crew would undertake the mission of planting their mass driver on Na and using it nudge the asteroid into a new trajectory.

We were told not to panic, that the authorities were on top of the situation, and that doomsday was not inevitable. And for the most part, people took it well. Generally speaking, there wasn't the mass hysteria and anarchy that many predicted would come from an announcement like that. To be sure, there were those who fortified their homes, grabbed every firearm they could lay their hands on, and prepared themselves for the end of the world (for which, I suspect, many of them secretly hoped). By and large, though, the vast majority of individuals determined that they would do what they could to help their friends and family survive. Some found solace in religion, others in a steadfast faith in the human spirit. Some even believed that the whole thing was either a hoax or just a scare that would soon blow over, and everyone would wake up on June 18 to find that the world was just the same and nothing had changed.

In any case, the public was repeatedly assured that there was a strong probability that *Comstock's* mission would be a success and that the mandatory evacuations were only a precaution. Relatively few people knew that the mission was a long shot. Until then, asteroid miners had only succeeded in moving NEOs no more than a few hundred feet in diameter. Na was much larger than that, and its greater mass meant a correspondingly higher inertia; *Comstock's* mass driver might not be adequate for the task. And blowing up the asteroid was out of the question; even if *Comstock* were carrying explosive charges sufficient for a job of that magnitude—which it wasn't—it would have only meant that, instead getting hit by one big rock, Earth would be subjected to a rain of smaller rocks, some of which might come down in populated areas. Not only that, but it would take the mining team almost three weeks to reach Na, during which time the asteroid would have traveled over twelve million miles closer to Earth, shaving the odds of success that much finer.

The authorities deliberately overstated the chances for a successful diversion in order to avoid a mass panic, and for a while, they were successful. Life went on as usual. But as the realization of the magnitude of the disaster and its long-term consequences—namely, a global winter that could last several years—slowly sank in, even communities far from the projected impact zone began making preparations.

The week after the announcement was made, the Amherst board of education voted to suspend school indefinitely so that children could help their families do whatever needed to be done. Suddenly, I no longer had a job. Which was just as well, because a couple of days later, Grandpa called and asked me to come home.

Grandma had passed away a couple of years earlier, leaving him and Mom alone on Juniper Ridge. So he'd been forced to divide his time between monitoring the MC and taking care of her, and although she'd lately become a little more independent, it was still a stretch for a man in his eighties who'd passed the age for retrotherapy. But that wasn't all.

"Dhani, your mother's scared," Grandpa said. "She'd been doing better, but now . . ."

"Is she pulling back into her shell?"

"I'm afraid so, yeah. There are days when I can barely get her out of the house, and when I talk to her, she keeps saying that she wishes you were still around." A sigh. "I know it's a lot to ask, but if you and Robert could bring yourselves to come home, even for a little while . . ."

His voice trailed off. He didn't say the rest; he didn't need to. Mom had accepted Robert only grudgingly, and not without some initial suspicion. She'd never trusted strangers very much; in her mind, Robert was the outsider who'd taken her daughter away from her. Robert had done his best to get along with her, but she'd never completely warmed up to him, and so our visits had been for only a few days at a time. What Grandpa was talking about, though, was a longer stay. Much longer.

I glanced across the living room at Robert. He'd linked his ear jack to the house phone and was quietly listening in. Our eyes met, and he answered my silent question with a nod. "Of course we will," I replied. "Just give us a few days to board up the place, and we'll be back there."

"Thanks. I appreciate it." He let out his breath in relief. "Tell you what—I'll even move upstairs and let you two have the downstairs bedroom."

"That's all right, Grandpa. I think we can manage without it." Hearing this, Robert gave me a grim smile. We'd have less privacy upstairs, with Mom's room next to mine, but I didn't want Grandpa to have to climb stairs more than he had to. I decided to change the subject. "How's *Galactique* doing? What's the latest?"

Another pause, this time longer. "I don't know," he said at last. "I didn't want to tell you this, but we lost contact about ten days ago. The lunar station hasn't received any telemetry for over a week."

"Nothing?"

"Nothing. Not even a status report. *Galactique*'s gone dark."

Again, Robert and I traded a look. He knew what that might mean as well as I did.

"We'll be home as soon as we can," I said.

11

In hindsight, it's fortunate that Juniper Ridge had always been self-sufficient. Because my father and grandparents dreaded having the MC knocked out of commission by a local power failure, they'd set up solar panels to provide the observatory with electricity, and the rest of our power came from the town's wind turbine on a nearby hilltop. The house drew its water from deep artesian wells, and Mom's obsession with the greenhouse meant that we'd have food even though we would probably have to tighten our belts a bit. And there were other things, like the snowplow Grandpa had attached to the front of his truck and the stockpiles of canned food we customarily kept for the winter months when we couldn't easily go shopping. So we were better prepared than most.

Still, Robert and I had our hands full as soon as we arrived. The roof of the main house badly needed to be reshingled, the firewood supply was down to half a cord, and the windows would have to be freshly weather-stripped. Grandpa was in no shape to tackle these jobs on his own, so it fell to us to prepare for Na's aftermath. Luckily, the asteroid had picked a good time to make its appearance; in New England, late spring is the best season to take care of such matters.

But Mom was in bad shape. As Grandpa told me, the news about

Na had messed up her mind, sending her back into the depression she'd struggled with for as long as I could remember. She welcomed me with open arms and tears but only gave Robert a tentative handshake and stared in horror as he carried our bags inside. Things might have been a little better if we'd been officially married, but . . . well, too late for that now. She gradually accepted the fact that he was living in the same house, but it took her a week just to get used to the idea that she'd have to share the upstairs bathroom with a strange man.

Yet we received aid from an unexpected source: Joni Ogilvy.

In the years since I'd grown up and moved away, my teenage best friend had changed, as well. While her twin sister, Sara, had moved to London and become an executive at Lloyd's, Joni had remained in Crofton after her parents' death to get married and take over the family's horse farm.

Tall and well built, with long corn-silk hair and cool green eyes, Joni could have been a runway model if she'd cared to go that way, but she was as direct and no-nonsense as only a country lady could be. It had been quite a few years since I'd last seen her, so I was surprised the day she and Brett walked down the road to our house. Noticing Robert climbing a ladder to the roof, Joni told me that they had a couple of pallets of leftover shingles from their own re-roofing job and that we were welcome to them. Considering that every hardware store in western Massachusetts was being cleaned out of stuff like that, it was an offer that was both generous and impossible to refuse.

Teddy Romero was long gone. After his father died, he'd sold the trailer and left Crofton. No one had ever seen him again. Good riddance. At least I wouldn't have to worry about having him show up at the house. On the other hand, having Joni and Brett as neighbors was a comfort. Once she and I renewed our friendship, I knew that our families would be able to rely on each other during the tough times ahead.

If only all our problems could have been solved as easily. The MC was something else entirely. While it wasn't critical to our survival, nonetheless it was the reason my family had remained on Juniper Ridge in the first place. Yet the Arkwright Foundation had suffered greatly from Grandma's death. Member donations had dwindled to a trickle, and while the computers in the MC were old and badly in need of an upgrade, replacing them was out of the question. Grandpa had kept them going as best as he could, but without Mom helping him, his efforts were inadequate at best.

I knew how to run the MC, but I didn't know how to fix it. The computers were still operational, more or less, but the radio dish no longer had a full range of motion; we could hear the gears of its platform creak from the floor above when it moved. And the screens remained resolutely dark whenever we tried to download new data from the lunar tracking station.

Was *Galactique* no more? Was its long silence an indication that the ship had somehow been destroyed? Or was it simply a communications blackout, and eventually we'd receive new data? We had no way of knowing. Every day, Grandpa sent a new query, one which approximately asked, "Hello? How are you? Where are you? Please respond at once!" No reply. Just more silence.

"You realize, of course, there's great irony to this," Grandpa said one afternoon.

"How's that?" I took a sip of water from a canteen and passed it to Robert. The three of us were sitting in a clearing on the hillside below the observatory, taking a break from using a chain saw to cut up some dead trees on our property. Mom was in the dome, taking her turn at what had begun to appear to be an exercise in futility, waiting for *Galactique* to tell us that it was still alive and well.

"Your great-great-great-grandfather started this whole thing because he was concerned about the human race getting wiped out by an asteroid." I must have had some sort of expression on my face, because he grinned and nodded. "It's true. Not many people know it, but that's the reason he willed his estate to the Arkwright Foundation in the first place."

"I thought it was because he wanted to build a starship. That's what Mom told me." I might have added that my father told me the same thing too, but it had been so many years since the last time I'd seen him that I seldom even thought about him anymore.

"Oh, I'm sure that was a reason too. Otherwise, he would've had us digging bunkers." Grandpa shrugged. "But going to the stars says something that digging a hole in the ground doesn't. It says you've got hopes for the future that goes beyond mere survival. Maybe it's because he was a science fiction writer that he saw things that way, but . . . well, at any rate, he was ahead of the curve."

"But the human race isn't going to get wiped out," Robert said. Then he added, with just a touch of uncertainty, "Is it?"

Grandpa didn't say anything for a moment. Instead, he gazed down the hill. It was a lovely afternoon; blue sky, no clouds, warm breeze, fresh leaves on the trees. Hard to believe anything bad could ever happen to a world as perfect as this.

"Probably not," he said at last. "We survived the global climate change of the last century, what with droughts and superstorms and coastal flooding and all that. The world lost a billion and a half people, but it took decades for the population to drop. Humans are adaptive creatures and pretty resilient when push comes to shove." He picked up a small log we'd just cut and idly began to strip off the bark. "This is different. Even if they manage to evacuate everyone from the coastal areas before the tsunamis come in, Na's going to vaporize a lot of seawater when it hits the ocean. That's going to cloud the upper atmosphere and in turn cause a climatic chain reaction." He looked up at the sky. "We may not have another day like this for a very long time. And not everyone has a greenhouse out back."

"But *Comstock* might still succeed, right?"

Grandpa and I shared a look. We understood the physics of the situation better than most people, my partner included, so we knew what a crapshoot the asteroid-deflection mission really was. "Sure . . . sure, it's got a chance," Grandpa said, and then he dropped the log and bent down to pick up the chain saw. "Well, c'mon, this wood isn't going to cut itself."

We spent a couple of more hours on the firewood, and then Grandpa and Robert went back to the house and took the truck to Joni and Brett's house to start loading the shingles they were giving us. We'd soon be repaying the favor by helping them bale hay for their horses. There was a lot of high grass growing in the mountain meadows abutting her property and ours, so the seven horses she owned would have enough to eat. They would be useful if and when there was no longer enough sunlight to adequately recharge the solar panels of our cars and the truck. And although no one spoke of it, we all knew that, if things got bad enough that we couldn't feed either them or ourselves, Joni's beloved horses might have to serve another purpose, as well.

I finished stacking the wood we'd just cut and then went back up to the house. I was about to go inside and start work on dinner when I heard a vehicle coming up the road. It was still out of sight around a bend and behind the trees, so at first I believed it was Grandpa's truck—which was a little odd; it takes time to load several pallets of shingles. Then it came into view, and I saw that it was a big black sports van.

No one we knew drove anything like that, so I raised my wrist phone and called Mom. "We've got company," I said when she answered. This was something we always did, giving her a chance to hide if she wanted to. My mother never liked unexpected visitors.

"All right," she replied. "Tell me when they're gone."

By then, I could see that it had tinted windows and light-blue all-state plates. I walked down the front path to the end of the driveway and waited until it came to a stop. The driver's-side door opened, and a young guy in an air force uniform got out.

"Can I help you?" I asked.

He seemed to hesitate, as if uncertain who I was. "Are you Chandraleska Skinner?"

An odd question. It was rare that people mistook me for my mother. We bore a certain similarity, but you could only mix us up if you hadn't seen her in quite a while, and most people hadn't. "No, I'm her daughter, Dhani."

He said nothing but instead went to the back of the van, slid open the rear door, and spoke to whoever was seated in back. I couldn't hear what he said. A couple of moments passed, and then two people climbed out. One was a heavy-set woman with ginger hair, who wore a pantsuit that, like the van and its driver, looked government issue. The other was a middle-aged man with white hair, thin and slightly stooped. He came out last, and for a long time, he simply stared at me, as if waiting for me to say something.

"Dhani," he said at last. "You've grown up."

If he hadn't spoken, it might have taken me a couple of minutes to recognize him as my father.

12

At the same moment, relativistically speaking, that I was looking at my father for the first time in fourteen years and trying to figure out what to say to him, *Galactique* was trying to bridge a communications gap of its own.

The spider-bots had taken only a few days to repair the laser array; it was just a matter of taking a little extra cable from the ship's spare-parts supply and splicing it into the main bus. Once power was restored to the lasers, the array was redeployed to the outer hull, where a quick test confirmed that the system was back on line.

Now came the hard part: locating Earth's position so that communications could be restored. *Galactique*'s planet of origin, along with its sun and all its neighboring worlds, had vanished into the cone of darkness that lay behind the ship; the Doppler effect caused by the ship's .5c velocity had rendered them invisible. To further complicate matters, no navigation updates from Juniper Ridge had been received during the blackout. So the ship had to rely entirely upon itself to determine Earth's location and send a laser pulse in that precise direction—a feat roughly equivalent to a sharpshooter with a high-powered rifle trying to hit a sparrow sitting on a tree branch ten miles away while wearing a blindfold.

Fortunately, *Galactique*'s quantum AI had something our hypothetical sharpshooter didn't have: detailed star maps that included the precise locations of known pulsars in the galaxy. Since each pulsar emitted radio beams on a unique frequency, the ship was able to use them as beacons, sort of like interstellar lighthouses. Together with superb sense of direction based upon the ship's current position and estimated trajectory and the internal chronometers accurate to the nanosecond, *Galactique* had the ability to predict where Earth and the Moon would be located, not just then but also in the future. All this involved a very difficult set of parallel calculations in four dimensions. It may have even taken as long as two or three minutes.

Then it fired off a message and waited for a reply.

13

It hardly needs to be said that I wasn't the only one who was stunned by Dad's return. When my mother walked into the living room to find her husband, whom she'd all but given up for dead, sitting there along with me and the two people who'd brought him back to Juniper Ridge, she didn't do anything but stare at him with wide, unblinking eyes. Her mouth opened, shut, opened again; I could tell that she was having trouble breathing, let alone finding anything to say. She swayed back and forth on her feet, and for a moment, I was afraid that her legs would give out from under her. As I rose from the couch, though, so did my father from the armchair that had been his usual place many years ago.

"Chandi . . . I'm home." Stepping toward her, he started to raise his hands. "Honey . . . I'm so, so sorry. I—"

"Don't." Her left hand shot up, palm open and facing outward. "Just"—she looked away, her hand trembling—"don't. I don't want . . ."

"Mom?" I headed for her. "Mom, are you okay?" Stupid question. Of course she wasn't okay.

"No . . . no . . ." Looking away from both Dad and me, she wheeled about and staggered away. My mother never had a drink for as long as I knew her, but just then, she looked just the way Dad did those nights when he came home late from the Kick Inn. "Just . . . everyone, just leave me alone."

Then she was gone, stumbling back through the door from which she'd just emerged, heading back to the observatory, where she'd been until I'd made the awful mistake of asking her to come over to the house without telling her who was waiting for her. I wasn't trying to be mean, and it wasn't as if I'd meant to say, "Surprise! Look who's home!" It was simply that I'd had no idea how to tell her that Dad had suddenly reappeared, and I decided that maybe it was best if she saw it for herself. Which only goes to prove that you can be intelligent and still be pretty stupid.

I turned to Dad. He was still standing there, face as white as his hair had become, hands still raised to embrace his wife. He looked at me and said, "Dhani, I didn't . . . I don't . . ."

"Shut up." I've never hit anyone in my life, but in that moment, all I wanted to do was deck him. Somehow, I managed to control myself. "Sit down," I said, pointing to his chair. "Now talk . . . no, wait." I took a second to use my wrist phone to call Grandpa. "Come home at once," I said when he answered. "Dad's come back." I didn't wait for a reply but simply clicked off. "Okay . . . start talking."

"Perhaps it would better if I explained," said the woman who'd shown up with my father. She and the air force officer were sitting on the other side of the room. "I'm Cassandra O'Neill, and this is Captain Philip Jensen, and we're—"

"No. Him first, and then you." I didn't even look at them; my attention was solely upon my father. "Go."

Dad dropped his hands and let out his breath, and then he slowly lowered himself into his chair. "Dhanishta, I don't know where to begin, but . . ." He shook his head. "All right, I'll try."

Fourteen years ago, he and the woman he'd met in town—it took a while for him to even speak her name, Sally Metcalfe—had taken off for what he originally thought would be no more than a few weeks, maybe a few months at most. Their destination was Denver, her hometown, where she'd told him that she still had friends, family, a job, and something like a future.

But first, they decided to have a little adventure. After abandoning his car in Boston, they'd boarded the transtube and used it weave their way across the country, getting off the maglev every now and then to sample the nightlife in the places where they landed. In this way, they'd drifted from bar to bar, motel to motel, eating in crappy restaurants, nursing hangovers, doing all the things two people did when they were on a long binge and running away from whatever it was they had left behind.

It may or may not have been fun, because Dad had little memory of that time. Blackouts were part of the ride, I guess. The next time he was able to think clearly at all, it was when he woke up to find himself in a jail cell in Denver, with no recollection of how he'd gotten there. Sally was gone, and somewhere along the line, his belongings had vanished, as well. He never saw her again.

The biggest shock, though, was discovering that seven months had passed since the day he'd walked out of my life and my mother's.

Dad was picked up by the Denver cops after he was found on the sidewalk outside a downtown wino bar. Someone had taken his wallet and what little money he had left, so being charged with vagrancy and public drunkenness was only the least of his problems. He was homeless, and just to put the icing on the cake, he began to suffer the DTs within hours of waking up in jail.

"Being taken to the hospital was probably the best thing that could have happened to me," Dad said. "After I got out and had my day in court, the judge realized that I needed treatment more than jail time. So I was sent to a substance abuse center and—"

"You're still not telling me where you've been for the last fourteen years." I didn't mean to be cold, but I was becoming impatient with him. "Not to mention why you've picked this time to come back."

"Maybe I can answer those questions," Grandpa said.

He and Robert had come into the living room so quietly that I hadn't noticed either of them. Dad looked around as he spoke. "Hi, Papa," he said quietly. "Good to see you again."

"You're looking better, son. Staying off the bottle, I hope?"

"Clean and sober for thirteen years."

"Glad to hear it. And the new job's working out?"

"Well, it's not so new anymore." Dad smiled just a little. "I've been there about—"

"Wait a minute!" I stared first at Dad and then Grandpa. "Am I getting this straight? You knew where he's been all this time?"

Grandpa slowly let out his breath. There were no vacant chairs left in the room, so he leaned against a wall, folding his arms across his chest. "Robert, do you think you could make some coffee, please? Thanks." Robert nodded and left the room, and Grandpa went on. "I heard from your father shortly after he went into treatment. He wanted to come back, but I didn't want to have a repeat of what happened here."

"Which is probably what *would* have happened," Dad said. "If I'd returned, it would've been only a matter of time before I became a barfly again." He couldn't look at me as he said this. "I'm sorry, Dhani, but I'd hurt you and your mother enough already, so I took your grandfather's advice and stayed away."

"I didn't let either you or your mother know," Grandpa said, speaking to me, "because you were both in a lot of pain, and it would take a long time for the wounds to heal. So I quietly kept in touch with him while he rebuilt his life, and when he was ready to leave the halfway house . . ."

"I was there for two and half years. It took me a long time to get over drinking." Dad paused, looking down at the floor again. "And when I did, I just couldn't face either of you again. Not after what I'd done."

"So we decided that it was probably just as well if he made a clean break of it, started over again out west." Grandpa was looking embarrassed, as well. Perhaps he'd never expected this day to come. "I called Win and Martha Crosby and asked them if they could find a job for him in California, and they managed to get him a staff position at UC–Davis."

My mouth fell open. "I almost transferred there!"

"I know." My father slowly nodded. "I was hoping that, once you did, I might be able to reconnect with you, get you back into my life again. But—"

"I met Robert and stayed here."

"So I figured that perhaps it was just as well and kept my distance." Again, he sighed. "Dhani, you don't know . . . you can't know . . . how hard it's been. Even after I got straight, there hasn't been a day that I don't regret everything I did to you and your mother. But I was so afraid that, if I came back, I'd wind up in the Kick Inn again."

"Okay, so you stayed in California. Good for you." I wasn't ready to forgive him, but at least I understood his long absence a little better. Perhaps he was right. As hard as his departure had been for Mom, returning home only to start drinking again would have killed her. "But that doesn't explain why you've picked this time to come home." I glanced over at O'Neill and Jensen. "Who are these people, anyway?"

"I'd like to know that myself," Grandpa said.

"This is where I come in." Cassandra O'Neill cleared her throat. "Dr. Skinner, Ms. Skinner, Phil and I are with DARPA . . . perhaps you've heard of us?" I nodded, and she went on. "We belong to the special task force assigned to finding a way of deflecting Na before it hits Earth, and it's because Matt got in touch with us that we've come out here."

Jensen spoke up. "Dr. Skinner neglected to mention what Matt has been doing in California the last decade or so. He's been working with the Crosbys on applied high-energy research, contributing his knowledge of the Galactique Project to their efforts to develop alternate propulsion systems for the next generation of interstellar vessels. Ones large enough to carry living people."

"Specifically, we're looking at the using outer system resources for fusion engines," Dad said. "There have been proposals to extract helium-3 from Jupiter's upper atmosphere. Or maybe even Saturn's; its radiation fields aren't nearly as intense, so it would be easier to reach it. A high-power beamer like the foundation's is an optimal way of getting there . . . we kinda leapfrogged over fusion when we built *Galactique*."

"There's another application, as well," O'Neill said. "It's something of a long shot, but Win Crosby has calculated that it may be possible to use the foundation beamer to deflect Na. It's a 120-terawatt system, after all—much more power than the 38-gigawatt beamer the consortium built."

Grandpa let out a low whistle. "I'll be damned. Why the hell didn't I think of that?"

I didn't say so, but I knew the reason. He'd had other things on his mind, like fretting over *Galactique*'s loss of telemetry and taking care of Mom, to think much about a microwave satellite he'd shut down the day I was born. "Does that thing even work?" I asked. "It's been out of service for years."

"We sent a crew out there just last week to examine it," Jensen said. "It needs some repair work, but otherwise, it's still in operational condition. However, it can't be reactivated or maneuvered except from here because—"

"We're the only ones who have the operating system," Grandpa said.

"Right. And that's why I've come back." Dad looked straight at me as he said this. "Once we get the beamer up and running again, we might be able use it to push Na just enough to nudge it from its current trajectory." He shrugged. "I mean, it was built to boost a three-hundred-foot starship up to half the speed of light, so it should be able to shove a big, dumb rock just a few hundred feet. That's all it would take, really."

"We may be able to do that, yes." Grandpa slowly nodded as he looked away from us. "I think the three of us know enough about the beamer to get it to do what needs to be done. Isn't that right, Chandi?"

I looked in the direction he was gazing. Unobserved by any of us, my mother had come back into the house. I had no idea how long she'd been standing there or how much she'd heard; she said nothing, but instead stared at Dad with dark and haunted eyes. My father turned to gaze at her, and she visibly flinched when their eyes met, but she didn't flee as I expected her to.

"It's possible," she said so quietly that it was almost a whisper.

14

This was as close to a happy family reunion as we got. The knowledge that for every minute we wasted Na traveled another 450 miles meant that Grandpa, Mom, and I didn't have time to reconcile our feelings toward Dad. Robert had barely returned to the living room with coffee before O'Neill and Jensen hustled us over to the dome so they could inspect the MC. One look at the antique computers Grandpa had been pampering for years because the foundation no longer had the money for regular upgrades, and O'Neill was on her phone. Late that evening, a USAF gyro touched down on the lawn outside the house, bearing state-of-the-art computers and the best technicians the Pentagon had to offer.

From that moment, Juniper Ridge and the Galactique Project fell under military jurisdiction. No one was allowed to leave the premises, and all outside phone calls or email messages were screened. Jensen would have placed soldiers at a roadblock leading to the observatory if Grandpa hadn't pointed out that doing so would have attracted the attention we didn't want. Except for Joni, people seldom visited the observatory, but everyone in Crofton would have known something was going on if they'd seen military people swarming in. He reluctantly agreed that the low-key approach was probably the best, and that's how we handled it. I went down the road and asked Joni and Brett to stay away for a few days; I didn't tell them why, and they didn't ask too many uncomfortable questions.

Along with Jensen and O'Neill, my father was installed in the cottage, which had gone largely unused since the Crosbys moved out years earlier. I don't think they saw much of the place, though. Along with Grandpa, they spent most of their time in the MC, working around the clock to help the technicians replace the old computers with the new ones and make sure the data and operating systems were successfully transferred from one to another. In the meantime, another group of technicians worked on the dish upstairs, restoring it to full operating condition. They napped in their chairs and gobbled down the sandwiches and soup Robert and I carried over from the house, and if there hadn't been a restroom in the observatory, I think they would've been urinating in the bushes.

At first, Mom kept her distance. She went up to her room and hid there for the first day, emerging only to go downstairs for a quick meal. But her memory of the beamer operating systems was sharper than my grandfather's, so it was only a matter of time before Grandpa came over to the house, went upstairs to her room, closed the door behind him, and had a long talk with her. When he came out, Mom was with him. She'd put on a fresh change of clothes and pulled her hair back, and she didn't say a word to Robert and me as she followed my grandfather over to the dome.

Robert waited until they were gone and then turned to me. "If she tries to murder your dad, do you think the air force guys will stop her?"

"They'd better," I murmured. "I won't."

When I went over to the MC a couple of hours later, though, I found Mom and Dad seated side by side at the master console, reading information to each other as they made their way through a complex checklist. They weren't exactly holding hands, but for a moment, it almost seemed as if my father had never left. Then Dad's elbow accidentally touched hers, and she immediately recoiled, and I knew that her forgiveness wasn't likely to come anytime soon.

By late that afternoon, the MC was back on line, this time with new computers and an operating system capable of handling the new information that had been uploaded from a NASA database. The irony couldn't have been thicker. NASA had become little more than an office building in Washington, D.C., and the Arkwright Foundation had once been the target of a congressional investigation, but now the fate of the world rested upon a neglected federal agency and an impoverished nonprofit organization. It would have been sweet if Representative Dulle was still around to see this, but a heart attack had killed him a few years after his constituents voted him out of office.

While this was going on, a space construction team had been working on the beamer itself, replacing the photovoltaic panels punctured by micrometeor impacts and upgrading the focusing elements. They finished their work just a few hours after the Juniper Ridge group finished theirs, and once they'd moved away, Mom and Grandpa ran a test to make sure that the beamer was once again capable of projecting a high-power microwave beam by aiming it at a small NEO that was passing Earth at a harmless distance of about three million miles. The beam was invisible, of course, but the satellite's instruments registered it nonetheless; a few minutes after it fired, space telescopes detected a tiny dust plume rising from the asteroid's surface.

The beamer worked, but no one was ready to break out the champagne quite yet. Hitting a little NEO was one thing. Hitting Na, and having it do any good, was another. However, my father pointed out something that Win Crosby's group had determined might be in our favor. Since Na was a class-C asteroid, it was very likely that deep beneath its crust lay primordial deposits of gaseous hydrogen, oxygen, carbon, perhaps even water ice. If the beam could penetrate the surrounding rock to heat these volatiles, it was theoretically possible that they might vent outward through the crust, therefore forming plumes that would help disturb Na's trajectory.

No one knew for sure whether this would be the case. But *Comstock* was still several days away from reaching Na, and this made *Galactique*'s beamer our best hope, if not our last. So my parents, Grandpa, and Cassandra O'Neill turned the beamer so that it was aimed at the asteroid, locked on to its position, and made sure that it was being precisely tracked.

And then they fired the beam, and everyone on Juniper Ridge began holding their breaths.

15

You know the rest of the story. Or at least you may think you do, if you were alive at the time and remember hearing the news. But you weren't there on Juniper Ridge, so you don't. Here's what I saw:

For the next six days, the sat tracked Na as it fell toward Earth, its microwave beam continuously pressing the rock while toasting its surface. *Comstock* followed it from a safe distance, its crew carefully keeping out of the beam's path while constantly monitoring Na's position, watchful for any significant changes in trajectory or surface appearance. And meanwhile, back home . . .

Back home, we did what we'd always done. We waited. This time, though, it was for a different reason. For the first time, *Galactique* was all but forgotten. The fate of our little lost starship was the furthest thing from our minds.

None of us slept well during those days. We took shifts in the MC, but more often than not, there were two or three people in the MC. There was a certain fascination with the screen displaying Na's position. It never seemed to change, but we watched it constantly, hoping for the moment the asteroid would deviate from the dotted line of its projected course. Sometimes there were periods when Mom and Dad would both be there. At first, they said little to each other, but as the hours became days and the days stretched into a week, they gradually began to talk a little more.

Early one evening after dinner, I stepped out of the house for a little fresh air. The sun was just beginning to go down, and the crickets and tree frogs were commencing their nocturnal symphony. I'd only strolled as far as the driveway, though, when voices came to me from the side of the yard. Looking around, I saw my mother and father sitting together on a bench beneath a maple tree overlooking the hillside. What they were talking about, I didn't know, but the conversation was relaxed, not angry . . . and then, unexpectedly, I heard something I thought I'd never hear again.

I heard my mother laugh.

I didn't say anything but instead quietly turned around and walked back into the house. Next morning, though, I had my own conversation with Dad. I won't bore you with the details, but we had a long talk that cleared the air about a lot of things, and when it was over, I put my arms around him and gave him a long hug, and there were tears on both of our faces when we finally stepped apart.

We were a family again.

Late that afternoon, Jensen rushed into the house, where everyone else was beginning to gather for dinner. He'd just received word from *Comstock* that they had spotted a large gaseous plume jetting from Na's surface, on the side of the asteroid facing them and perpendicular to Earth. Everyone dropped what they were doing and rushed back to the observatory, where we crowded around the console and studied the real-time images from the mining ship. Nearly all the pictures were remote and fuzzy; nonetheless, something that looked like a geyser was streaming outward from Na. *Comstock*'s mass spectrometer identified it as water vapor with traces of carbon; apparently, the beam had found a subsurface ice deposit and, over the course of the last several days, heated it to the point where it finally burst through the surface as a steam jet.

And then, even as we watched in awe, Na began to move from its projected course.

Here's what everyone knows: combined with the steady pressure of the beam itself, the jet caused Na to slip the necessary few degrees from its fatal trajectory until, three weeks later, it sailed harmlessly past Earth. It came close, all right—130,000 miles, a little less than half the distance to the Moon—but just far enough away that it wasn't captured by our gravity well and pulled in. Observatories and backyard astronomers in the Pacific caught telescopic pictures of a bright spot of light that slid across the predawn sky far above the ocean, but within less than a minute, Na was gone.

But Dad stayed.

16

And so did Robert and I.

There was no reason for us to remain together on Juniper Ridge, really. Grandpa was getting up in years, but now that my father had returned, he and my mother could continue monitoring the instruments in hopes that *Galactique* might one day resume contact. Yet I didn't want to leave my parents alone while they were still mending their relationship, and since the Galactique Project was now receiving generous funds from DARPA, I didn't necessarily have to go back to teaching.

So Robert and I sold our house in Leverett and moved to Crofton, where we took up residence in the cottage. I took a new job with the state as an online tutor, and we built a studio for Robert, where he could continue sculpting—he moved from holos to old-fashioned ceramic pottery and became pretty good at that—and time passed as it always did in the Berkshires: slowly and gracefully, the seasons marking the accumulating years.

In this way, we quietly entered the twenty-second century. There had once been a time when all I'd wanted to do was leave this place. If Na had taught me one thing, though, it was the same lesson others had learned. Our lives are short, our friends and family are precious, and sometimes it's okay to stay in one place if that's where you find your life's true purpose. Mine was on Juniper Ridge. I understood that now, and I no longer minded.

My son Julian was born a couple of years later. Again, a midwife delivered him at home . . . indeed, the very same one who'd helped Mom bring me into the world thirty-two years earlier. Mom, Dad, Robert, and Joni were with me, and Joni had to catch Robert when he nearly fainted, but this time, no one went down to the Kick Inn and got drunk.

In fact, never again did I see my father take a drink of anything stronger than coffee or iced tea. He remained sober ever since. And not long after he and Mom started sleeping in the same bed again, my mother surprised us all by saying, ever so casually one Saturday morning over breakfast, that she'd like to go into Pittsfield and do a little shopping. It was the first time she'd been off the mountain in many years, and from what I could tell, she enjoyed every minute of her return to the world.

Grandpa remained with us long enough to see Julian take his first steps, and then late one afternoon, he took a nap and rejoined Grandma. His grave is on the hillside not far from the observatory, and every once in a while, I'll go down there, freshen up the roses on his stone, and have a little talk with him.

And we finally heard from *Galactique* again.

I'd just come home from driving Julian and Joni's daughter Kate to middle school—from the day my son was born, I was determined that he'd grow up with other kids, even if Robert and I had to take him ourselves every day—when Robert rushed out of the studio and grabbed me in his arms. He was still whirling me around and laughing his head off when Mom came out of the observatory. She was smiling as she told me the news: she'd just received a message from *Galactique* informing us that there had been minor accident with the communications laser but that it was fixed and the ship was still on course for Gliese 667C-e.

I only wished that Grandpa could have been there, yet he'd died still believing that *Galactique*'s silence was only temporary and we'd eventually hear from it again. Faith is a great thing. The trick is keeping it.

Dad sent a brief message acknowledging the signal, yet we knew that it wouldn't be received until the ship had reached its destination. Indeed, that was the last transmission from Juniper Ridge; there was no point in any further communiqués from us.

Yet *Galactique* continued to send us regular updates of its condition. Over the next twenty years or so, we received word of what it was doing as it closed in on Eos. A couple of months after Mom passed away, Dad and I were in the MC when we learned that *Galactique* reached Gliese 667C. The AI had jettisoned its beamsail and had deployed its magnetic brake and was now guiding the ship for a close flyby of the star so that it could capture its solar wind and commence the braking maneuver in preparation for orbital rendezvous with Eos. Julian was on his honeymoon, but he was happy to hear the news.

Dad left us again ten months later, this time for a place where no one could follow. Robert and I were now alone on Juniper Ridge, although Julian and his wife Clarice would occasionally come to visit us. I'd just read a letter from him, telling me that I'd soon become a grandmother, when Robert walked into the room. He was carrying a printout, and from the grin on his face, I knew at once that it was the message from *Galactique* I'd been expecting.

"It made it, didn't it?" I asked.

"Uh-huh. Right on schedule. And there's this too."

He handed the message to me. It was short:

SANJAY HAS WOKEN UP, AND HE SAYS HELLO.

Robert rested his hands on the back of my chair and leaned over my shoulder. "Who is Sanjay?" he asked.

"Someone my father told me about," I replied, "a long time ago."

INTERLUDE

Arrival

Galactique reached the end of its journey as a seed falling from the stars.

As it entered the outermost limits of the heliosphere surrounding Gliese 667C, the starship jettisoned the enormous beamsail that had served as its primary means of propulsion. The sail—riddled with micrometeorite holes, its once-silver outer surface blotched by radiation a cancerous shade of gray—fell away like an enormous portobello mushroom. The AI controlling the vessel observed its disappearance with no sense of loss. It was a component that had served its purpose well but was no longer needed and thus could be discarded.

It's important to know this about *Galactique*'s AI: it was not a human intelligence. It had no emotions. It did not possess a sense of wonder. It did not even reckon the passing of time the same way its creators did. This nameless, voiceless, but nonetheless cognitive machine was a quantum computer more technologically advanced than any other AI built on Earth at the same time, but a human would have had more in common with a bumblebee than this cold automaton. It observed, analyzed, and made decisions in a purely logical manner, obeying conditions and precepts programmed into its memory core by the people who'd created it. At the same time, though, it was capable of independent thought, reaching conclusions and acting upon them of its own volition.

Therefore, as it entered the solar system that had been its destination for over half a century, *Galactique* was no longer a mere vessel but instead an intelligent being. But it wasn't born of flesh and blood, and this was both its strength and its vulnerability.

Once the sail was gone, the ship fired its midsection maneuvering thrusters and performed a 180-degree turn that put its aft end in the direction of travel. Once this was done, a small, drum-shaped module located at the sail's base sprang open, and a coiled metallic hoop unfolded. Attached by a network of cables, the magnetic sail gradually expanded to several times its original size; once it was fully deployed, an electromagnetic charge was introduced to the hoop. This formed a magnet bubble around the ship that captured and deflected Gliese 667C's solar wind, thus causing a braking effect.

Slowly yet inexorably, *Galactique* began to decelerate from its .5c cruise speed. As it did so, the AI repeatedly fired its thrusters, making minute course changes so that the ship entered the system on a proper heading. It did not head straight for its target world, though, but instead vectored toward the outermost planet, Gliese 667C-g, otherwise known as Gaea. By the time it reached the immense rocky world, *Galactique* had shed most of its interstellar velocity. It jettisoned the magnetic sail and, at the lander's aft end, inflated a large ballute heat shield. It then performed an intricate aerobraking maneuver that used the ballute to reduce its speed even further against Gaea's dense methane atmosphere.

Galactique slingshot around Gaea and emerged from the other side. Its two-step deceleration procedure successfully accomplished, it continued to approach Gliese 667C's family of planets in a slower and more sedate fashion.

As it continued its journey into the system, the ship raised its sensory antenna and commenced a careful survey of the remaining seven planets, confirming and updating the information learned about them by astronomers on Earth. By human standards, the Gliese 667C system was uninhabitable. The outermost of a triad of three class-M stars in the Scorpius constellation, the star the International Astronomical Union had decided to name Calliope—the two companion stars had been christened Aether and Bacchae—was only one-third the size of Earth's sun and considerably cooler as a result. Indeed, even though it was called a red dwarf, its proper color was more a pale orange, like that of a stoplight that needed to be replaced. Moreover, the orbits of all seven of its planets were less than 60 percent of an astronomical unit, the average distance of Earth from its sun, and most of them were less than .22 AUs from their primary, putting them closer to Calliope than Mercury was from Sol.

However, the similarities ended there. Because Calliope was much smaller than Sol, its habitable zone was closer to the sun, as well. Thus, while Gaea's closest neighbor, Demeter, also lay beyond the habitable zone, the two inmost planets—Gliese 667C-b and 667C-h, or Bona Dea and Hestia—were too hot to sustain liquid water on their surfaces. From long-range instruments raised from their bays in its service module, *Galactique* determined that Bona Dea, located a mere .05 AU from its sun, was a molten world of active volcanoes much like Io, while Hestia, just .08 AU away, was little more than a small, burned-out cinder.

Galactique dismissed them as unworthy of further attention and focused on the three planets within Calliope's foreshortened habitable zone.

Gliese 667C-c and 667C-f, Chronus and Faunus, were located at distances of .12 AU and .15 AU, respectively. Both were so-called superearths, terrestrial planets larger and more massive than Earth and therefore having higher surface gravities. In addition, Chronus was still much too warm, and since it was rotation-locked as well, with one hemisphere perpetually facing Calliope, its carbon-dioxide atmosphere was too tenuous to sustain life. Faunus wasn't much better. It, too, was rotation-locked, and while its far side was just cool enough to be livable, its surface gravity would have crushed any human who tried to make it home. *Galactique* took their measure and rejected them without a second thought.

But Eos . . . Eos was something else entirely.

Gliese 667C-e had always been a controversial destination for the Galactique Project. Indeed, shortly after the discovery of Calliope's planetary system in the early twenty-first century, the very existence of the fifth planet had been disputed, considered by some to be a mistake made in the optical interferometry methods used to spot it. Yet further observations by advanced orbital telescopes confirmed that Eos was really there, and in time, it went to the top of the list of likely candidates for human colonization.

As *Galactique* approached Eos, it made a closer observation of the planet. Occupying a semielliptical orbit at the outer edge of Calliope's habitable zone, the planet had a diameter of 10,533 miles, making it approximately one-third larger than Earth, and a surface gravity of 1.5 g, half again higher than Earth's. The planet was not rotation locked but turned on its axis every twenty-six hours, with Eos itself making a full revolution around Calliope every sixty-two days. So while the planet's slight orbital eccentricity allowed for a regular change of seasons, those seasons were incredibly short—only fifteen and a quarter days each for winter, spring, summer, and autumn.

Eos possessed a thin atmosphere chiefly composed of carbon dioxide. Nonetheless, there was enough oxygen and hydrogen present to allow liquid water to form and produce broad, shallow oceans and seas across most of its surface, with its poles surrounded by glacial regions. Since the planet had no moons, there were no lunar tides. However, the proximity of its neighboring planets meant that the sea levels rose and fell ever so slightly when Faunus and Demeter rose above the horizon. There were no obvious signs of life, though, let alone habitation. There were few indications of photosynthesis; the atmospheric carbon dioxide was probably the result of volcanic activity. That was a good thing; everything was predicated upon the discovery of an unoccupied world.

Geographically, Eos bore some resemblance to Earth. Its dry land was mainly comprised of large continents, with smaller islands and archipelagos scattered here and there. An abundance of volcanoes both active and dormant, along mountain chains and rift valleys, hinted at a geologically unstable past in which tectonic shifts had carved up the landmasses while the oceans were being formed. The global climate was most temperate at the equator; even as *Galactique* made its preliminary survey, it tentatively identified a coastal region of a major continent just south of the equator, along with a small chain of islands just offshore, as being a likely target for colonization.

Remote observation could only reveal so much. Before *Galactique* left Earth, mission planners knew that the mission's final make-or-break point would be when the ship reached its final destination. And so, as *Galactique* fired its thrusters for its primary approach to Eos, it entered the phase in which it would decide whether the efforts of its creators and their descendants had been a colossal waste of time.

Once again, *Galactique* made a long, shallow dive through the planetary atmosphere, using the heat shield to brake itself. From the ground on the night side, the arriving starship appeared as a fireball streaking across the dark sky. Firing its lateral thrusters, *Galactique* emerged from the atmosphere and assumed geosynchronous orbit above the planet's equator.

Then it went to work.

A small port in the module housing the biopods opened, and a small probe was jettisoned. The probe fell into the atmosphere, and shortly after entry, it discarded its outer aeroshell and deployed its parachute. The probe drifted to a soft landing near the region *Galactique* had tentatively selected as the primary site for colonization, where it immediately opened the half dozen panels protecting its instrument array.

For a very long while—time was unimportant to *Galactique*, so it paid almost no attention to measuring its passage—the probe sampled the atmosphere, dug soil from the ground and analyzed its composition, and studied the chemistry of this world. It quickly determined that the DNA of its organic molecules was left-handed, which was crucial to the future habitability of Eos. If their chirality had been right-handed, it would have immediately doomed any attempt to transplant Earth life to this planet, for even the simplest of plants would have been poisoned by the Eosian soil. So this was a fortunate outcome.

On the other hand, in making this determination, the probe also learned that Eos was not entirely lifeless. As a red dwarf, Calliope was a young star, and its planets were also young. Thus, Eos's native species were primitive as well, still on the lowermost rungs of the evolutionary ladder. Yet even the lichen, sponge molds, and tiny ferns of its flora and the multilegged worms and trilobite-like crustaceans that occupied the top of the food chain for the fauna were evidence that the planet was not barren.

Many years earlier, Arkwright Foundation scientists and mission planners had argued long and hard over the ethical problems just such a discovery would present. The intent all along had been to reshape Gliese 667C-e into a world that, while perhaps not being earthlike, would nonetheless support bioengineered Earth species: plants, animals, and, yes, humans. Yet, was it morally right to condemn an entire planetary ecology to death so an Earth colony could thrive and survive? No one had an easy answer to this, for humankind had already made extinct millions of planet and animal species on its own world. So a compromise had been reached. *Galactique*'s AI was programmed with a series of protocols that would help it determine whether life on Eos was sufficiently evolved to make their destruction an act of genocide.

Had the answer been yes, then *Galactique* would have stopped there, and its last act would have been to transmit its data via laser to Earth so that, twenty-two years in the future, whoever was still running the Arkwright Foundation could scream in frustration. But it took the AI, with its coldly ruthless logic, only a few seconds to determine that the answer was no.

From that moment, Eos's destiny was forever changed.

BOOK FOUR

The Children of Gal

1

Sanjay Arkwright's mother was sent to Purgatory on Monone, the second day of Juli. As dawn broke on Childstown, Aara was escorted from her home by a pair of Guardians, who silently walked two-legged on either side of the heretic as they marched her to the beach. Sanjay and his father, Dayall, quietly accompanied them; carrying belly packs and walking on all fours, they kept their heads down to avoid meeting the gaze of the townspeople who'd emerged from their cottages and workshops to observe Aara's passage into exile.

It was a day of shame for her family, and yet Aara maintained an upright stance. Even after a Guardian prodded the back of her neck with his staff, she refused to lower her head or place her fores against the cobblestoned street but instead strode forward on her hinds, gazing straight ahead in almost haughty dismissal of her neighbors. For this alone, Sanjay was proud of his mother. She would obey the Word of Gal, but not with the humiliation expected of her.

On the beach, a group of Disciples had already gathered to form a prayer circle. They squatted in a semicircle facing the Western Channel, where the sister suns Aether and Bacchae were beginning to set upon the distant shores of Cape Exile. Illuminated by the bright-orange orb of Calliope rising to the east, they cupped their fores together beneath their lowered faces and chanted words passed down to them from their mothers and grandmothers:

> *Gal the Creator, Gal the All-Knowing,*
> *Forgive our sister, who denies your love.*
> *Gal the Creator, Gal the All-Knowing,*
> *Guide our sister as you watch from above . . .*

Their voices fell silent as Aara and her guards approached. If they'd expected Aara to join them, they were disappointed. Aara barely glanced at them as she walked by, and Sanjay had to fight to keep his expression neutral.

Dayall noticed this. "Don't smile," he whispered to his son, "and don't stand. Everyone is watching us."

Sanjay didn't reply but only gave his father a brief nod. His father was right. This was a sad moment and also a dangerous one. Most of those who'd followed them to the waterfront were Galians, and even if some were friends of the family, a few were pious enough to report the slightest impropriety to the Guardians. Any sign of support from Aara's family, and the deacons could easily extend the same sentence to her husband and son, as well. It had been many yarn since the last time an entire family was sent to Purgatory, but it had been done before.

R'beca Circe, the deacon of the Childstown congregation of the Disciples of Gal, stood on all fours beside Aara's sailboat, accompanied by the deacons from Stone Bluff, Oceanview, and Lighthouse Point who'd traveled across Providence to attend Aara's trial. The Guardians led Aara to them and then stepped aside, standing erect with their staffs planted in the sand. R'beca rose from her fores to look Aara straight in the eye; the other deacons did the same, and for a long moment, everything was still, save for the cool morning breeze that ruffled their ceremonial capes and Aara's braided red hair, revealed by the lowered hood of the long black robe she'd been given by the Guardians.

Then R'beca spoke.

"On the first day of the Stormyarn," she recited, "when the Disciples were separated from the Children who stayed behind, Gal told his people, 'Follow my Word always, and obey the lessons of your Teachers, for my way is survival, and those who question it shall not.' Aara Arkwright, it is the finding of the Deacons of the Disciples of Gal that you have questioned the Word of Gal and therefore committed the sin of heresy, for which you have refused to repent. How do you plead?"

"I plead nothing." There was no trace of insolence in Aara's voice; as always, when she was given a direct question, she delivered a direct answer. "I am neither guilty nor innocent. I saw what I saw . . . and there is nothing in the Word that says it cannot exist."

R'beca's eyes grew sharper. She pointed toward the sky. "Clearly, there is no light there save that of Gal and her suns. Even at night, when Aether and Bacchae rise to cast away the shadows and the stars appear, Gal remains in her place, bright and unmoving. Stars do not suddenly appear and vanish, and none may approach Gal."

Almost unwillingly, Sanjay found himself following Deacon R'beca's raised fore with his gaze. As she had said, Gal the Creator hovered almost directly overhead, a bright star that never rose or set but remained a fixed point in the sky. It had been this way throughout the one hundred and fifty-two sixyarn of Eosian history, from the moment when Gal had carried the Chosen Children from Erf to the promised land of Eos.

None but fools or heretics ever questioned this. Those who did were purged from Providence, sent alone to the mainland to live out the rest of their days in a place where survival was unlikely.

Yet Aara wouldn't recant. "I did not lie then, and I'm not lying now. I saw a new star in the sky during my turn on night watch, one that moved in the sky toward Gal."

"So you question Gal's dominance? Her status as creator who cannot be challenged?"

"I question nothing. This was not an act of blasphemy, Deacon . . . it was an obligation to my duty to report anything unusual."

Hearing this, the Disciples crouched on the beach wailed in bereavement. As they slapped their fores against their ears, R'beca's mouth curled in disgust. She'd offered Aara a chance to repent and beg for mercy, only to receive a stubborn reiteration of the same defense she'd given during her trial. Again, Sanjay felt pride surge past his sadness. His mother had never been one to back down, and she wasn't about to do so now.

Yet her courage wasn't met with sympathy. As the other three deacons lowered themselves to their hinds and cupped their fores together, R'beca reached beneath her cape and produced the symbol of her office, a large white knife she carried with her at all times. Made of the same material as the large block of Galmatter that, along with the Teacher, resided within the Transformer inside the Shrine, it was one of the few remaining relics from the yarn before the Great Storm, when the Chosen Children had first come to Eos from Erf. R'beca clasped the pale blade in her left fore and, raising it above her, intoned the words everyone expected to hear:

"In the name of Gal, creator of Eos and mother of her children, I send you, Aara Arkwright, into exile. May Gal grant you safe passage to Purgatory, where you shall live the rest of your days."

Then she brought the knife forward and, with one swift stroke, whisked its blade across the right side of Aara's face. Sanjay's mother winced, but she didn't cry out when the blade cut into her cheek; it would leave a scar that would mark her as an outcast for the rest of her life, making her a pariah to any community on Providence to which she might try to return. She could be put to death if she was ever seen on the island again.

R'beca turned her back to her and, still on her hinds, walked away. "You may say farewell to her now," she murmured to Dayall and Sanjay as she strode past. "Be quick."

Sanjay and his father were the only ones to approach his mother. By custom, everyone else who'd witnessed the ceremony stood erect and silently turned their backs to her. Through the crowd, Sanjay caught a glimpse of Kaile Otomo. Her long black hair was down around her face, making it hard to see her expression, yet she briefly caught his eye and gave him the slightest of nods. Then she turned away as well.

Dayall stood erect to pull off his belly pack. It was stuffed with clothes, a couple of fire starters, fishing tackle, and his best knife, all permitted by the Guardians to be given to someone facing banishment. Aara took it from him and then let her husband wipe the blood from her face and take her in his arms. Sanjay couldn't hear what his father whispered to her, but he saw the tears in her eyes, and that was enough. After a few moments, Dayall let her go, and then it was Sanjay's turn.

"Aara . . ."

"It's all right. Everything will be all right."

He wasn't expecting the wan smile that crossed her face as she accepted the belly pack bulging with food he'd taken from their pantry. She dropped it on the ground next to his father's.

"I'm even sadder about this than you are," she said, "because I won't be around to see you and Kaile become bonded, but—"

"It's not fair!"

"Hush. Keep your voice down." She glanced over his shoulder, wary of being overheard by the Disciples or the deacons. "Of course it's not fair. I was only doing my duty. But the Guardians have their duties, as well, and R'beca"—another smile, this time sardonic—"well, she would call it blasphemy if winter came late. My only sin was not realizing this before I opened my mouth."

Sanjay started to reply, but then she wrapped her arms around him and pulled him close. "This is not the end," she whispered. "We'll see each other again."

Sanjay knew this wasn't true. Once someone was sent to Purgatory, he or she never returned from the other side of the Western Channel. Yet perhaps his mother wasn't facing reality or she was speaking of the afterlife promised by the deacons, when all who believed in Gal would join once their souls had departed Eos. So he simply nodded and told her that he loved her, and she borrowed his fish-bone knife to cut a lock of his red hair to take with her, and then a Guardian stepped forward to impatiently tap the sand with his staff.

It was time for her to go.

The catamaran was sound and sturdy, its outrigger hull constructed from cured umbrella palm, its mainsail woven from bambu threads. Sanjay had built the boat with his own fores, with help from his friend Johan Sanyal; they'd done this while Aara was under house arrest, awaiting the arrival of the other deacons and the commencement of the trial whose outcome was all but certain. They'd made the boat quickly but carefully, taking time from the spring fishing season to fashion the small craft for his mother. The master boat-builder, Codi Royce, hadn't objected when the two boys didn't work on the fishing fleet's boats for several precious days; as Sanjay's mentor, he knew just how important this was.

Although it wasn't strictly permitted, no one had objected when Sanjay discreetly hid a harpoon beneath the oars. It wasn't likely that Aara might encounter an ocean monarch while crossing the channel. The leviathans were nocturnal; along with the receding tide, this was a reason outcasts were sent away at dawn, to give them time to reach Cape Exile before the creatures rose to the surface and started hunting. Nonetheless, it might give her some measure of protection if she encountered one during her journey.

Like all Providence inhabitants, Aara was an expert sailor. Once she'd stowed the packs, she didn't immediately raise the sail but instead used the oars to push herself away from the beach and out into the Childstown bay. As a small measure of respect for her, none of the fishing boats set out when they were supposed to. On the nearby docks, their crews silently waited as Aara paddled away, allowing her a chance to begin the long, sixty-kilm journey from the island to the mainland.

Aara was a small figure sitting in the catamaran's stern when she finally lowered the outrigger and raised the mainsail. As it unfurled to catch the morning wind, there was a single, long gong from the watchtower's bell, the ritual signal that an islander was being sent into exile. As it resounded across the waters, Aara raised a fore in a final wave.

Sanjay and his father waved back, and then they stood together on the shore and quietly waited until her boat couldn't be seen anymore.

2

In the days that followed, Sanjay did his best to put his mother's banishment behind him. With only two weeks left in summer, there was much that needed to be done before the season changed: fish to be caught, dried, and preserved, seeds planted and spring crops tended, houses and boats repaired. He and his father put away Aara's belongings—they couldn't bring themselves to burn her clothes, a customary practice for the families of those sent to Purgatory—and accepted the sympathy of those kind enough to offer it, but it took time for them to get used to a house that now seemed empty; the absence of laughter and the vacant seat at the dinner table haunted them whenever they came home.

Sanjay didn't feel very much like attending the Juli service at the Shrine, but Dayall insisted. If he didn't make an appearance, the more inquisitive Disciples might wonder whether Aara's son shared her blasphemous beliefs. Dayall was an observant Galian if not a particularly devout one, and the last thing they wanted to do was draw the attention of the Guardians. So Frione morning, they joined the Disciples in the dome-roofed temple in the middle of town. Once they'd bowed in homage to the sacred genesis plant that grew beside the Shrine, they went in to sit together on floor mats in the back of the room, doing their best to ignore the curious glances of those around them. Yet as R'beca stood before the altar, where the boxlike frame of the Transformer stood with its inert block of Galmatter in the center, and droned on about how the souls of the Chosen Children were gathered by Gal from the vile netherworld of Erf and carried "twenty-two lights and a half through the darkness" to Eos, Sanjay found himself studying the Teacher resting within his crèche behind the altar.

Even as a child, Sanjay had often wondered why the Teacher didn't resemble the Children or their descendents. Taller than an adult islander, his legs had knees that were curiously forward-jointed and hinds lacking the thin membranes that ran between the toes. His arms, folded across his chest, were shorter, while the fingers of his fores were long and didn't have webbing. His neck was short, as well, supporting a hairless head whose face was curiously featureless: eyes perpetually open and staring, a lipless mouth, a straight nose that lacked nostrils. And although the Teacher wore an ornate, brocaded robe dyed purple with roseberry, every youngster who'd ever sneaked up to the crèche after services to peek beneath the hem knew that the Teacher lacked genitalia; there was only a smooth place between his legs.

These discrepancies were explained by the Word: the Teacher had been fashioned by Gal to resemble the demons who ruled Erf, and the Creator had made him this way to remind the Children of the place from which they'd come. This was why the Teacher was made of Galmatter instead of flesh and blood. According to the history everyone diligently learned and recited in school, the Teacher and the Disciples had fled the mainland for Providence just before the Great Storm, leaving behind the unfaithful, who'd ignored Gal's warning that their land would soon be consumed by wind and water.

The Teacher no longer moved or spoke, and he had not done so in recent memory. Yet his body didn't decay, so he was preserved in the Shrine. Along with the Transformer and the Galmatter block, they were regarded as holy relics, reminders of the Stormyarn. In her sermons, R'beca often prophesized the coming of the day when the Teacher would awaken and bring forth new revelations of the Word of Gal, but Sanjay secretly doubted this would ever occur. If it did, he hoped to be there when it happened; he'd like to see how someone could walk on all fours with limbs and extremities as misshapen as these.

Kaile kept a discreet distance from Sanjay after Aara left. He missed her but understood why; her parents, Aiko and Jak, were strict Disciples who'd become reluctant to have their daughter associating with a heretic's son. And while she wasn't as rigid in her beliefs as her parents, nonetheless, Kaile was a Galian who did her best to adhere to the Word. So he saw her only on occasion, sometimes in town but more often in the morning on the waterfront. While Sanjay was a boatbuilder—indeed, his family name, which his father had taken after he bonded with his mother, was an old Inglis word for those who built watercraft—Kaile was a diver, trained from childhood to descend deep beneath the channel to harvest scavengers from the seafloor. When they spotted each other during those days, they'd exchange a brief smile and a wave, a sign that she still cared for him and would return once her parents let her.

Dayall, on the other hand, retreated into himself. As Juli lapsed into Aug and then Sept, Sanjay watched as his father became increasingly morose. He seldom spoke to anyone, let alone his son, instead adopting a dull daily pattern of getting up, having breakfast, opening his woodworking shop, and puttering around in it all day until it was time to close up and go home, where he'd eat and then go to bed.

Although he was still bonded to Aara, it was understood that this no longer mattered; other women could come to him as prospective suitors, and he could bond with them and take their name if he so desired. But Dayall was approaching middle age, and it was unlikely any woman in Childstown would want to take as her mate someone who'd once had a heretic as a wife. So Sanjay could only watch as his father came to terms with his loss; he was helpless to do anything about it.

More than once, Sanjay found himself cursing his mother for not having the foresight to keep what she'd seen during night watch to herself. He began to suspect that her eyes may have been playing tricks on her. It wasn't uncommon to see streaks of light in the night. Old Inglis teachings, passed down through generations, called them meteorites, small rocks that occasionally fell from the sky. Perhaps Aara had seen something like that and had mistaken it for a moving star. She'd sworn otherwise when she'd been called before the Council of Deacons, though, and Aara was an intelligent woman who wasn't likely to mistake a meteorite for anything else. Nonetheless, Sanjay wondered whether, just this once, his mother may have been a fool . . . or even the heretic the deacons had proclaimed her to be.

When Monthree came around in Sept, the last week of summer, it was his turn again to take the night watch. Garth Coyne, Sanjay's uncle and the mayor of Childstown, dropped by the boat shop that afternoon to let him know that he could skip his turn if he wished. Garth would assign someone else instead, and Sanjay could wait three weeks to take the Monthree watch in Dec.

Garth meant well, of course. Part of the purpose of the night watch was to look out for anyone who might try to cross the channel from Cape Exile, whether it be a sinner attempting to abduct an islander for their own vile purposes—which was the Disciples' explanation for the occasional disappearance of someone from a village—or an exile attempting to return. Garth was the mayor, but he was also

Dayall's brother, so he was more sympathetic than most and also aware of the bitter irony of having Sanjay stand watch to prevent his own mother from coming home. Yet Sanjay turned him down. He didn't want anyone to think that he was reluctant to assume the task that had led to Aara's downfall.

That night, he stood in the wooden watchtower, anxiously watching the sky in hopes that he'd spot the same mysterious star Aara had seen. Yet thick clouds had moved in shortly after Calliope went down, so all he could see was the diffuse glow that its distant companions, Aether and Bacchae, made through the overcast. Even Gal was nowhere to be seen. The only light he saw was the luminescent glow of nightjewels floating on the bay. Sanjay ended his turn in the tower with nothing more interesting to report than an ocean monarch breaching the surface a short distance out beyond the reefs; with summer coming to a close and the waters becoming colder, the predators were more often to be seen off the Providence shores.

He'd become accustomed to the fact that he'd never see his mother again when Kaile came to him on Thursthree morning. He was sitting beside a fishing canoe, patching a tear in its mainsail, when she walked across the beach on all fours and stopped beside him.

"'Lo, Sanjay," she said. "How are you?"

Sanjay looked up at her, surprised by the casualness of her greeting. She hadn't spoken to him all season. Many of his friends had distanced themselves from him, but he'd missed her more than anyone else. Summer was a time for lying down with one's lover, and his bed had been cold and lonely without her. Sanjay had lately begun to wonder if he'd lost her for good, so her abrupt return caught him unprepared.

"Good, thanks. Just working on this boat." He tried to pretend that her appearance meant little to him, but his fores slipped as he attempted to slide a threaded fish-bone needle through the sail patch. He nicked his right forefinger instead.

"Oh . . . watch yourself!" Kaile exclaimed as he hissed in pain. "Here. Let me."

Before Sanjay could object, she bent closer, took his fore in her own, and gently slipped his finger into her mouth. Her lips formed a sly smile around his finger, and her eyes gleamed mischievously as her tongue, warm and moist, played with his fingertip. Sanjay felt himself becoming aroused. He shifted his hinds nervously, hoping she wouldn't notice, but if she did, she gave no sign.

"There," she said, withdrawing his finger from her mouth. "All better?" He nodded, and she smiled. "So . . . I was just wondering if you'd like to go diving with me today."

"Diving?" He'd done it before, but he wasn't trained the way she was. "Why?"

"Just because." A shrug. "We haven't seen much of each other lately, and I thought . . . well, it might be a way of getting back together again." Another smile. "Besides, my crew is running a little behind, and we could use some extra help."

Sanjay looked across the keel of the upended canoe. Codi was squatting nearby, working with Johan to finish a new boat. He didn't have to ask whether they'd overheard the conversation; Codi and Johan traded an amused look, and then his mentor nodded.

"Sure, go ahead. We can take care of things today."

Sanjay hesitated, but only for a moment. "Of course. I'd love to." Leaving the patch unfinished, he removed his tool kit from his vest and gave it to Johan for safekeeping. "After you," he said, and she smiled again and turned away, leading him on all fours down the beach toward the nearby docks.

He was just beginning to admire the way Kaile's body moved beneath the diaphanous shawl she wore over her halter and thong when she paused to let him catch up. At first, he thought she was merely expressing fondness when she raised herself erect on her hinds and slid her fore through the crook of his elbow, but when he stood up so she could pull him closer as if to give him a kiss, she murmured something only he could hear.

"There's something I need to tell you," she whispered.

"What about?" Sanjay glanced around to see if anyone else was nearby.

They weren't alone; others were walking past. The waterfront was as busy as it always was this hour of the morning.

"Not here," she said softly. "Wait until we're out on the water, where no one can hear us." She paused and then added even more quietly, "It's about what Aara saw . . . I've seen it too."

3

The fishing fleet bobbed on the warm blue waters of the bay, six canoes with sails furled and anchors lowered. This late in the season, it was necessary for them to venture farther away from shore in order for the divers to catch anything of significance; it would take the nine weeks of autumn, winter, and spring for the breadfish and scavengers born the previous yar to grow large enough to be caught. So the boats had to spread out in order for their crews to bring home a decent catch; this made for conditions suitable for a conversation that wouldn't be easily overheard.

Nevertheless, Sanjay had a hard time containing himself from asking Kaile what she had meant. Two others were on her boat: Sayra Bailee, a young girl who'd become a diver only three yarn earlier, and Ramos Circe, the boat captain. Neither Sanjay nor Kaile were very much concerned about Sayra—she wasn't terribly bright and tended to keep to herself, anyway—but Ramos was another matter entirely. He was the Guardian appointed to the fleet to observe the fishermen and help them maintain spiritual purity while they worked, and the fact that he was also Deacon R'beca's son only made him more dangerous. They would have to be careful of him.

So he and Kaile had made small talk with Sayra as they paddled out into the bay, saying nothing that really mattered while ignoring Ramos. They were about a half kilm from the reefs that separated the outer reaches of the bay from the Western Channel when Ramos called for them to take down the sails and drop anchor. By then, their craft was a hundred rods from the next nearest boat, all the better for the privacy they sought.

Sanjay watched as Kaile stood erect, dropped her shawl, and, as an afterthought, discarded her halter, as well. She wore nothing now except her thong, which covered very little of herself. He'd never forgotten how beautiful she was; with the orange sun on her light-brown skin, she was as radiant as Gal herself. Taking off his vest and kilt, he was glad that he'd decided to wear a thong himself that day; otherwise, his reaction would have been obvious to all. Sayra also chose to dive almost entirely nude, but at sixteen sixyarn, she hadn't yet blossomed into the full-breasted womanhood Kaile had achieved at twenty-two.

In keeping with his position as a Guardian, Ramos pretended not to notice either of the women. He waited while everyone buckled on diving belts and attached knife sheaths and woven collection bags. "All right, over you go," he said once they were ready. "Good hunting. May Gal keep you safe."

"Thank you." Raising her fores level with her shoulders, Kaile dove headfirst into the water, disappearing with barely a splash. Sayra followed her a moment later, leaping from the other side of the canoe. Sanjay took a few more breaths to fill his lungs, and then he joined them, although not nearly as gracefully.

The instant he was submerged, he instinctively squinted, forcing shut the watertight nictitating membranes of his eyes that Gal in her wisdom had provided her children. At the same time, the fingers of his fores and the toes of his hinds spread apart, opening the webs between his digits, which allowed his people to be fast and effort-less swimmers. Although he wasn't the practiced diver Kaile and Sayra were, he could nonetheless stay underwater for three or four mins at a time, allowing him to descend the twenty rods it took to reach the bottom. Although the sunlight faded, he could still see Kaile clearly, swimming toward the seafern jungle that lay across the bay floor.

It was here that they searched for scavengers, the spidery crusta-ceans that prowled among the ferns, feeding on the remains of nightjewels, breadfish, and other pelagic species that had died and drifted to the bottom of the sea. Because they tended to blend in to their environment, catching them was easier than finding them. Kaile was much better at this than he was; she'd collected two while he was still searching for one, and shook her head when he picked up a half-grown crustacean and showed it to her: *too small, let it go.*

His lungs were beginning to hurt by then, so he followed her back up to the boat and watched as she tossed her bag over the side and took another one from Ramos. The scavengers died as soon as exposed to the air, of course, but it didn't render the tender flesh beneath their carapaces inedible. Kaile and Sanjay took a min or two to replenish their lungs, and then they went down again. They ignored the fat breadfish that occasionally swam past, leaving them for the long-line anglers in other boats, and they stayed clear of the reefs, which tended to be patrolled by seaknives who'd attack any humans who dared enter their domain.

Over the next couple of hours, they made seven descents, stop-ping for a few minutes after every second or third dive to float on their backs and rest a little. Sanjay noticed that, while Sayra stayed fairly close to the boat, Kaile was gradually leading him farther away. Apparently, Ramos expected her to do this, because he didn't seem to mind that they'd have to swim quite a few rods to reach the boat again. By late morning, he'd decided to take a little nap, lying back against the stern with an arm across his eyes.

On their last dive, Sanjay caught a full-grown scavenger, but when he held it up for Kaile to see, she surprised him by shaking her head. Instead, she pointed to the surface. Looking up, he saw that the keel of the boat was nowhere to be seen. Understanding what she meant, he dropped the scavenger and then rose with her to the top.

Once they had surfaced, she paddled over to him and, to his delighted surprise, draped her fores across his shoulders and pulled him close. "Kiss me," she whispered, and he was only too happy to oblige. "Good," she said once they'd parted. "Now hold me close while we talk. This way, everyone will think we're just making love and leave us alone."

By then, he'd almost forgotten the reason she'd asked him to go diving with her. "Can't we do both?" he asked, playfully stroking her breasts. Her skin was warm against the cool water; he could feel it pimple beneath his fores.

"Maybe later." A wry smile quickly vanished as she pushed his fores away. "For now, just listen. I was standing watch last night . . ."

In furtive tones quietly spoken while she allowed him to caress her, Kaile told Sanjay about her turn in the watchtower the night before. The night was clear, without the clouds that had ruined his own attempt to observe the sky, but she hadn't been making any particular effort to see anything unusual. All the same, it was in the darkest hour of the night, when the sisters were setting to the east and before Calliope had risen to the west, her eye was drawn to a peculiar movement in the zenith.

"A small star, quickly moving from east to west." As she said this, Kaile glanced up at the sky. "It went straight toward Gal, quickly at first, and then . . ." She hesitated, looking down at Sanjay again.

"Then what?" he asked.

"It slowed down and . . . Sanjay, it merged with Gal." Her mouth trembled as she said this, her eyes wide. "It was as if the two became one. For just a few secs they became brighter, and then Gal went back to normal."

Losing interest in her body, he let his fores fall to his sides, moving back and forth to keep himself afloat. "How could—"

"That's not all. I kept watching, and it was almost first light when something else happened. The little star parted from Gal again and went back in the direction it had come, but this time, instead of vanishing beyond the horizon, it started going faster and getting brighter, until it formed a tail. I heard thunder, like a storm was coming in, but there were no clouds. Then . . ."

Again, Kaile looked away, but this time not at the sky but to the west. "It came down over there," she said softly, and when Sanjay followed her gaze, he saw that she was staring at the distant gray line that marked the shores of Cape Exile.

"Purgatory?" He could scarcely believe her. "Are you sure?"

Kaile glared at him. "Of course I'm sure!" she snapped, her voice rising a little as she swam back from him. "I'm telling you, I saw what I—"

She stopped herself. Like Sanjay, she remembered that this was exactly what Aara had said when she'd defended herself before the deacons. And Sanjay had spent enough time in the tower himself to know that the view of Cape Exile from up there was excellent. Save for the high cliffs of Stone Bluff to the north and the summits of Mount Lookout and Mount Roundtop in the island's forest interior, there was no higher vantage point on Providence. Indeed, it was whispered among islanders that, from these places on clear nights, one could see faint, glimmering lights on the mainland, a sign that at least some of those who'd been banished there still lived, struggling to survive in the terrible place from which Gal had rescued her most devout followers.

"I believe you," he said quietly, paddling closer to her again. "It sounds like you saw the same thing my mother did. Something like it, at least."

"No. That was *more* than what Aara saw." Glancing past him, she returned her fores to his shoulders once more. "Kiss me," she whispered. "Ramos is watching."

Again, their mouths came together. This time, though, Sanjay took little pleasure from it. He was thinking about something else. "Have you told anyone?" he said softly, his face against her wet hair.

"No." She sighed, and despite the warmth of the water, Sanjay felt her tremble. "After what happened to Aara, how could I?"

"No, of course not." As obedient to Gal as Kaile was, it would have been mad to repeat Aara's mistake. Deacon R'beca wouldn't have given any more credence to a second act of blasphemy than she had the first. He found himself wondering whether anyone else who'd recently stood watch might have seen the same thing Kaile did but had likewise remained silent about it, for fear of following Aara Arkwright into exile. But if there had been any similar sightings, they would never know, unless . . .

"There's only one way we'll ever know," he said quietly, thinking aloud.

Kaile looked him straight in the eye. "How?" Then she realized what he meant, and her mouth fell open. "No . . . no, you can't be serious."

She was right. Even as the notion entered his mind, Sanjay thrust it away. None but those whom the deacons cast out of Providence ever made the dangerous crossing of the Western Channel. In fact, no one was allowed to leave the island except fishermen and those who used sailboats to travel from one coastal village to another. All that was known of the rest of Eos came from ancient maps belonging to the First Children that had been handed down through the generations. They depicted great continents separated from one another by vast seas, with Providence the largest island of a small equatorial archipelago just off the coast of the landform known as Terra Minor. Gal had forbidden any exploration of these distant lands, though, so her children knew almost next to nothing about the rest of the world. Even the maps were closely held by the Council of Deacons, rarely seen by anyone else.

"No, you're right." He shook his head. "We can't do that. We'd—"

A shrill whistle from their boat, and then Ramos's voice came to them from across the water. "All right, you two, enough of that! Back to work!"

Then Sayra called to them, as well. "Yes, enough!" she yelled, childishly scolding them. "Save it for your bed, Sanjay, if she'll let you take her to it!"

Kaile forced a smile and raised a fore, but Sanjay wasn't about to let her go quite yet. "It's not a bad suggestion," he said. "I've missed you very much. Will you—"

She laughed, this time with genuine amusement, and pushed herself away from him. "Help me gather a few more scavengers," she said, "and I'll think about it."

Then she upended herself and, with a kick of her hinds, disappeared beneath the surface. But not before Sanjay caught the coy wink of an eye that told him that she'd already made up her mind.

4

Kaile kept her side of the bargain. When Calliope was going down and the boats returned to shore, she came home with Sanjay.

Dayall was already there, working on dinner. He was surprised when Kaile walked in with his son, and it was the first time in weeks that Sanjay saw him smile. As if nothing had ever changed, he put another plate on the table and then pulled some more mockapples and vine melons from the pantry and put them out along with a jug of wine. Sanjay had brought home a scavenger he'd caught, and it wasn't long before it was steamed, shelled, and on the table. They talked about his diving trip while they ate, and for once, Dayall's part of the conversation wasn't limited to monosyllables. The main room had the comfortable aroma of peeled fruit and cooked food, and for just a little while, it was as if everything had gone back to the way it had been before Aara left.

Once the meal was over and the kitchen was cleaned up, Dayall murmured something about how he thought it might be nice to spend the night at Garth's house. Sanjay politely objected, but he knew why his father was going over to his uncle's place. Dayall gathered a bedroll, took another jug from the wine cabinet, and was gone before Kaile could thank him for dinner.

Sanjay lit a fire and took the small wooden box of dreamer's weed down from the mantel. Kaile blew out the candles, and they shared a pipe by firelight, saying little as they gazed into the flames and let the pipe smoke soften their senses. The night was cool, so he closed the window shutters. The fire warmed them, and it wasn't long before their fores wandered to each other's bodies. Soon they were curled up together upon the rug, rediscovering the pleasures they'd been denied all summer.

Kaile considered going home but decided that the hour was late enough already that any excuses she might make for her absence would be transparent. Besides, it was time for her parents to learn that she wasn't going to leave Sanjay no matter what they thought of his family. Sanjay couldn't have agreed more. As the fire began to gutter, he led her through the darkened house to his bedroom. They made love again before exhaustion caught up with them, and wrapped within warm blankets, they fell asleep in each other's arms.

Sanjay had no idea what hour it was when he felt a fore upon his shoulder and heard a voice quietly say his name. Slow to emerge from the depths of sleep, his first thought was that Kaile trying to rouse him for another round of lovemaking, but when the voice repeated itself, he realized that it wasn't her who was speaking to him. Kaile was still asleep beside him, while the person trying to wake him up was crouched next to his bed. He opened his eyes and turned his head, and in the wan amber light of the sisters seeping in through a crack between the closed shutters of his bedroom window, he saw Aara.

He jerked upright in bed, not quite believing what he was seeing. Before he could say anything, though, his mother laid a fore across his mouth.

"Shhh . . . be quiet!" she hissed, barely more than a whisper. "Don't wake your father."

"Sanjay?" Kaile twisted beside him, still more asleep than awake. "Sanjay, what's going on?"

Aara's eyes widened, her mouth falling open in dismay. "Is that Kaile?" she asked softly, as if it would be anyone else. Still stunned by his mother's presence, he gave a dumb nod, and she sighed. "Oh no . . . I wasn't expecting this."

"Aara?" Kaile woke up as suddenly as Sanjay had and was just as astonished. "Aara, what are you—"

"Hush." Aara lifted a finger to her mouth. "Keep your voice down. I don't want Dayall to know I'm here."

Kaile went silent, but Sanjay could feel her trembling beside him. "He's not here," he whispered. "He's spending the night at Garth's house."

Aara let out her breath in relief. "Good . . . that's good. Wait a sec."

She moved away from the bed, and a moment later, there came the tiny sparks and soft sounds of flints being scratched together. The fish-oil lamp on his clothes chest flickered to life, and now they could see her clearly. Aara wore the same black robe she'd been wearing the last time Sanjay had seen her; although its hood was drawn up over her head, he could see the facial scar left by R'beca's knife, a reminder that she was an exile who could be killed if anyone found her back on Providence.

The thought must have occurred to her, as well, because Aara's expression was wary when she turned to them again. "Kaile," she said quietly, "I can trust you, can't I? You're not going to run straight to the Guardians, are you?" She looked straight at the girl, meeting her gaze with suspicious eyes.

Kaile hesitated just long enough for Sanjay to realize that she was wrestling with her conscience. "No . . . no, I won't," she said at last, much to his relief. "I'm not Aiko or Jak. I didn't want you to be banished. But Aara, why—"

"I can't tell you that. Not now, anyway. No time." A nod toward the closed window. "It'll be morning soon, and we must be gone by then." A pause. "Sanjay, I mean . . . Kaile, you're staying here, and I'm going to have to ask your word not to tell anyone that I was here or where—"

She stopped herself, but not before Sanjay knew what she meant to say next. "You want me to go with you?" he asked, and she nodded. "To Purgatory?" Again, a solemn nod. He felt a cold sensation in the pit of his stomach. "Why?"

Before Aara could respond, Kaile spoke up again. "I saw a light in the sky last night while I was on watch. Just like the one you saw, but instead, it merged with Gal before it came down on Cape Exile. That has to do with this, doesn't it?"

A grim smile. "Yes, it does." The smile disappeared, and Aara was thoughtful for a moment. "How many people know you spent the night here?"

"My parents. Dayall." Kaile laid a fore on Sanjay's shoulder. "Just about everyone who saw us leave the beach together after we went diving yesterday."

Aara sighed again, this time shaking her head. "So the Guardians will question you when he goes missing. I don't want you to have to face them or R'beca on my account. I can't make you come with us, but—"

"No. I want to come."

Startled, Sanjay stared at her. She met his gaze and gave him a brief nod. Yes, she was aware of what she was getting into. And she was doing it, anyway.

"Very well," Aara said as she turned away again. "Get up and get dressed, and be quick about it. I've got a boat waiting for us."

"A boat from Purgatory? Who—"

"Never mind that now. We're leaving in two mins."

Before Sanjay could ask any further questions, his mother left the room. No more lamps were lit, but as he and Kaile climbed out of bed, the soft creak of the pantry door told him that she was gathering food. He wondered why she'd bother to do so, but there was no time to ask.

"Are you sure you want to do this?" he asked Kaile as he dug into his chest to give her a sarong, tunic, and calf boots that would be warmer than the thin shawl she'd worn the day before. Autumn was only a couple of days away, and they would be traveling far from home. "You know what this means, don't you?" he added as he put on nearly identical clothes.

Kaile didn't say anything, but the silent nod she gave him told all that he needed to know. For better or worse, they were about to join his mother in Purgatory.

5

The sisters were beginning to set when the three of them slipped out through the back door. Kaile had mentioned that it was Johan's turn to stand watch, which Sanjay took as a good sign; he knew that his best friend often stole a few hours of sleep in the tower so that he'd be rested enough to go to work the next day. In any case, though, they avoided the streets as much as they could and instead quietly made their way on all fours through shadowed alleys between cottages, sheds, and shops until they reached the forest on Childstown's eastern border. No one spotted them; in the coldest hours of the night, the town was asleep.

Aara led Sanjay and Kaile to the footpath leading south to Mountain Creek, which flowed through the forest from Mount Lookout to the northeast. The trail would take them to the coastal estuary where the creek drained into the bay. It was there, Aara told them, the boat that had carried her back across the channel was awaiting her return.

"You came over tonight?" Although they were now out of earshot from the village, Sanjay was careful to keep his voice down. "How were you not spotted?"

The forest they walked through was dark, the black fronds of the umbrella palms and sunshade trees forming a shadowed canopy that blotted out all but thin slivers of sisterlight. All the same, Sanjay could see the soft smile that played across Aara's face.

"The exiles have ways of getting here," she said. "You'll see."

"But the monarchs—"

"That's . . . something else entirely." Her smile disappeared. "Now hush. No more questions."

Sanjay and Kaile exchanged glances but obediently fell silent. Sanjay knew better than to argue with his mother. Still, he thought as he shifted the straps of his belly pack, she was being a little too mysterious about all this.

About three kilms from Childstown, they reached the end of the trail. Through the wild roseberry and bambu that grew along the shore, the estuary lay before them, its waters faintly shimmering with the reflections from Aether and Bacchae. From the other side of a genesis plant that rose beside the trail, Sanjay could make out a catamaran resting upon the narrow beach. As they approached the genesis plant, though, he heard a soft voice, male yet unlike any he'd heard before.

"The specimen appears to be fully mature, approximately 1.8 meters in height, its width . . . call it a little less than one meter at its base. As with all pseudonative species, its leaves are matte-black in pigmentation, a genetically engineered adaptation to the primary's lesser magnitude and, in this instance, generation of cyanobacteria and the subsequent production of atmospheric oxygen and nitrogen. Its form clearly indicates its descent from the giant hosta, albeit considerably larger. Altogether, it appears that the alteration of its basic genetic pattern has been remarkably successful, especially considering the—"

"We're here," Aara said, raising her voice just a little.

Realizing that he was no longer alone, the person speaking abruptly stopped talking, but not before Sanjay spotted the individual to whom the voice belonged. Taller than any of them—as tall, in fact, as the genesis plant he stood beside—he stood upright on his hinds, his figure concealed by the hooded cloak that covered him from head to toe. Indeed, as they came closer, Sanjay was surprised to see that, beneath the cowl, he wore a dark veil across the lower part of his face, a mask that completely hid his features.

Yet it was his voice that intrigued Sanjay the most. Although the stranger had been speaking Inglis, many of the words he'd used were unfamiliar; Sanjay had clearly heard what he'd said but didn't understand its meaning. And the accent was strange: sharper, with an odd inflection of the syllables.

"Oh, good. You made it back." The figure stepped away from the genesis plant, and for an instant, Sanjay noticed something held in his right fore before it disappeared within the cloak. "No trouble, I hope?"

"None. We got out of there without being spotted. But"—Aara hesitated and then stood erect to indicate Kaile—"I had to bring someone else. This is Kaile, my son's betrothed. She was with him when I found them. We couldn't leave her behind."

A disgruntled sigh from the other side of the veil. "Are you sure? This could complicate things, you know."

"If she stays, the Guardians will know that she was with Sanjay when he disappeared, because they were seen together all day yesterday and last night. They'll try to work the truth out of her, and

R'beca is very good at that. With any luck, my husband and her family will believe that the two of them simply ran away for a while, as young people sometimes do."

Sanjay now understood why Aara had taken food from the pantry. Once he and Kaile were found to be missing, which was inevitable, the most likely explanation would be that they'd taken off into the wilds for a little while, perhaps to a little lean-to shed Sanjay had secretly built in the mountains. Unbonded lovers occasionally did this when they wished to be free of the prying eyes of family and neighbors; it wasn't a practice condoned by the Disciples but tolerated nonetheless. If they were fortunate, no one would search for them for a little while, preferring to give them their privacy while they rehearsed their future roles as a bonded couple.

"Very well. If we have no choice." The figure nodded his hooded head toward the boat. "Teri is waiting for you on the boat. If you'll give me a second . . . a sec, I mean . . . to cut a leaf . . ."

He stepped back toward the genesis plant. "Stop!" Kaile snapped, raising her fores. "You can't do that!"

The stranger halted, looked around at her again. "I'm sorry, but what—"

"It's forbidden to touch genesis plants." Kaile was horrified by what she'd seen, but also perplexed. "It's in the Word . . . everyone knows that!"

Sanjay was just as confused. One of the most basic tenets of the Word of Gal was that even wild genesis plants such as this one must never be harvested. They were the means by which Gal had created Eos, and touching them without the supervision of a deacon during the spring and autumn solstice rituals was considered a sacrilege. Every child was taught that the first time they were taken into the forest for their first lessons in wood lore. How could this person be unaware of this?

"My apologies. I . . ." The stranger stopped. "Perhaps I should introduce myself. I'm Nathan."

This was a common enough name among islanders. In Galian lore, it was said to have belonged to the archangel who beseeched Gal to carry the Chosen Children from Erf to the new world. Yet Sanjay noticed that he didn't mention a family name, as well.

"Sanjay Arkwright," he replied and gave a formal bow, clasping his fores together as he bent forward from his knees.

"I know." When Nathan returned the bow, it was in a peculiar fashion: stiff-legged and from the waist, fores still hidden by his cloak. "I've wanted to meet you ever since your mother told me about you. In fact, you're the very reason we're here."

"I am?"

"We don't have time to discuss this," Aara said. "Calliope will be coming up soon. We need to be away before we can be spotted from town." She pointed to the nearby boat. "Hurry, please."

They followed her to the beach, where a man about Aara's age was already raising the catamaran's sail. As they walked toward the boat, Sanjay noticed that Nathan remained upright, apparently preferring to walk on his hinds even though the others dropped to all fours. His gait was also slow, as if each step was an effort. Was he crippled? Perhaps, but if so, why risk undertaking a sea journey?

Sanjay tried to put all this aside as he helped his mother and Kaile stow the belly packs they'd brought with them, and then he helped the captain push the boat out into the water. He could now see the reason the boat had been able to travel across the channel without being detected. Its wooden hull, mast, benches, and oars were painted black, and even the sails had been dyed the same way. Against the dark waters of the bay at night, the craft would have been very hard to spot.

He wondered if the inhabitants of Purgatory had ever crossed the channel before, using that very same boat. Perhaps. There were rumors that exiles had sometimes returned to Providence for one nefarious reason or another; every so often, a relative or close friend who'd been left behind had disappeared for no accountable reason. But maybe . . .

"All right, everyone settled in?" The captain, who'd given his name as Teri Collins, glanced around from his seat at the tiller.

Sanjay and Kaile had taken seats amidships, while Aara and Nathan sat in the bow—Nathan awkwardly, hunched slightly forward with his hinds stretched out straight before him, still covered by the long folds of his cloak.

"Very well, then," Nathan said as he used an oar to push away from the shore. "Sanjay, raise sail, please."

Sanjay turned around to grasp the line dangling from the mast and pulled it down, unfurling the black sail. The tide was beginning to go out, and the morning breeze was starting to come in; the sail bellowed outward, and the boat quietly slipped away, its outrigger skimming the water surface.

"We need to be silent now," Aara whispered, bending forward to speak to Sanjay and Kaile. "No talking, no movement, until we're well past the reefs. Understood?"

Sanjay nodded, as did Kaile. It was still dark, and Calliope hadn't yet risen. If they were lucky, no one in Childstown would see a boat heading out into the bay. Nonetheless, he hoped that Johan was asleep in the tower.

As the boat entered the bay, though, and the town came within sight, no lights appeared within its windows, and there was no gong of the warning bell. Childstown remained peaceful, unknowing of the intrusion that had happened during the night. Teri must have sailed these waters before, because he accurately steered the boat through the break in the reefs that lay a couple of kilms offshore. The hull sliced through the glowing nightjewels and scattered the curious knifefish who'd ventured close to the boat. High above, Gal observed their passage with an unblinking and omnipresent eye.

Looking up at her, Sanjay hoped that Gal would forgive her children for their transgressions. Providence had become a long, black shape gradually receding behind them, its inland mountain range rising as three low humps. He'd rarely been that far out on the channel, and only then in the light of day. The sea was a dangerous place to be at night.

He prayed that the monarchs wouldn't notice them.

His prayers went unanswered.

6

"Monarch," Teri said. "Off starboard bow."

He spoke calmly, yet there was no missing the urgency of his tone. Sanjay turned to look. At first he saw nothing; the sea and the night both were still dark. Then, about three hundred rods from the boat, he caught sight of a dorsal fin, light gray and shaped like the tip of a knife, jutting upward from the dark water. It was running parallel to them, neither approaching nor moving away, as if the massive form to which it belonged was swimming along with the catamaran. Tracking, observing, waiting for the moment to strike.

To the east, the first scarlet haze of dawn had appeared upon the horizon, tinting the curled gauze of the high clouds with shades of orange and red. He'd hoped that, with the passing of night, the danger of being noticed by an ocean monarch would pass, as well. But this one hadn't yet descended to the channel's lowest depths. It was still prowling the waters midway between Providence and Cape Exile in search of prey.

And now it had found them.

There was a harpoon lying on the deck at his hinds. Sanjay started to reach down to pick it up, but Teri shook his head. "No need," he said, his fores steady on the tiller. "Just wait." He glanced at Aara. "Move to the center of the boat, Aara. Everyone, hang on."

Sanjay stared at him in disbelief. Surely he didn't think they could possibly outrun a monarch. Many had tried to do this, but they'd only succeeded if they were already far enough away that it couldn't catch up . . . and this one was pacing them. Their only hope of survival lay in using a harpoon against it when it attacked.

He began to reach for the harpoon again, but then his mother, who'd walked back from the bow, laid a fore against his wrist. "Just watch," she said quietly. "The same thing happened to us on the way over."

"A monarch attacked you last night?" He had trouble believing her. "How did—"

"Wait and watch." Aara smiled as she squatted across from him and Kaile and then nodded toward Nathan.

The stranger remained in the bow. Until then, Sanjay hadn't taken much notice of the long object wrapped in waterproof bambu cloth that lay on the deck before him. Picking it up, Nathan removed the covering, revealing something the likes of which Sanjay had never seen: a slender, rodlike thing, broad in the center but tapering to what appeared to be a hollow tube at one end, with a handle fitted with a small ring projecting from its lower side. Its surface gleamed dully in the wan light of the coming dawn, and Sanjay realized to his surprise that it was made entirely of metal: very rare and almost never found in such a quantity.

"What is that?" Kaile asked.

No one answered her. Nathan rose from his bench and, hinds firmly planted against the gentle rocking of the boat, cradled the object in his fores. Turning away from them, he lowered his hood and pulled down his veil. Sanjay couldn't see his face, though, only the short-cropped red hair on the back of his head.

"Coming at us!" Teri snapped.

Sanjay looked in the direction the captain pointed. The monarch had veered toward the catamaran, its fin creating a frothy furrow through the water. Fifty rods from the boat, the fin abruptly disappeared beneath the surface. Sanjay knew that the monarch was diving in preparation for an attack, but even as he grabbed the harpoon and stood erect to do battle, he heard a faint, high-pitched whine from the object Nathan was holding. From the corner of his eye, he saw that the stranger had raised it level with his shoulders and appeared to peering straight down the length of its tube.

Sanjay barely had time to wonder what Nathan was doing when the monarch breached the surface. A massive wall of flesh, gray on top and white across the bottom, the leviathan shot up from the water only a few rods from the starboard side. Large as the boat itself, its mouth was wide enough to swallow a human whole and lined with rows of serrated teeth. Sanjay caught a glimpse of black eyes, small yet malevolent, and with an angry scream, he raised the harpoon in both fores . . .

It was if a beam of starlight had erupted from the hollow end of Nathan's object, a thin white ray that briefly and silently erased the darkness. It lanced straight into the underside of the monarch's mouth, and for an instant, Sanjay saw it reappear within the creature's jaws. A smell like fish being broiled as the beam burned through the monarch's head and a loud, agonized groan, and then the monarch fell back into the water, making a tremendous splash that threw a wave over the side of the boat.

The monarch was still spasmodically flopping on the surface, its fins and tail thrashing back and forth, when Nathan pointed his weapon—for this was obviously what it was—at it again. Once more, the thin beam cut into the creature's head, this time between the eyes. The monarch jerked and then became still, a dying mass floating on the water.

"A gift from Gal," Kaile whispered.

"No." For the first time since they'd left shore, Nathan spoke. "Not Gal. A plasma-beam rifle."

Sanjay hadn't the slightest idea what Nathan meant by that, but as Nathan turned to him, he suddenly didn't care. Nathan's cloak had fallen open, and now he could see the rest of the stranger's body: forward-jointed legs and slender hinds, a waist that was a little thicker, a neck not as long as his own. The breeze caught the robe and pulled it back from the stranger's shoulders, revealing long-fingered fores that lacked webbing between the digits.

But it was his face that startled Sanjay the most. Except for his red beard, the open nostrils of his nose, and eyes that possessed visible pupils, Nathan's face was nearly the same as that of the Teacher.

Kaile whimpered, clutching Sanjay's shoulder in fear. Sanjay stared at the apparition before them, not knowing what to say or do. When he glanced at Aara, though, he saw the calm and knowing smile on her face. She'd been aware of this all along.

"Who are you?" he asked.

"You won't believe this"—Nathan stopped and then corrected himself—"but I hope you eventually will. Sanjay, I'm your cousin."

7

Nathan refused to say any more about himself for the rest of the journey across the channel. He spent the remaining hours sitting quietly in the bow, rifle propped up on his forward-jointed knees, an enigmatic smile on his face as he politely listened to the younger man prod him with questions. He finally raised a fore and shook his head.

"Enough," he said. "You're just going to have to wait until we reach shore. Once we're there and we meet up with my friends—"

"There are more of you?" Sanjay stared at him.

"—then I'll tell you everything you want to know."

"So there are other Teachers like you." Kaile was no longer as fearful as she'd been, but she continued to hold tightly to Sanjay's fore.

A dry laugh. "I'm not a Teacher, and neither are they. We're human, just like you . . . only a bit different, that's all."

"Then why do you look like—"

"Be patient. All will be explained." He then turned away and spoke no more.

Sanjay looked at his mother, and Aara silently shook her head. Neither she nor Teri would tell them anything. They would just have to wait.

Calliope came up a little while later, revealing the mainland before them. By the time the sun was high above the channel, they could clearly make out the black forests that lay beyond the coast, gradually rising to meet the inland mountain range known as the Great Wall. This was the most anyone could see of Cape Exile from Providence, and although it soon stretched across the visible horizon, Sanjay was surprised to see how much the eastern peninsula of Terra Minor resembled Providence. He'd been told since childhood that anyone who dared to approach Purgatory would hear the mournful cries of the banished, but instead, the only sound that reached his ears were the screech of seabirds spiraling above the coastal shallows.

And once they were only a couple of kilms away, he saw more than that.

The white sand beach had just become visible when sails came into view, fishing boats plying the offshore waters. The men and women within them raised their fores in greeting as their catamaran sailed past, and Teri did the same in return.

"Wave back," Aara quietly urged her son. "We're among friends."

Sanjay gave her a doubtful look but did as he was told. He noticed that Nathan made no effort to hide his features or misshapen limbs. His hood remained lowered as he smiled at the fishermen, and although a couple of them stared at him, no one seemed surprised by his appearance, let alone regarded him as an emissary of Gal. Indeed, they treated him as if he was what he'd claimed to be: just another person, albeit one who looked a bit different.

There was no settlement visible from the water, yet canoes and sailboats were lined up on the shore, with nearly as many people around them as there would be on the Providence waterfront. A couple of men waded out to meet their boat; they grasped its sides and pulled it the rest of the way onto the beach, and one of them helped Nathan climb out. As before, Sanjay noticed that Nathan walked with a stiff, almost arthritic gait. It occurred to him that the stranger not only wouldn't walk on all fours but in fact could not. He always stood on his hinds and never used his fores for anything except grasping and holding objects. Yet it seemed as if there was a heavy load on his back, for he walked with a perpetual slump, shoulders hunched forward and head slightly bowed.

Aara caught him staring at Nathan and walked around the beached catamaran to stand beside him. "He was born that way," she murmured, "but he's not a freak. It's not polite to stare."

"He's . . . not from here, is he?" he whispered, and Aara shook her head. "Then where is he from?"

"You'll find out soon enough. Come."

With Kaile walking behind them, Aara led Sanjay from the beach. There were no structures on the shore, yet a trellis gate at the edge of the tree line marked the opening of a raised boardwalk leading into the woods. Nathan was already ahead of them; he'd just reached the gate when a bearded older man emerged from the boardwalk. He rose up on his hinds to greet Nathan; instead of the customary exchange of bows, they clasped each other's right fore, a gesture Sanjay had never seen before. Then he turned to Aara, Sanjay, and Kaile.

"Aara . . . so glad to see that you've returned. Any trouble along the way?"

"Not at all." Apparently, Aara didn't think that a close encounter with a monarch was worth mentioning. They exchanged bows, and then she raised a fore to Sanjay and Kaile. "Let me introduce my son, Sanjay, and his betrothed, Kaile Otomo. It was necessary to bring her along, I'm afraid."

"I'll trust that it was." A kindly smile. "No worries. I'm just happy you managed to get away safely." The older man dropped to all fours to approach Sanjay and Kaile. "Welcome to First Town. I'm Benjam Hallahan, the mayor. Pleased to meet you both."

"An honor to meet you." Sanjay rose to offer a formal bow, as did Kaile. "I'm sorry, but I don't understand . . . where did you say we are?"

"First Town." Benjam's smile became an amused grin. "We don't use the name Purgatory. In fact, it's what this place was called before the Stormyarn. The Disciples . . ." He shrugged. "Let's just say for the moment that most of what you were taught is wrong."

Hearing this, Sanjay instinctively glanced about to see if anyone was listening. Aara noticed this and laughed. "Don't worry, there are no Guardians here. No deacons, either. In fact, I don't think you'll find any Galians in First Town."

"We have a shrine," Benjam added, "but only a few people worship there. Mainly older folks who've come here from Providence as exiles and still have trouble accepting the truth."

"What truth is that?" Kaile asked.

Benjam started to reply, and then he paused to gaze over his shoulder at Nathan. The stranger shook his head, and the mayor looked back at her and Sanjay again. "That's a question with a long and difficult answer," he said, and his smile faded. "I'm afraid some of us have recently learned a few things we ourselves didn't know before." His eyes met Sanjay's. "One of them involves you, my friend."

"Me? How am I—?"

"Maybe we should find a place where we can speak a little more privately." When he spoke, Nathan seemed a bit wearier than he'd been before they'd come ashore. "And more comfortably."

"Of course. You must be exhausted." Benjam went down on all fours to lead them toward the boardwalk. "This way, please."

8

First Town was located deep in the forest, on a low plateau that had been cleared of the surrounding trees. When Sanjay reached the stairs leading to it at the end of the boardwalk, he was amazed by what the forest and adjacent marsh concealed from the channel. The settlement was larger than Childstown and, if anything, more prosperous. The houses and workshops were bigger, more solidly constructed; they had glazed windows, and quite a few even had second floors, something he'd never seen before. Elevated aqueducts supplied the town with fresh water from mountain springs; he saw waterwheels turning millstones and lathes, and Benjam told him that a buried network of ceramic pipes fed water into individual homes and businesses. It was the last day of summer, but there seemed to be no anxious rush to prepare for the cold weeks ahead. He smelled wood fires and drying fish, heard chatter and laughter. Townspeople were calmly going about their daily affairs, and there seemed to be no shortage of children playing in the schoolyard.

He'd been expecting a crude camp filled with starving peasants mourning their banishment from Providence, not a content village inhabited by happy, well-fed people. There was a Galian shrine, just as Benjam said, but it was small and neglected. The genesis plant that grew beside it appeared to be regularly tended, but it wasn't cordoned off by a ring of stones. One look at it, and it was clear that the Disciples had little or no authority there.

What was more surprising was a row of pens near the community gardens. Inside the pens were flocks of what appeared to be large, flightless birds, fat and white, which incessantly clucked and pecked at the soil. Never having seen the like before, Sanjay and Kaile stopped to stare at them, causing the others to come to a halt.

"Chickens," Benjam said as he walked up behind them. "And those are turkeys." He pointed to another flock of larger and even fatter birds in another pen. "We raise them for food."

"Food?" Kaile asked, and Benjam nodded. "Where did you find them? There's nothing like that on Providence."

"No, there isn't. They're not even indigenous to Eos. They came from Earth."

"Erf?" Sanjay drew back from the pens.

"No . . . *Earth*." Again, Benjam smiled. "Come. You've got a lot to learn."

Sanjay glanced at Aara. His mother gave him a knowing nod but said nothing. Yet as they turned to follow Benjam again, Sanjay noticed that, while he and Kaile had been examining the . . . the *chickens* and *turkeys* . . . Nathan had disappeared. Looking around, he saw the stranger walking away, apparently heading for another part of the village. A few passersby gave him curious glances, but no one seemed to be startled by his appearance. It was obvious that he was known there.

Benjam brought them to a large, slope-sided building near the center of town. Opening its front door, he led them into what appeared to be a meeting hall. With its carefully arranged rows of mats facing a high rear wall whose stained glass windows formed an abstract pattern, it bore superficial resemblance to a shrine, yet there was no altar, no crèche containing a sleeping Teacher, only a low table. The room was cool but comfortable. The mayor gestured to the front row of mats, and once Sanjay, Kaile, and Aara were seated, he squatted before them in front of the table.

"Nathan will be back soon," he began, speaking to Sanjay and Kaile, "but before he does, I'll get started by telling you what Aara learned when she came here—namely, that much of what you grew up accepting as fact is . . . well, to put it bluntly . . . wrong."

"Heresy." Folding her hinds beneath her, Kaile crossed her fores and glared at him.

"No. Not heresy . . . history. History that has been lost to generations of people living on Providence." Benjam paused. "You grew up in a proper Galian household, didn't you?" he asked, and Kaile nodded. "You can't be blamed for believing that anything contrary to the Word of Gal is blasphemous. But you'll have to believe me when I tell you that the Word is a distorted version of what actually occurred many yarn ago and that the true events are more complex than anything you've been taught."

Kaile scowled and started to rise from her mat, but Sanjay stopped her with his fore. "Let's just listen to what he says. We've come all this way. Maybe it'll explain what you and Aara saw."

Kaile hesitated and then reluctantly sat down again.

Benjam let out his breath and patiently went on. "First . . . to begin, Erf is not what you've been led to believe it is, a netherworld filled with damned souls. It's called Earth, and it's a planet much like Eos, only about one-third smaller. It revolves around a single star called Sol, which is much larger and brighter than Calliope . . . it's white, not orange, and Earth is much farther away from it than Eos is from Calliope."

"Did Gal create sisters for it, as well?" Sanjay asked.

Benjam shook his head. "No, there's only that one sun . . . and Gal didn't create either Calliope or Sol—or even Earth or Eos, for that matter. They existed long, long before Gal . . . because Gal itself isn't a deity but rather a vessel created by humans. Our own ancestors, in fact."

Kaile hissed between her teeth. "Blasphemy!"

"Listen to him." Aara glared at her. "He's telling the truth. Go on, Benjam."

"Gal is a vessel . . . what people like Nathan call a starship." Benjam continued. "About 440 sixyarn ago—or years, the way his people reckon time—our ancestors built a ship called *Galactique* for the purpose of carrying the seed of men and women to this world, which they knew was capable of sustaining life."

"Why?" Unlike Kaile, Sanjay wasn't upset but intrigued by what he was hearing.

"The reasons are complicated." Benjam frowned and shook his head. "I'm not sure I completely understand them myself. Nathan and his companions have told us that *Galactique* was built because the people of that time believed that life on Earth was in peril of being destroyed, and they wanted to assure the survival of the human race." A crooked smile. "It's still there, but it isn't a terrible place filled with tortured souls. The Chosen Children, as we call them, were simply the seed of those who'd spent years building the ship. In fact, they resembled Nathan himself . . . those we call the Children were altered before birth so that they could live comfortably on Eos, which *Galactique* had changed to make suitable for human life."

"Then Gal . . . I mean, *Galactique*"—Sanjay stumbled over the unfamiliar syllables—"is our creator."

"Just as the Word says," Kaile quietly added.

"*Galactique* created our people, yes, and also the world as we know it, but it is not a deity. Those of us here in First Town and the other mainland settlements—yes, there are other villages like this one, although not as large—knew this even before Nathan and his companions arrived a few weeks ago. People here have long been aware of the fact that we're descended from the human seed—the sperm and eggs, as they call it—transported from Earth aboard *Galactique* and that Eos itself was a much different place before *Galactique* transformed it over the course of nearly 300 sixyarn into the world we know now."

Benjam pointed beyond the open door of the meeting hall. "Those birds you saw, the chickens and turkeys . . . they were brought here, too, in just the same way. In fact, everything else on Eos—the forests, the insects, the fruit we eat, the fish in our seas—is descended from material carried from Earth by *Galactique,* which was then altered to make them suitable for life here."

"Nathan calls this 'genetic engineering,'" Aara said, slowly reciting words she herself had apparently learned only recently. "It's really very complicated. I'm not certain I understand it myself."

"It all was done aboard *Galactique* during the time it circled Eos." Benjam nodded in agreement. "Nathan and his people have told us that, during this same time—hundreds of yarn, longer than our own history—*Galactique* also deposited across Eos dozens of tiny craft called 'biopods,' which in turn contained the genesis plants. Eos was a much different place back then. Its atmosphere was thin and unbreathable, and the only life here was insignificant—lichen and such. The genesis plants were scattered all over Eos, and as they took root and grew to maturity, they absorbed the atmosphere that was already here and replaced it with the air we breathe while also making it thick enough to retain the warmth of Calliope and her sisters. Once that was accomplished, the plants distributed the seeds of all the other plants we know, none of which existed on Eos before *Galactique* came. Other biopods followed them, bringing down the infant forms of fish, birds, insects, and animals that had been gestated aboard the ship. Once they were here—"

"Then came you," Nathan said.

He'd entered the room unnoticed, and he wasn't alone. Looking around, Sanjay saw that he was accompanied by a man and a woman, both walking upright on forward-jointed legs and curiously small feet. This time, though, instead of the hooded cloak that concealed his form on Providence, Nathan wore a strange outfit over his clothes, a jointed framework of pipes and molded plates made of some metallic material that softly whirred and clicked with every move he made. The other two wore similar outfits.

Nathan noticed that Sanjay was staring at him. "It's called an exoskeleton," he said as he walked over to where he and the others were seated. "The surface gravity on Eos—the force that causes you to stay on the ground—is half-again higher than it is on Earth. Without these to help us stand and move about, we'd get tired very quickly.

Our hearts would have to work harder, as well, and before long, it would be very unhealthy for us to live here. The exoskeletons compensate for this."

Sanjay stood erect to tentatively lay a fore on the exoskeleton's chest plate. It was hard and cool, reminding him somewhat of a scavenger's carapace. "Why weren't you wearing this on Providence?"

"Unfortunately, it doesn't float. If I'd have fallen out of the boat, it would have dragged me to the bottom. Leaving it behind was the wisest thing to do." A wry smile. "Fortunately, I'm in pretty good shape. I could handle the stress for a little while." Nathan turned to the two who'd walked in with him. "Let me introduce my companions. This is Marilyn Sanyal, and he's Russell Coyne. Like myself, they're related to people you may already know."

"I have a friend named Johan Sanyal. And my father's family name is Coyne."

"Is it really?" Russell appeared to be Sanjay's age, differences notwithstanding. He grinned as he extended an oddly shaped fore and then apparently thought better of it and bowed instead. "I believe that makes us relatives."

Sanjay didn't return the bow. Instead, he looked at Nathan. "You said on the boat that you and I are cousins. Are you also . . . ?"

"Even more so than Russell, yes. My last name is Arkwright . . . Nathan Arkwright II." He raised a fore before Sanjay could ask another question. "There's a lot of complicated family history involved here, but you should know that we both bear the last name of the person who was responsible for *Galactique* in the first place, and I was given his first name as well." He touched his hair and then pointed to Sanjay's. "Same hair color, in fact . . . it's hereditary."

"So you're telling us that Sanjay comes from the seed of someone on Erf who was brought here by Gal—" Kaile began.

"No." Nathan turned to her. "Not the way you're saying it, at least. As Benjam just told you, Erf is a world called Earth, and Gal is a starship called *Galactique* that's still in orbit above Eos. Over time, their names were shortened, just as their true nature has been forgotten."

"Otherwise, you've got it right." Marilyn appeared to be a little older than Kaile, although not quite as old as Aara. Of the three, she alone had skin the same dark shade as the native inhabitants; the others were nearly as pale as the Teacher. "What's your family name, if I may ask?"

Kaile hesitated. "Otomo."

Marilyn pulled a small flat object from a pocket in the clothes she wore beneath the exoskeleton. Holding the object in her left fore, she tapped her finger a few times against it and then studied it for a moment. "There was a Katsumi Otomo among those who built *Galactique*," she said. "A propulsion engineer . . . never mind what that means. She was your ancestor . . . one of them, at least."

"Everyone you know, everyone on this world, is descended from least two of the two hundred men and women who contributed reproductive material to *Galactique*'s gene pool," Russell said. "First, the ship distributed genesis plants across the planet, which in turn introduced cyanobacteria into the atmosphere to reduce the carbon dioxide content, raise the oxygen-nitrogen ratio, and thereby make Eos human habitable through ecopoiesis—"

"Russ, don't get technical," Nathan said quietly. "They're not ready for that yet." Russell nodded, albeit reluctantly, and Nathan went on. "The point is, although we don't look alike, we're humans just as you are. *Galactique* altered the embryonic forms of your immediate ancestors so that they could survive this planet's higher gravity while also making them amphibious—"

"And you're telling me not to get technical," Russell said, raising an eyebrow.

"So the Word is correct," Kaile said. "Even if what you say is true, it still means that Gal is our creator."

Nathan shared an uncertain glance with Russell and Marilyn.

"Well . . . yes, I suppose you could say that, but not in the sense you mean."

"But she's in our sky every day and every night, watching every move we make." Kaile remained adamant. "She's been there for as long as our mothers and grandmothers and great-grandmothers—"

"A matriarchal mythology as well as a society," Marilyn said softly. "Interesting."

Nathan ignored her. "Once humans were brought down here, *Galactique* moved into a geosynchronous orbit"—he caught himself—"a place in the sky that is always above the same place on the ground, where it was supposed to function as a . . . um, a source of information for the original colony. That's why you can see it all the time. It rotates at the same angular velocity as Eos, so it's always directly above you."

Russell picked up the thread. "The ship also carried with it two . . . ah, artificial beings, what we call robots . . . that were meant to be your instructors. They raised the first children who came here, teaching them how to survive."

"You mean the Teacher. There were two?" Sanjay said.

"Yes, there were." Benjam had been quiet for a while; now he spoke up. "There was one here in First Town like the one in Provincetown, along with another Transformer." He looked over at Russell. "Which, as you say, manufactured the first tools used by our people, made from blocks of the material we call Galmatter."

"Correct." Russell was obviously relieved that someone here understood what he'd been trying to explain. "The Transformers are what we call three-dimensional laser manufacturers. They took information stored within *Galactique*'s data library and—" He caught a stern look from Nathan. "Damn, I'm doing it again, aren't I?"

Nathan nodded and then spoke to Sanjay again. "The Teachers, the Transformers, the stuff you call Galmatter . . . they were all sent down here to help the original colonists—the ones you call the

Chosen Children—grow up and survive in their new home. But then, there was an accident."

"Enough." Kaile raised her fores in protest. "You tell us these things and ask that we believe them, but you offer no proof." She cast an angry glare at Nathan. "Perhaps you've managed to fill their minds with lies—"

"We're not lying," Nathan said, his voice flat and steady.

"—but I refuse to accept what you're saying on your word alone. Prove it!"

No one said anything for a moment. Then Benjam stood up. "Then I'll give you proof. Something that's been here since the beginning of our history, which we've long accepted as evidence that life began out there."

"And you'll also see what caused that light you saw in the sky," Nathan added. Marilyn opened her mouth as if to object, but he shook his head. "No, she needs to see this. It's the only way."

"Follow me," Benjam said, and then he dropped to all fours and began to walk toward the door.

9

Another path, this was on the far end of town, led uphill into the dense forest at the base of the mountains. As Benjam led the group through the black woodlands, Nathan picked up where he'd left off in the meeting hall.

"First Town was the original colony, and for the first few years— um, sixyarn—it was the only settlement. During this time, the Teachers nurtured the hundred children who'd been gestated and born aboard *Galactique* . . . building shelters for them, providing them with food from the mockapples, roseberries, and vine melons that they cultivated, and educating them as they raised them from infancy to childhood. It helped a great deal that Eos has very short seasons. Unlike Earth, your winters last only three weeks, and the equatorial region is relatively mild."

"Have you ever seen snow?" Marilyn asked.

Sanjay and Kaile shook their heads. "What's that?" Sanjay asked. "It's . . . um . . ."

"Don't interrupt," Nathan said to Marilyn. She grinned and became silent, and he went on. "The colony was approaching self-sufficiency when an unforeseen occurrence happened, one that changed every-thing . . . your sun, Calliope, underwent a variable phase."

"Calliope is what's known as a red dwarf." As Russell spoke, he turned to walk backward on his curiously shaped hinds. Sanjay was amazed by the improbable and yet so casual movement, but Russell didn't seem to notice the way he stared at him. "They're generally smaller and cooler than Earth's sun, but every now and then—a few thousand years or so—they tend to spontaneously enter phases in which they grow hotter and brighter due to solar prominences—"

"Russell." Again, Nathan was concerned that Sanjay and Kaile wouldn't understand him.

"No, don't stop," Sanjay said. "I think I understand what you're saying."

"You do?" Russell said. Sanjay nodded, and after a moment, Kaile reluctantly did, as well. "All right, then. Anyway, when Calliope started to undergo one of these variable phases, *Galactique* detected the change that was about to occur—"

"Of course she did," Kaile said. "Gal knows all and sees all."

Marilyn sighed, shook her head. "Please try to understand . . . Gal isn't a deity. It's a machine." Seeing the confused expression on the young woman's face, she tried again. "It's like a tool, just far more complicated than anything you've ever seen. One of the things it can do is think and reason for itself, just as you can."

"This tool has a mind?" Even Aara was startled by this revela-tion.

"Of a sort, yes." This time, Russell made a stronger effort to speak in terms the islanders could understand. "Not exactly like your own, but . . . yes, it can observe, gather facts, and make its own decisions. *Galactique* also provided the Teachers with information and instructions, just as it provided the Transformers with their own instructions."

"Unfortunately, it can also make mistakes." Nathan had become pensive. He walked with his head down, gazing at the ground as he spoke. "When it saw that Calliope was entering a variable phase, it calculated the probable effects upon the planetary climate and realized that severe storms—typhoons, we call them—would occur in this region. The colonists were still quite young, and the settlement had been established in a coastal area that would probably experience high winds, flooding, perhaps even forest fires."

"The Great Storm," Sanjay said.

"We know all about that." A vindicated smile appeared on Kaile's face. "This was when Gal separated those who believed in her and took them to Providence, leaving behind those who'd sinned."

"Again, you're only half-right." As Nathan said this, Sanjay could tell that he was trying to be patient. "It wasn't a matter of who'd sinned and who hadn't. *Galactique* determined that the odds of survival would be increased if the colony was divided, with half of the children sent elsewhere while the other half remained here to protect the settlement. So it instructed the Teachers to build boats to take fifty children to the nearby island, whose western coast *Galactique* calculated would be less vulnerable to storm surges from the east, where they would remain until the variable phase came to an end and the climate restabilized."

"My ancestors were among the fifty who stayed here." Benjam walked slowly, turning his head to Kaile and Sanjay. "They were given a Teacher and one of the Transformers, just as your ancestors were, and then they relocated to higher ground away from the beach—the place where First Town stands today."

"It was supposed to be only temporary," Marilyn said, "but then—"

"We're here," Benjam said.

The path came to an end in a clearing where the slope was level and only chest-high grass and clumps of dreamer's weed grew. From its center rose a tall object, off white and partially covered with vines, that Sanjay first took to be a large, tooth-shaped boulder tilted slightly to one side. As they walked a little closer, he saw that it wasn't a natural object at all. Darkened on the bottom, tapering upward as a conical shape with mysterious markings along its sides, it had a round opening midway up, a rope ladder dangling from it.

Whatever it was, clearly it had been made by human fores.

"This is where it all began." Benjam stopped and stood erect. "This is the craft in which all our ancestors were brought down to the surface."

Nathan pointed to dark-blue markings along its upper surface, just visible through the clinging vines. "See? $G \ldots A \ldots L \ldots$" He shrugged. "The rest got rubbed off some way or another."

"Probably atmospheric friction during entry and landing," Russell said. "Sun and rain too. Still, it's in amazing condition, considering how long it's been here."

Walking a little closer, Sanjay rose on his hinds to peer in the direction Nathan was pointing. All he saw was something that looked like a snail, something that looked a little like a harpoon tip, and a right angle. "I don't know what you're talking about."

"You can't see that?" Marilyn asked. "How can you not—" Then she stopped and stared at him. "Oh, my god. You can't read, can you?"

"No," Benjam said quietly. "For the islanders, Inglis—what they call English—is entirely a phonetic language, with no written counterpart." He regarded Sanjay and Kaile with a pitying expression. "The children who were sent to Providence lost their ability to read and write when their Teacher was disabled and they lost communications with *Galactique*. It's the main reason their understanding of history became diluted by myth."

"Oral history." Marilyn nodded with sudden understanding. "Unwritten, malleable, and all too easy to be misunderstood. Everything they know, or they think they know, has been—"

"What are you saying?" Sanjay glared at them, annoyed by their condescension but also confused. "Are you trying to tell us that everything the Deacons have told us is . . . is . . . ?"

"Wrong," Nathan said, finishing his thought for him. "I'm sorry, but that's what we've been trying to explain." Stepping past Benjam, he slowly walked through the high grass, approaching the craft as respectfully as if it was a shrine. "You wanted proof," he said over his shoulder to Kaile. "Well, here it is. Want to come closer and see?"

Kaile hesitated. Then, visibly shaken but nonetheless curious, she followed Nathan and Benjam, walking on her hinds so that she could see the craft more clearly. Sanjay and Aara fell in behind her, with Russell and Marilyn following them. As the group made its way across the clearing, Nathan continued.

"When our ship arrived a few weeks ago—that's the light your mother saw, Sanjay—one of the first things we did was rendezvous with *Galactique* and access its memory . . . talk to it, if you will. We learned a lot of what had happened here over the last hundred and sixty years—sixyarn, I mean—but there were still some mysteries that remained unsolved until we came here and made contact with Benjam and his people."

"By then, I'd been told the truth, as well," Aara said quietly, looking at Sanjay. "Like everyone who's been exiled here, the first thing that I learned was how wrong the Disciples are. Our whole history, everything we know . . ." Her voice trailed off.

Nathan continued to speak. "One of the worst effects—in fact, probably the single worst effect—of Calliope's variable phase was the enormous electromagnetic surge that occurred during its peak." He glanced over his shoulder at Sanjay and Kaile. "I know you're not going to understand this, so I'll try to make it simple. Stars like Calliope emit more than just heat and light. They also cast other forms of radiation that you can't hear, see, or feel but that are present, anyway. The radiation became so intense that it not only destroyed *Galactique*'s ability to . . . um, talk to the Teachers and the Transformers but also the islanders' ability to communicate with those who stayed on the mainland."

"We didn't lose our Teacher the way you did," Benjam explained, "because it took shelter within this craft, which has adequate shielding to resist against this intense radiation. So we still had the means by which to learn the things we needed to know, including our history and origins. But our Transformer was destroyed, as well as the high-gain antenna. Those had been built up and couldn't be deconstructed in time."

"Almost all electrical technology was lost," Russell said. "Except for the emergency radio beacon. That was inside the lander, where it runs off a nuclear power cell. Once we learned its frequency from *Galactique*, we were able to use it to figure out where this colony was located."

"That's the light you saw, Kaile," Aara said.

She said nothing. By then, the group had reached the landing craft. It was over forty rods tall, and Sanjay could now see that it was made entirely of metal, its paint chipped and faded with age. The opening midway up its flank was a hatch from which a ladder made of woven vine and bambu had been draped.

"The children who'd been taken to Providence remained there," Benjam said. "Their Teacher and Transformer ceased to function, and they lost contact with those who'd been left behind. By the time the Great Storm finally ended four yarn later, they'd come to believe everyone there was dead. Without a Teacher to lead them, much of their knowledge was lost. They couldn't even cross the channel without risking being killed by monarchs."

"What we call great white sharks back on Earth," Marilyn added. "Like everything else, they've been adapted to provide Eos with a diverse ecosystem. Unfortunately, they also became a barrier between the two colonies."

"So the colony on Providence formed its own culture," Benjam continued, "without the benefit of written language or history or even science. In time, their children and children's children came to believe in Gal, but here"—he laid a fore against the lander's hull—"we didn't lose those things. Before our own Teacher ceased to function, it taught our grandparents all that we needed to know. By the time they were ready to build boats and try to restore contact with those who lived on island, the Disciples had made anything contrary to the Word of Gal—*Galactique*'s final instructions to the island colony, passed down by word of mouth over the yarns, all the time being reinterpreted and misunderstood—an act of heresy. Even trying to come over could get us killed. All we could do was stay away and accept those your people banished. Do you see?"

"Yes," Sanjay said.

"No," Kaile said. "All I see is something left to us by Gal. It could be anything but what you say it is."

"Kaile . . ." Aara shook her head, more disappointed than angry. "Everything they've told you is true."

"If you still don't believe us, go in and see for yourself." Benjam tugged at the bottom of the ladder. "Here . . . climb up and look."

Sanjay didn't hesitate. Taking the ladder from him, he grasped the rungs with his fores and carefully began to climb upward. As Nathan took the ladder to follow him, Sanjay paused to look back down. Kaile was still standing on the ground; when she caught his eye, she reluctantly began to scale the ladder herself.

The compartment on the other side of hatch was dark. As Sanjay crawled through the hatch, he found that he could see very little. There was a gridded metal floor beneath his fores and hinds and some large oval objects clustered along the circular walls, but that was almost all he could make out. Nathan came in behind him, and Sanjay was startled by a beam of light from a small cylinder he'd pulled from his pocket. But this was nothing compared to the shock he felt when the bright circle fell upon an object on the far side of the compartment.

"A Teacher!" Kaile had just entered the craft. She crouched beside the open hatch, staring at what Nathan's light revealed.

Sanjay felt his heart pound as he stared at the solitary figure seated in a chair in front of what appeared to be some sort of glass-topped desk. Like the Teacher in Childstown, it had a featureless face and oddly formed limbs; this one, though, wore a loose, single-piece outfit that had moldered and rotted over time, exposing the gray and mottled skin beneath. Yet the Teacher's eyes were as blank as those of his long-lost companion, and it was obvious that it too hadn't moved in many yarn.

"Benjam tells me it managed to survive the solar storm." Nathan's voice was quiet, almost reverent as Sanjay crouched beside the Teacher. "It took refuge in here, and that's how it was able to remain active long after the one you have on the island became inert. Unfortunately, it appears that they couldn't disassemble the replicator—the Transformer, I mean—or the communications antenna in time to save them, so this was the only place where any electronic equipment—"

"I don't know what you're talking about." Sanjay continued to peer at the Teacher. He prodded its face with a fingertip, something he'd always wanted to do with the one in Childstown. The Galmatter felt nothing like human flesh or indeed like anything that had ever lived.

"I know. I'm sorry. It's going to take a while for you to—" Nathan stopped himself. "Anyway, here's something else you need to see." He looked back at Kaile. "Come closer. You ought to see this too."

"No. I'm staying where I am." She wouldn't budge from the hatch. Sanjay could tell that she was frightened.

"Suit yourself." Keeping his head down so as not to bang it against the low ceiling, Nathan came farther into the compartment. "Look at these, Sanjay," he said, running the light beam across the ovoid shapes arranged along the walls. "What do you think they look like?"

Sanjay approached the egg-like objects and examined them. Although they were covered with dust, he could see that their top halves were transparent, made of substance that looked like glass but resembled Galmatter. Raising a fore to one of them, he gently wiped away the dust. Nathan brought his light a little closer, and Sanjay saw that within the cell was a tiny bed, its covers long since decayed yet nonetheless molded in such a way that would accommodate an infant.

"They look like cradles," he murmured.

"Exactly. They're cradles meant to carry down from orbit one hundred newborn babies." Nathan shined the light upward, and Sanjay looked up to see an open hatch in the ceiling. "There are three more decks just like this one above us, and in two of them are more cradles, along with places for all the equipment that was transported here from Earth. But the babies were the most important cargo."

Returning the light back to the cradle Sanjay had been inspecting, Nathan reached past him to tap a finger against a small panel on its transparent cover. "You can't read what this says, I know, but it's a name . . . 'Gleason.' That's the last name of the child who was in this particular egg, and it's also the last name of the person who donated his reproductive material to *Galactique*'s gene pool. All these cradles have names on them, and I bet that if you went through the lander and looked at them, you'd find the last names of everyone you know . . . except one. And you know whose that is?"

"No."

"Yours."

Sanjay turned to look at him. "I don't understand. You said—"

"There's no cradle here with the name of Arkwright, but that doesn't mean our common ancestor wasn't aboard the lander. These names were put on the cradles before *Galactique* left Earth, and the Arkwright genome—our family, that is—is supposed to be represented by the Morressy genome. But there are no cradles here labeled Morressy, which means something else unforeseen happened after *Galactique* arrived. And that's why your mother and I came to find you."

"What was it?"

Nathan didn't respond at once. "I could tell you, but maybe you ought to hear this for yourself." He turned about to look at Kaile. "Do you still not trust me?" he asked, not in an unkindly way but rather with great patience. "Do you still think all this was performed by some all-powerful deity?"

Kaile was quiet. Her gaze traveled around the compartment, taking it all in. Then she said, softly yet with determination, "I believe in Gal."

"Very well . . . then let's go meet Gal."

10

From space, Eos looked like nothing Sanjay had ever imagined. His people knew that they lived on a planet, of course; no one but small children thought the world was flat. But since only the deacons saw the global maps dating back before the Stormyarn—one more aspect of their history lost to Galian superstition—his people's knowledge of the place where they lived was limited to Providence, the Western Channel, and Cape Exile.

So he was unable to look away from the windows of the winged craft that had carried him, Kaile, Nathan, and Marilyn into space. On the other side, an immense blue hemisphere stretched as far as the eye could see, its oceans broken by dark-hued landmasses, its mountains and deserts shadowed by gauzy white clouds. The world slowly revolved beneath them, so enormous that he could barely believe that it could even exist.

"Beautiful, isn't it?" Marilyn spoke quietly from the right front seat of the spacecraft she and Nathan had led Sanjay and Kaile through the forest to find. It had been left in a meadow about a half kilm from *Galactique*'s lander, where the expedition's contact team had touched down three weeks earlier.

"Yes . . . yes, it is." Sanjay could barely speak. Fascination had overcome the terror of liftoff, the noise and vibration of the swift ascent, the invisible pressure that had pushed Kaile and him into soft couches barely suitable for their bodies despite the changes Nathan had made to accommodate them (during which Sanjay learned that the visitors had other words for their fores and hinds: *hands* and *feet*). The pressure was gone, and now his body felt utterly without weight, as if he were floating on the sea except without having to make any effort to stay buoyant; only the straps kept him in his seat. "Never thought it was . . . so big."

"Eos is about 8,500 kilometers in radius and 17,000 kilometers in diameter." Nathan didn't look away from the yoke-like control bar in his lap. "Kilometers are what you call kilms. Anyway, it's about one-third larger than Earth but just a little more than one-fifth of the distance Earth is from Sol . . . about .2 AUs, but you don't need to worry about that. The important thing is that it isn't rotation locked, which helped make it habitable."

Sanjay looked over at Kaile. She'd closed her eyes shut the moment the spacecraft left the ground and kept them closed all the way up, but now she'd opened them again and was staring at Eos with both awe and dread. She clutched the too-short armrests, and when Sanjay reached over to lay a fore across hers, she barely noticed.

"And you say it . . . it wasn't always like this?" she asked, her voice barely more a whisper.

"No. Before *Galactique* arrived and began dropping its biopods, Eos was a largely lifeless world. The oceans were there, but they were almost sterile, and what little life existed on the surface was . . . well, very small and very primitive. The biopods and genesis plants changed all that, and very quickly too—just under three centuries." Again, Nathan glanced over his shoulder. "That's about eighteen hundred yarn by your reckoning. A very short time . . . but then, your seasons are so much shorter, so it just seems long to you."

"And you say you came here in another craft?" Sanjay asked. "One that's bigger than this?"

"Oh, yes, much larger." Marilyn reached forward to press her fingers against a row of buttons between her and Nathan, and a moment later, a small glass plate above the buttons lit up to reveal an image of something that looked like an hourglass, with a drumlike cylinder at one end with spheres clustered around its midsection. Sisterlight reflected off its silver skin, and tiny windows gleamed in the forward cylinder; as Sanjay watched, the night side of Eos glided into view in the background. Although he couldn't understand how, he realized that he was viewing the vessel from a distance. This alone was just as miraculous as the craft itself—but then, he was becoming accustomed to miracles.

"That's our ship . . . the *Neil deGrasse Tyson*," Marilyn continued. "It's a Daedalus-class starship over six hundred meters long—a meter is about the same length as your rod—and there are over two hundred people aboard. It took us over sixty-seven years for us to get here."

"That long?" Sanjay was becoming accustomed to their way of counting the time.

"Yes, but we slept most of the way, so—"

"You *slept*? How did you—"

"It's rather complicated." Marilyn shook her head. "Anyway, it's on the other side of the planet, where it can't be seen from Providence, but that's what your mother saw . . . its main engine firing to decelerate." Again, she let out her breath in frustration as she gave Nathan a helpless look. "I never thought I'd have to explain so much."

"No one did," Nathan murmured.

"Where is Gal?" Kaile asked abruptly. "You said we could meet her. So where is she?"

Her expression had tightened, her eyes no longer filled with wonder. She had endured enough already; now she wanted to see what she'd been promised, the face of her creator. Sanjay was almost embarrassed for her. He'd become convinced that what Nathan and Marilyn had told them was the truth, but she remained stubborn in her beliefs.

"Just ahead." Marilyn pointed. "There . . . look."

Stretching forward as much as he could against the straps, Sanjay peered through the bubble. At first he saw nothing but stars. Then something came into view, a small, bright dash of light that twinkled in the sun. It steadily grew larger, gradually gaining shape and form.

"It was much larger when it left Earth," Nathan said as he guided their craft closer. "It once had a sail larger than Providence, but that was discarded once it reached Eos. The lander we visited was once attached, as well. Now there's only this."

Hovering before them, slowly tumbling through the night, was a slender, cylindrical object about a hundred rods in length. Sunlight reflected from its silver hull, and what looked like sticks, dishes, and barrels stuck out here and there. In no way did it look like a deity, though, or in fact like anything except a toy some imaginative child might have cobbled together from discarded household implements.

"This is Gal?" Kaile's eyes were wide, her voice weak.

"This is what you call Gal." Marilyn was apologetic. "I'm sorry, Kaile, but yes, this is all there is."

Sanjay looked down at Eos again. It took him a few moments to recognize the shape of the land that lay below, but the finger-shaped peninsula protruding from the northeast corner of an equatorial continent was probably Cape Exile, which meant that the large island just off its coast was Providence. Calliope was beginning to set to the west, which meant that anyone looking straight up from the island would see the very same thing they saw.

"He's telling the truth." Sanjay's mouth was dry as he turned to Kaile. "We're above Childstown." He pointed through the windows. "This is what we've seen whenever we've looked at the sky."

Kaile didn't speak, but when she peered in the direction he was pointing, her face became ashen.

"Now I want you to hear something, Sanjay," Nathan said as he did something with his controls that caused the yoke to lock in place, and then he bent forward to push more buttons. "Many, many years ago, while *Galactique* was on its way here, one of your ancestors on Earth sent a message. Her name was Dhanishta, and her father, Matt, helped her send this to *Galactique*. The ship received the message and stored it in memory, and we found it when we arrived. Here's what Dhani had to say."

The glass panel lit again, this time to display a child's face: a little girl, probably no older than seven or eight sixyarn, as dark skinned as any islander but with a yellow flower in her long black hair. She was sitting upright in a chair, smiling brightly, and as Sanjay watched, she began to speak.

"Hello, Sanjay. My name is Dhanishta Arkwright Skinner, and I'm calling you from Earth . . ."

The image was grainy and occasionally shot through with thin white lines. The girl's cheerful voice had a blurred tone to it, but nonetheless her words were distinct. *"I know you're still asleep and so it will be many years before you see this, but when* Galactique *finally gets to Eos, I hope you will . . ."*

A slight pause; she looked flustered. *"I mean, I hope you'll see this. Anyway, I wish I was there with you, because I'd love to know what the new world looks like. I hope it's as nice as Earth and that you'll have a great time there. Please think of me always, and remember that you have a friend here. Much love, Dhani."*

The girl stopped speaking. She blinked and then looked away. "*Is that okay? Did I—*"

Then the glass panel went dark.

Sanjay didn't know what to say. He couldn't tell which astonished him more, the fact that he could see and hear a little girl speaking to him from across the worlds and yarn or what she'd said. When he raised his eyes again, he found both Nathan and Marilyn smiling at him.

"She said her name is Arkwright," he said.

"That's correct." Nathan nodded. "Dhanishta Arkwright Skinner . . . Arkwright is her middle name. She's your ancestor. Mine too."

"But how did . . . how did she know I was here?"

"When she was much older," Marilyn said, "Dhani wrote her memoirs . . . her life story. She explained that Matt Skinner, her father, had told her that there was a little boy named Sanjay aboard *Galactique,* and he let her send that message to him."

"But the little boy didn't really exist," Nathan continued, "so her father sent another message to *Galactique,* telling its AI—its machine mind—to alter its original instructions. As I said, many of the people who helped build *Galactique* were allowed to contribute eggs and sperm who'd later become the original colonists . . . the people you've called the Chosen Children. One of them was a woman named Kate Morressy, who was Dhanishta's great-grandmother and also the granddaughter of Nathan Arkwright."

"The person you're named after."

"Correct. Well, without telling anyone, Matt instructed the AI to rename that particular genome *Arkwright* instead of *Morressy* and that its first offspring was to be a male child named Sanjay."

"He did this as a gift for his daughter but never told her about it," Marilyn said. "In fact, we didn't know about it, either, until we reached *Galactique* and downloaded—I mean, listened to—its AI."

"My great-great-grandfather's name was Sanjay Arkwright." Sanjay could barely speak; his voice came as a dry-throated croak. "He was one of the Chosen Children."

"That was the little boy Dhani imagined was aboard *Galactique*," Marilyn said. "He never heard it, though, so in a way, the message was meant for you."

Something small and wet touched Sanjay's face. Reaching up to brush away the moisture, he looked over at Kaile and realized that she was crying. Her tears didn't roll down her cheeks, though, but instead clung to her skin as tiny, glistening bubbles.

"Do you believe us now?" Marilyn asked, quietly and with great sympathy.

Kaile didn't say anything. She simply nodded and continued to weep for the god who'd just died.

"Yes . . . yes, I think we do," Sanjay said quietly. "So what do we do now?"

Nathan and Marilyn looked at each other. For once, they were the ones who were at a loss for words.

"That's up to you," Nathan said quietly. "What do you think we should do?"

Sanjay gazed out the window for a little while. "I think I know," he said at last.

11

The craft shook violently as its wings bit into the atmosphere, and for several minutes, its canopy was enveloped by a reddish-orange corona. Sanjay clenched his teeth and held Kaile's fore tightly within his own; he felt weight returning and regretted losing the brief euphoria he'd experienced high above Eos. Nathan had warned them that returning to the ground would be like that, but it didn't make it any less frightening. He just hoped it would be over soon, although he wasn't looking forward to what was coming next.

The trembling gradually subsided, and the corona faded, revealing the darkening blue sky of early evening. Through the canopy windows, the ocean came into view; Aether and Bacchae were coming up over the horizon, and Sanjay gazed at them in wonder, understanding now that they weren't really sisters but instead two dwarf stars just like Calliope, the three of them sharing the same center of gravity.

Indeed, everything familiar seemed new again. Eos, his people, their place in history, even Gal . . . no, *Galactique* . . . itself. What had once been the works of an all-powerful creator, he now understood to be something different, small yet significant aspects of a vast but knowable universe.

"Are you sure you want to do this?" Although Nathan didn't look away from his controls, Sanjay knew that he was speaking to him and Kaile. "You can always change your mind, y'know."

"I'm not sure we're doing the right thing." Marilyn spoke to Nathan, ignoring the passengers seated behind them. "It's a primitive culture. The shock . . . maybe we should take this slowly, introduce it over time."

"No." Just as Sanjay was feeling weight return to his body, so he also felt the responsibility of telling others what he'd learned. "My father, my friends, even the Disciples . . . they have to know the truth." He glanced at Kaile. "Yes?"

She lay back in her seat, gazing through the windows. "Yes," she said at last, turning her face toward his to give him an uncertain smile. "They won't like it, but they deserve to know what everyone in Purgatory already knows."

Nathan nodded and then looked at Marilyn. "Very well, then," he said, letting out his breath. "We're go for touchdown."

"Make it the beach," Sanjay said. "Plenty of room there."

Far below, Providence was coming into view. The last light of day was touching the thin white strip of its coast, and although he still couldn't make out Childstown, he knew that those who lived there had probably seen the bright star descending from the sky and the birdlike object it had become. The bell in the watchtower was being rung, and townspeople were emerging from their homes and workshops to stare up at the strange thing descending upon them.

He smiled to himself, imaging R'beca's reaction when she saw the craft alight upon the waterfront and who would emerge from it. Soon, there would be no more heretics. Another thought amused him, and he laughed out loud.

Kaile looked at him sharply. "What's so funny?"

"I'm going to be busy soon," he replied. "We're going to need more boats."

Puzzled, Kaile shook her head. Sanjay didn't explain what he meant, though, but instead gazed up at the sky. *Galactique* was there, as it had always been, but he now knew that its long journey had finally come to an end.

And another journey was about to begin.

EPILOGUE

The meeting hall of First Town was filled almost to capacity when Nathan Arkwright stood up to speak. Most of the people who'd gathered there that winter morning were mainly townspeople, but quite a few of them were recent immigrants from Providence who'd come to the place once known as Purgatory of their own free will, while a dozen or so were newly arrived Earth colonists who'd lately established the new settlement just south of First Town. On the second day of Feb, springtime was still another week away, so there was time for everyone to relax from their chores and hear what the expedition commander had to say.

A podium had been set up at the front of the room, a handsome bambu lectern that was a little short for him but nonetheless would serve as a convenient place to lay his reading matter. Nathan pulled a book from the jacket he wore over his exoskeleton and was about to speak when something like a distant thunderclap caused him to look up. Many of the people seated on the floor mats did the same, particularly the Eosians, who'd only lately heard a sonic boom, let alone know what caused them. They were startled by the roar of another shuttle from the *Tyson* entering the atmosphere, but Nathan's shipmates just looked at one another and smiled knowingly.

Nathan waited for the noise to subside. "Sounds like we'll soon have company," he said, and his audience gave an appreciative, if somewhat nervous, laugh. "Perhaps it's appropriate," he continued. "A long time ago, the man who made it possible for us to be here today would have enjoyed hearing that. He was my ancestor and namesake, and I think he probably would've dropped everything and run outside to watch. When he was alive, humans had only recently begun to venture beyond Earth. In his time, relatively few people like him even dared to imagine that something like this"— he raised his hands to encompass the room—"would ever occur beyond the confines of the stories he and his colleagues told."

Those from Earth nodded in agreement. Those who'd been born on Eos, though, gazed at him in confusion, not understanding what he meant.

"My ancestor was Nathan Arkwright," he continued. "I share his name, but the truth of the matter is that some of you are more directly related to him than I am. In terms of the Arkwright family tree, I'm just a distant relative, the scion of cousins who barely knew him when he was alive. But his genome was represented on the *Galactique* and therefore became part of the gene pool whose blood now flows in many of your veins. So I know that I'm speaking to not only his direct descendents but also those of his family and friends. And I consider this to be an honor."

As he spoke, Nathan absently tapped his fingers against the cover of the book he'd brought with him. It was a very old volume, published over five hundred years earlier, one of only a small handful of copies that still existed—a miracle in itself, considering how cheaply it had been printed. Nathan could have read electronic text, which would have been just as good, but this book was a family heirloom that he'd brought with him from Earth in hopes that, one day, he'd be able to do this very thing.

"So I want to read to you a little bit of what Nathan Arkwright imagined all those centuries ago . . . before Eos, before *Galactique,* before the very idea of traveling to the stars was anything but the wildest fantasy." Nathan felt a rawness in his throat; he coughed in his hand, blinked back the tears that threatened to run from the corners of his eyes, and went on. "I like to believe that his stories inspired the voyages that brought us to this world, but I know that his were only a few of many. There were countless other visionaries like him, and all had faith in the future."

With this, he opened the book and began to read *The Galaxy Patrol*.

ACKNOWLEDGMENTS

Arkwright was inspired in large part by the 100 Year Starship Symposium, cosponsored by DARPA and NASA and held in Orlando, Florida, in October 2011, and also by the Starship Century conference, sponsored by the Arthur C. Clarke Center for Human Imagination and held at its location on the University of California–San Diego campus in May 2013. I was a participant at both conferences, and it was during the second in particular that this novel was conceived.

So it's to the organizers and my fellow participants of these two conferences that I owe my gratitude. I'm especially grateful to Greg and Jim Benford for inviting me to the Starship Century conference and for giving me feedback for this book, Geoffery Landis for helping me understand the technical details of microwave beam propulsion systems, and Microwave Sciences for the fundamental design of *Galactique*'s beamer and beamsail.

In addition, I'd like to thank Bob Madle and David Kyle for sharing their memories of the 1939 World Science Fiction Convention, Betsy Wollheim for letting me know a bit about her father, Donald A. Wollheim, that I wouldn't have learned otherwise, Gardner Dozois, Susan Casper, and Michael Swanwick for acquainting me with Philadelphia's neighborhoods, Jack McDevitt for educating me in the rules of softball and an imaginary political cartoon, and

ACKNOWLEDGMENTS

Rob Caswell and Deb Zeigler for a fine interior illustration and for letting me bounce ideas off them.

I'm very grateful to Sheila Williams for making it possible for parts of this novel to first appear as a series of stories in *Asimov's Science Fiction,* my editor at Tor, David Hartwell, for coming to the rescue, and his assistant, Jennifer Gunnels, for becoming the book's guardian angel. My literary agent, Martha Millard, stood by me even when she probably would have liked to strangle me instead.

As always, my deepest gratitude to my wife, Linda, who has watched me write twenty novels and lived to talk about it.

—Whately, Massachusetts
September 2013–November 2014

BIBLIOGRAPHY

Anglada-Escudé, Guillem, et al. "A Dynamically Packed Planetary System Around GJ 667C with Three Super-Earths in Its Planetary Zone." *Astronomy & Astrophysics* 556 (August 2013): A126.

Asimov, Isaac. *In Memory Yet Green: The Autobiography of Isaac Asimov, 1920–1954*. New York: Doubleday, 1979.

———. *In Joy Yet Felt: The Autobiography of Isaac Asimov, 1954–1978*. New York: Doubleday, 1979.

Beech, Martin. *Terraforming: The Creating of Habitable Worlds*. New York: Springer-Verlag, 2009.

Benford, James. "Sailships." In *Starship Century*, edited by James Benford and Gregory Benford. Lafayette, CA: Microwave Sciences / Lucky Bat Books, 2013.

———. "Starship Sails Propelled by Cost-Optimized Directed Energy." *Journal of the British Interplanetary Society* 66 (2013): 85–95.

Cowl, Adam. "Starship Pioneers." In *Starship Century*.

Dyson, Freeman. "Noah's Ark Eggs and Vivaparous Plants." In *Starship Century*.

Hearth, Donald P., ed. *A Forecast of Space Technology 1980–2000*. Washington, D.C.: NASA SP-387, 1976.

Kiang, Nancy Y. "The Color of Plants on Other Worlds." *Scientific American* 298 (April 2008): 48–55.

Knight, Damon. *The Futurians*. New York: John Day, 1977.

Kyle, David. "Caravan to the Stars." *Mimosa,* no. 22 (June 1998): 4–8.

Landis, Geoffrey. "Microwave Pushed Interstellar Sail: Starwisp Revisited." American Institute of Aeronautics and Astronautics presentation, July 2000.

Madle, Robert T. "Fandom Up to World War II." In *Science Fiction Fandom,* edited by Joe Sanders. Santa Barbara, CA: Greenwood, 1994.

Mallove, Eugene, and Gregory Matloff. *The Starflight Handbook: A Pioneer's Guide to Interstellar Travel.* New York: Wiley & Sons, 1989.

Meloshi, H. J., et al. "Nonnuclear Strategies for Deflecting Comets and Asteroids." In *Hazards Due to Comets and Asteroids,* edited by Ron. T. Gehrels. Tucson, AZ: University of Arizona Press, 1994.

Moskowitz, Sam. *The Immortal Storm.* Concord, NH: Hyperion Press, 1954.

———. "1939—Nycon: Fandom Before Glasnost." In *Noreascon Three Program Book.* Framingham, MA: NESFA Press, 1989.

Newitz, Annalee. *Scatter, Adapt, and Remember: How Humans Will Survive a Mass Extinction.* New York: Doubleday, 2013.

Patterson, William H. *Robert A. Heinlein: In Dialogue with His Century: Volume 2, 1948–1988: The Man Who Learned Better.* New York: Tor Books, 2014.

Pohl, Frederik. *The Way the Future Was.* New York: Ballantine / Del Rey, 1978.

Rhodes, Richard. *The Making of the Atomic Bomb.* New York: Touchstone / Simon & Schuster, 1986.

Scott, David Meerman, and Richard Jurek. *Marketing the Moon: The Selling of the Apollo Lunar Program.* Cambridge, MA: MIT Press, 2014.

Vulpetti, Giovanni, Les Johnson, and Gregory L. Matloff. *Solar Sails: A Novel Approach to Interplanetary Travel.* New York: Copernicus Books, 2008.

Wright, Jerome L. *Space Sailing.* Amsterdam: Gordon and Breach, 1992.

Young, James. "Beyond This Horizon: The Potential for Commercial Spaceflight." *Minnesota Technology* (March 1974).

Zubrin, Robert. "On the Way to Starflight: Economics of Interstellar Breakout." In *Starship Century.*